D1109732

Hark!

Also by Ed McBain
in Large Print:

Gladly the Cross-Eyed Bear
The Last Best Hope
Fat Ollie's Book
The Frumious Bandersnatch

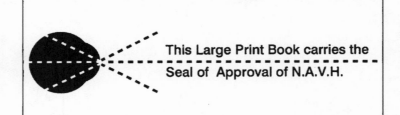

Hark!

A Novel of the 87th Precinct

Ed McBain

Thorndike Press • Waterville, Maine

Published in 2004 by arrangement with
Simon & Schuster, Inc.

Thorndike Press® Large Print Mystery.

The tree indicium is a trademark of Thorndike Press.

The text of this Large Print edition is unabridged.
Other aspects of the book may vary from the original edition.

Set in 16 pt. Plantin by Minnie B. Raven.

Printed in the United States on permanent paper.

Library of Congress Cataloging-in-Publication Data

McBain, Ed, 1926–
    Hark! : a novel of the 87th precinct / Ed McBain.
      p. cm.
    ISBN 0-7862-6934-0 (lg. print : hc : alk. paper)
    1. 87th Precinct (Imaginary place) — Fiction.
  2. Shakespeare, William, 1564–1616 — Appreciation
— Fiction.   3. Police — United States — Fiction.
4. Large type books. I. Title.
PS3515.U585H36 2004
813'.54—dc22   2004053723

This is for my wife,
DRAGICA —
the very beginning of everything for me.

As the Founder/CEO of NAVH, the only national health agency solely devoted to those who, although not totally blind, have an eye disease which could lead to serious visual impairment, I am pleased to recognize Thorndike Press★ as one of the leading publishers in the large print field.

Founded in 1954 in San Francisco to prepare large print textbooks for partially seeing children, NAVH became the pioneer and standard setting agency in the preparation of large type.

Today, those publishers who meet our standards carry the prestigious "Seal of Approval" indicating high quality large print. We are delighted that Thorndike Press is one of the publishers whose titles meet these standards. We are also pleased to recognize the significant contribution Thorndike Press is making in this important and growing field.

Lorraine H. Marchi, L.H.D.
Founder/CEO
NAVH

★ Thorndike Press encompasses the following imprints: Thorndike, Wheeler, Walker and Large Print Press.

1

Gloria knew that someone was in her apartment the moment she unlocked the door and entered. She was reaching into her tote bag when a man's voice said, "No, don't."

Her fingertips were an inch away from the steel butt of a .380 caliber Browning.

"Really," the voice said. "I wouldn't."

She closed the door behind her, reached for the switch to the right of the door jamb, and snapped on the lights.

He was sitting in an easy chair across the room, facing the entrance door. He was wearing gray slacks, black loafers, blue socks, and a matching dark blue, long-sleeved linen shirt. The throat of the shirt was unbuttoned two buttons down. The cuffs were rolled up on his forearms. There was a hearing aid in his right ear.

"Well, well," she said. "Look what the cat dragged in."

"Indeed," he said.

"Long time no see," she said.

"Bad penny," he said, and shrugged almost sadly.

It was the shrug that told her he was going to kill her. Well, maybe that and the gun in his right hand. Plus the silencer screwed onto the muzzle of the gun. And their history. She knew he was not one to forget their history.

"I'll give it all back," she said at once. "Whatever's left of it."

"And how much is that, Gloria?"

"I haven't been frugal."

"So I see," he said, and with a slight arc of the gun barrel indicated her luxurious apartment. She almost reached into the tote again. But the gun regained its focus at once, steady in his hand, tilted up directly at her heart. She didn't know what kind of gun it was; some sort of automatic, it looked like. But she knew a silencer when she saw one, long and sleek and full of deadly promise.

"What's left of the thirty million?" he asked.

"I didn't get nearly that much."

"That was the police estimate. Thirty million plus."

"The estimate was high."

"How much *did* you get, Gloria?"

"Well, the smack brought close to what

10

they said it was worth. . . ."

"Which was twenty-four mil."

The gun steady in his fist. Pointing straight at her heart.

"But I had to discount it by ten percent."

"Which left two-sixteen."

Lightning fast calculation.

"If you say so," she said.

"I say so."

A thin smile. The gun unwavering.

"Go on, Gloria."

"The police sheet valued the zip at three mil. I got two for it."

"And the rest?"

"I'm not sure I have all this in my head."

"Try to find it in your head, Gloria," he said, and smiled again, urging her with the gun, wagging it encouragingly. But not impatiently, she noticed. Maybe he didn't plan to kill her after all. Then again, there was the silencer. You did not attach a silencer to a gun unless you were concerned about the noise it might make.

"The rocks brought around half a mil. The lucy was estimated at close to a mil. I got half that for it. The ope, I had a real hard time dealing. The cops said eighty-four large, I maybe got twenty-five for it. If I got another twenty-five for the hash, that was a lot. The gage brought maybe one-fifty large for the bulk. The fatties, I smoked myself." She smiled. "Over a period of time," she said.

"Over a *long* period of time," he said. "So let me see. You got two-sixteen for the heroin and another two for the coke. Half a mil for the crack and another half for the LSD. Twenty-five for the opium and the same for the hashish. Another one-fifty for the marijuana. That comes to two hundred and nineteen million, two hundred thousand dollars. The cigarettes are on the house," he said, and smiled again. "You owe me a lot of money, Gloria."

"I spent a lot of it."

"How much is left?"

"I haven't counted it lately. Whatever's left is yours."

"Oh, you bet it is," he said.

"Maybe two mil, something like that? That's a lot of cash, Sonny."

The name he'd used on the job was Sonny Sanson. Sonny for *"Son'io,"* which in Italian meant, "I am." The Sanson was for *"Sans son,"* which in French meant, "without sound." I am without sound. I am deaf. Maybe.

"Where's the money?" he asked.

"In a safe-deposit box."

"Do you have the key?"

"I do."

"May I have it, please?"

"And then what? You kill me?"

"You shouldn't have done what you did, Gloria."

"I know. And I'm sorry. Put down the gun. Let's have a drink, share a joint."

"No, I don't think so. The key, please. And let me see your hands at all times."

He followed her into a lavishly decorated bedroom, a four-poster bed, a silk coverlet, a chest that looked antique Italian, silk drapes to match the bedspread. From a drop-leaf desk that also looked Italian, hand-painted with flowery scrollwork, she removed a black-lacquered box, and from it took a small, red snap-button envelope. The printing on the envelope read *FirstBank*.

"Open it," he said.

She unsnapped the envelope, took out a small key, showed it to him.

"Fine," he said. "Put it back, and let me have it."

She put the key back into the envelope, snapped it shut, and held it out to him. He took it with his left hand, the gun steady in his right, and slipped it into his jacket pocket.

"So here we are in my bedroom," she said, and smiled.

"Took me a long time to find you, Gloria."

"Thought you'd never get here," she said. Still smiling.

"Didn't even have a last name for you," he said.

"Yes, I know."

"All I knew was you'd been a driver since you were sixteen, that your end of a bank job in Boston enabled you to buy a house out on Sand's Spit. . . ."

"Sold it the minute I came into some money."

"*My* money."

"Well, actually the ill-gotten gains from narcotics the police were going to burn anyway."

"Still *my* money, Gloria."

"Well, yes, it *was* your plan, so I suppose the dope was rightfully yours. And we all got paid for what we did, so it wasn't really right of me to . . . well . . . run off with the stash, I know that, Sonny. The plan was a brilliant one, oh, *God,* what a plan! First the diversion in the Cow Pasture. . . ."

"I see you remember."

Smiling.

"How could I forget? And then the heist

itself, at the Department of Sanitation incinerator. . . ."

"Yes."

Nodding. Remembering.

"Houghton Street on the River Harb Drive," she said. "Remember, Sonny? Me driving the truck, you sitting right beside me?"

"Went off like clockwork," he said.

Still smiling, remembering.

"Like clockwork," she said. Smiling with him now. Beginning to feel this would go all right after all.

"I found the house you used to live in, Gloria. Took me a while, but I found it."

"What took you so long?"

"Recuperating. You almost did me in. A doctor named Felix Rickett fixed me up. Dr. Fixit, I called him," he said, and smiled again.

"Yeah, well, like I said, I'm sorry about that."

"I'm sure you are," he said, and glanced knowingly at the gun in his hand. "The present owner of the house told me he'd bought it from a woman named Gloria Anstdorf."

"Yep, that was me, all right."

"German ancestry?"

"I suppose so. I know the *dorf* part

means 'village' in German. My grand-mother thinks the *anst* may have come from 'badie*anst*alt,' which means 'baths' in German. A village where they had thermal baths, you know? She thinks the Customs people at Ellis Island shortened it when her parents got to America. To Anstdorf, you know?"

"But that's not the name in your mailbox, Gloria."

"No, it isn't."

"You bought this apartment as Gloria Stanford."

"Yes. What I did was rearrange the let-ters a little. From Anstdorf to Stanford. Made the name a little more American, you know?"

"A *lot* more American."

"Never hurts to rearrange the letters of your name here in the land of the free and home of the brave, does it? Especially when someone might be looking for you."

"It's called an anagram, Gloria."

"What is?"

"Rearranging the letters to form another word."

"Is that right?"

"Anstdorf to Stanford. An anagram."

"Is that what I did? An anagram? I'll be damned."

16

"Never hurts to use anagrams here in the land of the free and home of the brave."

"I suppose not."

"But I found you anyway, Gloria."

"So you did. So why don't we make the most of it?"

"Was that your German ancestry, Gloria?"

"Pardon?"

"Tying me to the bed that way?"

"I thought you liked that part."

"The Hamilton Motel, remember, Gloria?"

"Oh, *how* I remember."

"In the town of Red Point. Across the river."

"And into the trees," she said, and smiled.

She was feeling fairly confident now. She sat on the edge of the bed, patted it to indicate she wanted him to sit beside her. He kept standing. Kept pointing the gun at her chest. She took a deep breath. Never hurt to advertise the breasts here in the land of the free and home of the brave. He seemed to notice. Or maybe he was just searching for a spot on her chest to shoot her.

"Was that German, too?" he asked.

"Little bit of Nazi heritage there?"

"I don't know what you mean, Sonny."

"Shooting me twice in the chest that way?"

"Well . . ."

"Leaving me tied to the bed that way?"

"Speaking of beds . . ."

"Leaving me there to bleed to death?"

"I'm really sorry about that, I truly am. Why don't you let me show you just how sorry I am?"

"Turnabout is fair play," he said.

"Come over here, honey," she said. "Stand right in front of me."

"Fair is foul, and foul is fair," he said.

"Unzip your fly, honey," she said.

"*Macbeth*," he said. "Act One, Scene One."

And shot her twice in the chest.

Pouf, pouf.

2

"Now that is what I call a zaftig woman," Monoghan said.

"How do you happen to know that expression?" Monroe asked.

"My first wife happened to be Jewish," Monoghan said.

Monroe didn't even know there'd *been* a first wife. Or that there was now a second wife. If in fact there was a second wife. The woman's skirt had pulled back when she fell to the expensive Oriental carpet, exposing shapely thighs and legs, which, in concert with her ample breasts, justified the label Monoghan had just hung on her. She was indeed zaftig, some five feet nine inches tall, a woman of Amazonian proportions, albeit a dead one. The first bullet hole was just below her left breast. The second was a bit higher on her chest, and more to the middle, somewhere around the sternum. There were ugly blood stains around each bullet hole, larger stains in the weave of the thick carpet under her. The detectives seemed to be staring down at the wounds, but perhaps they were just admiring her breasts.

Today was Tuesday, the first day of June, the day after Memorial Day. The dead woman lying there at Monoghan's feet looked to be in her mid-thirties, still young enough to be a mother, though not what anyone would call a young mother, which was the juiciest kind. Monroe's thoughts were running pretty much along similar lines. He was wondering if the woman had been sexually compromised before someone thoughtlessly shot her. The idea was vaguely exciting in an instinctively primitive way, her lying all exposed like that, with even her panties showing.

Monoghan and Monroe were both wearing black, but not in mourning; this was merely the customary raiment of the Homicide Division. Their appearance here was mandatory in this city, but they would serve only in an advisory and supervisory capacity, whatever that meant; sometimes even they themselves didn't know what their exact function was. They *did* know that the actual investigation of the crime would be handled by the detective squad that caught the initial squeal, in this instance the 8-7 — which, by the way, where the hell were they? Or the ME, for that matter? Both detectives wondered if they should go down for a cup of coffee, pass the time that way.

The handyman who'd found the dead woman was still in the apartment, looking guilty as hell, probably because he didn't have a green card and was afraid they'd deport him back to Mexico or wherever. The super had sent him up to replace a washer in the kitchen faucet, and he'd let himself in with a passkey, figuring the lady . . .

He kept calling her the lady.

. . . was already gone for the day, it being eleven o'clock in the morning and all. Instead, the lady was dead on her back in the bedroom. The handyman didn't know whether or not it was okay to go back downstairs now, nobody was telling him nothing. So he hung around trying not to appear like an illegal, shifting his weight from one foot to the other as if he had to pee.

"So how do you wanna proceed here?" Monoghan asked.

Monroe looked at his watch. "Is there traffic out there, or what?" he said.

Monoghan shrugged.

"You wanna hear what happened yesterday?" he asked.

21

"What happened?"

"I go get some takee-outee at this Chinese joint, you know?"

"Yeah?"

"And I place my order with this guy behind one of these computers, and I tell him I also want a coupla bottles non-alcoholic beer. So he . . ."

"Why you drinking non-alcoholic beer?"

"I'm tryin'a lose a little weight."

"Why? You look okay to me."

"I'm tryin'a lose ten, twelve pounds."

"You look fine."

"You think so?"

"Absolutely."

Together, the detectives looked like Tweedledum and Tweedledee. But Monroe didn't seem to realize this.

"Anyway, that ain't the point of the story," Monoghan said. "I told him I wanted two non-alcoholic beers, and he told me I'd have to get those at the bar. So I go over to the bar, and the bartender — this blonde with nice tits, which was strange for a Chinese joint . . ."

"Her having nice tits?"

"No, her being blonde . . . can you please pay attention here? She asks me, 'Can I help you, sir?' And I tell her I'd like two non-alcoholic beers, please."

"When you say 'nice tits,' is that what you really mean? 'Nice tits'?"

"What?"

"Is that a truly accurate description? 'Nice tits'?"

"Can you please tell me what that has to do with my story."

"For the sake of accuracy," Monroe said, and shrugged.

"Forget it, then," Monoghan said.

"Because there's an escalation of language when a person is discussing breast sizes," Monroe said.

"I'm not interested," Monoghan said, and looked down again at the breasts of the dead woman.

"The smallest breasts," Monroe said, undeterred, "are what you'd call 'cute boobs.' Then the next largest breasts are 'nice tits' . . ."

"I told you I'm not . . ."

". . . and then we get to 'great jugs,' and finally we arrive at 'major hooters.' That's the proper escalation. So when you say this blonde bartender had nice tits, do you really mean . . . ?"

"I really mean she had 'nice tits,' yes, and that has nothing to do with my story."

"I know. Your story has to do with ordering non-alcoholic beer when you don't

23

even need to lose weight."

"Forget it," Monoghan said.

"No, tell it. I'm listening."

"You're sure you're not still distracted by the bartender with the great tits or the cute hooters or whatever the hell she had?"

"You're mixing them up."

"Forgive me, I didn't know this was an exact science."

"There's no need for sarcasm. I'm tryin'a help your story, is all."

"So let me tell it then."

"So tell it already," Monroe said, sounding miffed.

"I ask the bartender for two non-alcoholic beers, and a Chinese manager or whatever he was, standing there at the service bar says, 'We can't sell you beer to take home, sir.' So I said, 'Why not?' So he says, 'I would lose my liquor license.' So I said, 'This isn't alcohol, this is non-alcoholic beer. It would be the same as my taking home a Diet Coke.' So he says, 'I order my non-alcoholic beer from my liquor supplier. And I can't sell it to customers to take home.' So I said, 'Who *can* you sell it to if not customers?' He says, 'What?' So I say, 'If you can't sell it to *customers*, who *can* you sell it to? Employees?' So he says, 'I can't sell it to *anyone*. I would lose my liquor license.' So I say, 'This is *not* liquor! This is non-alcoholic!' And he says, 'I'm sorry, sir.' "

"So did you get the beer or not?"

"I did not get it. And it wasn't beer. It was non-*alcoholic* beer."

"Which you don't need, anyway, a diet."

"Forget it," Monoghan said, sighing, and a voice from the entrance door said, "Good morning, people. Who's in charge here?"

The ME had arrived.

Detectives Meyer and Carella were just a heartbeat behind him.

You couldn't mistake them for anything but cops.

Monoghan and Monroe might have been confused with portly pallbearers at a gangland funeral, but Meyer and Carella — although they didn't look at all alike — could be nothing but cops.

Detective Meyer was some six feet tall, a broad-shouldered man with China-blue eyes and a completely bald head. Even without the Isola PD shield hanging around his neck and dangling onto his chest, even with his sometimes GQ look — on this bright May morning, he was wearing brown corduroy slacks, brown socks and loafers, and a brown leather jacket zipped up over a tan linen shirt — his walk, his stance, his very air of confident command warned the criminal world at large that here stood the bona fide Man.

Like his partner, Detective Stephen Louis Carella exuded the same sense of offhand authority. About the same height as Meyer, give or take an inch or so, dark-haired and dark-eyed, wearing on this late spring day gray slacks, blue socks, black loafers, and a blue blazer over a lime-green Tommy Hilfiger shirt, he came striding into the room like an athlete, which he was not — unless you counted stickball as a kid growing up in Riverhead. He was already looking around as he came in just a step behind both Meyer and the Medical Examiner, who was either Carl Blaney or Paul Blaney, Carella didn't know which just yet; the men were twins, and they both worked for the Coroner's Office.

In answer to Blaney's question, Monroe said, "We *were* in charge until this very instant, Paul, but now that the super sleuths of the Eight-Seven . . ."

"It's Carl," Blaney said.

"Oh, I beg your parmigiana," Monroe said, and made a slight bow from the waist. "In any event, the case is now in the capable hands of Detectives Meyer and Carella, of whose company I am sure you already have had the pleasure."

"Hello, Steve," Blaney said. "Meyer."

Carella nodded. He had just looked down at the body of the dead woman. As always, a short sharp stab, almost of pain, knifed him between the eyes. He was looking death in the face yet another time. And the only word that accompanied the recognition was *senseless*.

"Nice jugs, huh, Doc?" Monoghan remarked.

"*Great* jugs," Monroe corrected.

"Either way, a zaftig woman," Monoghan said.

Blaney said nothing. He was kneeling beside the dead woman, his thumb and forefinger spreading her eyelids wide, his own violet-colored eyes studying her pupils. A few moments later, he declared her dead, said the probable cause of death was gunshot wounds, and ventured the wild guess that the lady had been shot twice in the heart.

Same words the handyman had used.

The lady.

The handyman told them the lady's name was Gloria Stanford. He told Meyer and Carella what he'd already told the Homicide dicks. He'd come up to change a washer in the kitchen faucet and had found the lady dead on the bedroom floor.

"What were you doing in the bedroom?" Meyer wanted to know.

"Señor?"

"If you came up to change a washer in the kitchen, what were you doing in the bedroom?"

"I alwayss check the apar'menn, make sure anybody's home."

"So you went into the bedroom to see if the lady was in there, is that right?"

"Sí. Before I begin work."

"And what if the lady'd been in bed or something?" Meyer asked.

"Oh no. It wass eleven o'clock. She hass to be gone by then, no?"

"Then why'd you go look in the bedroom for her?"

"To see if she wass there," the handyman said, and shrugged elaborately.

"This guy sounds like my Chinese manager," Monoghan said.

"What'd you do when you found her in here dead?" Carella asked.

"I run down get the super."

"He's the one called it in," Monroe said. "The super."

"Where is he now?"

"You got me. Probably hiding in the basement, keeping his nose clean."

The boys from the mobile crime lab were just arriving.

It was going to be a long day.

Along about three-thirty every afternoon, the squadroom's often frantic boil dissipated, to be replaced by a more relaxed ambience. The shift would be relieved in fifteen minutes, and usually all the clerical odds and ends were tied up by now. This was a time to unwind, to relax a little before heading home. This was a time to enter the mental decompression chamber that separated the often ugly aspects of police work from the more civilized world of family and friends.

Meyer and Carella had jointly composed the Detective Division report on Gloria Stanford, the woman who'd been found dead this morning in a fourteenth-floor apartment on Silvermine Oval, an area that passed for the precinct's Gold Coast. One copy of this DD report would go to Homicide, another would go to the Chief of Detectives, and the third would be filed here. Meyer was on the phone with his wife, Sarah, discussing the bar mitzvah of his nephew Irwin's second son — my how the time does fly when you're having a good time; it seemed like only yesterday that they'd attended Irwin the Vermin's own bar mitzvah. But Irwin was a grown man now — albeit a lawyer, so perhaps the sobriquet still applied.

Carella was on the phone with his sister, Angela. She had just told him he was a cad. Not in those words, exactly. What she'd actually said was "Sometimes you behave like a spoiled brat."

This from his kid sister.

Not such a kid anymore, either.

All grown up, divorced once, and about to marry the district attorney who'd let their father's killer escape justice. Or so it seemed to Carella. Which was probably why his sister expressed the opinion that he sometimes behaved like a spoiled brat.

"I don't know what you're talking about," he said into the phone, unconsciously lowering his voice to a whisper because a squadroom was not particularly the most private place in the world.

"What you said to Mama," Angela said.

She was referring to dinner at their mother's house yesterday. Carella felt like telling her that what had made that Memorial Day memorable for a woman named

Gloria Stanford was getting shot twice in the chest, with both bullets passing through her heart, and that this morning, he had looked down into that woman's dead eyes, staring up at him wide open before the ME gently lowered her lids. He wanted to tell her that it had been a long, tiring day, and that he had just finished typing up the details of the case, and was ready to call home to tell Teddy he'd be on the way in fifteen — he glanced up at the wall clock — make that thirteen minutes, and he didn't need a scolding just now from his kid sister, was what he felt like telling her.

Instead, he said, "I told Mama I was very happy. In fact, I told *both* of you . . ."

"It was your tone," Angela said.

"My what?"

"The tone of your voice."

"I meant what I said. I'm very happy Mama is getting married so soon after Papa got killed, and I'm very happy you're . . ."

"That's exactly what I mean. That sarcastic, sardonic tone of voice."

"I did not mean to sound either sarcastic *or* sardonic. You're both getting married, and I'm very happy for you."

"You still think Henry ran a shoddy trial."

"No, I think he did his best to convict Papa's murderer. I just think the defense outfoxed him."

"And you still hold that against him."

"Sonny Cole is dead," Carella said. "It doesn't matter anymore."

"Then why do you keep harping on it?"

"I don't."

"Why do you keep *behaving* as if I shouldn't marry Henry, and Mama shouldn't marry Luigi?"

"I wish he'd change his name to Lou," Carella said.

"That's just what I mean."

"And I wish he'd move here instead of taking Mama with him to Italy."

"His business is in Italy."

"And mine is here."

"You're not the one marrying Mama!" Angela said.

"That's true," Carella said. "I'm not the one marrying Henry Lowell, either."

There was a long silence on the line. In the background, Carella could hear the voices of the other detectives in the squad-room, all of them on their own phones, at their own desks.

At last, Angela said, "Get over it, Steve."

"I'm over it," he said. "You're both getting married on June twelfth. I'm giving both of you away. Period."

"You even make that sound ominous. Giving us away. You make it sound so final. And yes, ominous."

"Sis," he said, "I love you both. *You* get over it, okay?"

"Do you really?" Angela asked. "Love us both?"

"With all my heart," he said.

"Do you remember when you used to call me 'Slip'?" she asked.

"How could I forget?"

"I was thirteen. You told me a thirteen-year-old girl shouldn't still be wearing cotton slips."

"I was right."

"You gave me an inferiority complex."

"I gave you an insight into the mysterious ways of womanhood."

"Yeah, bullshit," Angela said, but he could swear she was smiling.

"I love you, bro," she said.

"I love you, too," he said, "I have to get out of here. Talk to you later."

"Give my love to Teddy and the kids."

"I will," he said. "Bye, sweetie."

He pressed the receiver rest button, waited for a dial tone, and then began dialing home.

33

★ ★ ★

A relationship can settle down into a sort of complacency, you know. You forget the early passion, you forget the heat, you begin to feel comfortable in another sort of intimacy that has nothing to do with sex. Or if it does, it's only because the idea of being loved so completely, of loving someone back so completely, is in itself often sexually exciting. This profound concept did not cross the minds of either Bert Kling or Sharyn Cooke as they spoke on the telephone at eighteen minutes to four that afternoon. They simply felt snug and cozy with each other, sharing their thoughts as their separate days wound down in separate parts of the city.

Sharyn worked in the police department's Chief Surgeon's Office at 24 Rankin Plaza, over the bridge in Majesta. As the city's only female Deputy Chief, she was also its only black one. A board-certified surgeon with four years of medical school, plus five years of residency as a surgeon, plus four years as the hospital's chief resident, she now earned almost five times as much as Kling did. Today, one of the cops she'd seen on a follow-up had been shot in the face at a street demonstration six months earlier. Blinded in the left eye, he was now fully recovered and wanted to go back to active duty. She had recommended psychiatric consultation first: a seriously wounded cop is often thought of as a jinx by his fellow officers, who sometimes tended to shun him. She told this to Kling now.

"I'm seriously wounded, too," he said.

"Oh? How's that, hon?"

"We've been on the phone for five minutes, and you haven't yet told me you love me."

"But I *adore* you!" she said.

"It's too late to apologize," he said.

"Where do you want to eat tonight?"

"You pick it, Shar."

"There's a place up in Diamondback serves real down-home soul food. Want to try it?"

"Wherever."

"Such enthusiasm," she said.

"I'm not very hungry. Cotton and I were working a burglary over on Mason, we stopped for a couple of late pizzas afterward."

"Shall we just order in?"

"Whatever," he said. "*Law and Order* is on tonight, you know."

"*Law and Order* is on *every* night," she said.

"I thought you liked *Law and Order.*"

"I adore *Law and Order.*"

"That's just what I mean," he said. "You say you adore me, but you *also* adore *Law and Order.*"

"Ahh, yes, but I *love* you," she said.

"At last," he said.

Not exactly hot and heavy.

But they'd been living together for quite a while now.

And neither of them ever once thought trouble might be heading their way.

Had they but known.

This was still the early days of their relationship. Everything was still whispers and heavy breathing. Innuendos. Promises. Wild expectations. Covert glances around the room to see if the phone conversation was being overhead. Hand cupped over the mouthpiece. Everything hot and heavy.

Honey Blair was in a large, open room at Channel Four News, sitting at a carrel desk, her back to the three other people, two men and a woman, occupying the room at the moment. What they were doing was frantically compiling some last-minute news segments that would go on the air at six p.m. Honey was telling Hawes that before she saw him tonight, she would have to run downtown to do a remote from the Lower Quarter, where some guy had jumped out the window of a twenty-first-floor office. She'd be heading out in half an hour or so.

"I can't wait," she whispered into the phone.

"To scrape your jumper off the sidewalk?" Hawes asked.

"Yes, that, too. But, actually . . ."

She lowered her voice even further.

". . . I can't wait to jump on *you!*"

"Careful," he warned, and glanced around to where the other detectives all seemed preoccupied with their own phone conversations.

"Tell me what *you* can't wait to do," she whispered.

"I'd get arrested," he whispered.

"You're a cop, tell me, anyway."

"Do you know that little restaurant we went to the other night?"

"Y-e-ess?"

"That very crowded place where everyone turned to look at you when we walked in . . . ?"

"Flatterer."

"It's true. Because you're so beautiful."

"Don't stop, sweet talker."

"I want you . . ."

"I want you, too."

"I'm not finished," he said.

"Tell me."

"I want you to go to the ladies room . . ."

"Right now?"

"No, in that restaurant."

"Y-e-ess?"

"And take off your panties . . ."

"Oooo."

"And bring them back to the table and stuff them in the breast pocket of my jacket."

"Then what?"

"Then you'll be sitting there in that crowded room with everyone knowing you're Honey Blair from Channel Four News . . ."

"Honey Blair, Girl Reporter."

"Yes, but I'll be the only one who knows you're not wearing panties."

"Even though they're sticking out of your jacket pocket like a handkerchief?"

"Even though," he said.

"And then what?"

"Then we'll see."

"Oh, I'll just *bet* we will," Honey whispered.

Hot and heavy.

Like that.

Not a worry in sight.

Little did they know.

38

★ ★ ★

The bicycle courier was a Korean immigrant who not five minutes earlier had almost caused a serious accident when he ran a red light on Culver Avenue and almost smacked into a taxi driven by a Pakistani immigrant whose Dominican immigrant passenger began cursing in Spanish at the sudden brake-squealing stop that hurled her forward into the thick plastic partition separating her from the driver.

Now, safe and sound, and smiling at the desk sergeant, the courier asked in his singsong tongue if there was a Detective Stephen Carella here. Murchison took the slender cardboard envelope, signed for it, and sent it upstairs.

The packet was indeed addressed to Carella, the words DETECTIVE STEPHEN LOUIS CARELLA scrawled across the little insert slip, and below that the address of the precinct house on Grover Avenue. He pulled on a pair of latex gloves, ripped open the tab along the top end of the stiff envelope, and found inside a white business-size envelope with his name handwritten across it again, DETECTIVE STEPHEN LOUIS CARELLA. He opened this smaller envelope, and pulled from it a plain white sheet of paper upon which were the typewritten words:

WHO'S IT, ETC?
A DARN SOFT GIRL?
O, THERE'S A HOT HINT!

"Who's it from?" Meyer asked, walking over.

"Dunno," Carella said, and turned the packet over in his hands. The return name on the delivery insert, in the same hand-writing as Carella's scribbled name, was ADAM FEN. The return address was for a post office box at the Abernathy Station downtown.

"Anybody you know?" Meyer asked.

"Nope," Carella said, and looked at the note again.

WHO'S IT, ETC?
A DARN SOFT GIRL?
O, THERE'S A HOT HINT!

"He spelled *oh* wrong," Genero said. "Didn't he?" he asked, not certain any-more. He had walked into the squadroom as part of the relieving night-shift team, and was now at Carella's desk, peering at the two envelopes and the note. "Isn't *oh* supposed to be spelled with an *h?*"

"It's sexier without the *h*," Parker said.

He, too, had just walked in as part of the relieving team. All in all, there were now six detectives crowded around Carella's desk, all of them looking at what he'd just received by same-day delivery. Cotton Hawes, all suffused with heat from his conversation with Honey Blair, had to agree that *o* was sexier than *oh*, even if he couldn't say exactly why. Detective Richard Genero was still pondering the exact spelling of the word *oh*, when Hal Willis suggested that perhaps Adam Fen was an Irishman, a "fen" being an Irish bog or marsh . . .

". . . or swamp or something like that, isn't it?" he asked.

. . . and the Irish sometimes waxing a bit romantic, which might account for dropping the *h* in the word *oh*, confirming Genero's lucky surmise.

Kling had already gone home, so he didn't have any opinion at all. Eileen Burke was just coming through the gate in the slatted rail divider that separated the squadroom from the corridor outside. She hadn't yet seen the stuff on Carella's desk, so she didn't have an opinion, either. As yet.

Meyer was remembering that Monoghan

41

— or Monroe, or one or the other of them — had remarked earlier today that the dead woman on the bedroom floor of the Silvermine Oval apartment was "zaftig," which in Yiddish meant "juicy" or "succulent," but which in everyday English slang meant "having a full or shapely figure," which Meyer supposed could be translated as "a darn soft girl." He hesitated before mentioning this aloud because he knew in his heart of hearts that Detective Andy Parker was at best a closet anti-Semite and he didn't want to introduce religious conflict into what seemed to be a mere note from a possible homicidal nut named Adam Fen. But the coincidence seemed too rare not to have specific meaning.

"You know," he said, "the word *zaftig* . . ."

And Carella immediately nodded and said, "Gloria Stanford."

"You think there's a connection?"

"Some crazy trying to tell us he did it?"

"Did *what?*" Parker asked. "And what the hell is zaftig?"

"A darn soft girl," Meyer said.

"Is that some kind of sexist remark?" Eileen asked.

Unlike the female detectives she saw on television, Eileen was not wearing a tight sweater. Instead, she had on an olive-green pants suit that complemented her red hair and green eyes. On every cop television show, at least one of the leading characters was a female detective. Sometimes, you had two or three female detectives in the same squadroom. Sometimes, even the *lieutenant* in command of the squad was a woman. In Eileen's experience, this was total bullshit. Of the eighteen detectives on the 87th Squad, she was the only woman.

"We caught a shooting death this morning," Meyer explained.

"Beautiful woman."

"Gloria Stanford."

"Two in the chest."

"So is this a written confession?" Genero asked hopefully.

"Oh, *there's* a hot hint!" Parker said, and rolled his eyes.

"Where's the Abernathy Station?" Willis asked.

"Downtown near the Arena," Hawes said.

"Should be easy to check that P.O. box."

"You don't think Mr. Fen here would give us a real address, do you?" Parker asked.

"What's the name of that courier service?" Hawes asked.

Carella turned the envelope over again. "Lightning Delivery."

"Shy and unassuming," Eileen said.

"Modest, too." Willis agreed.

"Fen sounds Chinese to me," Genero said. "Like Moo Goo Gai Fen."

They all looked at him.

"No, Fen is American," Parker said. "There was once an actor named Fen Parker, no relation. Played Daniel Boone on TV."

"That was *Fess* Parker," Hawes said.

Parker shrugged.

"Anyway," Genero said, nodding in agreement with himself, "Adam Fen is most definitely Chinese. Adam is a popular name in Hong Kong."

"How do you happen to know that?" Parker asked.

"It's common knowledge," Genero said.

Willis almost sighed. He turned to the three detectives who were now fifteen minutes late getting relieved.

"Go home," he told them. "We'll get on this shit." He tapped the courier envelope. "Maybe we'll learn something."

"*Mazeltov,*" Meyer said.

"Which means *what?*" Parker asked, making it sound like a challenge.

"Which means 'good luck,' " Carella said.

He had no expectation that either Lightning Delivery *or* the Abernathy Station would provide any clue to Adam Fen.

He was right.

3

It would seem odd that in this vast and bustling metropolis, in the mightiest nation on earth, a message from someone intent on mischief could enter a police station unchallenged. After the anthrax mailings — and what with Homeland Security and all — one might have thought that a barrier of screening machines would have been erected at the portals of every police station in the country. Nay.

In the good old days (ah, the good old days) whenever you were in trouble, you ran right into a police station, any police station, past the hanging green globes flanking the wooden entrance doors, and you rushed to the desk sergeant and yelled, "I've been raped!" "I've been robbed!" "I've been mugged!" and somebody would take care of you. Nowadays, there was a uniformed cop standing guard at the entrance, and he asked you to state your business and show some ID before he let you inside. This was still the big bad city and a great many choices were available to you. "I've been stabbed, I've been axed, I've been shot in the foot!" But he wouldn't let you inside there unless he felt you had legitimate business with the police.

Well, a same-day, courier-service messenger certainly has legitimate business with the police if he's delivering a letter. Besides, what are you supposed to do? Examine each and every letter in his pouch? Impossible. In fact, what you do is you say, "How goes it today, Mac?" and you let him in. Same way you let in the courier from Lightning Delivery yesterday, whom you also called "Mac" even though you didn't know him from Adam.

Adam Fen was the return name on the letter the messenger carried to the muster desk at six-thirty that Wednesday morning, the second day of June. The letter was once again addressed to Detective Stephen Louis Carella. Sergeant Murchison asked an officer to take the letter upstairs.

Upstairs in the squadroom, Bob O'Brien shouldn't have opened it because it wasn't addressed to him, but he thought if a person used a same-day delivery service, there might be some urgency involved. Besides, the graveyard shift still had an hour-fifteen to go, and things were pretty quiet. So he pulled on a pair of latex gloves, ripped open the MetroFlash envelope, and plucked from it a white business-size envelope. The note folded inside it read:

A WET CORPUS?
CORN, ETC?

O'Brien figured their trigger-happy lunatic from yesterday was still bragging about his dead broad.

Early stages of a romance, when you go to the bathroom to pee, you make sure the door is locked, and you run water in the sink to cover the sound of your urination, lest it be your ruination. When Hawes came back into the bedroom, Honey was awake and sitting up in bed.

"I have to pee, too," she said, and climbed over the side of the bed, long legs flashing beneath the hem of a white babydoll nightgown. On her way to the bathroom, she tossed him a sassy moon, grinned over her shoulder, and then disappeared behind the closed door. He did not hear the lock clicking shut. Neither did he hear water running in the sink.

He wondered if he should call in sick. If

the squad hadn't caught a homicide yesterday, he might have given it serious thought. Was there time, anyway? He looked at his watch. Six forty-five. Figure half an hour to get uptown to the precinct. No way he could manage it.

Honey came out of the bathroom.

Reading his mind, she asked, "Do we have time?"

"I have to be in at a quarter to eight," he said.

She looked at the bedside clock.

"Nuts," she said, and went to him and kissed him anyway.

It was almost a goodbye kiss.

The first shot cracked on the early morning air the moment Hawes stepped out of the building. He was about to say "Good morning" to Honey's doorman when he heard the shot and instinctively ducked. He had been a cop for a good long time now, and he knew the difference between a backfire and a rifle shot, and this was a rifle shot, and he knew that even before he heard the bullet whistling past his right ear, even before he saw brick dust exploding from the wall of the building where the first slug hit it.

Because he was an officer of the law, and

because he was sworn to protect the citizenry of this fair city, the first thing he did was shove the doorman back into the building and out of harm's way, and the second thing he did was drop to the sidewalk, which was when the second shot came, ripping air where Hawes' head had been not ten seconds earlier. On his hands and knees, he scrabbled for cover behind a car parked at the curb to the left of the building's canopy, reaching it too late to drag his right foot from the sniper's line of fire.

He felt only searing pain at first, and then a wave of fleeting nausea, and then anger, and then immediate self-recrimination — how could he have let this happen to himself? His gun was already in his hand, too late. He was already scanning the rooftops across the way, too late. The doorman was starting out of the building . . .

"Stay *back!*" Hawes shouted, just as another shot splintered the suddenly surreal stillness. There were two more shots, and then a genuine stillness. He signaled to the doorman with his outstretched left hand, patting the air, wait, wait, his hand was saying. There were no further shots.

The doorman came rushing out of the building.

"Call an ambulance," Hawes said.

A small puddle of blood was forming on the sidewalk.

Sharyn Cooke was asleep in Bert Kling's bed when the phone rang in his apartment near the Calm's Point Bridge. He was not due in until seven forty-five, and this was now a quarter past seven and he was just heading out the door. He picked up the phone, said, "Kling," listened, said, "Just a moment, please," and then went to the bed and gently shook Sharyn awake. "For you," he said.

Sharyn scowled at him, but she took the phone.

"Deputy Chief Cooke," she said.

And listened.

"What?" she said.

And listened again.

"Where is he?"

She looked at Kling, shook her head. Her face was grim.

"I'll get there right away," she said. "Thanks, Jamie," she said, and hung up.

"What?" Kling asked.

"Cotton Hawes got shot," Sharyn said. And then immediately, seeing his face, "It's not serious. Just his foot. But he's at Satan's Fluke, and I want him moved out of there fast."

"I'll come with you," Kling said.

She was already in the bathroom.

"Who's Jamie?" he asked.

But she'd just turned on the shower.

The second note that day arrived at twenty minutes to eight. Sergeant Murchison handed Carella the envelope the moment he walked into the muster room.

"Arrived five minutes ago," he said.

Carella nodded, said, "Thanks, Dave," and studied the envelope as he climbed the steps to the second floor of the old building. Name of the courier service was Speed-O-Gram. The envelope was addressed to Detective Stephen Louis Carella. The return name on it was Adam Fen, the return address P.O. Box 4884, Abernathy Station. Willis had drawn a blank on each of those yesterday. There were only five Fens listed in all of the city's telephone directories. None of them was an Adam. Willis had called each and every one of them, with no luck. He got Chinese accents each and every time, "So solly, no Adam Fen here"; for a change, Genero had been right. There were only 300 post office boxes at the Abernathy Station downtown. A box numbered 4884 simply did not exist.

"See you got another one," O'Brien said.

Carella didn't know what he was talking about.

O'Brien handed him the MetroFlash envelope and the note that had been inside it:

A WET CORPUS?
CORN, ETC?

"Meaning?" Carella asked.

"You're the detective," O'Brien said.

"He's still trying to confess," Carella said.

"You think?"

"Telling us there's a dead body wet with her own blood."

"Maybe so," O'Brien admitted dubiously, not wishing to press his good fortune by venturing a true opinion. O'Brien was known far and wide as a hard-luck cop. Not only just here in the confines of the Eight-Seven. Everywhere in the city. Far and wide. Walk down the street with Detective Bob O'Brien, there'd be shooting. Just standing beside him here in the squadroom, Carella was wondering if a bullet would come smashing through one of the windows.

"But what does he mean by 'corn, etc'?" O'Brien asked, stepping out boldly.

53

"He's referring to the same old routine," Carella said. "A body, an investigation, like that. He's telling us this is all corny by now. We've seen it a thousand times on television."

"You think?" O'Brien said again.

"I'm guessing. Same as you."

"What's the new one say?" O'Brien asked.

He knew his own hard-luck reputation. Shrugged it aside. He'd had to shoot only six, or maybe seven, people in his entire career, but who was counting? And, anyway, that wasn't so much. Besides, if they couldn't take a joke, fuck 'em.

Carella fished a pair of latex gloves from his desk drawer, pulled them on, opened the Speed-O-Gram envelope. A business-size envelope inside. A pattern here. Same lunatic. He slit open the inner envelope, removed from it a folded white sheet of paper. The message on it read:

BRASS HUNT?
CELLAR?

"So what's that got to do with your wet corpse?" O'Brien asked.

"I haven't the foggiest," Carella said.

Which was when the telephone rang.

It was Bert Kling telling him that Cotton Hawes had been shot and that Sharyn was having him moved from the notorious St. Luke's to Boniface, one of the city's better hospitals.

On the way to Boniface, Carella and Meyer tried to dope out what the three notes meant. The first one said:

WHO'S IT, ETC?
A DARN SOFT GIRL?
O, THERE'S A HOT HINT!

"Okay, the darn soft girl is the female stiff we caught. That's obvious."

"Then why's he asking us who it is?" Carella asked.

He was driving. Meyer was riding shotgun.

"Cause he's a madman," Meyer said. "Lunatics don't behave like normal people."

"He asks us who it is, etcetera, etcetera, and so on, and then he tells us that's a hot *hint?* Right after he's already *told* us the vic is a darn soft girl who we already *know* is Gloria Stanford? I don't get it, Meyer, I really don't."

"He's confessing, is all. He wants us to

55

catch him, is all. It's like that nut years ago who wrote in lipstick on the mirror, whatever his name was."

"Here? One of our cases?"

"No, Chicago. Catch me before I kill more. Whatever it was he wrote on the mirror."

"That's what he wrote."

"He wanted them to stop him."

"But this guy *doesn't* want us to stop him. He doesn't say '*Stop* me!'"

"'*Catch me*' was what he said. Heirens, that was his name. William Heirens. The guy in Chicago."

"*Our* guy says I killed this girl and I'm giving you a hint who she is, that's what he says in his note."

"In his *first* note. What about the other two?"

A copy of the second was on Meyer's lap.

A WET CORPUS?
CORN, ETC?

"Same thing. He's telling us to pay attention here. I killed this woman, her nice white blouse is all covered with blood . . ."

"Where does it say that?"

"Metaphorically. A wet corpus. A bloody

56

body. Is what he's saying. Do your usual corny thing, he's saying."

"And the third note?"

Carella glanced at the copy:

BRASS HUNT?
CELLAR?

"I don't know," he said.

"I mean, she was killed in her own *bedroom*. What's he talking about, a cellar?"

"I don't know. The techs didn't find any spent cartridge casings, so he can't mean brass in that way."

"You're thinking, like, a hunt for brass *shell* casings?"

"Yes, but we already . . ."

"Like he's telling us we won't *find* any shell casings cause the murder gun was an automatic?"

"But we already *know* that. Ballistics already *told* us it was a forty-five."

"So he's telling us again."

"Why?"

"Because he thinks he's smarter than we are. He's telling us we're still in the cellar on this thing. No spent cartridge cases, we don't know what kind of gun, we don't know who the body is, we're totally lost, we're in the cellar. He's giving us all these hints, but we're just plain stupid. Is what he's saying."

"Maybe," Carella said.

"It's the next driveway," Meyer said. "Where it says 'Main Entrance.' "

"You think he may have tossed the weapon in the basement?" Carella asked. "On his way out of the building?"

"I don't think so," Meyer said. "But we can ask Mobile to check again."

"If not, why's he pointing us to the cellar?" Carella asked, and shook his head, and pulled the police sedan into Boniface's parking lot.

Detective/Second Grade Cotton Hawes was enormously pissed off. Sitting up in bed, wearing a blue-striped hospital gown, a shaft of sunlight streaming through the bedside window to highlight the white streak in his otherwise red hair, he fumed and snorted about having been cold-cocked by a rooftop sniper, and having to spend the day here . . .

"For *observation!*" he shouted. "What do they have to observe? They've already cleaned and dressed the wound, what the hell do they have to observe?"

"You got shot, Cotton," Carella observed.

"In broad daylight!" Hawes said. "Can

you imagine someone shooting a cop in broad daylight?"

Meyer could imagine it.

"What was he *thinking?*" Hawes said. "A cop? Broad daylight? A good thing Sharyn yanked me out of Fluke's. They wanted to *amputate* the foot!"

"You didn't happen to see the shooter, did you?" Carella asked.

"I was too busy ducking. He was on one of the rooftops across the way."

"The Eight-Six is already up there looking around," Meyer said.

"Silk Stocking precinct."

"Who's on it, do you know?"

"Kling didn't say."

"Not often the Eight-Six gets a sniper."

"Tell them one of the slugs is in the wall to the left of the entrance doors."

"Guy's probably in China by now."

"Maybe not," Hawes said, and looked suddenly concerned. "This guy was serious. I got the distinct impression he wanted me dead."

Carella looked at him.

"Yeah," Hawes said, and nodded. "And also, I have to wear like this open kind of boot for the next little while."

The next note arrived ten minutes after

59

Meyer and Carella got back to the squadroom. Yet another courier service. Same phony Adam Fen return name, same non-existent Abernathy Station P.O. Box 4884. The note read:

PORN DIET?
HELL, A TIT ON MOM!

"Party's getting rough," Meyer said.

Carella merely nodded.

"I think he's beginning to lose it," Meyer said. "I mean, this is pure *bullshit*, is what this is here."

"You know what I think?"

"No, *what* do you think?" Meyer asked. He sounded angry. Not as angry as Hawes had sounded half an hour ago, but angry enough for a man who hadn't been shot in the foot.

"I think it's coffee and donuts time."

The Thursday Morning Meeting wasn't supposed to take place till tomorrow, this still being Wednesday and all, but when Carella laid out the five notes for Lieutenant Byrnes to study, he agreed that the changing of the guard this afternoon might be a good time to summon together the great minds of the 87th Squad. Coffee and donuts were *de rigueur,* paid for from the squad's slush fund, and arranged on top of the long bookcase on one wall of the lieutenant's corner office.

The team being relieved was Meyer, Kling, and Carella; Hawes would have been there, too, but he was in the hospital, still fuming. The relieving team was Willis, Parker, Genero, and Brown. Andy Parker, relieving five minutes late, was nonetheless the first to pour himself a cup of coffee and heap three donuts onto his paper plate.

"So what've we got here?" Byrnes asked. "A nut?"

He sounded annoyed. White-haired and blue-eyed, the map of Ireland all over his craggy phizz, he sat behind his desk in his corner-windowed office, glaring out at his men as though challenging them to tell him this nut was as sane as any of them.

"Beginning to ramble a bit, right," Meyer agreed, and rolled his eyes.

"Whose mom is he referring to?" Parker asked.

Naturally, his interest would have been drawn to mention of a porn diet and a tit, *any* tit. He had not shaved this morning. Upon awakening, he'd told himself he would shave this afternoon, before coming in. But it was now a little past four p.m., and he still hadn't shaved, and he wouldn't be relieved until midnight, so he probably wouldn't shave at all today. But such were the vagaries of police work; one never knew when he might be called upon to impersonate some kind of shabby street person.

"Who *cares* whose mom?" Meyer said. "Mom's tit is where he starts to lose it."

"*And* us," Carella added.

"When were you not lost?" Byrnes wanted to know.

"Well, at first we thought he was referring to the homicide we caught yesterday morning. In his first note . . ."

"Let me see that again," Byrnes said, and extended his hand across his desk. Carella gave him the note in its plastic shield:

WHO'S IT, ETC?
A DARN SOFT GIRL?
O, THERE'S A HOT HINT!

"And this arrived when?" Byrnes asked.

"Around this time yesterday afternoon."

"So you figured the 'darn soft girl' was . . . what was the vic's name again?"

"Gloria Stanford. Yes."

"And *that* was the perp's hot hint, is *that*

what you figured? That Gloria Stanford was the darn soft girl?"

"Yes. Well . . . yes."

"Some hint," Parker remarked.

"He spelled *oh* wrong," Genero said, sure of it now. He'd looked it up in the dictionary last night. At five feet nine inches tall, Genero thought he was very tall. From his father, he had inherited beautiful curly black hair, a strong Neapolitan nose, a sensuous mouth, and soulful brown eyes. From his mother, he had inherited the tall Milanese carriage of all his male cousins and uncles — except for his Uncle Dominick, who was only five-six.

"Tell me something," Byrnes said. "Doesn't the perp *realize* we know this girl's name? I mean, he left her in her own apartment, he didn't dump her in the park someplace without any ID on her, he's got to realize we already *know* who she is. Isn't that so?"

"It would appear to be so, yes, sir," Carella said.

Byrnes looked at him. He was not used to being sirred by his detectives.

"So why is he asking us who she is? And why is he telling us there's a hint in his note? Where's the hint? Do any of you see a hint? Hot or otherwise?"

"Am I the only one eating here?" Parker asked.

"I can use some coffee," Brown said.

He appeared to be scowling, but that was merely his normal expression. A big man . . . well, a *huge* man . . . with eyes and skin the color of his name, Arthur Brown was the sort of detective who reveled in playing Bad Cop because it fulfilled the stereotypical expectations of so many white people. He particularly enjoyed being partnered with Bert Kling, whose blond hair and healthy cornfed looks made him the perfect Good Cop honkie foil. Going to the bookcase feast now, eating a donut in three bites before he poured himself a cup of coffee and put two more donuts on a paper plate, Brown said, "Could we see that second note, please?"

Carella passed it around:

A WET CORPUS?
CORN, ETC?

"He's telling us we've got a bleeding corpse here," Brown said.

"Just what *I* thought," Meyer said.

"Then why the question marks?" Genero asked.

"He's saying 'Get it?' " Kling said.

"Wake up here! I'm spelling it all out for you, dummies."

"Pay *attention* here!"

"*Listen* to me."

"*Hark!*"

They all turned to look at Willis.

"Is actually what he's saying," Willis said, and shrugged. Dark-haired and dark-eyed, he was the shortest man on the squad, but he was a black belt in karate, and he was ready to knock any one of his colleagues flat on his ass in ten seconds flat if they questioned his use of a perfectly legitimate synonym for "listen carefully."

"The third note is where he begins to lose it," Meyer said. "In my opinion, anyway."

"Could we see it again?" Kling asked.

Carella placed it on Byrnes's desk. They crowded around it, munching donuts.

BRASS HUNT?
CELLAR?

"Was there any top brass at the scene?" Byrnes asked.

"Not a big enough case to draw their attention," Carella said.

"So what's this about a 'brass hunt'?"

"I figured he might be referring to spent cartridge cases."

"Did Mobile find any?"

"No, but . . ."

"What'd Ballistics say the weapon was?"

"A forty-five automatic."

"So there wouldn't have been any."

"So what does 'brass hunt' mean?"

"And why's he sending us to the cellar?"

"Which, by the way," Meyer said, "Mobile went down there this afternoon and found zilch."

"Down where?" Genero asked.

"The basement of the building," Carella said. "Where the girl was killed."

"She was killed in the basement?"

"No, in her bedroom. I meant the *building* where she was killed."

Genero looked bewildered.

"The last note is where he loses it entirely," Meyer said. "In my opinion, anyway."

"Let's have a look," Byrnes said.

PORN DIET?
HELL, A TIT ON MOM!

"Maybe he's referring to the girl again," Genero said.

"Did he shoot her in the breast?"

"Not according to the ME's report. She was shot twice. Both slugs took her in the heart. Just *below* the left breast."

"Was she sexually assaulted?"

"No."

"Then what's this 'porn diet' shit?" Parker asked.

"What's *any* of it?" Genero asked.

"Who's this Adam Fen?" Byrnes asked.

"I checked the phone books yesterday," Willis said. "Fen is a Chinese name . . ."

"Told you," Genero said.

". . . but I didn't get an Adam anyplace in the city."

"Was there an *Eve?*" Parker asked. "Adam and *Eve? Porn* diet?"

Byrnes glared at him.

"Just a thought," Parker said, and picked up another donut.

"What about this P.O. box number?" Byrnes asked.

"Nonexistent," Willis said.

"Why'd he pick 4884?"

"Why'd he pick *us?*" Genero asked.

"He's crazy is why," Meyer said.

"Like a fox," Carella said.

"Let's go over it again," Byrnes said.

In a penthouse apartment not a mile from where the detectives mulled over the various missives he'd sent them, the Deaf Man was trying to explain the meaning of the word *anagram* to the girl who sat beside him on his living room couch.

The girl was blond, and perhaps twenty-three years old, certainly no older than that. He had helped her to remove her white blouse not three minutes ago, so she was at the moment wearing only a black miniskirt, black panties and bra, and black, high-heeled, strapped sandals. Altogether a dangerous look.

"Think of it this way," he said. "Suppose I told you your breasts are as ripe as berries."

"Well, you don't know that yet, do you?" the girl said.

"I can speculate," the Deaf Man said.

"I suppose we can all speculate," she said.

"As ripe as berries," he repeated, and lifted a clean white pad from the coffee table, and with a marking pen wrote on it:

AS BERRIES

"Is that for emphasis?" the girl asked.

Her name was Melissa, Lissie for short. She'd told him this at the bar in the cocktail lounge of the Olympia Hotel, where he'd picked her up. He knew she was a hooker. A hooker was what he needed. But he had never in his life paid anyone for sex, and he did not intend to pay for it now.

"Now if we rearrange those letters," he said, "placing them in a different order, we get the word . . ."

And here he wrote on the pad again:

BRASSIERE

. . . and reached behind her back to unclasp it, freeing her breasts.

"As ripe as berries," he said, and tried to kiss her nipples, but she crossed her arms over her breasts, and crossed her legs, too, and began jiggling one black-sandaled foot.

"And *what'd* you call that?" she asked. "Rearranging the letters that way?"

"An anagram," he said.

"That's a neat trick," she said. "Can you do an anagram for Melissa?"

"Aimless," he said at once. "But how about this one?" he asked, and on the pad he wrote:

A PET SIN

. . . and reached under her skirt to lower them over her thighs, before writing on the pad:

PANTIES

"Neat," she said, and uncrossed her legs and her arms, and lifted herself slightly so he could lower the panties to her ankles. She kicked them free. They sailed halfway across the room, hitting the sliding glass doors that opened onto the seventeenth-floor terrace and a spectacular view of the city.

"Let's hope no one can spy us," he said, and wrote the last two words on the pad:

SPY US

"Can you rearrange those?" he asked.

"Sure," she said, and took the marker from his hand, and wrote:

PUSSY

"Neat," he said.

"But," she said, and wrote:

MORE'S NIFTY

"I'll bet it is," he said.

"Oh, you bet your ass it is," she said. "But it's your game, Adam."

"Which game do you mean?" he asked.

His hand was between her legs, but her thighs were closed tight on it, refusing entrance.

"This one," she said, and wrote on the pad:

SNAG A RAM

"Anagrams, do you mean?"

"Bingo," she said.

"You want an anagram for 'more's nifty.' Is that it?"

"Try it," she said, and handed him the marker.

He thought for merely an instant, and then wrote:

MONEY FIRST

"How clever of you," she said, and spread her legs wide, and held her hand out to him, palm upwards.

"I think not," he said, and slapped her so hard he almost knocked her off the couch.

Later, while Melissa was still tied to the bed, he asked if she knew that "Adam Fen" was an anagram for "Deaf Man."

Aching everywhere, she said she guessed she did.

He wrote both words on the pad for her, one under the other:

ADAM FEN
DEAF MAN

"Gee, yeah," she said.

Along about then, a courier was delivering the final note in what the Deaf Man thought of as the first movement of his ongoing little symphony.

The note in the inside envelope read:

We wondred that thou went'st so soon
From the world's stage, to the grave's
    tiring room.
We thought thee dead, but this thy
    printed worth,
Tells thy spectators that thou went'st
    but forth
To enter with applause.

An Actor's Art,
Can die, and live, to act a second part.

I'M A FATHEAD, MEN!

There was also a line drawing in the envelope:

72

"Who the hell is *that* supposed to be?" Parker asked.

"Looks like a rag picker," Byrnes said. "You have rag pickers in your neighborhood?"

"We called him the Rags Man," Brown said, nodding.

"Why would he be sending us a picture of a rag picker?" Meyer asked.

"No, Artie's got it," Carella said. "It's a rags man. Oh, Jesus, it's a rags man!"

They all looked at him.

He seemed about to have a heart attack.

"It's an anagram!" he said.

"Huh?" Genero said.

"An anagram, an anagram, a rags man! That's an anagram for *anagrams!*"

"Huh?" Genero said again.

All at once the letters under the note's

poetry seemed to spring from the page, I'M A FATHEAD, MEN, leaping into the air before Carella's very eyes, rolling and tumbling in random order, I A F M H A T D E A N M E, until at last they fell into place in precisely the order Adam Fen had intended.

I AM THE DEAF MAN!

"Shit," Carella said, "he's back."

And now, of course, all of it made sense.

All of the notes, when read as anagrams, clearly told them what the Deaf Man had done and possibly why he had done it.

WHO'S IT, ETC?
A DARN SOFT GIRL?
O, THERE'S A HOT HINT!

Rearranged in their proper order, the letters became:

SHOT TWICE?
GLORIA STANFRD?
SHOT IN THE HEART!

Move that dangling "O" from the third line to the first line and you had her full last name: STANFORD.

74

Similarly:

A WET CORPUS?
CORN, ETC?

. . . became:

COW PASTURE?
CONCERT?

. . .the scene of the Deaf Man's last chaotic diversion in Grover Park.

And once they rearranged:

BRASS HUNT?
CELLAR?

. . . they got:

STASH BURN?
RECALL?

. . . which merely asked them to remember his true target the last time out, the incinerator on the River Harb Drive, where thirty million dollars worth of confiscated narcotics was scheduled to be burned by the police.

And lastly:

75

PORN DIET?
HELL, A TIT ON MOM!

Put in their intended order, the letters in both lines formed the words:

RED POINT?
HAMILTON MOTEL!

. . . the name of the motel in a town across the river where a man who'd registered as Sonny Sanson had left behind a bloody trail apparently inspired by a woman who'd betrayed him.

Had that woman been GLORIA STANFORD?

A DARN SOFT GIRL-O!

Because, boy-o-boy-o, Sonny Sanson was sure as hell *Son'io Sans Son,* who was in turn ADAM FEN, who was none other than the DEAF MAN, who'd entered with fanfare and flourish to act yet another part.

I'M A FATHEAD, MEN?

Oh, no, not by a long shot.

I AM THE DEAF MAN!

Bravo, lads, that was more like it!

He was back, and the very thought sent a collective shudder through the detectives gathered in the lieutenant's office.

"Anyone care for another donut?" Byrnes asked.

4

Rough winds do shake the darling
  buds of May
And summer's lease hath all too short
  a date . . .

"Actually, that's kind of nice," Genero said.
  "He's back, all right," Willis said.
  "With more poetry, no less."
  " 'The darling buds of May,' " Eileen
said. "That's Shakespeare, isn't it?"
  "Sure sounds like Shakespeare."
  " 'The darling buds of May.' "
  "But it's June already," Carella said.
  "Just barely," Meyer said.
  This was Thursday morning, the third
day of June. The lieutenant had virtually
double-teamed the squad because when-
ever the Deaf Man put in an appearance,
his people all suddenly began behaving like
Keystone Kops, and one could not be too
careful lest disapprobation thunder down
from the brassy skies above. The nine
Shakespearean scholars grouped around

Carella's desk were Carella himself, Meyer, Kling, Genero, Parker, Hawes, Willis, Brown, and Eileen Burke.

"Kind of nice, though," Genero said. " 'The darling buds of May,' you know? I really like that."

All the squadroom windows were open to the balmy breezes of early June. The note on Carella's desk was the first one delivered today. He felt sure there'd be more.

"What's he trying to tell us this time?" he asked.

"Nothing about the homicide, that's for sure."

"He's already said enough about that," Meyer said. "I killed Gloria Stanford, I shot her twice in the heart, now come find me, dummies."

"Where does it say that?" Parker asked.

He had shaved this morning. Maybe he expected another round of coffee and donuts.

"In his previous notes," Meyer explained. "All those anagrams."

"Yeah, anagrams, right," Parker said, not giving a shit one way or the other.

"What does he mean about 'summer's lease'?" Willis asked.

"When does summer start this year?" Eileen asked.

Limping around the lieutenant's office in his soft cast, Hawes didn't much care *when* summer started this year. Or *any* year. He was still fuming because the dicks from the 8-6 hadn't found any ejected shells on any of the rooftops opposite Honey Blair's building, and so far nobody knew nothing about whoever had fired half a dozen shots at him yesterday morning. It was one thing to get all excited about someone who might or might not be the Deaf Man perhaps being responsible for the death of a woman named Gloria Stanford, but bygones were bygones, easy come, easy go, and Hawes himself was still in the here-and-now and luckily among the living, and whoever had tried to render him otherwise was still out there someplace, on the loose, so where the hell was a cop when you needed one?

"Miscolo!" Brown yelled.

" 'Summer's lease hath all too short a date,' " Eileen quoted.

"Nice," Genero said again, smiling wistfully.

Miscolo came in from the Clerical Office down the hall. He'd put on a little weight and lost a little hair at the back of his head. But he still resembled a somewhat moist-eyed basset hound. "You want coffee, right?" he said.

"Have you got a *Farmer's Almanac* in the Clerical Office?" Brown asked.

"Why would I have a *Farmer's Almanac*?"

"We're trying to find out when summer comes this year."

"Why?"

"Because it hath all too short a date," Genero explained.

"You guys," Miscolo said, and walked out shaking his head.

"Anybody got a calendar?" Brown asked, and went to his own desk. He flipped open the pages to June, ran his forefinger across the dates. The words *Summer begins* were printed in the box for June 21. "Here it is," he said. "June twenty-first. First day of summer."

" 'Summer's lease,' " Eileen said.

"Is he planning something for the twenty-first?"

"Or *not* planning it, as the case may be," Meyer said. "He *never* tells us exactly what he's up to."

" 'All too short a date,' " Willis reminded them.

"So it could be short of the twenty-first."

"Closer to May," Kling suggested. " 'Rough winds do shake the darling buds of May.' "

81

"That reminds me of teenage girls," Parker said.

Then again, *many* things reminded him of teenage girls.

" 'The darling buds of May,' " he explained, and shrugged.

"You know what he *might* be doing?" Carella said. "He might be sending us a new batch of notes just to divert us from the homicide investigation."

But even he didn't believe this.

The lieutenant's door opened.

"Eileen?" he said. "See you a minute?"

"Have a seat," Byrnes said.

She took one of the chairs opposite his desk.

Waited.

"I want you to know I appreciate your input on this case," Byrnes said.

"Thank you, sir."

"Pete," he said. "Please. Pete."

"Yes, sir. Pete."

"Eileen," he said, "I don't want you to take what I'm about to say the wrong way."

Uh-oh, she thought.

"This isn't just because you're a woman."

Am I being transferred? she wondered. To a precinct where a *woman* — Fat

Chance Department — commands the detective squadroom?

She waited.

"I want you to go over to the Stanford apartment. Now that Mobile's cleared it, I want you to go through her things, her personal items, everything she left behind. Bring a fresh eye to it. Bring a *woman's* eye to it. See if you can spot anything a man might have missed."

"Yes, sir," she said.

"It's not just because you're a woman," he said.

Then what is it? she wondered.

"I understand, sir," she said. "Pete."

"In my experience," he said, "aside from crimes of passion, which this might have been . . ."

"Yes, sir."

". . . the man coming back to take revenge on the woman who done him wrong, that sort of thing . . ."

"Yes, sir."

"But if this *wasn't* simply that, if instead the man *wanted* something from her, which in my experience is the motive for many murders, hasn't that been your experience, too? A person *wants* something very badly, he *gets* it, and then, to protect his identity or whatever, he kills the person he took it from. Like an arsonist setting a fire to cover some other crime. Hasn't that been your experience, Eileen?"

"Well, I haven't investigated that many homicides, Pete. Sir," she said. "Or arsons, either, for that matter."

"So what did the Deaf Man want from her?" Byrnes asked rhetorically. "He mas-terminded a multimillion-dollar narcotics theft, you know . . ."

"Yes, sir, I know."

". . . so was he coming back after that stash? If so, where is it? Where's the dope? Or the dope money? I don't think he's the sort of man who'd kill someone merely for revenge, do you? So why *else* might he have killed her? That's what I want you to bring your woman's eye to."

"I understand, sir. It's like what the Walt Disney studio did a few years back."

"The what?"

"The movie company."

"Yes?"

"They hired a nineteen-year-old girl to bring a teenager's sensibility to a script a man had written for them."

"Oh," Byrnes said.

"Turned out she was in her thirties. The female writer they hired."

"Oh," Byrnes said again.

"But they figured a man couldn't possibly know what a woman was thinking or feeling."

"That's right," he said.

"Even if he was a writer."

"I can understand that."

"So that's why you want me to shake down Gloria's apartment. Find out what she might have been thinking or feeling."

"Find out why he *killed* her," Byrnes said, nodding grimly.

Melissa Summers didn't know quite what she was feeling.

Never in her entire life had she ever met anyone like Adam Fen, or whatever his name was. Never anyone like him in all the guys she'd fucked for free when she was still just a girl and an amateur, never anyone like him in all the guys she'd fucked since turning pro at the age of sixteen in Los Angeles, California. Well, sort of *dabbled* at being a pro. She didn't *really* become a pro till she came to this city, thank you for that, Ambrose Carter.

But never had she met anyone like Adam Fen.

Never.

A *deaf* guy, no less!

If he was, in fact, deaf.

Actually, she didn't know *what* he was.

One minute, he was kind and gentle with her, stroking her like a kitten, the next he was fierce as a tiger, slapping her around, making her do things even none of the freaks in LaLaLand had asked her to do, some of them movie stars even, would you believe it? Well, TV actors, anyway. Some of them. *One* of them, actually. Well, a walk-on part in a weekly sitcom, actually. Tipped her five hundred bucks. Told her to catch the show on NBC next Friday night. And there he was! Actually on the show! Walked into this executive's office, said, "someone to see you, sir," and walked right out again. Looked innocent as an angel, the things he'd asked her to do.

Adam Fen was worse. Or better, depending how you looked at it. *If* that was his real name. Which she sincerely doubted. But Melissa Summers wasn't her real name, either, so what difference did it make? He'd told her Adam Fen was an anagram for Deaf Man, which was certainly true, the anagram part, but whether or not he was really deaf was another matter. Not that she cared. What she was worried about was getting involved with him. She had the feeling that getting involved with him could be dangerous. Well, getting involved with *any* man, getting *really* involved with any man, was a dangerous thing to do.

Take the money and run, that was her motto.

Even when she was still *giving* it away (boy, talk about naïve!) she'd realized that getting *involved* with a man — though back then they were all still boys, kids, you know, fifteen, sixteen, a bit older than she was, she'd started when she was fourteen, with a cousin of hers from New Jersey — getting involved meant letting them have the upper hand, and that was putting yourself in a vulnerable position.

He had a gun.

She'd seen the gun.

He'd showed her the gun.

Actually cocked the trigger and used it on her like a cock. The gun. Inserted the barrel inside her. Got her so scared, she almost peed on it. Turned out there were no bullets in it.

But she was afraid if she got involved with this guy, *really* involved with him — he might one day actually use the gun on her.

That was her fear.

He seemed unpredictable.

Exciting but dangerous.

So why was she running this errand at the bank for him today?

There was something eerily frightening about the murder scene. Maybe it was the yellow tape on the bedroom carpet, the outline of where Gloria Stanford's body had lain. Maybe it was the silence. Eileen guessed it was the silence.

A stillness so complete that it seemed to exclude the sounds one normally associated with big-city living, the ambulances and police sirens outside, the occasional toilet being flushed somewhere in the building, the low whine of an elevator, the rumble of television voices. All seemed subordinate to the utter silence.

She stood in the entrance door to the dead woman's bedroom, looking in at the yellow tape on the floor. The stillness was oppressive. It seemed to be challenging her to enter the bedroom. She hesitated on the door sill. At last, she took a step into the room, walked gingerly around the taped outline on the floor, and directly to a drop-leaf desk that must have cost her yearly salary. As a detective/third, Eileen currently earned $55,936 a year; her own one-bedroom flat was furnished with stuff she'd bought at IKEA, across the River Harb.

She lowered the drop-leaf front and sat in a chair upholstered with a satin seat and back.

In one of the desk's warren of cubbyholes, she found a box of checkbook inserts. Blank checks for FirstBank's Salisbury Street branch right here in the city. Top sheaf of checks numbered from 151 through 180. Sheaves below it numbered to follow. Lettering across the top of each check was:

GLORIA STANFORD
1113 SILVERMINE OVAL
ISOLA, 30576

In another of the cubbies, she found FirstBank's most recent statement. Gloria's checking account balance at the end of March had been $1,674.18. On the third of April, she'd made a cash deposit of $9,800. Another cash deposit on April 12, this time for $7,200. Yet another on April 23, for $8,100. Total cash deposits for the month: $25,100. Total amount of checks written: $24,202.17; her closing balance on April 30 was $2,573.01.

By law, all banks were required to report to the Internal Revenue Service any cash deposits in excess of $10,000. Was it mere coincidence that Gloria's cash deposits had been for amounts somewhat less than the ten grand? She looked for a savings account passbook and could find none.

So where had those cash deposits come from?

Eileen went through Gloria's appointment calendar and her address book.

She went through her closets and her dresser drawers.

She went through her medicine cabinet and her refrigerator.

Her "woman's eye" caught nothing a man's eye might have missed.

In the living room, on a counter to the right of the entrance door, she found a tote bag with a small-caliber pistol in it. She wondered if Carella and Meyer had simply missed the gun. Or had they turned it over to Ballistics for testing, and then brought it back to the apartment on their second go-round? A place for everything and everything in its place. She would have to ask them. Meanwhile, the apartment had been cleared, so she felt free to take the gun out of the bag (although using a pencil passed through the trigger guard) and sniff the barrel. It did not seem to have been fired recently.

Sliding the gun off the pencil, she

dropped it back into the bag. Digging around the way only a woman could — the lieutenant was right in that respect, at least — she also found a tube of lipstick, a mascara pencil, a packet of Kleenex tissues, a small vial of Hermès' *Calèche*, and a red leather Coach wallet. Oddly, there was no identification in the wallet. No driver's license (but that was possible in a big city), no credit cards (which was unusual), no social security card (but you weren't supposed to carry that with you), not anything with Gloria Stanford's name or her signature on it.

She went back to the drop-leaf desk in the bedroom, opened the FirstBank statement again.

The statement showed checks written in April to American Express, Visa, and MasterCard.

So where were the credit cards?

Was *that* what he'd been after?

The lady's credit cards?

The Deaf Man?

Planning to charge a camcorder or a stereo to the lady's credit cards?

Come on now.

That hardly seemed his style.

And yet . . .

**Rough winds do shake the darling
buds of May . . .**

Maybe the poor man had fallen upon
hard times.

**And summer's lease hath all too short
a date . . .**

Maybe he needed a new wardrobe for
the coming summer season.
Still and all . . .
Credit cards?
Such small-time shit for such a big-time
schemer.
She decided to pay a visit to the
FirstBank branch on Salisbury Street.

Melissa had practiced signing the name
a hundred or more times. Copying it from
Gloria Stanford's driver's license and
credit cards. Gloria Stanford, Gloria Stanford, again and again. She now knew it almost the way she knew her own name.
Melissa Summers, Gloria Stanford. Inter-
changeable.
There was a photo of a good-looking
blonde on both the license and in the
corner of one of the credit cards. But except for the blond hair, Gloria Stanford —

whoever the hell *she* might be — bore no resemblance to Melissa Summers, none at all.

Melissa had pointed this out to Adam.

"We don't look at all alike," she'd said.

"No problem," he'd assured her. "One thing certain about a so-called personal banker is that he wouldn't know you if he tripped over you in his own bathroom."

She hoped so.

She did not know what crime it might be to try getting into someone else's safe-deposit box, but she had a feeling she could spend a lot of time upstate if she got caught doing it. Be ironic, wouldn't it? Get sent up for signing someone else's name on a bank's signature card, after she'd been hooking all these years with never so much as a blemish on her spotless career — well, that one prostitution bust in L.A., but she was still Carmela Sammarone then.

Her high-heeled shoes clicked noisily on the bank's polished marble floor as she approached the desk at the rear. A bespectacled woman looked up at her, smiled. Handing her the little red envelope with the key in it, Melissa returned the smile. The woman shook the key out of the envelope, opened a file drawer with numbered index cards in it, fingered swiftly through them, yanked one out, silently read the name on it, looked up, asked "Miss Stanford?," and without waiting for an answer, handed the card to Melissa for signature. Gloria Stanford's true signature marched down the length of the card like so many identical siblings:

Gloria Stanford
Gloria Stanford
Gloria Stanford
Gloria Stanford
Gloria Stanford
Gloria Stanford
Gloria Stanford

Melissa added her forgery just below the last true signature:

Gloria Stanford

Close, but no cigar.

On the other hand, who was watching the store?

The lady in the eyeglasses glanced cursorily at the signature, and then opened the gate in the railing and led Melissa back to the rows upon rows of stainless steel boxes. She used first Gloria's key and next the bank's own key to open the door to one of the boxes, and then yanked the box out of the row and handed it, deep and sleek, to Melissa.

"Will you need a room, Miss Stanford?" she asked.

"Yes, please," Melissa said.

Her heart was pounding.

In the small room, with the door locked, Melissa lifted the lid of the box and peered into it.

There seemed to be a whole big shitpot full of hundred-dollar bills in that box.

She wondered if Adam would find her and shoot her if she ran off with all that money.

She decided he would.

When Eileen Burke got to the bank, the woman in the eyeglasses told her that Miss Stanford had been there not ten minutes earlier. She showed Eileen the signature card Miss Stanford had signed. Eileen knew she'd now have to go all the way downtown for a court order to open that safe-deposit box. She also knew that when she opened it, she would find it empty.

Just as she was going down into the subway kiosk to catch a train to High Street, the second message that day was being delivered to the stationhouse.

Shake off slumber, and beware:
Awake, awake!

"There he goes again!" Meyer said. "Taunting us with Shakespeare."

"If it *is* Shakespeare," Kling said.

"What else could it be but Shakespeare?"

"Calling us dummies," Meyer said.

"Maybe we *are* dummies," Genero said.

No one disagreed with him.

"Let's try to figure out what he's saying," Carella said. "That shouldn't be too difficult."

"I got better things to do," Parker said, and went off to the men's room to pee.

"He's telling us to wake up."

"Or else."

" 'Shake off slumber and beware.' "

" 'Awake, awake!' "

"It doesn't even rhyme," Genero said.

Dr. James Melvin Hudson was head of the Oncology Department at Mount Pleasant Hospital, not too distant from where Sharyn Cooke maintained her private practice in Diamondback. As a member of the medical team in the Deputy Chief Surgeon's Office in Majesta, however, he reported only to

96

Sharyn, his immediate superior.

At twelve noon that Thursday, while Detective Eileen Burke was on her way downtown for her court order, Hudson asked Sharyn if she'd like to go down for lunch, and they both went downstairs to a sandwich joint called the Burger and Bun, right there in the Rankin Plaza complex. The strip mall in which the Deputy Chief Surgeon's Office was located also housed a dry-cleaning establishment, a fitness center, a Mail Boxes, Etc., and a branch of the Lorelie Records chain of music shops. A cop who'd recently been shot or merely kicked in the ass could therefore have coffee or lunch before being examined by a doctor, get his uniform jacket pressed while he was having his chest X-rayed, develop his pecs or his abs after his exam, and then buy and mail a CD to his mother for her birthday, all in the same little mall. Location, location. All was location.

Timing was important, too.

At a quarter past noon, when Hudson and Sharyn entered the Burger and Bun, it was jammed with similarly minded lunchers. Heads turned nonetheless. Here was a strikingly good-looking black couple, both obvious professionals, both wearing white tunics, a stethoscope hanging

97

around Sharyn's neck, another one dangling from Hudson's pocket. He was six-feet two-inches tall. She was five-nine. All conversation almost stopped when they came through the door. The proprietor showed them to a booth near the rear of the shop. They ordered soups and sandwiches, and then earnestly and seriously discussed a patient they'd both seen earlier that morning, Sharyn because the cop had been shot two months ago, Hudson because the cop had revealed to him that two non-malignant tumors had been removed from his bladder three weeks before the shooting. When their food came, they dropped shop talk for a while, Sharyn mentioning a movie she and Kling had seen over the weekend, Hudson telling her he was getting sick and tired of movies aimed at fifteen-year-old boys.

"There's nothing made for grownups anymore," he said.

"Not *all* movies are that bad," Sharyn said.

She was bone weary.

Her police workday was only three hours old, and she was ready to go home. Still had to bus back to the city for her own office hours this afternoon. Sometimes, she wondered.

"I'd rather stay home and listen to music," Hudson said. And then, without preamble, "Are you familiar with the work of a rap group called Spit Shine?"

"No," she said. "I don't much like rap."

"Well, it's come a long way from 'Let's All Kill the Police,' if that's what you're thinking."

"I don't know what 'Let's All Kill the Police' is."

"I'm categorizing a form of gangsta rap," Hudson said. "Spit Shine went beyond that. Spit Shine addressed the ills of black society itself. Didn't try to lay it all on Whitey. Asked us what we *ourselves* were doing to denigrate . . ."

"I don't like the expression 'Whitey,'" Sharyn said.

"Sorry. Didn't mean it in a derogatory way. In any case, Spit Shine no longer exists. Guy who wrote their stuff got killed in the Grover Park riot a few years back. Remember the riot there?"

"Yes."

She remembered. The day after the riot, a white detective named Bert Kling had called her from a phone booth in the rain to ask if she'd like to go to dinner and a movie with him.

"Twenty-three years old when a stray

99

bullet killed him," Hudson said. "His name was Sylvester Cummings, his rapper's handle was 'Silver.' Wrote wonderful lyrics. Wonderful." And again without preamble, he began beating out a rhythm on the table top, and began singing in a low, somehow urgent voice.

"You dig vanilla?
"Now ain't that a killer!
"You say you hate chocolate?
"I say you juss thoughtless.
"Cause chocolate is the color
"Of the Lord's first children
"Juss go ask the diggers
"The men who find the bones
"Go ask them 'bout chocolate . . .
"Go ask them 'bout niggers . . ."

"I don't like *that* word, either," Sharyn said.

"Man was trying to make a point," Hudson said.

Their food arrived.

He seemed about to say something more. Instead, he just shook his head, and began eating.

Go apart, Adam, and thou shalt hear how he will shake me up.

"Adam," Meyer said.

"Adam Fen," Carella said.

"The Chinese guy again," Genero said.

"The Deaf Man," Kling said.

"If he's deaf, then how can he *hear?*" Parker asked. " 'Thou shalt *hear.*' " "And what's with all this Quaker talk all at once?" Willis asked. " '*Thou* shalt hear?' What's that supposed to be?"

" 'Thy hat and thy glove,' " Eileen said. "That was a good movie."

This was now ten minutes past three. She'd been back in the squadroom since a quarter to. As she'd suspected, the FirstBank safe-deposit box was empty. She was wondering now if it was worth sending Mobile over there to dust it for prints. Had "Gloria Stanford" put on gloves before opening it?

"*Friendly Persuasion,*" Kling said, remembering.

They had seen it together on television, Eileen lying in his arms on the couch in his studio apartment near the Calm's Point Bridge. That was when they were still living together. That was a long time ago, in a galaxy far far away.

" 'Thee I love,' " Eileen said, remembering.

"He's telling us he plans to shake us up," Parker said.

He *hated* this fucking Deaf Man. Made him feel stupid. Which maybe he was. But he didn't even like to consider that possibility.

"Shake us up *how?*" Brown asked.

"You think he's gonna tell us all at once?"

"Oh no, not him."

"Piece by piece."

"Bit by bit."

"Listen."

"Go apart and listen."

"Hark!" Willis said.

And this time, no one questioned his use of the word.

The call from Milan came at three-thirty, which Carella figured was either nine-thirty or ten-thirty over there in Italy. The call was from Luigi Fontero, the man who was about to marry Carella's mother on June twelfth and whisk her off to Italy shortly thereafter. *Life With Luigi,* he thought.

"Hey, Luigi," he said, feigning a jovial camaraderie he did not feel. "What a surprise! How are you?"

"Fine, Steve, and you?" Fontero said.

Mild Italian accent. Somehow it grated.

"Busy, busy," Carella said. "We're having

trouble again with a criminal we call the Deaf Man. That would be *'El Sordo'* in your language."

"Il *Sordo*," Fontero corrected.

"Right," Carella said.

Thanks, he thought.

"So what can I do for you?" he asked.

"I don't know how to begin."

Carella immediately thought *He's calling off the wedding!*

He waited.

"About the wedding . . ."

Breathlessly, he waited.

"I don't know how to say this."

Just say it, Carella thought. Just tell me you've made a terrible mistake, you've now met a lovely Italian girl drawing water from the well in the town square, and you'd like to call off the entire thing. Just *say* it, Luigi!

"I don't wish to offend you."

No, no, Carella almost said aloud. No offense, Luigi, none at all. I quite understand. We all make mistakes.

"I want to pay for the cost of the wedding," Fontero blurted.

"What?" Carella said.

"I know this is not customary . . ."

"What?" he said again.

"I know the groom is not supposed to

make such an offer. But Luisa is a widow . . . your mother is a widow . . . and we are neither of us youngsters, there is no father of the bride here, there is only a loving, devoted son who has taken it upon himself . . ."

He's rehearsed this, Carella thought.

". . . to shoulder the burden of a *double* wedding, his mother's *and* his sister's. And, Steve, I cannot allow this to happen. You are a civil servant . . ."

Oh, *please*, Carella thought.

". . . and I cannot allow you to assume the tremendous expense of a double wedding. If you will permit me . . ."

"No, I can't do that," Carella said.

"I've offended you."

"Not at all. But I'm perfectly comfortable paying for both weddings. In fact it's been fun talking to caterers and musicians and . . ."

"I can hear it in your voice."

"No, Luigi, truly. It's very kind of you to make such an offer, but you're right, this isn't something the groom should have to do, pay for his own wedding, no, Luigi. No. Truly. When do you plan to come over?"

"Are you certain about this, Steve? I'm ready to wire to my bank there . . ."

"No, no. Not another word about it. How's the weather there in Milan?"

"Lovely actually. But I long to be there. I miss your mother." He hesitated. "I love her dearly," he said.

"I'm sure she loves you, too," Carella said. "So when do you think you'll be here?"

"I fly in on the eighth. Four days before the wedding."

"Good, that's good," Carella said.

There was a long silence on the line.

"Well, I'd better get back to work here," Carella said.

"Are you sure I haven't offend . . . ?"

"Positive, positive. See you next week sometime. Have a good flight."

"Thank you, Steve."

Carella broke the connection.

He wondered now if actually he *had* been offended.

Here at the ragtag end of the day's shift in this grimy squadroom he had called home for such a long time now, he wondered if the offer from the rich furniture-maker in Milan had offended him.

As a working detective, Carella currently earned $62,857 a year. By his most recent calculation, the double wedding was going to cost almost half that. Without doubt, Mr. Luigi Fontero could more easily afford to pay for the coming festivities than could Detective/Second Grade Stephen Louis Carella.

But there was this matter of pride.

When he was still in college, one of his professors — and he truly could no longer remember which class this had been — called him in to discuss his term paper and his final grade. The professor told him it was a very good paper, and he was grading it an A, and then he said he was giving Carella a B-plus for the semester.

He must have seen the look on Carella's face.

"Or do you really *need* an A?" the professor asked.

Carella didn't know what that meant. Did he really *need* an A? *Everyone* really needs an A, he thought.

He looked the professor dead in the eye.

"No," he said. "I don't really need an A. B-plus will be fine."

And he'd picked up his term paper and walked out.

A mere matter of pride.

So what the hell? he thought now.

My mother and my only sister are getting married. So thanks, Mr. Fontero, but

no thanks. I'll find a way to pay for it myself. Even if it takes me to the poorhouse.
Which was just when the Deaf Man's
final note of the day arrived.

And now I will unclasp a secret book,
And to your quick-conceiving
**   discontents**
I'll read you matter deep and
**   dangerous,**
As full of peril and adventurous spirit
As to o'er-walk a current roaring loud
On the unsteadfast footing of a spear.

"Now we're getting there," Meyer said.
"*Where* are we getting?" Parker wanted
to know. "It's just more damn Shake-
speare."
"But he'll be sending us a book!"
" 'A *secret* book,' " Kling corrected.
"Didn't Shakespeare write sonnets?"
Genero asked. "I hope it's a book of his
sonnets. I like his poetry."
"Personally, I find it somewhat shitty,"
Parker said.
"We've got to put them all together,"
Carella said. "His notes. The four notes we
received today."
"Why?"
"Because they won't make sense other-

107

wise. Same as the anagrams."

"You're right," Willis said. "We've got to look at them as a whole. Otherwise they're just nonsense."

"You want my opinion," Parker said, "they're just nonsense, anyway. I mean, what the fuck — excuse me, Eileen — is *this* supposed to mean? 'As to o'er-walk a current roaring loud on the unsteadfast footing of a spear.' I mean, that isn't even *English!*"

"Let's take a look at the other ones," Carella suggested, and removed the previous three notes from the center drawer of his desk.

Rough winds do shake the darling buds of May
And summer's lease hath all too short a date . . .

"He's telling us he's planning something for the summer."

"Or maybe even *sooner.*"

"Sometime closer to May . . ."

" 'The darling buds of *May,*' " Eileen said.

" 'Rough winds do shake the darling buds of May.' "

"He's telling us the party's gonna get rough."

"Let's see the second note."

Shake off slumber, and beware:
Awake, awake!

"Previews of coming attractions," Meyer said. "Nothing more, nothing less."

"We can expect a full-screen ad for a furniture store next," Parker said. "I *hate* going to the movies nowadays."

"Oh, me, too," Eileen agreed.

"Wake up, he's telling us. 'Shake off slumber.'"

"Let's see the third one."

Go apart, Adam, and thou shalt hear
how he will shake me up.

"Uses the name 'Adam' this time," Willis said.

"Lets us know this is the same Adam Fen who sent us the anagrams."

"Same Deaf Man who told us who he killed last Sunday."

"Whom," Genero corrected.

"Same fuckin *murderer*," Parker said heatedly. "Excuse me, Eileen."

"Going to shake us up with what he's planning next."

"Big summer movie."

"Coming attractions."

"You notice they release the lousiest movies in the summer and around Christmastime?"

"There's that word again."

"What word?"

"Shake. He's gonna shake us up. That's what he's telling us."

"Oh *shit!*" Eileen said. "Excuse me, Andy."

"What?" Carella asked at once.

"Check out these first three notes again. What's the word common to all of them?"

They all studied the notes again:

Rough winds do SHAKE . . .

SHAKE off slumber . . .

SHAKE me up . . .

"Now take a look at this last note."

I'll read you matter deep and
  dangerous,
As full of peril and adventurous spirit
As to o'er-walk a current roaring loud
On the unsteadfast footing of a spear.

"And single out the last line . . ."

On the unsteadfast footing of a spear.

"Then skip to the last word in that line. . . ."

. . . footing of a SPEAR.

"Put them all together . . ."

". . . they spell MOTHER," Parker said.

"No," Eileen said. "They spell Shakespeare. *Shake* and *spear* spell *Shakespeare*."

"Doesn't Shakespeare have an *e* on the end?" Genero asked.

"Don't you see?" she said. "He's telling us all his references will be coming from Shakespeare."

"I doped that out from the very start," Parker said.

"How come everybody in the world always dopes out everything from the very start?" Willis asked.

"Well, I *did*," Parker insisted. "Right after we got all that anagram shit. I knew that would be his plan. All Shakespeare, all the time. Where's that note?" he asked, and began rummaging through the messages arranged on Carella's desktop. "Here," he said. "This one."

We wondred that thou went'st so soon

111

From the world's stage, to the grave's
    tiring room.
We thought thee dead, but this thy
    printed worth,
Tells thy spectators that thou went'st
    but forth
To enter with applause.

An Actor's Art,
Can die, and live, to act a second part.

"Now if that ain't Shakespeare," he said,
"then I don't know what is!"

When Carella got home that night, he
was carrying a thick book he'd borrowed
from the library three blocks from his
house.

His daughter, April, was curled up in the
armchair under the imitation Tiffany lamp,
reading.

"Hi, Dad," she said, without looking up.
"Catch any crooks today?"

"Hundreds," he said.

"Good work, Jones," she said, and tossed
him a salute. He went to her, kissed the
top of her head. "What are you reading?"
he asked.

"Math," she said.

"Where's your brother?"

112

"Here," Mark said, and came striding in from his room down the hall. The twins favored their mother more than Carella, he guessed. Or perhaps hoped. Mark gave him a hug. Carella went into the kitchen. Teddy was at the stove, cooking. She turned her face to him for a kiss. Raven hair pulled back into a ponytail. Long white apron made her look like a French chef or something. She lifted a cover, stirred something, put down the ladle, noticed the book. Her hands moved on the air, signing. He read her flying fingers, read the words she mouthed in accompaniment.

"Shakespeare," he answered. "The complete works."

Mark materialized in the kitchen doorway.

"Why Shakespeare, Dad?"

"Some guy's sending us quotes from Shakespeare. I want to find out where he's getting them."

"There's an easier way," Mark said.

Carella was thinking no home should be without a twelve-year-old boy going on thirteen. Sitting before the computer in his room, Mark went first to GOOGLE, and then typed in the keyword SHAKE-

113

SPEARE and from the seemingly hundreds of choices there, he zeroed in on a site called *RhymeZone Shakespeare Search*. To the right of a little picture of Shakespeare's face were the words **Browse:** *Comedies, Tragedies, Histories, Poetry, Coined words,* **Most popular lines,** *Help.*

Just below that was the direction **Find word or phrase,** with a narrow rectangular box to the right of that, and then the boxed word

Search

"All you do is type in the word or phrase you're looking for," Mark said. "Give me an example."

Carella took out his batch of photocopied notes.

"How about 'the darling buds of May'?" he said.

Mark typed in *darling buds.* He hit the search key. On the computer screen, Carella saw:

Keyword search results:

Rough winds do shake the **darling buds** of May, <u>Sonnets: XVIII</u>
<u>1 result returned.</u>

"Now we click on *Sonnets*," Mark said, and clicked on it. The screen filled with:

XVIII.

Shall I compare thee to a summer's day?
Thou art more lovely and more temperate:
Rough winds do shake the darling buds of May,
And summer's lease hath all too short a date . . .

"That's amazing," Carella said.
"Give me another one," Mark said.

Carella remembered the name of the course now. American Romantic Poetry.
And his term paper had been titled *"The Raven" and Poe's Philosophy of Composition.*
What had fascinated him most about the poem was Poe's subsequent admission that he'd written it *backwards*. He could still remember the key passages from the author's explanation:

Here then the poem may be said to have had its beginning — at the end where all works of art should begin —

for it was here at this point of my preconsiderations that I first put pen to paper in the composition of the stanza:

"Prophet!" said I, "thing of evil! — prophet still, if bird or devil!"

I composed this stanza, at this point, first — by establishing the climax . . .

Carella had read the entire poem aloud to the class. Wowed the girls. Got an A on the paper, too. But only a B-plus for his final grade. It still rankled.

Once upon a midnight dreary, while I pondered weak and weary,
Over many a quaint and curious volume of forgotten lore —

Still knew the entire poem by heart. Could recite it at the drop of a hat. Now, weak and weary after a long day in the salt mines, he pondered on his son's computer many a quaint and curious volume of forgotten lore. And because he'd once been a good student and was now a good cop, he composed a short list he would take to work with him tomorrow morning:

Rough winds do shake the **_darling buds_** of May: <u>Sonnets XVIII</u>
shake off slumber, and beware: <u>The Tempest: Act II, Scene i</u>
how he will **_shake me up:_** <u>As You Like It: Act I, Scene i</u>
On the unsteadfast **_footing of a spear:_** <u>King Henry IV, part I: Act 1, Scene iii</u>

Shake plus *spear* equals Shakespeare.

But he got no returns at all for any of the words or phrases in one of the earliest quotes they'd received:

We wondred that thou went'st so soon
From the world's stage, to the grave's tiring room.
We thought thee dead, but this thy printed worth,
Tells thy spectators that thou went'st but forth
To enter with applause.

An Actor's Art,
Can die, and live, to act a second part.

Nothing.
Nada.
Zero.
Zilch.

* ★ ★

Before she'd left Rankin Plaza that afternoon, Sharyn stopped in at Lorelie Records downstairs from her office, and bought Spit Shine's last CD. Titled after its hit song, "Go Ask," it was the final album they'd made before that fateful and fatal Cow Pasture Concert. The title song was on track number seven. In her bedroom that night, she played it for Kling. He listened intently.

"Can you understand what they're singing?" he asked.

"Sure," she said.

"I can't," he admitted.

"Guess you got to be black, sugah."

"They ought to put subtitles on rap music," he said, shaking his head.

"They already do, on TV," she said. "But here, read the liner notes. The lyrics should be there."

"Play it again," he said, and removed the little pamphlet from the CD's plastic jewel box, and opened it to the lyrics for "Go Ask."

Sharyn clicked back to band seven again.

"You dig vanilla?
"Now ain't that a killer!
"You say you hate chocolate?

"I say you juss thoughtless.

"Cause chocolate is the color
"Of the Lord's first children
"Juss go ask the diggers
"The men who find the bones
"Go ask them 'bout chocolate . . .
"Go ask them 'bout niggers . . ."

"Oops," Kling said.

"Why you denyin
"Whut should senn you flyin?
"Why you find borin
"Whut should senn you soarin?
"You a black woman, woman
"Who you tryin'a sass?
"You a black woman, woman,
"Why you tryin'a pass?"

"Juss go ask the diggers
"The men who find the bones
"Go ask them 'bout chocolate . . .
"Go ask them 'bout niggers,
"Go ask."

The song ended. Sharyn turned off the player.
"That's kinda nice, actually," Kling said. "How'd you come across it?"

119

"Colleague suggested I give it a listen. I thought you might like it."

"Well, it's not exactly Shakespeare . . ."

"Hey, what is?"

"But I like it. I really do."

"Do you think I'm like that woman in the rap?" Sharyn asked, straight out of the blue.

Kling blinked.

"Do you think I dig vanilla?"

"Well, I certainly *hope* so," Kling said, and she burst out laughing.

"You think I've forgotten I'm black?"

"I hope not."

"You think I'm trying to pass?"

"No way. Who's been telling you such things?"

"Nobody," she said, and went to him where he was sitting on the sofa, and curled up in his arms.

He turned the CD pamphlet over, looked at the picture on the back of it.

"You think any of these guys are handsome?" he asked.

She hesitated.

A tick of an instant too long, he thought.

Then she said, "No."

She took the pamphlet from his hand, thumbed through it till she found the lyrics for another of the songs, something called "Black Woman."

"I like these last few couplets, don't you?" she said.

"Couplets," he said. "Now *that's* Shakespeare for you."

She began reading them aloud.

"In the night, in the night,
"All is black, all is white
"Love the black, love the white
"Love the *woman* tonight."

She looked up into his face.
Batted her eyelashes like an ingenue.
"So what do you say, big boy?" she asked.

"Do you know how much money was in that box?" the Deaf Man asked her.

Melissa debated lying. But she figured it might not be such a good idea to lie to this man.

"Yes," she said.

He looked surprised. She did not think he was the sort of man a person could ever surprise, but he sure looked surprised now.

"How do you know?"

"I counted it," she said.

"Why?"

She again debated lying. No, she thought. Always tell this man the truth. Or one day he'll kill you.

"I counted it so I'd know how much I should ask. For what I did. For walking that money out of the bank for you."

"I see. You felt you were entitled to some sort of reward, is that it?"

"Well . . . a million-eight," she said, and raised her eyebrows. "Don't *you* think that's worth a tip?"

Stop thinking like a hooker, she warned herself.

"How big a tip, would you say?"

She knew better than to fall into this trap.

"I'll leave that entirely to your judgment," she said.

"Does a hundred thousand sound okay?" he asked, and smiled.

She smiled back.

"A bit low," she said, "but hey, you're the boss."

She figured he thought of himself as some kind of mentor.

The last time she had a mentor was right here in the big bad city, the minute she got off the bus from L.A. Enter Ambrose Carter in his shiny pimp threads, Hey, li'l girlfriend, welcome to town. Got a place to stay? Introduced her to twelve of his homies that very night, cheaper by the dozen, right? Twelve of them who took her under their collective wing, a sort of pimp conglomerate that proceeded to fuck her day and night in a tiny room off the Stem, everywhere, anyplace she had an opening, day and night, twelve of them coming into the room one after the other to let her know she belonged to them, day and night. "Turned her out," as the expression went in the trade. Taught her she was nothing but a cheap two-bit hooker now, even though in L.A. she'd been getting a hundred bucks a throw for a mere blowjob.

Well, boys, you should see me now, she thought.

Adam wasn't kidding when he'd said a hundred K.

That's what he'd given her, cold cash, and he'd also taken her to a fur salon on Hall Avenue, where they were having what they called their Fall Preview Sale, when it wasn't even summer yet, and he bought her a sable coat that came right down to her ankles, and a mink stole she could wrap around her three times.

He also told her she could now leave anytime she wanted, but that if she stayed she might learn a thing or two.

This was what made her think he might

want to be her mentor.

He did not tell her what he was up to, but she figured it had to be something grand. When a man already had a million-eight in the poke — less the hundred grand he'd laid on her, and the sable and the mink — he certainly didn't have to take risks on any penny-ante scheme. She knew this had something to do with misleading the police, though she didn't know exactly why he would want to do that. She also suspected that she would somehow figure into his plan later on, he wasn't just keeping her around because she gave great head, which by the way, she did, and that wasn't just her opinion.

She was curious to see how this thing might unfold.

She was also wondering if he'd cut her into it for another big chunk later on.

So she figured she *would* stick around, why not, even though the hundred K could take her around the world three times over, like the mink stole took her shoulders.

"Do you know the story Frank Sinatra used to tell on himself? Do you like Sinatra?"

"I don't know Sinatra all that well," she said.

The truth. With him, always the truth.

"When he was playing Vegas, he would put on his tux each night, and stand in front of the mirror tying his bow tie, can you visualize that?"

"Sort of," she said. She found it hard to visualize Sinatra himself. She concentrated instead on some guy trying to tie a bow tie.

"He'd tweak the tie this way and that . . ."

She loved him using words like "tweak," which most guys didn't.

". . . until finally he said to his mirror-image, 'That's good enough for jazz.' Do you understand the meaning of that?"

"No, I'm afraid I don't."

Never lie to this man, she thought again.

"He was going out there to sing jazz. This was not grand opera, this was merely jazz. And he wasn't going to fool around with that tie any longer, it was good enough for jazz. You have to remember, Lissie, that even in his later years, Sinatra could sing rings around any other singer, male or female. Any of them. Name one who could beat him. And he knew exactly how good he was. Never mind who hit the charts that particular week. He knew none of them could come anywhere near him. In fact, he knew how *bad* most of them really were, million-copy gold records or not. So he was just going out there to sing his splendid jazz in yet another barroom to yet another bunch of people who'd already heard all his tunes. The bow tie was good enough for jazz, do you see?"

"Gee," she said.

"Well, I can always tie my tie so that it's good enough for jazz, I can do what I plan to do without all this folderol before-hand . . ."

Folderol. Another word she liked.

"But then where would all the fun be?" he asked, and looked deep into her eyes. "Where would all the fun be, Lissie?"

5

"He's back to spears again," Genero said. The Deaf Man's first note that Friday morning, the fourth day of June, read:

Come on, come on; where is your
    boar-spear, man?
Fear you the boar, and go so unpro-
    vided?

"Or is he telling us he's just a bore?" Parker asked.

"Which he spelled wrong, by the way."

"Because, you want to know the truth, I think he *is* a bore. Him and his Shakespeare both."

"Never give critics a good line," Carella said.

Parker didn't know what he meant.

"Anyway, we don't know for sure that this one *is* Shakespeare," Kling said.

"Well," Eileen said, "he *told* us it was going to be Shakespeare from now on, didn't he? That's what he told us yesterday,

127

am I right? That's what the *spear* and all those *shakes* were about yesterday."

She was inordinately proud of her deduction yesterday, and did not much like Kling shooting her down this way now. In her secret heart, she also felt he wouldn't be talking this way if they hadn't once shared a relationship. This was some kind of man-woman thing between them, she felt, and had nothing whatever to do with sound police work.

"Who else but Shakespeare would talk like that?" Carella asked.

"Right," Genero said. "Nobody but Shakespeare talks like that."

"Well, *Marlowe* talked like that," Willis said.

"Marlowe said 'Where is your boar-spear, man?' "

"I don't know if Marlowe actually said that particular line. I'm just saying Marlowe talked a lot like Shakespeare."

"Did Raymond Chandler know that?" Kling asked.

"Know what?" Brown asked.

"Who's Raymond Chandler?" Genero asked.

"The guy who wrote the books," Meyer said.

"What books?"

"The Phillip Marlowe novels."

"Did he *know* he sounded like Shakespeare?"

"I'm talking about *Christopher* Marlowe," Willis said.

"What's a boar-spear, anyway, man?" Brown asked.

"They had these wild boars back in those days," Parker said.

"The question is," Eileen said, "why's he going back to *spears* again?"

"Maybe he's gonna throw a spear at somebody," Genero suggested.

"This city," Parker said, "I'd believe it."

As Hawes was leaving the squadroom for his eleven o'clock doctor's appointment, Genero sidled over to him.

"I know how it feels to get shot in the foot," he said. "I'm with you, guy."

"Thanks," Hawes said.

Actually, he didn't appreciate the comparison. The way he recalled it, Genero had shot *himself* in the foot. This was on the eighth day of March during a very cold winter many years ago, the second time the Deaf Man had put in an appearance. What he'd done *that* time around was demand $50,000 in lieu of killing the deputy mayor, asking that the Eight-Seven leave the money in a lunch pail on a bench in Grover Park.

If Hawes remembered correctly, the fuzz staked out in the park that day had included a detective recruited from the Eight-Eight, who was posing as a pretzel salesman at the entrance to the Clinton Street footpath. Meyer and Kling, disguised as a pair of nuns, were sitting on a park bench saying their beads. Willis and Eileen were pretending (or not) to be a passionate couple necking in a sleeping bag on the grass behind another bench. Genero was sitting on yet another bench, wearing dark glasses and scattering bread crumbs to the pigeons as he patted a seeing-eye dog on the head.

Genero was still a patrolman at the time. He'd been pressed into undercover service only because there was a shortage of detectives in the squadroom that Saturday. Unaccustomed to the art of surveillance, he jumped up the moment he saw somebody picking up the lunch pail, yanked off his blind man's dark glasses, unbuttoned the third button of his overcoat the way he'd seen detectives do on television, reached in for his revolver, and promptly shot himself in the leg.

This was not the same thing as getting

shot by a sniper from a rooftop across the way.

Or maybe it was.

Grumbling to himself, Hawes threw open the front door of the stationhouse, nodded to the uniformed cop bravely protecting homeland security on the steps outside, and limped down to the sidewalk, where he planned to make a right turn that would take him to the subway kiosk up the street.

A black stretch limo was standing at the curb, its engine running. Stenciled onto the rear door of the car was the Channel Four logo — a silhouette of the city's skyline with the huge numeral 4 superimposed on it. The tinted rear window on the street side slid down noiselessly. Honey Blair's grinning face appeared in the opening.

"Want a lift, gorgeous?" she asked.

Hawes walked over to the car. "Hey!" he said. "What're *you* doing here?"

"Thought I'd surprise you," she said.

He climbed in beside her, pulled the door shut behind him. "Nice wheels," he said.

"One of the perks of being a media *staaah*," she said, rolling her eyes on the last word.

"Five seventy-four Jefferson," Hawes told the driver.

"I've already got that, sir," the driver said.

Honey tapped a button. The tinted glass partition between the driver's seat and rear compartment slid up, closing them off, sealing them in a soundless, moving cocoon.

"Here's another perk," she said, and unzipped his fly.

"Uh-oh," Hawes said.

"You know why Clinton got impeached, don't you?" she asked.

"I think so, yes."

"It was because right-wing conservatives didn't know what the word 'blowjob' meant."

"Is that right?"

"Uh-huh. They thought 'blowjob' was the code word for two villains running around the White House."

"Now where'd they get *that* idea?"

"From James Bond."

"I see. Two villains from James Bond, huh?"

"Yep."

"Which ones?"

"Blofeld and Oddjob," she said.

She didn't say anything else after that. Or if she did, he didn't hear her.

★ ★ ★

Dr. Stephen Hannigan was one of the orthopedists approved by the PD for the treatment of police personnel injured in the line of duty. Whether getting shot as you left your girlfriend's house in the early morning qualified as "injured in the line of duty" was a matter for the Police Benevolent Association to sort out later. Meanwhile, a civil servant who earned $62,587 a year as a Detective/Second Grade pulled up in a stretch limo in front of 574 Jefferson Avenue at the corner of Jefferson and Meade. Hawes kissed Honey goodbye, and was just stepping out on the curb side of the car, when —

He hurled himself and Honey to the floor of the car the instant he heard the first shot. He wasn't counting, but enough shots were fired in the next thirty seconds to shatter the tinted glass window of the limo, rip through the Channel Four logo on the rear door, tear up the interior upholstery, smash the whiskey and brandy decanters in both side door panels, and narrowly miss killing Honey and Hawes both.

Picking himself up off the floor of the car, Hawes yelled "I wasn't angry until right *now!*" never realizing how close he'd come to echoing Shakespeare's "I was not angry since I came to France" line in *King Henry V*, Act IV, Scene vii.

The second note that day read:

I am disgraced, impeach'd and baffled here,
Pierced to the soul with slander's venom'd spear

"That first line is intended for us," Meyer said. "He's telling us by now we should be feeling disgraced, impeach'd . . ."

"Which he *also* spelled wrong," Genero said.

". . . and baffled here. That's what he's saying."

"No, I don't think any personal message is intended here," Eileen said. "I think he's simply calling our attention to the last word in the couplet. *Spear.* It's *spear* again."

"I quite agree," Genero said, sounding somewhat Shakespearean himself. "But what's a couplet?"

"And *why?*" Kling asked.

"Why what?" Parker said.

"Why's he pointing us to *spear* again?"

"A *poisoned* spear."

134

"Where does it say that?"

"Venom'd. That means poisoned."

"Shakespeare keeps dropping his e's, you notice that?"

"What's slander?" Genero asked.

"A lie," Carella said.

"Meanwhile we've got a dead girl here," Lieutenant Byrnes said.

He had asked Willis and Eileen to step into his office, and now they were sitting in chairs opposite his desk, listening attentively. Eileen figured the Loot was old enough to call a thirtysomething dead woman a "girl" and get away with it, so she forgave him. "Let's forget what this hard-of-hearing shmuck plans to do *next*," Byrnes said, "and concentrate instead on what he's *already* done. He's committed murder, is what he's done. He can quote Shakespeare from here to Christmas, and that won't change the fact that he *killed* that girl!"

"Yes, sir," Eileen said.

Byrnes glared at her.

"Pete," she corrected.

"What'd the FBI report tell us, Hal?"

"Nothing," Willis said. "No matching prints anywhere. Means she doesn't have a record, was never in the armed forces, and never worked for any governmental agency."

"Which is not surprising," Byrnes said. "How many people do you know who have their fingerprints on file?"

Willis thought this over. Except for the hundreds of assorted thieves he met in this line of work, he couldn't think of a single soul.

"I want both of you to go back to the girl's building," Byrnes said. "He got into that apartment somehow. How'd he get past the doorman? Did anybody see him going in or coming out? He's not invisible, how'd he manage it? Talk to everybody and anybody. Get a description, get *something*."

As they started out of his office, he added, *"Anything."*

The caterer was as gay as a bowl of fresh daisies.

His name was Buddy Mears, and he was wearing a fawn-colored suit with a lavender shirt open at the throat. He had blond hair and blue eyes. A nose Caesar would have died for. High cheekbones. Taut skin. Teddy Carella wondered if he'd had a face lift. They were sitting in his office on Henley and Rhynes, in Riverhead, not far from the hall in which the reception would take place on June twelfth. Carella had driven here on his lunch hour. Teddy had taken a bus over. Sample menus were open on Buddy's desk. Several framed culinary awards were hanging on his walls. Plaques, too. Early June sunshine streamed through the windows and splashed onto the open menus.

"How many guests are we expecting?" he asked.

"About a hundred," Carella said.

Teddy signed to him.

Buddy looked politely puzzled.

"A hundred and *twelve*," Carella corrected.

Buddy already knew that Teddy Carella was a deaf-mute, speech-and-hearing impaired as they were calling it these days, but nonetheless a woman with devastating black hair and luscious dark brown eyes to match, absolutely gorgeous even when her fingers were flashing on the air, as they were now.

Carella watched her flying fingers.

"The numbers keep changing every day," he translated for her. And then added, "Either my mother or my sister keep inviting new people all the time."

"This is *so-o-oo* cute, what they're doing," Buddy said. "The double wedding.

Adorable. So let's figure a hundred and ten people . . ."

Reading his lips, Teddy again signed, *A hundred and* twelve.

"Yes, I know, darling," Buddy said, almost as if he could read her hands. "I'm approximating. But let's say a hundred and ten, a hundred and twelve. Will we be passing fingerlings around before dinner?"

"Fingerlings?" Carella said, and looked at Teddy.

Finger food, she signed.

"Fig with liver mousse," Buddy said, nodding. "Seared tuna on toast tips . . . well, here," he said, and moved one of the sample menus to where Carella and Teddy sat opposite him. "Potato pancakes with avocado salsa . . . salmon and cucumber bites . . . goat cheese tartlets . . . and so on. We've got fifty or more fingerlings we can pass around before dinner is served."

"Do you think we'll want fingerlings?" Carella asked.

I think they might be nice, Teddy signed. *With the drinks. Beforehand.*

"How many different kinds of fingerlings would you suggest?" he asked Buddy.

"Oh, four or five. Half a dozen. That should be enough. We don't want to get too complicated. And we don't want to

138

spoil our appetites for dinner, do we?"

Reading his lips, Teddy signed, *Maybe we should choose the dinner menu first.*

Carella translated.

And come back to the hors d'oeuvres later.

Hors d'oeuvres was a difficult word to sign. Or to read. She saw the puzzled look on her husband's face. She corrected it at once.

Finger food.

Carella told Buddy what she'd said.

"Well, yes, certainly, we can do it *backwards* if you prefer," he said, sounding miffed.

For the appetizers, he suggested three dishes from which the guests could choose. Either the lobster salad with black truffle dressing, *or* the Hamachi tuna tartare with caviar crème fraiche and smoked salmon, *or* the jumbo shrimp cocktail. For the main course, again a choice of three dishes. Either the roasted branzino stuffed with seafood, button mushrooms, roasted artichokes, and fennel, *or* the chicken curry with pearl onions, red peppers, and madras rice, *or* the braised rabbit in Riesling with spaëtzle, fava beans, and wild mushrooms.

"All served with a baby-greens-and-tomato salad with lemon, extra virgin olive oil, and century-old balsamic vinegar

139

dressing," he said, grinning in anticipation.

Carella looked at Teddy.

She looked back at him.

"Isn't there anything . . . *simpler?*" Carella asked.

"Simpler?" Buddy said.

"Well . . . it's just . . . I don't think many of the invited guests would appreciate such a . . . such an ambitious menu."

"These *are,* believe me," Buddy said, "some of our very *simplest* selections. Virtually *basic,* in fact."

"Well," Carella said, and shrugged and turned to Teddy. "Hon?" he said.

Some of the guests will be coming from Italy, she signed.

Carella told Buddy what her hands had just said.

"So what would you *like* to serve them?" Buddy said, somewhat snippily. "Spaghetti and meatballs?"

"No, but . . ." Carella started.

"Or maybe you should just take them over to McDonald's," Buddy snapped.

"Maybe so," Carella said, and rose abruptly. "Let's go, hon," he told Teddy, who had stood up at almost the same moment.

"We also make a nice risotto," Buddy offered as they went out the door.

"Anybody coming in the building has to talk to me first," the doorman told them. "Has to state his business with me," he said. "I clear all visitors with the tenant. That's the rule here. No exceptions."

"So if anyone had come here for Ms. Stanford . . ."

"That's right."

". . . on Memorial Day . . ."

"Correct."

". . . he'd've had to talk to you."

"Which is what I just told you," the doorman said, "din't I?"

"So how'd he get in her apartment?" Eileen asked.

"I got no idea," the doorman said.

"Is there a service entrance?"

"Yes, there is a service entrance."

"Where's that?"

"Around the back of the building. On Eleventh. But the man taking deliveries there has to call up to the tenant, same as me. Before he lets anything or anyone go upstairs. So you can save yourselves a walk around there."

"Is there a door to the roof?" Willis asked.

"Of course there's a door to the roof."

"Is it kept locked?"

"All the time."

"Mind if we take a look up there?"

The doorman looked at them, and then wagged his head as if to say there was no accounting for people who wished to waste their time. "Let me get the super to take you up," he said, and yanked a wall phone off its hook.

The building superintendent seemed surprised.

"Looks like somebody smashed the lock," he said, studying the door to the roof.

"Looks that way, doesn't it?" Willis said.

"Sure does."

"When's the last time you were up here?"

"Can't recall."

"Try," Eileen said.

"Must've been last week sometime. Water tank was leaking. Had to bring a plumber up."

"When last week would that have been?"

"Friday, must've been. Had a tough time getting a plumber cause the long weekend was coming up. Well, it's *always* tough getting a plumber. Plumbers are the divas of the building trade, you know. Guys fixing toilets, can you imagine? Divas!"

Eileen had already taken out her pocket calendar.

"So this would've been Friday, May twenty-eighth, is that right?" she said. "When you last came up here?"

"If that's what it says," he said, and leaned over to look at the calendar in her hand.

"And the lock was okay at that time?" Willis said.

"Had to use my key to open the door," the super said.

"Anybody been up here since?"

"Not to my knowledge."

"Let's see what's on the other side," Eileen said.

A doorknob was lying on the floor inside the door. The super poked a screwdriver into the hole the missing knob had left, angled it upward, and used it for leverage to pull open the door. They stepped out onto the roof.

There were times when this city took your breath away.

The day was sunny and bright, with wisps of white clouds scudding across an immaculate blue sky. At this time of day, the sun glinted on the gray-green waters of the River Harb below in the near distance, causing dancing sparkles of silver to glimmer on its surface. There was enough breeze to encourage the city's sailors; at least a dozen boats skimmed along the river's surface, bright sails billowing in the sunlight. Across the river in the next state, a non-competitive skyline seemed modestly secure in its own stark beauty. And to their right, the city's rooftops stretched far and away to the distant River Dix.

"Is the building next door a doorman building?" Eileen asked.

"Don't think so," the super said.

"So he could've got onto this roof from the one next door," Willis said.

"If he was of a mind to, yes," the super said.

"Could've jumped right over."

"If he was intent on doing mischief, yes."

They turned back to the door behind them.

Someone had worked long and hard on the knob in order to get to the lock. Removed the knob, approached the lock from inside the door.

"No alarm on this door?" Willis said.

"No," the super said.

"You ought to look into that," Willis said.

Why? Eileen wondered. Horse is already out of the barn.

The super was thinking the same thing.

"Can we go down to her apartment again?" Eileen asked.

This time they concentrated on the door and the lock. And this time, now that they were looking for them, they found the discreet marks a burglar's jimmy had left. So now they knew how he'd got in. Jumped onto the roof from the building next door, forced the lock on the roof door, did the same thing to the lock on Gloria Stanford's apartment. Was waiting for her when she got home that day. He'd used a gun with a silencer, Ballistics had confirmed that. So no one had heard any shots, no one had raised an alarm. Had he left the building the same way he'd got in? Probably. Easy come, easy go.

They thanked the super for his time, and left 1113 Silvermine Oval.

"Want to do a canvass next door?" Willis asked.

"I doubt if anyone spotted him going in or out," she said. "But if you want to knock on doors, I'm with you."

"For the sake of closure," he said.

"I hate that word," she said. "Closure."

"So do I."

"It's a lawyer's word."

"I also hate lawyers," Willis said.

"Me, too."

They were out on the street now. It was almost three-thirty. Their shift was almost over.

"So what do you say?"

"Let's do it," she said. "Keep the Loot happy."

The Deaf Man's third and final note that day cleared up any lingering doubt that he was trying to spear the word *spear*, so to speak:

Yea, and to tickle our noses with spear-grass to make them bleed, and then to beslubber our garments with it and swear it was the blood of true men.

"What the hell is spear-grass?" Parker asked.

"Some kind of grass they have over there in England," Genero said.

"How do you happen to know that?"

"Common sense. If it's Shakespeare, it has to be England."

"This doesn't even *look* like Shakespeare," Hawes said.

"That's right. It's not even poetry."

"Shakespeare also wrote prose," Carella said.

"And this time, there *is* a message," Kling said, "prose or whatever."

"What's prose?" Genero asked.

"What's the message?" Hawes asked.

"That it's all fake. He's misleading us. It's slander, the venom'd spear. It's a lie again."

"Same as always."

"Tickle your noses to make them bleed . . ."

"Must be some kind of sharp grass, don't you think? That spear-grass?"

". . . and then beslubber your garments . . ."

"I love that word."

"Sounds like be*slobber*," Brown said. "Beslobber the Johnson . . ."

"Be*slubber* the garments . . ."

"The clothes . . ."

". . . with the blood from the nose, make it look like battle wounds. That's what he's saying. It's all *fake*. He's leading us to *spear*, but he's going someplace else."

"Then why's he leading us to *spear*?"

"Cause he's a rotten son of a bitch," Carella said.

The building next door to 1113 Silvermine Oval was a seventeen-story edifice with six apartments on each floor. By five-thirty that night, Willis and Eileen had knocked on the doors to a hundred and two apartments, and spoken to eighty-nine tenants who were home and who answered their knocking. The first time they'd ever dealt with the Deaf Man, they'd got a description of him from a doorman named Joey. This was a long time ago, after he'd fired a shotgun blast into Carella's shoulder and slammed the stock of the shotgun into his head again and again and again. One could understand why Carella considered any encounter with the Deaf Man a highly personal matter.

He's around my height, Joey had told Lieutenant Byrnes. *Maybe six-one, six-two, and I guess he weighs around a hun' eighty, a hun' ninety pounds. He's got blond hair and blue eyes, and he wears this hearing aid in his right ear.*

This was the description they gave the tenants now. Had anyone seen a white male fitting that description, in or around the building, at anytime on Memorial Day?

No one had seen anyone fitting that description.

Not on Memorial Day or any other day.

Outside the building again, Willis said, "Wanna catch a bite to eat?"

148

Eileen looked at him.

"Maybe go see a movie afterward?" he said.

She hesitated a moment longer.

Then she said, "Sure. Why not?"

That evening, Channel Four's Six O'Clock News had a big story to tell.

Someone had tried to kill their star investigative reporter, Honey Blair.

Avery Knowles, the show's co-anchor, first announced it on the air at five minutes past six, following the breaking news about a big fire in Calm's Point, where two children left alone had been playing with a kerosene burner while their mother was out scratching numbers off a lottery ticket at the corner grocery store.

"Earlier today," Avery said, "an armed assailant tried to murder someone with whom all of our viewers are familiar. You can only see the story now, here on Channel Four, in Honey Blair's own words."

Only a handful of literate viewers knew that if they could only *see* the story now, right here on Channel Four, then they could not also *hear* the story. However, these were probably not Avery Knowles's own words, but instead the words of some network employee who didn't realize that the correct language should have been "You can see the story now, only here on Channel Four."

Standing before the camera in her trademark legs-slightly-apart pose, wearing a mini that was also something of a trademark, Honey said (not in her own words, either, even though they were coming from her own mouth), "This morning at approximately five minutes to eleven, in front of five-seventy-four Jefferson Avenue, a gunman fired some dozen or more shots into a Channel Four vehicle that was driving me here to the studio. I have no idea why I was the target, but if any of our listeners have any information whatsoever regarding the shooting, please call either the police hotline number at the bottom of the screen or our own hotline number listed just below it. Meanwhile, hear this loud and clear, Mr. Shooter! I don't know what might have ticked you off, but I'm going to keep doing my job, rain or shine, bullets or not! Just keep that in mind, mister!"

The camera cut back to the co-anchors. Millie Anderson, the woman on the team, said, "We're with you, Honey. Folks, if you have *any* information at all, please call one of those hotlines, won't you?"

She glanced at Avery and said, "A terrible thing, Ave." Avery nodded in solemn agreement. Millie looked back into the camera again. "At the Federal Courthouse downtown this afternoon," she said, "two women accused of . . ."

Cotton Hawes snapped off his television set.

He was wondering why Honey hadn't mentioned he'd been in the car with her. Or that someone had tried to kill him as he'd come out of her building Wednesday morning. He was merely a cop, but it seemed to him that in all probability he himself, and not Honey Blair, had been the intended target.

But he guessed that was show biz.

Eileen didn't think she should ask him anything about Marilyn Hollis.

Willis didn't think he should ask her anything about Bert Kling.

So over dinner, they talked mostly about the case. The *two* cases actually. One past, one future. The murder of Gloria Stanford and whatever monkeyshines the Deaf Man might be cooking up for the days ahead. They had worked together for a good long while now — from way back to when

Eileen was still with Special Forces — but they'd socialized only once before, dinner with the four of them, Willis and Marilyn, Eileen and Kling. So to make dinner tonight a bit less awkward, they tried to figure out why the Deaf Man had anagrammatically confessed to the murder of Gloria Stanford, and why he was now taunting them with Shakespearean quotes that might or might not indicate some crime he was planning for the future.

"Why us?" Willis wondered aloud.

"I think it's something personal," Eileen said. "I think he has something personal against Steve."

"Or maybe each and every one of us."

"Maybe. But why? What'd we ever do to him?"

"He's annoyed because we always mess him up."

"Wellll," Eileen said, "I'm not sure I'd say exactly *that*, Hal. We've never been the ones who actually foiled his plans."

"Foiled," Willis said. "I love that word. Foiled."

"So do I."

"You think we'll *foil* his plans this time?"

Smiling. Stressing the word. He had a nice smile, Eileen noticed.

"How can we foil his plans if we don't

even know what they are?" she asked.

"Oh, he'll tell us, never fear."

"You think so, huh?"

"I really do."

"Dream on," Eileen said.

When Melissa got back to the apartment that evening, the first thing he did was ask her to model the wigs.

Her natural hair color — well, as natural as Miss Clairol could make it — was what they called "Spring Honey," a sort of soft blondish hue that she felt suited her chocolate-brown eyes. In a wig shop on Sakonsett Street — which name she supposed derived from the American Indians who had once inhabited this island — she'd found a wig shop named Hair Today that was having what it called its "Late Spring" sale. There were sales going on all over this city, and nobody could tell her this had nothing to do with the shitty economy. She'd bought two wigs — well, gee, these prices! — a red one in a sort of feather cut like the one she wore her own hair in, and a black one, shoulder length with bangs across the forehead. Looked *s-o-oo* natural with her brown eyes. Cost a bit less than a hundred each, including tax.

"Nice," he said. "You don't look at all like yourself."

"Is that supposed to be a compliment?" she asked.

She'd gone to bed with guys who'd asked her to wear wigs, and then complained that the drapes didn't match the carpet, any excuse to bat her around, some of these creeps you met.

She sure hoped this wasn't going to be the case here tonight.

The wigs and all.

"Well, I have to tell you," Willis said, "this only confirms my theory that you should never go see a movie anybody both wrote *and* directed."

They had just come out of the theater and were strolling up the avenue, most of the shops already closed, the evening still somewhat balmy.

"I kind of liked it," Eileen said.

"You did? Even though it withheld facts we needed to know? I mean, to solve the *crime?*"

"Well, you're a cop. You'd naturally be looking for something like that."

"You're a cop, too. Don't you think he should have given us, like . . . some *clues?*"

"I was more interested in the personal

story. I think women look more for that."

"Withholding evidence doesn't bother you?"

"Only if the Deaf Man does it."

"This was *worse* than what the Deaf Man's doing. At least he's playing fair. He gives us everything we need to know . . ."

"We hope."

". . . and if we're too dumb to figure it out, that's our own hard luck."

"Wanna go for some coffee or something?" she asked.

"Yes," Willis said, but he was just gathering steam.

As they walked up the avenue toward a coffee shop on the corner, and while they ordered, and even after they'd been served, he went on to say that a lot of the movies he saw nowadays claimed to be mysteries in one way or another, and being a cop whose profession was *investigating* crime, he felt like *shooting* the damn *auteur* directors who made these films.

"Uh-huh," Eileen said. "Like which movies do you mean?"

"Any movie that says 'written and directed by.' "

"You've got a real thing about that, huh?"

"No, it's just that . . . well, figure it out

155

for yourself. Most writers can't direct, am I right? And most directors can't write. So when you get a movie that's both written *and* directed by the same person, run for the hills!"

"You really think so, huh?"

"I really think so. Male or female, if it's written and directed by, that's exactly like 'Conspiracy to Commit,' or 'Criminal Facilitation,' or 'Hindering Prosecution,' all of them pretty damn serious crimes."

"My, such passion!" Eileen said.

"Well, it just isn't *fair,*" he said, and ducked his head and smiled sheepishly, as though he'd revealed something about himself that might better have stayed concealed. Again, she felt like reaching across the table and taking his hand.

Outside the coffee shop, they went their separate ways. After all, this hadn't been a real date. This had just been two cops having dinner together, and seeing a movie afterward, sharing coffee, sharing a bit of movie criticism.

She hadn't asked him anything abut Marilyn Hollis.

And he hadn't asked her anything about Bert Kling.

And tomorrow was another working day.

"Starting tomorrow morning," the Deaf Man was saying, "there'll be notes delivered to the 87th Precinct every day but Sunday."

"Why not Sunday?" Melissa asked.

"Because even God rested on Sunday."

"Oh, I see. And what will these notes say?"

"You don't have to know that."

"Starting tomorrow, you say?"

"Yes. And continuing through Saturday."

"That means . . . what's today?"

"The fourth." He looked at his watch. "Well, it's almost midnight, almost the fifth."

"That means the last notes will be delivered on June twelfth."

"Yes."

"Is that when you're going to do this thing, whatever it is? On June twelfth?"

"Yes."

"What is it you're going to do?"

"You don't have to know that."

"Then why are you telling me all this?"

"Because *you'll* be delivering the notes."

"Oh no. *Me* walk into a police station? Not on your life!"

"Not you personally," he explained patiently. "You'll have to *find* people who'll deliver the notes for you."

"It'll *still* come right back to me. There's no way I would *ever* do anything like that. Why would I want to do anything like that?"

"Because I'm going to give you thirty-five thousand dollars to do it."

"You are?"

"I am. Five thousand dollars a day for tomorrow, and the six days next week."

"Gee," she said.

"That should be enough to buy you the people you need, don't you think?"

"Well, I guess so, yes."

"With quite a bit left over for your trouble, I would expect."

"I would expect."

"You could buy yourself some nice lingerie."

"I certainly could."

"Or something."

"Or something, yes."

"And there's a lot more coming, Lissie. We're talking seven figures in the coffers here."

She was remembering that she'd taken a million-eight out of that safe-deposit box for him. Was he talking about seven figures in *addition* to that? Should she ask? Why not?

"In *addition* to the other money, you mean?" she said. "The money from the bank?"

"In addition, yes."

"Seven figures has to be at least another million, right?"

"At least," he said.

"And what's my share of that?" she asked.

"Mustn't be greedy, girl," he said.

Why not? she thought. And don't call me girl, she thought. But did not say.

"How does a vacation in Tortola sound?" he asked. "After this is all over?"

"A vacation in Tortola might be very nice," she said, "but . . ."

"I've already booked the flight," he said. "We leave at nine-thirty Sunday morning, the thirteenth of June. Doesn't that sound nice?"

"Not as nice as a piece of seven figures."

He chuckled. Actually chuckled. Still chuckling, he said, "Well, I suppose one can never be too rich or too thin."

"I'll say."

"Do you know who said that, Lissie?"

"No, who?"

"The Duchess of Windsor."

"Who's that?"

"A king gave up an empire for her."

"She must have been very beautiful."

"Not half as beautiful as you."

Melissa wondered if he was telling her he'd give up an empire for her. Maybe cut her in on that seven figures he'd just mentioned? She didn't ask. Play the cards you're dealt, she thought. So far, she was a hundred thousand K richer than she'd been before she picked him up in that hotel bar. Or vice versa. Not to mention the sable coat and the mink stole.

"Do you think you can get those notes delivered when they're supposed to be delivered?"

"I think so, yes," she said. "But . . . uh . . . these people I hire to deliver them?"

"Yes?"

"They'll be able to describe me, won't they? They'll tell the police exactly what I look like."

"That's where the wigs come in," he said.

6

Melissa figured this was what she usually did, anyway, except in reverse. Haggle over a price, that is. What usually happened, the john said, "Two hundred for the night," and then you said "Five hundred." He said "Three," you said "Four." You settled for three and a half and everybody was happy — especially you, if he fell asleep after the first go-round.

This was Saturday morning, the fifth day of June. Very *early* Saturday morning.

Before she left the apartment, Adam had given her five thousand bucks in hundreds. Five thousand dollars! Which didn't seem like very much when you broke it down to a mere fifty $100 bills, oh well.

"That's your outside limit for the day," he'd told her. "You get your people for less than that, whatever's left over is yours, you can buy yourself that lingerie we were talking about."

She had a better idea of what to buy with what was left over, but first she had to buy what she needed to make this work at all.

She figured, correctly as it turned out, that not too many people would be eager to take a letter into a police station. Not with the anthrax scare still a very much alive issue. Would've been different if any of the brilliant masterminds in Washington — some of them should meet Adam Fen, they wanted mastermind — knew what to do about it except stick their thumbs up their asses. As it was, the first three men she approached said flat out, "What are you, crazy?" This after she'd offered two hundred bucks just to carry a friggin letter inside a police station and hand it to the desk sergeant!

The next person she approached was in a coffee shop on Jefferson. Six in the morning, the girl sitting there drinking coffee was a working girl like herself, Melissa could spot them a hundred miles away. Black girl with hair bright as brass, nail polish a purple shade of Oklahoma Waitress. She'd had a hard night, too, judging from the bedraggled look of her. Melissa started low, no sense spoiling her, and the hell with sisterhood. Turned out the girl was nursing a horrendous hangover, figured Melissa was looking for a little early-morning girlie-girlie sex, told her any muff-diving would cost her two bills.

Melissa tried to explain that no, what she wanted was a letter delivered to a police station. She showed her the letter. It was addressed to Detective Stephen Louis Carella. Melissa told the girl this was her boyfriend. She told the girl they'd had an argument last night. She told the girl she was desperate to make up with him. The girl said, "Honey, you a hooker same as me. If yo boyfrien's a *po*-lice, I'm the queen of England."

It sort of insulted Melissa that she'd been spotted for a hooker straight off like that.

After three more tries and three more turndowns, she remembered something her mother had told her as a child: Desperate people do desperate things. So what she needed here was somebody desperate to carry that letter in. For a minute, in fact, since she herself was starting to get a little desperate here — it was already seven a.m. — she thought she might carry it in personally. Tell the cops some guy wearing a hearing aid had given her nine hundred bucks to deliver it, show them nine bills, tell them she was just a hard-working girl worked nights at a Burger King and had met this guy over the counter, asked her to deliver the letter. She didn't know nothing at all about who he was or what was inside the letter. So please let me go, sirs, as my mother will be wondering why I'm not home yet, my shift ending at eight in the morning and all.

Decided against it.

If that girl in the coffee shop had spotted her for a whore, the cops would make her in a minute.

Was it really that easy to see what she was?

Maybe she'd buy a new dress with whatever the residuals turned out to be today.

At seven-fifteen that morning, she taxied down to a skid row area of flophouses, homeless shelters, bars, and electrical supply houses. First crack out of the box, she found a doorway wino who said he'd deliver the letter for fifty bucks. She taxied uptown again, the wino sitting beside her on the back seat, stinking of piss and belching alcohol fumes. At five past eight, she dropped him off three blocks from the stationhouse, the letter in one pocket of his tattered jacket, and pointed him in the right direction. Told him she'd be watching him so he'd better make sure he kept his end of the bargain. Guy swore on his sainted mother.

Melissa figured he'd be stopped the minute he set foot on the bottom tread of the stationhouse steps, and he was.

Which was why she'd bought the wigs, right?

Her waspish-headed son has broke his arrows,
Swears he will shoot no more but play with sparrows

That's what the first note read.

"Is that correct English?" Genero asked.
" 'Has *broke* his arrows'?"

Nobody answered him.

" 'Shoot no more,' " Meyer said. "He's telling us he's not going to shoot anybody else. Gloria Stanford was the last one."

"Unless he plans to use *arrows*," Willis said.

"Or spears," Kling suggested.

"No, he's finished with the spears," Carella said. "Now he's onto arrows."

" 'Swears he will shoot no more.' "

"Gonna 'play with sparrows' instead."

"Little birdies," Parker said sourly.

"Did you see that movie Hitchcock wrote?" Genero asked.

"Hitchcock didn't write it," Kling said.

"Then who did?"

"Daphne somebody."

"*Twice*," Willis said.

"She wrote *The Birds* twice?" Genero asked, puzzled now.

"No, *arrows*. He uses arrows twice this time."

Carella was at the computer again, looking for his rhyme zone. Parker glanced down at the Deaf Man's note.

"I only see *arrows* once," he said.

"The second one is buried in another word," Willis said. "*Arrows* in *sparrows*."

"So what's the significance of *that?*" Parker asked, sounding angry.

"*The Tempest*," Carella announced. "Act Four, Scene One."

Captain John Marshall Frick should have retired ten years ago, but he liked to tell himself the 87th Precinct couldn't get along without him. Byrnes thought of him as an old fart. There were men who were Frick's age — sixty, sixty-five, in there, whatever he was — who still thought like much younger men, carried themselves like much younger men, sounded like much younger men, actually *looked* far younger than they were. John Marshall Frick was not one of them.

Frick belonged to that other category of older men who thought of themselves as "senior citizens," men who had nothing to do anymore except send each other old fart jokes via e-mail every day. Men who'd retired from life and living too damn early — although Frick was old when he was fifty and should have retired then.

"Tell us your name," he told the wino.

"Freddie."

"Freddie *what*, Freddie?"

"Freddie Apostolo. That means Freddie the Apostle."

"You been drinking a little today, Freddie?"

"A little. I drink a little every day."

"Why'd you write that note, Freddie?"

"I didn't."

Byrnes looked at his boss. Did the Captain really think this old wino had pulled up a Shakespeare quote from the internet and delivered it in person to the precinct? Did he really think this slovenly old bum stinking of body odor and urine and sweet wine was the notorious Deaf Man who'd slain Gloria Stanford and who so far had delivered all these tantalizing notes designed to infuriate and . . . well . . . intoxicate? He wasn't even wearing a hearing aid!

"Then who wrote it, Freddie?"

"I got no idea."

"Then where'd you get it?"

"This girl gave it to me."

"What girl?"

"Pretty girl with black hair and bangs."

Byrnes almost said She does?

"What's her name?"

"Don't know."

"Just gave you this note, is that . . ."

"No."

". . . right? Just handed you . . ."

"No."

"Then what?"

"Gave me fifty bucks to deliver it. Said I should hand it to the desk sergeant, that's all. Which I tried to do but you guys stopped me at the front door. I used to play piano, you know."

"Is that right?"

"That's how I started drinking. There's always a drink on a piano, did you ever notice? A drink and a cigarette. I'm lucky I didn't get throat cancer. You play piano, you drink and you smoke, that's it. I guess I drank a little too much, huh?"

"I guess so. Where'd you conduct this transaction with your mysterious black-haired lady?"

"She wasn't mysterious at all. It was

down near the Temple Street Shelter. She came over to me and asked would I like to make fifty bucks. So I said yes."

"Who wouldn't?" Frick said.

"Sure. So what did I do wrong, can you please tell me?"

"Did she tell you her name?"

"No. I didn't tell her mine, either."

"How'd you get uptown here, all the way from Temple?"

"We took a taxi. She dropped me off on Fourth, said she'd be watching. I believed her."

"Why's that?"

"She looked like I'd better do what she said."

"How's that?"

"Her eyes. There was a look in her eyes."

"What color?" Frick asked. "The eyes."

"Brown," Freddie said.

"How tall?"

"Five-seven, five-eight?"

"White?"

"Sure." Freddie paused. "Her eyes said she'd kill me if she had to."

Byrnes looked at the captain again.

"Okay, go home," Frick told Freddie.

"Home?" Freddie said.

She had watched from the park across

the street, and had seen the uniformed cop on the front steps first challenge and next detain the wino she'd enlisted. But that was okay because she knew the letter would now be delivered one way or another, and she didn't much care if they later locked the bum up, or hanged him by his thumbs from a lamppost, or whatever.

She now knew that whoever she might recruit to deliver all the remaining letters would also be stopped, but this didn't bother her, either. The letters would get inside the precinct, they would be read, the messengers would protest, "Hey, I'm only the messenger!", and that would be that. In this city, there had to be two million girls with shoulder-length black hair and bangs. Or feather-cut red hair, for that matter. Well, maybe a million, the redheads.

The problem was rounding up two more guys today, and however many more she'd need for every day next week, Monday through Saturday, the twelfth of June, which was the date Adam had announced for whatever it was, she didn't know. His caper? His escapade? His prank, his practical joke, his *whatever* it was that would add seven figures to the coffers, whatever *they* might be, coffers. She sometimes

170

wished she was smarter than she was.

But she was smart enough to know that she couldn't keep running back and forth between all the way downtown and up here to secure new messengers all the time. That would be both exhausting and time-consuming. So whereas she didn't like to cut anyone else in on the thirty-five grand Adam had allotted for the project, she knew that she needed a middleman here. And the only middleman she could think of was the first pimp she'd had, or vice versa, when she arrived in this rotten city five years ago.

Ambrose Carter was a black man who still ran a stable of eleven whores, four of them white, and he was very happy to see little Mela Sammarone again because he thought she might be coming back to work for him again. As it turned out, she wanted *him* to work for *her*.

"Now juss lemme get this straight," he said, putting on a baffled black man look. In truth, nothing ever baffled him. He was too damn smart to ever be baffled.

They were sitting in a bar in what was called the Overlook section of Diamond-back, appropriately named in that a lot of drug and prostitution shit was conveniently overlooked by the police here. Ambrose was nursing a Jack Daniels and Coca-Cola. Melissa was drinking a Coke without the bourbon. The two wigs she'd purchased were in her tote bag. Sitting there *au naturelle,* more or less, as it were, she looked as blond and as pert and as pretty as a young Meg Ryan. Ambrose really regretted not representing her any longer. He thought of himself as not a pimp but a representative.

He still considered her the one who'd got away. Partially because he hadn't been able to hook her on any kind of controlled substance, she'd been too smart for that, but primarily because she'd been socking away bit by bit, piece by piece, what came to a total of fifty-five grand over a period of five years, which she'd offered him in exchange for her freedom. Well, figure it out, man. He wasn't holding her passport or no shit like that, and fifty-five in the here-and-now was worth grabbing on the spot, you never knew how fast these girls would age and become worthless. So he'd said So long, darlin, and kissed her off. But here she was, back again. And asking him to represent her again in a different sort of way.

"You want me to fine however many

people it is you'll need in the next however many days . . ."

"That's right."

". . . screen them for you befo'hand so you'll be sure they willin to march into a *po*-lice station . . ."

"Yes, Ame."

". . . and then senn 'em to way'ever you be waitin for 'em, so you can pay 'em a hunnerd bucks each to deliver an envelope, *separate* envelopes actually . . ."

"Separate envelopes, yes."

". . . into this *po*-lice station, whichever one it may be."

"That's exactly right."

"And what's in this for me, may I be so bold? What do I *get* for fine-in' these people for you?"

"A thousand bucks today, and a grand a day starting Monday."

"Till when?"

"Last one'll be next Saturday."

"That's a total of seven large."

"Seven, correct."

Carter thought this over.

"How do I know this won't come back on me?" he asked. "These people marchin up to a *po*-lice station, they sure to be stopped, Mel."

"I know that. They tell the cops they got

173

the money from me. You're out of this completely. I'm the one pays them, I'm the one they describe."

"You don't mine bein' made?"

"Not at all."

Carter thought this over for another moment.

"Make it an even ten K," he said.

"You've got it," she said. "I'll need two people today. I'll tell you where they can meet me."

"Male or female? Or do it matter?"

"As suits you," Melissa said. "I wouldn't send me one of your whores, though. . . ."

"Now do I look stupid, Mel?" he asked.

"No one could ever say that about you, Ame," she said, and grinned.

"How do I get paid?" he asked.

"Three now," she said. "Two grand Monday morning, a grand every morning after that, straight through the twelfth."

"You trust me that far, huh?"

"Got no reason not to, Ame."

"That when it's going down?" he asked. "The twelfth? Whatever this thing may be?"

"Now do *I* look stupid, Ame?" she asked.

The second note that Saturday morning was addressed to Miss Honey Blair at

Channel Four News. It read:

DEAR HONEY:
PLEASE FORGIVE ME AS I DID NOT KNOW YOU WERE IN THAT AUTOMOBILE.

It was unsigned.

The Deaf Man's second note was delivered to the 87th Precinct at a little past noon that day by a man who admitted under intense questioning that a pretty redhead had paid him a hundred dollars to take it over here. Before he'd met her at a bar called the Lucky Diamond down on Lewis and Ninth, he'd never seen her in his life. Did this mean they would take the money from him?

"That's *Macbeth*," Genero said.

To be or not to be: that is the
   question:
Whether 'tis nobler in the mind to
   suffer
The slings and arrows of outrageous
   fortune,
Or to take arms against a sea of
   troubles
And by opposing, end them?

Even Parker knew this was definitely not *Macbeth*.

"It's *Romeo and Juliet*," he said.

Eileen did not think the quote on the lieutenant's desk was from *Romeo and Juliet*. She knew that play virtually by heart, or at least she knew the Baz Luhrmann movie version, which she'd seen seven times when it was first released, falling in love with Leonardo di Caprio, who now seemed rather pudgy and middle-aged to her. But this was definitely not *Romeo and Juliet*.

Carella knew the quote was from *Hamlet* because back in his green and salad days, he'd played a bearded drama-club Claudius to a zaftig Sarah Gelb's Gertrude. Sarah had thrown herself much too seriously into the Oedipal theory of Hamlet's relationship with his mother, French-kissing twenty-year-old Aaron Epstein during the famous "Now, mother, what's the matter?" scene in the Queen's closet. "What have I done that thou dar'st wag thy tongue in noise so rude against me?" young Sarah had demanded, her breasts heaving in the low-cut Elizabethan gown she wore, a crown tilted saucily on her reddish curls.

After the opening night party, Sarah performed the same osculatory acrobatics with Carella, in the back seat of his father's automobile, which led to a somewhat steamy interlude interrupted by two uniformed cops driving past in a radio motor patrol car. Tossing the beams of their torches through both open back windows, surprising the coupling young lovers — Sarah pulling up her panties, Carella zipping up his fly — those two diligent vigilantes caused him to hate all cops for a good long time. But he would never forget *Hamlet*, oh no, and this now was most definitely *Hamlet*.

Hal Willis was wondering why the Deaf Man — if indeed the *Hamlet* quotation had been sent by him — had chosen to bring up the second-act curtain on their dreary Saturday morning routine with perhaps the most famous soliloquy in all literature. Did he feel he had given them information enough about spears and such, and was now ready to move on to another topic? In which case, what might this new topic be, hmmm?

The note had undoubtedly been computer-generated, printed on the same white bond paper he'd used for his previous messages.

"Why *Hamlet*?" Willis asked.

"Why *Macbeth*?" Genero insisted.

"Something in Grover Park again?" Brown suggested. "Like his mischief last time around? Some kind of event in the Cow Pasture?"

"When does Shakespeare on the Green start?" Eileen asked.

"Sometime later this month?"

"Around the fifteenth?"

"Later, I think."

"But even if it *is* Shakespeare on the Green . . ."

"Right," Eileen said.

"Of course," Meyer agreed.

". . . it'd be bullshit, anyway."

"He never tells us what he's *really* up to."

"So toss the letter," Parker suggested, and shrugged.

"He's got to be telling us *something*," Carella said.

"Even if it's something misleading?"

"Poetry," Brown said, shaking his head.

"Shakespearean poetry, no less."

"*Macbeth*, no less!" Genero said, agreeing.

Melissa calculated that of the thirty-five large Adam was allotting for operating expenses, Carter was costing her ten, and the various messengers would cost her another, say, two, three thou, depending on how far upward any of them negotiated the basic hundred-dollar delivery fee. That would leave her with a cool profit of, say, twenty thousand.

She had already given Carter three as the down payment for his work, and had paid the twelve o'clock delivery boy a hundred. Because the girl looked so neat and clean and innocent and all, Melissa had given *two* hundred to the four o'clock messenger Ame had sent; she wondered where the hell in Diamondback he'd found somebody who resembled a college girl. So out of the five K Adam had laid on her this morning, she now had something like sixteen hundred left, after cab fares and drinks and coffees and such while she'd waited for the messengers to show up first at the Lucky Diamond and then at the Hotel Majestic lounge, the separate venues (she liked that word) she'd chosen for their meeting places.

Now what she *could* have done was take that sixteen hundred and buy herself some goodies with it, including the lingerie Adam had suggested, but she figured a more profitable investment would be a gift for Adam himself. She decided she'd look for a cashmere robe for him; a nice black cashmere robe would put him in a good mood, his blond hair and all.

But then, because at the back of her mind she still had the feeling that one day he might shoot her dead if he became dissatisfied with one thing or another . . .

. . . and since she was already uptown here where she knew most of the criminal element from the days when she was either on her back or her knees, working either day or night to fill the coffers, whatever they were, of her erstwhile representative, Ambrose Carter . . .

. . . she decided to visit a man named Blake Fuller, who sold her a neat little Kahr PM 9, which at only 16.9 ounces empty and measuring only four by five-and-a-half inches overall, would fit nicely into her purse, just in case push came to shove later on down the line.

Only cost her five bills, too, which Fuller advised her was a bargain.

That left eleven hundred for the robe.

Thinking she'd done a good day's work so far, she grabbed a taxi and headed for the big department stores midtown.

Along about then, the cute little college girl lookalike was delivering the Deaf Man's third and final note of the day.

***

The note read:

**Even such, they say, as stand in narrow lanes
And beat our watch, and rob our passengers.**

"At least he spelled everything right this time," Genero said. "Didn't he?"

Carella was already at his computer, looking for *RhymeZone Shakespeare Search*.

"An arrow again," Eileen said, just as Carella typed in "as stand in narrow lanes." "Buried in the word *narrow*."

"First spears, now arrows," Kling said.

"Arrows all day long."

"*King Richard II*, Act Five, Scene Three," Carella read from the screen.

"First *The Tempest*, then *Hamlet*, and now *Richard II*," Willis said.

"Any importance to these plays he's choosing?" Hawes asked. He was being very careful not to get his open-toed boot stepped on by any of the detectives milling around Carella's desk.

"He's just choosing them at random," Parker said. "It's all total bullshit."

"I don't think so," Carella said. "First off, he's telling us it's going to happen on

181

our watch. He's going to 'beat our watch.' "

"That's very clever," Genero said.

"Thanks," Carella said.

"I meant *him*. It's very clever of him to have found that reference."

"He's going to rob our passengers," Eileen said.

"We don't have any passengers," Parker said.

"It's something to do with passengers," she insisted.

"A train?"

"An airplane?"

"A boat?"

"Oh, Jesus, not another boat."

"Not another rock star, please!"

"Who stands in narrow lanes?" Hawes asked.

"Hookers," Parker said at once.

This he knew for sure.

Parker suggested that he should be the one who interrogated the girl because he was older and therefore more avuncular than either Hawes, Willis, Genero, or Kling, and perhaps younger but more experienced than Carella, which he wasn't; Carella had been a cop longer than Parker had, and Carella had just turned forty whereas Parker was forty-two.

In any case, because the police department was at best a sexist organization and Lieutenant Byrnes was still clinging to the notion that Eileen Burke could bring a woman's so-called intuition to this case, she was the one chosen to speak to Alison Kane that Saturday afternoon.

"So where'd you get that letter, Alison?" she asked.

Chummy sort of dormy school-girl approach.

"In the lounge at the Hotel Majestic."

"Is it nice there? I've never been there."

"Very nice, yes," Alison said.

She was perhaps twenty-four, twenty-five years old, some five-six or -seven, slender and curvy but not too buxom. Wearing a not-too-short dark green skirt, with a paler green twin sweater set, crew neck and buttoned cardigan. String of pearls around her neck. Truly looked Ivy League. Eileen figured her for a hooker.

"What were you doing at the Majestic?" she asked.

"Just stopped by for a cup of tea."

Sounded Ivy League, too.

"Happened to be strolling by the Majestic . . ."

"I'd been doing some shopping."

"Went into the lounge . . ."

"Yes. For a cup of tea."

"And happened to . . . well, how *did* that letter come into your hands, can you tell me?"

"A woman gave it to me."

"Ah. What woman?"

"A woman I met there. She said she'd had an argument with her boyfriend who was a detective up here, and she wanted someone to deliver this letter of apology to him."

"And you believed her."

"She seemed sincerely contrite."

"Uh-huh."

"Also, she offered me money to deliver the letter."

"Ah."

"Two hundred dollars."

"Ah."

"So I figured I'd help her out. Why not? Her boyfriend's name was on the letter, some Italian name, so I figured her story was genuine. Otherwise, where would she have got the name?"

"And *her* name? Did she tell you her name?"

"Cookie."

"Cookie, uh-huh."

"Yes."

"Cookie what?"

"She didn't say."

"What did this Cookie look like?"

"Red hair in a feather cut. Brown eyes. About my height, I would guess. Nice figure. About my age, maybe a little younger. Well-dressed."

"Like you."

"Thank you."

"Was she wearing gloves?"

"What?"

"Gloves."

"No. Gloves?"

"Gloves. I don't suppose *you* were wearing gloves, either, were you?"

"No, I wasn't. Gloves? It's June!"

"Miss Kane, would you mind if we took your fingerprints before you left the precinct?"

"Yes. I mean *no*. I mean yes, I *would* mind. Why do you want my fingerprints?"

"Because they're most likely on that envelope you handled, and we'd like to eliminate them when we run our check."

"What check?"

"To see what *other* prints may be on it."

"No," Alison said. "No fingerprints."

"Why not?"

"Because I haven't done anything wrong."

"Uh-huh," Eileen said, and looked her dead in the eye. "Ever been in trouble with the law, Miss Kane?"

She did not answer.

"Alison? Ever been . . . ?"

Which was when she gave up Ambrose Carter.

"Whut this is," Ambrose told Willis and Eileen, "is a tempest in a teapot."

He was thinking he'd like to put the red-head in his stable. What the hell could she be making as a cop?

"Girl told us you're her pimp," Eileen said.

"I been out of that trade a long time now," Carter said.

"We're not looking at a Two-Thirty bust," Willis said.

Carter knew the man was referring to Section 230.25 of the Penal Law, which stated that a person was guilty of promoting prostitution when he knowingly advanced or profited from prostitution by managing, supervising, controlling, or owning either a house of prostitution or a prostitution business involving two or more prostitutes.

Which Carter was, in fact, guilty of doing. Owning a prostitution business in-

186

volving two or more prostitutes. Eleven of them, in fact. But he didn't let on like he knew what Willis was talking about, because that would be the same thing as admitting he was a pimp, and not a mere agent of sorts.

"Then whut is it you *are* looking at, Detective?" he asked Eileen, deferring to her rank and her beauty and her big tits. "And whut do it have to do with me?"

"Alison Kane," Eileen said again, which was exactly how she'd opened the conversation.

"Said you sent her to meet some woman . . ."

"I *tole* you I am no longer engaged in that form of occupation."

"This wasn't a takee-outee call," Eileen said. "This woman needed someone to deliver a letter."

"To *us*," Willis said.

"At the Eighty-seventh Precinct."

"Woman gave her two bills to do it."

"I still does not know whut this possibly has to do with me," Carter said, spreading his hands wide in innocence.

"We want the woman's name."

"I do not know which woman you is talkin' about."

"The woman who gave Alison Kane two

hundred bucks to deliver a letter to us."

"I know of no such woman."

"Alison says you're the one who sent her . . ."

"I do not know anyone named Alison, either. Kane or otherwise."

"How about Gloria Stanford?" Willis said.

"Her neither. Who *are* all these women?"

"Gloria Stanford was murdered on Memorial Day," Willis said.

"And that ain't such a tempest in a teapot," Eileen suggested.

Which was when Carter gave up Carmela Sammarone.

The federal search came up with a hit for a prostitution arrest in Los Angeles six Decembers ago. A set of partials they'd lifted from the envelope Alison Kane had delivered matched the prints on file for **Sammarone, Carmela, NMI** in the AFIS system.

Before now, they'd had good reason to believe that the Deaf Man had killed Gloria Stanford. Problem was they didn't know who he might be, or where they could find him.

Now they also had good reason to believe he'd engaged a prostitute named

Carmela Sammarone to recruit at least one other person to deliver his messages to the precinct.

Problem here was they didn't know where *she* might be, either.

Or even that nowadays she was known as Melissa Summers.

7

The phone rang at a little past nine that Sunday morning. They were sleeping in Sharyn's apartment that night, and she always slept on the side of the bed closest to the phone because in this city you never knew when another cop would get shot, and the Deputy Chief Surgeon would have to respond.

Sharyn picked up the receiver and said, "Cooke here," and then listened, and said, "Where?" and listened again, and said, "I'm on the way," and hung up and threw back the covers and ran for the bathroom.

Kling was dressed before she was.

"I'll drive you," he said.

"You don't have to," she said.

"I want to," he said. "We'll get breakfast when you're finished there."

"My dollface," she said, and went to him and kissed him.

He drove them through a Mickey D's for coffee, and they started the drive to Majesta with the windows down and fresh morning breezes blowing through. There was very little traffic so early on a Sunday morning, and they made it over the bridge in ten minutes flat and were at Mount Pleasant in another ten. Mount Pleasant was one of the city's better hospitals. There'd be no need for Sharyn to arrange a transfer, but a cop had been badly cut trying to break up an early morning gang rumble outside St. Matthew's Church on Camden Boulevard, and she had to be here to make sure he'd get the best possible treatment.

That didn't explain why Dr. James Melvin Hudson was standing outside the main entrance to the hospital.

Kling suddenly remembered that this was where Dr. James Melvin Hudson worked. When he wasn't working at the office of the Deputy Chief Surgeon in Rankin Plaza, four miles and another world away. Medland versus Copland.

Dr. James Melvin Hudson was wearing his hospital togs this morning, looking all pristine and medical in a white tunic with a stethoscope hanging out of the right-hand pocket. Dr. James Melvin Hudson was tall and black and extremely handsome, and he'd been dating Sharyn when she and Kling first met, and here he was now. Standing outside Mount Pleasant Hospital. Where he was Head of the Oncology Department. Which was why he also worked at Rankin Plaza because cops didn't only get shot or knifed or bludgeoned or axed; they sometimes got cancer.

And then Kling remembered that it was someone named Jamie who'd called Sharyn to tell her Hawes had been shot.

And he suddenly wondered if the colleague who'd suggested she give a listen to "Go Ask" was none other than Jamie Hudson himself.

Sharyn got out of the car.

"Hi, Jamie," she said. "Where is he?"

And went into the hospital without telling Kling where they'd be meeting for breakfast later.

There was nothing he appreciated more than thoughtful solitude. Alone in the room he had set aside as his office, sitting behind his computer and contemplating the week ahead, he knew an intense satisfaction he felt lesser men could not possibly enjoy.

For him, the planning was far more exciting than the execution. He had read somewhere that Alfred Hitchcock felt a movie was finished the moment he laid out his storyboard. In many respects, he felt the same way.

The letters he would . . .

Or rather *Melissa* would . . .

Or rather Melissa's *minions* would deliver next week had already been composed and printed and placed in their separate envelopes, each of them addressed to Detective Stephen Louis Carella at the 87th Precinct. Step by step, bit by bit, Monday through Friday, the delivered messages would gradually unfold his meticulous plan, leading the Keystone Kops down the garden path until Saturday, ta-ra! when at last all would be revealed — if they were clever enough. But too late.

Smiling, he hunched over the keyboard and opened first the folder he had titled **SKED**, and next the file he had titled **CALENDAR**:

MON 6/7	**DARTS**
TUE 6/8	**BACK TO THE FUTURE**
WED 6/9	**NUMBERS**
THU 6/10	**PALS**
FRI 6/11	**WHEN?**
SAT 6/12	**NOW!**

He nodded in satisfaction.

Bit by bit, he thought.

Step by step.

The actual gig next Saturday held little or no interest for him. Neither did the eventual payoff. It was the planning that thrilled him to the marrow — to coin a phrase. And this was a magnificent plan!

He suddenly burst into jubilant song.

When Melissa heard him singing at the top of his lungs, she thought perhaps he'd finally lost it. Sighing, she picked up the receiver and punched out Ambrose Carter's number in Diamondback. He answered on the third ring.

"Ame," she said, "it's me."

"Li'l early to be callin, ain' it?"

She looked at the clock on the desk. It was ten minutes past ten.

"Sorry, Ame," she said, "but I was wondering about tomorrow."

"Whut about tomorrow?"

"Have you lined up your three people?"

"Whut three people?" he said.

She held the receiver away from her ear, looked at it the way a person might do on television when she'd just heard something she couldn't quite understand or believe. Eyes squinching up. Brow furrowing.

"For the letters," she said.

"Whut letters?" he said.

"The letters you were going to find people . . ."

"Whut letters?" he said again.

"The letters I advanced you three fucking thousand dollars to . . ."

"I don't know whut you talkin bout, girl," he said, and hung up.

She looked at the phone again.

Just like on television.

Hawes couldn't quite imagine himself dating a so-called celebrity, but he guessed that's what Honey Blair was. Which was why he didn't have to prod the detectives of Midtown South to follow up diligently on the drive-by shooting that had taken place outside 574 Jefferson at a few minutes before eleven on Wednesday morning, June second, four days ago. The other person in that perforated limousine had been Hawes himself, by the way, but this didn't seem of much interest to a detective named Brody Hollister, who was heading up the Mid South investigative team.

"Thanks, Colton," he told Hawes on the phone. "We'll keep that in mind, if, when."

"Thanks," Hawes said. "And it's Cotton, by the way. *Cotton* Hawes."

"Really?" Hollister said, and hung up.

Asshole, Hawes thought, and made his next call to the Eight-Six, where there was no question that he himself, Cotton (sometimes known as Colton) Hawes, had been the intended victim. The detective who'd caught the squeal there was a First named Barney Olson, and he told Hawes he was still working the case, but they'd had a rash of crib burglaries this past week, and he was sorry to admit he hadn't given the sniper case his undivided attention.

He sounded a bit distracted, but also somewhat sarcastic, landing a mite too heavily on the words "undivided attention," hmm? Crib burglaries were not the theft of infants' beds, but merely burglaries committed in dwellings rather than offices, and doubtless of vast importance in a Silk Stocking precinct like the 8-6. But, shit, man, a person — *Hawes* himself! — had been shot at from a rooftop, and it was very likely, in fact virtually indisputable that the Wednesday morning attempt on his life was linked to the subsequent Friday morning shooting outside his orthopedist's office on Jefferson Avenue. He still wondered what you had to do to get the "undivided attention" of a cop around here.

He did not yet know that a personal note of apology had been delivered yesterday to

Channel Four's seventh-floor offices on Moody Street.

Neither did Honey.

Her weekend off had started yesterday. This was still Sunday. This afternoon, in fact, they planned to go downtown to hear the visiting Cleveland Symphony Orchestra perform an all-Stravinsky program in Clarendon Hall's popular "Three at Three" series. Meanwhile, Hawes had finished making his calls, and Honey was taking a luxuriant bubble bath.

He wondered if he should go in there and offer to scrub her back.

Carella's mind was on the Deaf Man.

Watching his wife's moving fingers, translating for his mother and sister, his mind was nonetheless on where the Deaf Man might be, and what he might be planning on this Sunday, the sixth day of June.

Carella had checked with the desk sergeant at the 8-7 early this morning, as soon as he'd got up, but as of eight-thirty a.m, no message from Mr. Adam Fen had been delivered. He had checked again at twelve-thirty, just about when his mother, and Angela, and Angela's two daughters were arriving for lunch, but again, there had been nothing from the man who'd barraged them with missives the week before.

Now, reading and translating, Carella's mind wandered.

While Teddy explained that they had thought a Northern Italian menu might be appropriate, in honor of Luigi and his children and the dozen or more friends who were coming over from Milan for the wedding, Carella was thinking. Two days of anagrams, starting with **WHO'S IT, ETC?** on Tuesday afternoon and ending the next day with **I'M A FATHEAD, MEN!** All five notes designed to remind them of his previous mischief and to tell them he was the one who'd killed Gloria Stanford.

And, as Teddy's fingers signaled savory but difficult to sign pass-around starters like *bruschetta* and *crostata di funghi* and *tartine di baccala,* Carella simultaneously spoke the words aloud in his halting Italian while silently pondering the fusillade of Shakespearean quotes that had started on Thursday with three *shakes* and a *spear* . . .

Rough winds do SHAKE . . .
SHAKE off slumber . . .
SHAKE me up . . .

And finally . . .

. . . footing of a SPEAR.

Announcing without question that whatever might come next, it would most certainly come from Shakespeare. And indeed it had. On Friday morning . . .

"Steve? Are you listening to her?"

His sister's voice. Yanking him forward some five centuries in time.

"Sorry," he said.

Teddy was starting on the main course. *There'll be two choices,* she signed.

"There'll be two choices," Carella said, reading her hands. "Either the roast lamb loin encrusted with mixed Italian herbs . . ."

"Yummy," Angela said.

"Or the Tuscan-style veal tenderloin."

"I think I prefer the veal," his mother said.

"Well, there'll be a choice, Mom."

"I know, honey. I'm just saying I *love* veal."

I thought no fish, Teddy signed. *Fish can be tricky.*

Which was even trickier to sign.

She went on to explain the entrées would be accompanied by fresh sweet peas and pearl onions . . .

"And new potatoes," Carella said, reading.

And a spinach salad . . .

"With goat cheese, walnuts, and a warm pancetta dressing," Carella said.

And, of course, there'll be a choice of desserts, Teddy signed.

"It sounds *delicious*," Angela said.

"Steve?" his mother said. "Don't you think so?"

"Can't wait," he said, nodding, but his mind had begun to wander again.

So while the women lingered over coffee and cannoli, and the children ran around the house giggling and playing whatever game they'd invented *this* week, he went to the computer in Mark's room, and again called up the sources of the three "spear" notes they'd received on Friday.

Tickle our noses with spear-grass — from *Henry IV.*

Where is your boar-spear, man? — from *Richard III.*

And the last note that day — **Slander's venom'd spear** — from *Richard II.*

Was there any significance to the choice of plays, or the order in which the notes were delivered?

If so, what about yesterday's notes?

No more spears this time around. Now the Deaf Man was into arrows:

Her waspish-headed son has broke his
  arrows
Swears he will shoot no more but play
  with sparrows

Act Four of *The Tempest.*

The slings and arrows . . .

Act Three of *Hamlet.*
And lastly:

As stand in narrow lanes

Act Five of *King Richard II.*

One historical drama this time around.
Plus a straight play and a tragedy. Carella
could see nothing significant in their
choice.

Or in the sequence of their delivery, either.

He was left with solely spears and arrows, some of them buried, and he still
didn't know what the hell was about to
happen.

Hawes mentioned during the intermis-
sion that he was getting sort of a brush-off
from the upper-crust dicks at the Eight-Six

and the overworked ones in Mid South. Honey seemed surprised.

"Even after the show I did Friday night?" she asked.

"Oh, they're aware of *you*, all right. But they don't seem interested in finding a link to whoever took those potshots at *me*. Outside your building, I mean."

"You think the two shootings are linked?"

"Well . . . don't you?"

"Honestly? I don't know."

"You don't? Honey, it seems obvious that *I'm* the one they're after."

"You? Why on earth would anyone . . . ?"

"Maybe because I've put away one or two bad guys in my time. And some of those guys are out on the street again. And maybe they *still* don't like the idea of . . ."

"Excuse me, Miss Blair?"

Hawes turned. A tall thin man with a silly grin on his face was virtually leaning in over Hawes's aisle seat to extend his program to Honey in the seat next to his.

"Could you sign it 'To Ben,' please?" he asked, and handed her the program and a marking pen.

Hawes shifted his weight, giving Honey the arm rest and more room to write. Feigning indifference, he busied himself with his own program.

It appeared that next week's "Three at Three" series would kick off on Saturday afternoon with Beethoven's Violin Concerto in D major, Op. 61, his only full concerto for violin. Konstantinos Sallas, the guest violinist, would . . .

"There you go, Ben," Honey said, and handed the program and the pen across Hawes to the man, who was standing expectantly in the aisle, still grinning like a schoolboy.

"Thank you, Miss Blair," he said.

Honey smiled, and then squeezed Hawes's hand.

The house lights were beginning to dim.

At a little past four that afternoon, just as Eileen was searching through her refrigerator and discovering there was nothing but yogurt to eat for dinner tonight, her telephone rang. For some reason, she looked at her watch, and then went into the living room to pick up the receiver.

"Burke," she said.

"Eileen, hi. It's Hal."

"Hey, hi," she said.

"Got a minute?"

"Sure," she said. "What's up?"

"I've got some ideas about our Deaf Man."

"I'm all ears," she said.

Willis laughed.

"Wanna meet for a cup of coffee or something?"

"Sure," she said, and for some reason looked at her watch again.

"Horton's on Max?"

"Give me ten."

"See you."

There was a click on the line.

She looked at the receiver.

Gave a little puzzled shrug.

Shrugged aside the shrug.

Put the receiver back on its cradle, went into the bedroom to see what she looked like in the mirror there, decided she looked good enough for coffee at Horton's, looked at her watch again, and left the apartment.

Horton's on Max was one of a chain of coffee joints that took their separate names from the streets or avenues of their locations. Hence there was a Horton's on Howes and a Horton's on Rae and a Horton's on Granger and a Horton's on Mapes and so forth. The Horton's on Max took its name from its corner location on Maximilian Street, which had been named after Ferdinand Maximilian, the deposed emperor of Mexico, who — at dawn on the nineteenth of June, 1867 — was executed by firing squad on *El Cerro de las Campanas* . . .

"That means 'The Hill of the Bells' in English," Willis told her.

Maximilian Street was not located on or near any hill, nor was there a church close by that might have sounded bells every hour on the hour and therefore provided a modicum of credibility to naming the street after a long-forgotten and scarcely mourned Mexican emperor. But the street had been named during a heatedly fought mayoral election, when a brief influx of Mexican immigrants to this part of the city seemed to presage (wrongly as it turned out) a full-scale invasion of wetbacks. Ever mindful of the power of the ballot box, the city's incumbent mayor dug into his history books and — seemingly ignorant of the fact that Maximilian had been imported from Austria and was largely despised — changed the name of the erstwhile "Thimble Street" (but that was another story) to the more acceptable to Mexicans (he thought) "Maximilian Street."

The theme of "independence" being a

favorite one in any American election . . .

"The other one being 'patriotism,' " Willis said.

. . . perhaps the incumbent mayor was thinking of Maximilian's last words before the bullets thudded home: "I forgive everyone, and I ask everyone to forgive me. May my blood which is about to be shed, be for the good of the country. *Viva Mexico, viva la independencia!*"

"But I digress," Willis said.

"How come you know so much about Mexico?" Eileen asked.

Willis hesitated. Then he said, "Well, Marilyn spent a lot of time in Mexico, you know."

"Yes, I knew that."

"Yes," he said, and fell silent.

They were sipping cappuccino in a corner window, sitting in armchairs opposite each other.

"You okay with that now?" she asked.

She was talking about Marilyn Hollis getting shot to death by a pair of Argentinian hit men.

"Are you ever okay with something like that?" he asked, and suddenly reached across the table to touch her cheek. "Are you okay with this?" he asked.

He was talking about the faint scar on

her cheek where she'd been cut by the son of a bitch who'd later raped her.

"As okay as I'll ever be," she said.

"So," he said, and pulled back his hand, and nodded. He hesitated for what seemed a long time. Then he asked, "Is there still anything between you and Bert?"

"No," she said. "No. Why?"

"Just wanted to make sure I wasn't . . ."

"Yes?"

He shook his head.

"Wasn't what?"

"You know."

She looked at him, nodded. There was another long silence.

"Remember that time in the sleeping bag?" she asked.

"Oh, God, yes!"

Their first encounter with the Deaf Man. The stakeout in Grover Park. Eileen and Willis sharing a sleeping bag as pretend lovers. A decoy lunch pail on one of the benches, cut scraps of newspaper inside it, instead of the fifty thousand bucks the Deaf Man had demanded.

The "passionate couple" assignment had been the choice one; Hawes and Willis had drawn straws for it, and Willis had won. He'd worked with Eileen only once before then, on a mugging case. Now they were lying side by side, in somewhat close proximity, in a sleeping bag.

"*We're supposed to be kissing,*" he told Eileen.

"*My lips are getting chapped,*" she said.

"*Your lips are very nice,*" he said.

"*We're* supposed *to be here on business.*"

"*Mmmm,*" he answered.

"*Get your hand off my behind.*"

"*Oh, is that your behind?*"

"*Listen,*" she said.

"*I hear it,*" he said. "*Somebody's coming. You'd better kiss me.*"

She kissed him.

"*What's that?*" Willis asked suddenly.

"*Do not be afraid,* guapa, *it is only my pistol,*" Eileen said, and laughed.

Remembering now, sipping their coffees, they looked at each other across the round table between them. Eileen licked foam from her lips.

"I didn't know what *guapa* meant," Willis said.

"Rabbit," Eileen said.

"I know that now."

"The line was from *For Whom the Bell Tolls.* The sleeping bag scene between Robert and what's her name."

"Ingrid Bergman."

"I meant in the book."

"I forget."

"Ah, how soon we forget," she said.

They looked at each other again.

"What are these ideas you've got about the Deaf Man?" she asked.

"I don't have *any* ideas about the Deaf Man," he said. "None at all. Not a clue."

"Then . . ."

"I lied."

"You didn't have to," she said, and reached across the table and took his hand. "But promise me something, Hal."

"Yes?"

"Never lie to me again."

"Okay," he said. "I want to make love to you."

She burst out laughing.

"Eileen? I want to make love to you," he said.

"I heard you," she said.

"Eileen?"

"*Yes*, Hal, *yes*. I heard you."

"So . . . do you think . . . do you think you might . . . ?"

"Yes," she said, "I think so," and reached across the table, and took his other hand in hers. "Yes, Hal," she said softly. "Yes."

Melissa knew where to find him because she'd worked for the bastard. Knew all his haunts, all his hangouts, all the places he slept and didn't sleep. He was a busy little man, Ambrose Carter was. When she located him at seven o'clock that Sunday night, it was just beginning to grow dark.

She spotted him through the front plate glass window, sitting at the bar, nursing what was probably a Blackjack, his favorite drink. She knew better than to go inside there, confront him where there'd be all his homies to help him out. Drag her out of there, do her fore and aft to teach her a lesson, a dozen of them, two dozen of them, however many it took to teach the little whore a lesson once and for all.

Well, she was here tonight to teach *him* a lesson.

Teach Mr. Ambrose Carter a lesson.

Teach him you don't go taking money from a person, even if she was a whore, and then not deliver on your promise. You just don't do that.

Not to Melissa Summers, anyway.

She waited till he finished his drink, waited till he paid for it and came out of the bar, walking a bit unsteadily, watched him from across the street, and then caught up with him just as he was unlocking the door to his car.

"Ame?" she said.

He turned.

He was looking at a small gun in her hand. Seemed like some kind of toy gun made out of plastic.

"Well, look who the fuck's here," he said.

"I'll need my money back, Ame," she said.

"Get lost, ho," he said, and went back to unlocking his car door, turning his back on her.

It was calling her a whore that did it, she supposed. He shouldn't have called her a whore. Shouldn't have turned his back on her, either. Shouldn't have dissed her that way. She thought maybe that was why she shot him twice in the back, once while he was still standing, and another time after he'd crumpled to the sidewalk.

Or maybe it was because she'd sucked too many cocks for the son of a bitch in the five years she'd worked for him.

Maybe that was it.

She came out of the bathroom wearing only a white garter belt and red high-heeled pumps. The garter belt, white, made her look somewhat virginal. The pumps matched her lipstick, a red much brighter than her hair, too bright to be worn by anyone but a whore. She had pulled the hair back into a ponytail that again made her appear girlish, a teenager surprised, echoing the pristine white of the garter belt. The garter belt exposed the wild red tangle of her pubic hair, enforcing the whore image again. She was a study in contrasts tonight, Eileen Burke.

"I think I look beautiful," she said, sounding amazed by the discovery.

"You are beautiful," Willis said, and held out his hand to her.

She came to the bed and sat on the edge of it. He kissed first her hand, and then the faint scar on her left cheek. He kissed the hollow of her throat and her nipples. He kissed her below, where the red hair curled recklessly beneath and around the garter belt, and then he found her lips and kissed her longingly and tenderly, murmuring "Eileen, Eileen, Eileen" against her mouth, and her hair and her ears and her shoulders and her neck, making her feel beautiful, genuinely beautiful and clean for the first time since she was raped and stabbed.

He took her in his arms and lowered her onto the bed.

Discovering her, marveling at her presence beside him, he repeated over and over again, "Eileen, Eileen, Eileen, Eileen, Eileen."

Her name.

No one else's name.

Hers alone.

8

"Well, well, well, now what have we here?" Detective Oliver Wendell Weeks asked.

He was talking to the uniformed cops who'd called in what appeared to be a homicide at eight-fifteen this bright Monday morning, June 7, which was when Police Officers Mary Hannigan and Roger Bradley found what appeared to be a dead body on the sidewalk alongside what appeared to be a BMW sedan.

Long before the two officers happened across the stiff on their first circuit of Adam Sector during the first half-hour of the day shift, a great many other people had noticed it lying there on the sidewalk in a huge puddle of blood. All through the livelong night and early morning, these passersby glanced down at the body and hurried on along because, this neighborhood being what it was, nobody thought it prudent to report what sure as hell looked like a murder. Especially those good citizens who recognized the corpse as being the remains of one Ambrose Carter, an influential, what you might call, pimp.

Ollie recognized Carter the moment the ME rolled him over.

"Ambrose Carter, Pimp," he announced, spreading his hands on the air and raising his voice to the world at large, but especially to the two Homicide cops who'd been sent over to lend authority to the vile goings-on up here in the Eight-Eight.

"I know all the girls in his stable," Weeks said.

"Biblically, no doubt," the ME commented drily.

"You think one of them might've aced him?" Muldoon asked.

"It's been heard of," Mulready said.

The two Homicide dicks were wearing black suits, black socks and shoes, black ties, white shirts, black snap-brimmed fedoras. They looked like Tommy Lee Jones and Will Smith, except that they were both white. They had already decided there was nothing important for them up here. A dead pimp? Who cared?

"Shell casings there," Muldoon said, indicating them with a nod of his head.

"I saw them," Weeks said.

"By the way, you ever find the guy

who stole your book?"

"Not yet," Ollie said. "But I will."

"What book?" Mulready asked.

"Detective Weeks here wrote a book," Muldoon said.

"You're kidding me."

"Tell him, Ollie."

"I wrote a book, yes," Ollie said. "What's so strange about that?"

"Nothing at all," Muldoon said. "Every detective I know has written a book."

"Not me," Mulready said.

"Not me, neither," Muldoon said. "But we're exceptions to the rule, right, Ollie?"

"I don't need this," Ollie said.

"Can I buy this book on Amazon?" Mulready asked.

"It ain't been published yet," Muldoon said. "That's what's so fascinating about it. The manuscript was stolen from the back seat of Detective Weeks's car by some transvestite hooker."

"You're kidding me, right?" Mulready said.

"Who you ain't caught yet, am I right, Ollie?"

"Shove it up your ass," Ollie explained.

The Mobile Crime boys were just arriving.

215

★ ★ ★

Melissa had begun looking for her next three messengers immediately after she ran from what she supposed the cops would now be calling the "crime scene." Hadn't thought to clean up after herself, pick up those little brass thingies from the sidewalk, whatever you called them, she'd thought of that only later; they could identify a weapon from stuff like that, couldn't they? She just wanted to get the hell out of there fast. Before last night, she'd never shot a person in her life, no less killed one, and she was just plain scared.

But that was last night and now was now.

Sitting in the Starbucks on Rafer and Eleventh, her hand shaking only slightly as she lifted a cup of espresso macchiato to her lips, she read both morning newspapers and could not find a single article about the death of a pimp named Ambrose Carter. Not a single paragraph. Not a single word. As her mother was fond of saying: *Good riddance to bad rubbish.*

She was feeling exceptionally fine this morning.

'Tis pity she's a whore and all that, but it wasn't every day you got to kill the pimp who'd turned you out.

Smiling secretly, she sipped serenely.

Along about now, the first of the three envelopes should be arriving at the Eight-Seven. She had arranged to meet later with her next two chosen messengers, exchange cash for envelopes. One, two, three, and finished for the day.

The way she'd found all three delivery boys was by remembering once again what her mother had taught her at her knee: *Desperate people do desperate things.*

Only this time, she'd looked for the *most* desperate people she could find.

Simple.

She took another satisfying sip of espresso.

Maybe she'd even buy herself one more cup.

Maybe a double this time.

And a chocolate chip cookie.

What the hell.

You know his nature,
That he's revengeful, and I know his
    sword
Hath a sharp edge: it's long and, 't
    may be said,
It reaches far, and where. 'twill not
    extend,
Thither he darts it. Bosom up my
    counsel,

You'll find it wholesome.

"A *sword* now?" Meyer asked.

"From spears to arrows to a sword," Carella said.

He was already at the computer.

"Shouldn't it be '*Has* a sharp edge'?" Genero asked.

"*Hath* is what they said back in those days," Parker explained.

"Sounds like a lisp," Genero said.

"Maybe he's gay," Parker suggested. "This guy whose sword *hath* a sharp edge."

"Don't forget it's *long,* too," Eileen said, looking all wide-eyed and innocent.

"And reaches far," Willis added.

Kling darted a look at both of them.

"Party's getting rough again," Hawes said.

" 'Bosom,' yeah," Genero said, grinning.

"It's from *King Henry VIII*," Carella said. "Act One, Scene One."

"Which tells us nothing at all," Kling said.

"It tells us we *know* him," Brown said, "and we know he's out for revenge."

"That's for sure."

"You think he's *really* gonna use a sword?" Hawes asked. "For whatever he's planning?"

"Well, he *said* no more arrows, didn't he? Where's that other note?"

Carella went searching through the notes they'd received the week before. He found the one he was looking for, put it on the desk for the others to look at again:

Her waspish-headed son has broke his
   arrows,
Swears he will shoot no more but play
   with sparrows

"Doesn't say anything about swords," Parker said. "Just says from now on he's gonna play with sparrows."

"Does he mean girls?" Genero asked. "Chicks?"

"They call 'em birds in England," Willis said, nodding.

"Sparrows," Meyer said, and shrugged. "Could be. Who the hell knows?"

"The Shadow knows," Genero said.

"Dee Shadow know," Brown said, affecting a thick, down-home, watermelon-eating accent.

"*Sparrows* has *arrows* in it, you know," Willis said.

"*Hath,*" Parker corrected.

"I mean, the *word sparrows*. It has the word *arrows* in it."

"So you told us," Hawes said.

"Just mentioning it. I mean, if we're still on the spears-to-arrows-to-swords kick."

"Don't forget he hath a *long* sword," Eileen said, looking innocent again.

"And that thither he will dart it," Willis said.

"It doesn't say that," Kling said, sounding annoyed.

Carella looked at him.

"Well, more or less," Willis said, and shrugged.

Eileen shrugged, too.

"Or maybe we're missing the *point*," Hawes said, and grinned.

"Is that another sword joke?" Genero asked.

Konstantinos Sallas seemed to be a creature of habit.

The Deaf Man had been trailing him for the past week now, and his routine never varied. The man was staying at the new Intercontinental Hotel on Grover Avenue, at the high-rent reaches of the 87th Precinct, facing Grover Park. Enter the park at Sakonuff Street, follow the footpath uptown, past the zoo, wander crosstown past the lake, under the arches, and you'd come out a few blocks from the 87th Precinct stationhouse, where just about now — he glanced at his watch — someone should be delivering the second of his notes that day.

Every day since he'd arrived from Athens, Sallas left his hotel at 8:30 a.m. and in the company of his bodyguard walked directly to Clarendon Hall, which took him precisely seventeen minutes. At 8:48, he entered the concert hall by the stage door, where a uniformed guard challenged him on only the first day.

It was no different today.

It was now 8:48:17 by the Deaf Man's digital watch, and Sallas was just entering the hall, the bodyguard trailing dutifully behind him.

Later, the Deaf Man thought.

The Deaf Man was not the only cheap thief working the Eight-Seven and environs that Monday morning.

At a quarter past nine, Parker and Genero went to investigate the apparent strangulation of a seven-month-old baby in her crib. The father, a letter carrier, had left for work at five this morning. The mother was in hysterics when she let the detectives into the apartment. There were purple bruises on the infant's throat. Her tongue bulged out of her mouth. A window alongside the baby's bed was open to the fresh breezes of early June. The mother told them she was sleeping soundly when her husband left for work. She didn't know the baby was dead till she woke up around a quarter to nine. She'd called the police at once.

In the hallway outside, Genero said, "The father did it."

"Wrong, Richard," Parker said. "The mother."

Twenty minutes later, Willis and Eileen went out together to investigate a burglary in a lingerie shop the night before. The owner of the shop, a woman who spoke English with a French accent, told them she'd opened the shop at ten o'clock this morning to find everything "t'rown all over zee place like you see it now, eh?" Waving her hands on the air. Indeed, there were panties and slips, bras and garter belts, kimonos and teddies, tangas and boyshorts, merry widows and bustiers strewn all over the shop. The cash register drawer was open, but the lady told them she'd taken its contents home with her when she left last night at seven. Which might have accounted for why the intruder had gone berserk inside there.

"In England, they call these 'suspenders,' " Willis told Eileen, lifting from the floor a garter belt trimmed in black lace.

"Do you have this in white?" Eileen asked the lady.

Cost her sixty bucks.

She winked at Willis when they left the shop.

At ten-thirty that morning, Carella and Hawes went out to investigate an apparent suicide on Silvermine Oval, in a building not too far from where Gloria Stanford had been shot to death a week ago today. The woman in the tub was naked. The ME pronounced her dead, and suggested she'd electrocuted herself by dropping a hair dryer into the water.

"Nice tits, though," Monoghan said.

"Great jugs, you mean," Monroe corrected.

Carella wondered if someone other than the dead woman had dropped that dryer into the tub. The super of the building told them the woman's husband was a stock-broker downtown, left for work very early every morning. At a little before eleven, they headed down to the financial district to ask him a few questions.

Kling and Brown, the Good Cop/Bad Cop team, caught a squeal closer to home at five past eleven. Drive-by shooting. Gang stuff. Dead boy on the sidewalk. Nobody saw or heard anything. They were back in the squadroom by twelve-fifteen. Everyone else drifted in by the half-hour.

It was now twelve-thirty, and here came Konstantinos!

Striding out of the stage door, saying hello to the armed guard there, and then marching off up the avenue toward his favorite little deli.

Dutifully, the Deaf Man followed.

Every day so far, Sallas left the concert hall at twelve-thirty, walked to the Greek delicatessen — surprise! — on Sakonuff, had lunch there, and then walked back to the hall to resume rehearsal at 1:00 p.m. At 4:00 p.m. every day, he exited through the stage door, bodyguard beside him, violin case swinging from his right hand, took a brief brisk stroll up Grover Avenue, past the museum and the 87th Precinct stationhouse, and then turned back toward the hotel again.

Later, the Deaf Man thought.

It was only after the second messenger arrived that the police detected a pattern here: Carmela Sammarone was drafting

224

junkies to do her legwork. At least today, anyway. At least in the selection of her delivery boys.

It wasn't too difficult to find a junkie on any street corner in this city. Lay some shit on him, or just the cash to buy the shit, and he'd go out to kill his own mother for you. It wasn't difficult to recognize a junkie, either. There were always the red watery eyes, the pupils either too large or too small. There was the puffy face, or the cold, sweaty palms, or the shaking hands, or the pale skin. Sometimes there was the smell of this week's substance of choice — cocaine or heroin or ecstasy or meth or OxyContin — on the breath or the body or the clothes.

But more than any of these, there was the blank desperate stare of the addict. And behind those dead eyes, the knowledge that he or she was married to a tyrannical slaveholder. And the further knowledge that not a single soul on earth — sister, mother, brother, father, spouse, significant other, social worker, doctor, or cop — looked upon you with anything but pity or contempt because they felt you had no one but yourself to blame for your predicament.

"Where'd you get this letter, Joseph?"

they asked the first messenger.

At the time, they suspected he might be a junkie, but they didn't yet realize a pattern was about to emerge.

"Girl give it to me Langley Park."

"What girl?"

"Doan know who she was."

"She give you a name?"

"Nossir. Lay a C-note on me, say she be watchin me deliver the en'lope."

"Where was this, Joseph?"

"Tole you. Langley Park."

"How old was she?"

"Ain' no good with ages. Young."

"How young? Young like you?"

"Older."

"How old are you, Joseph?"

"Seventeen."

"What'd she look like?"

"Short red hair, brown eyes."

The second messenger was a girl with bleached blond hair and green eyes. Her hair was matted and stringy and greasy. Her eyes had lost all their luster, and she was as thin as a rail, and her clothes were bedraggled and stained and smelled of vomit and Christ knew what else. She was probably somewhere in her mid-twenties, but she could easily have been mistaken for a woman in her thirties. Maybe even older.

A tired woman in her thirties.

Speaking with a Calm's Point accent — the Irish, not the black or Italian variety — she told them she'd been an addict since she was seventeen, a hooker since she was eighteen. Started with crack, which was all the rage then, moved on to gremmies and sherms and even did some fry before starting to shoot hop directly into the vein, welcome to the club, sweetheart! She told them this girl with long black hair had made her an offer she couldn't refuse, two bills to deliver this envelope here, told her she didn't know who the girl was, didn't know her name, had never seen her before this morning, wouldn't recognize her again if she tripped over her in church.

She was stoned out of her mind when she delivered the envelope, and she couldn't remember where, or even when, she'd met the girl with the long black hair.

"I'm a natural redhead, wanna see?" she said, and lifted her skirt.

She spelled her name Aine Duggan, but she pronounced it Anya Doogan.

They figured her for a lost cause.

But now they knew for sure that Carmela Sammarone was finding her messengers in the city's pool of drug addicts.

And the pool was bottomless.

I may say, thrusting it;
For piercing steel and darts
  envenomed
Shall be as welcome to the ears

"He's sticking it to us," Parker said.

"That's what he means by 'thrusting it,' " Genero agreed.

"Sticking it right in our eye."

" '*Thrusting* it.' "

" 'I may say,' " Meyer said, quoting from the note. "He sounds like Rumsfeld. Next thing you know, he'll be saying 'Golly!' and 'Gee whiz!' "

"There's that sword again," Eileen said.

"Where?" Willis asked.

" 'Piercing steel.' "

"Poisoned darts, too," Kling said.

"I don't see any poisoned darts," Genero said.

" 'Darts envenomed.' That's poisoned darts, Dickie-boy."

"No one calls me 'Dickie,' " Genero told Parker.

"Not even your mama?"

"Everyone calls me Richard."

" 'Darts envenomed' are poisoned darts, Richard."

"Thanks for the information."

" 'Welcome to the ears,' " Carella said, typing the words into the computer.

"Joking about his own infirmity," Hawes said.

"You think so?"

"Signing the note, in effect. I am the Deaf Man, remember?"

"*Julius Caesar*, Act Five, Scene Three," Carella said, reading from the screen.

"How many is that so far?"

"How many is what?"

"The plays he's quoted from."

"Nine?" Kling said.

"No, ten, I think."

"No, wait . . ."

"Plus one from the sonnets. The one about the darling buds of May," Eileen said, and glanced at Willis.

"And we *still* don't know where the first one came from," Carella said.

"Which one?"

"About 'an actor's art,' all that."

" 'An actor's art can die, and live, to act a second part,' " Kling quoted.

"So how many is that?"

"Nine plays for sure. Or ten. Plus the sonnet."

"Out of how many?" Genero asked.

They all looked at him.

"How many did he write?"

"Thousands," Parker said.

"Must be a place we can find out," Genero said. "Isn't there a collection or something?"

"What difference does it make how *many* he wrote, Richard?"

"I thought if there was a collection someplace . . ."

"Yes, Richard?"

"We could figure out how many he wrote."

"And then what?"

"One thing could lead to another," Genero said, and shrugged.

The Deaf Man was thinking that almost anywhere in America, almost anyone could walk in with a bomb and blow the place to smithereens. Walk into any restaurant, any theater, any sporting event, any prayer meeting with a bomb strapped around your waist, and the rest was late-night news. When death was preferable to life, when death promised a heaven where there'd be seven, or seventeen, or seventy waiting virgins, however many there were supposed to be — he personally didn't think there were *any* virgins left in the entire world — then what was to stop any lunatic from walking in with his ticket to

230

paradise strapped around his waist?

Security?

Impossible to maintain in a free society.

Right this minute, he was walking into the biggest library in the city, stopping at a checkpoint where uniformed guards examined his briefcase, peering into it like the trained watchdogs they were, but never asking him to open his jacket or take off his shoes because so far no one in America had marched in loaded. Once that happened, things would change. Before long, you'd be strip-searched before you were permitted to watch the latest hit movie. But for now . . .

"Thank you, sir. If you'll check the bag, please."

He walked across the echoing, vaulted marble lobby to a cloakroom behind and to the right of the security guards. He handed the briefcase across the counter, received a claim check for it, and followed the signs to **FOLGER FIRST FOLIO.**

There used to be a time when Ollie frequented girls like the ones employed or previously employed by Ambrose Carter. Not that he'd been personally intimate with anyone in the man's stable. But he was certainly familiar with the species.

There was a time, too, when Ollie might have called a prostitute of the Hispanic persuasion a "spic slut," but that was before he'd met Patricia Gomez, who was Puerto Rican and a police officer besides and who was . . . well . . . not his girlfriend, quite, but someone he was . . . well . . . sort of seeing. And nowadays, he would break anyone's head who called Patricia a spic.

The first hooker he talked to was, in fact, a spic slut named Paquita Flores, a very dark-skinned voluptuous cutie dressed somewhat scantily for so early in June, not even summer yet here in the city, sitting on the front stoop of her own building, skirt up to her ass, long legs flashing, licking a lollipop, as if she needed further advertisement.

"Yo, *hombre*," she said, looking up, licking. "Long time no see."

He tried to remember those days back then when he frequently traded police lenience for sexual favors. Paquita had been sixteen or thereabouts. She was now, what, twenty, twenty-one? He sat down beside her. Her skimpy frilled skirt flapped about her knees in a mild breeze. She kept licking the lollipop.

"*Que pasa, maricon?*" she said.

232

"What's the word on Carter?" he asked.

"Oh, man, he's like dead, you dinn know?" she said, and grinned around the lollipop.

"The street guessing why?"

"Maybe he ratted out a whore."

"Which one?"

"Don't know, man."

"Who *would* know?"

"Carter wasn' my *abadesa*," Paquita said. "You axin the wrong person."

"Who *should* I ask?"

"Go the Three Flies. His girls hang there."

The book was in a thick glass case surrounded on all four sides by uniformed guards. The Deaf Man knew that the case was alarmed and that if anyone so much as touched the glass, the alarms would sound not only here on the second floor of the library, but also at the offices of Security Plus, who would immediately alert the Midtown South Squad, four blocks from the library.

A red velvet rope hanging on stanchions kept visitors back some four feet from the exhibit. The book in its glass case was opened to its title page:

A notice behind a Plexiglas shield was

Mr. WILLIAM SHAKESPEARES

COMEDIES,
HISTORIES, &
TRAGEDIES.

Published according to the True Originall Copies.

LONDON

Printed by Isaac Iaggard, and Ed. Blount. 1623

fastened to one wall of the library's Elizabethan Room, advising visitors that the book on display was on loan from the Folger Shakespeare Library in Washington, D.C., home to the largest collection of Shakespeare's printed works. Included in the Folger's collections were more than 310,000 books and manuscripts, 250,000 playbills, 27,000 paintings, drawings, engravings, and prints, and musical instruments, costumes, and films.

The notice further advised that the rare book on exhibit was one of only four copies of the earliest complete editions of plays written by William Shakespeare. Whereas only eighteen of his plays had appeared in print during his lifetime, the First Folio collection contained thirty-six of his plays, together with a list of the names of the principal actors in the company, as well as comments and eulogies from them. The book had been printed in London in 1623, at an estimated cost of a bit more than six shillings per copy, marked up to a London retail price of fifteen shillings for the unbound edition, and an even one pound for the edition bound in plain calf.

It was now worth 6.2 million dollars.

★ ★ ★

The Three Flies was a bar in what used to be a notorious red-light section of the Eight-Eight once upon a time before an off-duty cop got shot in the neighborhood by a pimp who didn't like one of his girls having sex with the cop a few dozen times. The girl's developing bad habit led to all the other neighborhood pimps calling the pimp in question — to his face, no less — *un ahuevado*. Which subsequently led to the hapless cop getting shot, and incidentally killed. So the other cops of the Eight-Eight took offense and went marching in there like it was Iraq. The area now relatively clean, but the Three Flies was still a hangout for hookers and college boys who wandered over from Beasley U across the park, looking for sex or dope or both.

When Ollie got there at three that afternoon, the place was still comparatively empty; the schoolboys were still at their studies, and most of the hookers were still sleeping off last night's revelries. The jukebox was playing some kind of bullfight music, and two girls were sitting in a booth bullshitting in time to it. Ollie walked over to them. He didn't know either one of them, so he flashed the buzzer to let them know this was the Law here, and sat down opposite them, and grinned across the table at them. The girls didn't look scared in the slightest; cops were some of their best customers.

"Ambrose Carter," he said.

One of the girls stared at him. She was a black girl with blond hair. The other one was white, also blond. Both of them in their twenties, Ollie guessed. Both of them smoking and drinking beer straight from the same bottle, passing it back and forth between them. Ollie wondered if they worked as a team, passing similarly shaped things back and forth between them.

"What about him?" the black blonde asked.

"Who'd he rat out? And why?"

The two blondes looked at each other.

Dead-panned, they turned back to Ollie.

"So?" he said.

"What's in it for us?" the white blonde asked.

"Look, *almeja*," Ollie said, which meant "cunt" in Spanish, but which the white blonde didn't understand because she happened to be of Scotch-Irish descent, "I don't have time to waste here, okay?"

The black blonde didn't know what *almeja* meant, either, her great-great grandparents having come from the Ivory

Coast. But she knew what the look on this fat hump's face meant.

So she said, "Carmela Sammarone."

Which was what led him to the Eighty-seventh Precinct.

Ollie arrived just a few minutes after the third note that day was delivered.

"She's got the city's whole damn powder crowd marching in here with her damn messages," Byrnes told his assembled detectives.

"Your needle freaks and sleepwalkers, too," Parker said.

This after they realized the third messenger was a heroin addict.

The third note read:

And that you not delay the present,
    but,
Filling the air with swords advanced
    and darts,
We prove this very hour.

"Swords again," Meyer said.

"Spears to arrows to swords."

"Or darts," Carella said. "Maybe that's where he's leading us. *Darts.*"

"Like you throw at a board," Genero said, nodding. "Like in a pub."

"What do you know about pubs, Richard?"

"They're like these bars they have over there."

"Over where, Richard?"

"In England. Where Shakespeare came from," Genero said, and hesitated. "Didn't he?"

"Smaller and smaller," Eileen said. "The weapons."

Willis looked at her. So did Kling.

"They're getting smaller and smaller."

"A sword ain't smaller than an arrow," Parker said.

"A dart is," Hawes said.

"He's gonna shoot somebody with a poisoned *dart!*" Genero announced triumphantly.

"Who is?" Ollie Weeks asked.

He had just pushed his way through the gate in the slatted rail divider that separated the squadroom from the corridor outside. Now, sauntering in as if he owned the place, he walked over to where the detectives were gathered around the note on Carella's desk, peeked at it, shrugged, and said, "Who's Carmela Sammarone?"

"Why?" Eileen asked.

"Hey, Cutie, how you like it up here?" Ollie said, referring to her recent transfer, and grinning like a shark.

"I like it fine, thanks," she said, almost adding "Fatso," but she felt he might be sensitive. "Why do you want to know about Carmela Sammarone?"

"Because I caught a dead pimp, and from what I understand, he gave up one of his girls to you. Is that correct?"

"One of his *former* girls, yes."

"So mayhaps his ratting her out pissed her off," Ollie said. "And mayhaps, as a consequence, she pumped a pair of nines into him."

"You speak Shakespeare, too?" Genero asked.

"Huh?" Ollie said.

"Mayhaps, I mean."

"Huh?" Ollie said again.

"We're getting notes from Shakespeare."

"Don't be ridiculous. Shakespeare's dead."

"*Quotes* from him," Genero explained.

"So what?" Ollie said.

"Sammarone is delivering them," Willis said.

"*Paying* people to deliver them."

"That's what Carter spilled."

Ollie thought this over for a moment.

"That doesn't sound like a reason to kill him," he said.

"Maybe it does," Parker said. "We think she's working for the guy who stiffed a broad last week."

"Puts a different slant on it, I will admit," Ollie said. "So why don't we just go bust her and the guy both?"

"Where?"

"Last address we have for her is L.A."

"I could go on the earie again," Ollie suggested. "See if any of the other girls know where she's at."

"You could do that," Willis agreed.

"It's from *Coriolanus*," Carella said at the computer.

"That makes an even ten plays. Or eleven maybe."

"I'd *still* like to know how many he wrote," Genero said.

"So go to the lib'ery, Richard."

"You know that one about Bush?" Ollie asked.

"What one?"

"When they asked him how he liked Liberia, he said 'I love it. Well, you know, my wife used to *be* a lib'erian.' "

"I don't get it," Parker said.

"What do you make of this last line?" Carella asked.

They all looked at it. Even Ollie looked at it.

We prove this very hour.

They all looked at the clock on the wall. It was 3:45.

"Maybe he's about to tell us *when* he's going to do it," Eileen said.

"Do what?" Ollie asked.

"Whatever he's planning. The *time* he's going to do it. The 'very hour.' "

"Who?"

"The Deaf Man."

"Do I know him?" Ollie said.

"*Nobody* knows him," Genero said.

"This is getting too deep for me," Ollie said. "I'm sorry I came up here. See you," he said, and started out.

"Wait up," Parker said.

The two men strolled out into the corridor together. Parker took Ollie's elbow, leaned in close.

"So you still dating her?" he asked.

"Who you mean?"

"The little spic twist."

"If you're referring to Officer Gomez, yes, we are still seeing each other."

"You get in yet?" Parker asked subtly.

"I got work to do," Ollie said, and shook his elbow free.

"Still tryin'a find that masterpiece of yours?"

"So long, Andy," Ollie said.

"Still tryin'a find the little spic faggot who stole your precious book?"

But Ollie was already going down the iron-runged steps that led downstairs.

The topic of discussion at Channel Four's afternoon meeting was what everyone was already calling "The Note."

DEAR HONEY:
PLEASE FORGIVE ME AS I DID NOT KNOW YOU WERE IN THAT AUTOMOBILE

Present at the meeting were Honey Blair, of course; Danny Di Lorenzo, the show's Program Director; Avery Knowles, its News Director and Head Anchor; his co-anchor, Millie Anderson; Jim Garrison, the Weekday Sports Anchor; and Jessica Hardy, the show's Weather Person, or — as she preferred being called — its Meteorologist.

"I think we should suppress the Note," Di Lorenzo said.

As news director, Avery Knowles felt the Note was indisputably newsworthy. But he wasn't the program director, so he listened.

"The Note specifically says Honey

wasn't the target . . ."

"Thank *God*," Jessica said.

She was a very religious person. She almost crossed herself.

". . . which is nice for Honey, but not so good for us," Di Lorenzo said.

"Who was in that car with you, anyway?" Millie asked.

"A friend of mine," Honey said.

"What friend?" Di Lorenzo asked.

"A detective I know."

"A police detective?"

"Yes."

"That makes it even worse."

"How so?" Avery asked.

"If he's a detective, he'll be trying to find out who did the shooting."

"So?"

"So that's *our* job. That's the job of Channel Four News. Find the demented individual who decided Honey Blair was a prime target for . . ."

"But I'm . . ."

". . . extermination."

". . . *not!* He says as much in his note. He didn't even know I was in the car. *Cotton* was the target."

"Cotton?"

"Cotton Hawes. The detective who was with me."

"Is that his name? Cotton?"

"Yes. Cotton Hawes."

She said this somewhat defensively. She didn't want to get into a brawl with Di Lorenzo because he was, after all, the program director, whereas she was but a mere roving reporter, though not quite so mere anymore, not after Friday's shooting had granted her America's seemingly obligatory fifteen minutes of fame. But shouldn't they go on the air to tell their viewers that she hadn't been the intended target at all, her fame had been ill-earned, the true focus of the attack was . . .

"Cotton Hawes," Di Lorenzo said, shaking his head in disbelief. "An insignificant little nobody."

Honey wanted to say that at six feet two inches, Cotton wasn't what anyone might consider "little." Not *anywhere,* as a matter of fact. Nor was he exactly a "nobody"; he was, in fact, the Detective/Second Grade who'd recently helped crack the Tamar Valparaiso kidnapping case. Nor was he "insignificant," either. He was, in fact, well on the way to becoming what Honey considered the "significant other" in her life. But she didn't mention any of this to Di Lorenzo because she was beginning to catch his drift and beginning to understand what his approach could mean to her career.

"What we've got here," Di Lorenzo said, "is someone shooting at one of our star reporters . . ."

"But he *wasn't*," Millie said. "His note . . ."

"Nobody's seen the Note but us," Di Lorenzo said.

"I'd have to show it to Cotton," Honey said.

"Why?"

"Because someone's trying to *kill* him, for Christ's sake!"

This time, Jessica actually did cross herself.

"You said he's a detective, didn't you?" Di Lorenzo asked.

"Yes, but . . ."

"So I'm assuming he knows how to take care of himself. The point is, for reasons as yet unknown to any of us, someone shot at your limo this past Friday morning. It's not our job to *find* this person, whoever he . . ."

"You said it was," Avery reminded him. "Our job."

"No. Our job is to keep this story *alive*. The longer we keep it alive, the longer the Great Unwashed will tune in to Channel

246

Four at six and eleven every night. I don't care if we *never* find him. The point is, somewhere out there . . ."

Where did I hear *that* line before? Honey wondered.

"Somewhere out there," Di Lorenzo repeated, pointing to the seventh-floor windows and the magnificent view of the skyline beyond, "there's a killer intent on slaying our own Honey Blair. Let's not let anyone forget that."

He'd already forgotten the Note that said Honey wasn't the target at all.

The last time he'd followed a woman he loved was when he was still married to Augusta. Top fashion model, should have known better than to marry her, a mere cop, should have known it would turn out the way it finally did. He hadn't felt good about following her, and he didn't feel good following Sharyn now.

He had been waiting across the street from her office on Ainsley Avenue since a quarter to five. Her usual routine was to subway over to Rankin Plaza and the Deputy Chief Surgeon's office there, where she'd stay till noon, break for lunch in Majesta, and then bus back to the city and uptown to her private practice. Deputy

Chief Surgeon Sharyn Cooke in the morning, Dr. Sharyn Cooke, internist, in the afternoon. He knew he was living with a Deputy Inspector whereas he was a mere Detective/Third. This didn't matter; he loved her. He was white and she was black. This didn't matter, either; he loved her.

What mattered . . .

He'd found Augusta in bed with another man.

Almost killed the son of a bitch.

His eyes had met Augusta's.

Their eyes had said everything there was to say, and all there was to say was nothing.

Across the street, Sharyn was coming out of her office.

He turned away, still watching her in the reflecting plate glass window of a pharmacy, a trained cop. When she started away from the building, stepping out with that quick, proud stride of hers, he turned and began trailing her, still on the other side of the street, a hat hiding his telltale blond hair. Black and blond. A doctor and a cop. Should he have known better this time, too?

She swung into a Starbucks up the street, came out five minutes later, carrying a cardboard container. Sipping at the coffee, she strolled along almost jauntily, enjoying the mild weather, walking right past the bus stop where she could have caught a bus that would have taken her crosstown to his apartment. Tonight was his place again; tomorrow night would be hers. They alternated haphazardly; they were in love. Or so he devoutly wished.

The neighborhood in which Sharyn maintained her office had been gentrified ten years ago and was already sliding inexorably back into the morass of a full-time ghetto and slum. What had once been a pool parlor and was later transmogrified to a fitness center was now a seedy cuchifrito joint catering to the area's small Hispanic population, a minority here among the predominant blacks. A similar transformation-retransformation process had taken place when condemned tenements became sleek brick apartment buildings that were already crumbling into decrepitude. Drugs — flourishing when crack was all the rage, virtually vanquished when the Reverend Gabriel Foster launched his famously popular *No Shit Now!* campaign — were back on the street with a vengeance, the preferred controlled substance now being heroin, seems like old times, don't it, Gert?

In this stretch of all too sadly familiar

black turf, blond Bert Kling followed the gorgeous black woman he adored, and hoped against hope that she was not hurrying to meet Dr. James Melvin Hudson.

But she was.

The name of the café was the Edge.

It was called this because it was on the very edge of Diamondback, in a sort of no-man's-land that separated the hood from the rest of the city. Jumping the season somewhat, the Edge had put tables out on the sidewalk, and as Sharyn approached, half a dozen patrons were sitting there in the quickly fading light, sipping coffees or teas, munching on cookies or cakes. One of them got to his feet, and walked toward her, hand outstretched.

Dr. James Melvin Hudson.

Kling hung back.

Ducked into a doorway.

She took his hand, Dr. James Melvin Hudson's hand, reached up, kissed him on the cheek, which Kling thought an odd greeting for a pair of physicians; cops never even shook hands with other cops. She sat opposite him, and he signaled to a waiter. She'd just had a coffee . . .

Kling could imagine her explaining this to him . . .

So if he didn't mind, she'd just sit here . . .

Turning away the waiter's proffered menu . . .

And then leaning into him over the table, Dr. James Melvin Hudson, her elbows on the table, heads close together, talking seriously and intimately as on the sidewalk passersby hurried on along, unknowing, uncaring, this was the big bad city.

Kling watched them for the next half-hour, hidden in his secret doorway, a cop, shoulders hunched as if it were the dead of winter and not the seventh day of June, hat pulled down low on his forehead, hiding his blond hair. The blond guy and the black girl. Had it been a mistake from the start? Was it now a mistake? Would black and white *ever* be right in America?

He looked at his watch, Dr. James Melvin Hudson did, and signaled to the waiter. Sharyn watched him as he paid the bill, rose when he did, kissed him on the cheek again when he went off, and then sat again at the table, alone now, seemingly deep in thought as the shadows lengthened and evengloam claimed the distant sky.

Genero hadn't been inside a public library since he was twelve years old and checked out John Jakes' *Love and War* with his new Adult Section card. His current reading ran to the Harry Potter books, but he actually bought those because he felt people should support starving writers who wrote on paper napkins in coffee shops.

The library he went to that Monday night was in his Calm's Point neighborhood and stayed open till ten p.m. He got there around eight, after having dinner with his mother and father in their little one-story house nearby. His mother made *penne alla puttanesca,* which she told him meant "whore style," in front of his father, too. When he asked the librarian if she had a book that had everything Shakespeare ever wrote in it, she looked at him funny for a minute, and then came back with a heavy-looking tome that he took to the reading room, which was as quiet as a funeral parlor.

He didn't plan to *read* everything Shakespeare ever wrote; he simply planned to *count* all the stuff he'd written. The numbers he came up with were thirty-seven plays, five long poems, and a hundred and fifty-four sonnets, which up to now he'd thought were also poems, but since they were in a separate section of the book labeled SONNETS, he now guessed otherwise. He also guessed this was a very large body of work. In fact, he could hardly think of anyone else who'd written so many wonderful things, he supposed, in his or her lifetime.

He didn't know to what use he could put this newfound knowledge, but he considered it very sound detective work. And besides, when he returned the book, the librarian looked at him with renewed respect, he also supposed.

Lying in bed, waiting for her to come to him, Kling told her they'd probably figured out what weapon — or weapons, actually — the Deaf Man planned to use, but not whom he planned to kill, or even *if* he planned to kill anyone at all.

"It's darts," he said. "Plural. D-A-R-T-S. Probably poisoned. We figured out it's, like, the law of diminishing returns. In his notes, he went from spears to arrows to darts, in descending order. Like backward. So we're pretty sure it's darts, but we don't know who or how — or even when, for that matter."

"Mmm," Sharyn said.

She was in the bathroom, brushing her teeth. She seemed preoccupied, but she often got that way while getting ready for bed. Lots of things a woman had to do before bedtime. Even so . . .

"Thing is, that's not his usual style," Kling said. "Announcing a murder, I mean."

Sharyn spit into the sink.

"We think he killed this woman last week, but that may have been getting even for her betraying him or something. Mayhem is more his style. Subterfuge. Leading us in one direction and then moving in another."

"He sounds like a real pain in the ass," Sharyn said, and came back into the bedroom. She was wearing a baby-doll nightgown, no panties, fuzzy pink slippers.

"A *supreme* pain in the ass," Kling said. "But dead serious."

"Are you cold in here?" Sharyn asked. "Or is it just me?"

"It is a little chilly," he said. "Such a nice day, too."

"Lovely."

The room was silent for a moment.

"How'd *your* day go?" he asked.

"Okay," she said.

He hesitated. Took the plunge.

"What'd you do?"

"The usual," she said. "Parade of the halt and lame at Rankin, lunch at a Chinese restaurant, march of the poor and op-pressed up in Diamondback. Same old, same old."

She took off her slippers, climbed into bed beside him.

"And afterward?" he asked.

"After what?"

"After work?"

"Bought a coffee at Starbucks, and caught a bus *home*. Come warm my feet," she said, cuddling close to him.

9

It was already one o'clock on Tuesday morning, the eighth day of June. Despite the light drizzle wetting the streets and dampening the libido, the stroll in Ho Alley had been underway since eleven or so last night.

There was a time when Ollie might have found these nocturnal adventures exciting . . . well, actually *had* found them exciting, never mind the "*might* have." Half the girls out here looked like they were parading in their underwear. The other half were wearing skirts cut high on their thighs, some of them slit up the side to expose even more flesh, barelegged, with strapped stiletto-heel sandals or boots of the dominatrix variety, leather laces up the side. If you were a red-blooded American male, how could you *not* get excited?

Especially when these girls reeked of everything forbidden. He didn't mean just the casual blowjob; junior high school girls were giving those away free nowadays. He meant the very *concept* of Anything Goes.

In a society becoming more and more restrictive, here on this five-block stretch of turf, everything was permitted. Anything imagined by the Great Whores of Babylon had been refined to perfection over the centuries and was now for sale in this outdoor bazaar where girls talked freely and seemingly without fear of arrest about such delicacies as the Moroccan Sip, and the Acapulco Ass Dip, and the Singapore Slide.

There ought to be a law, Ollie thought.

There *was*, in fact, a law, but you couldn't guess it existed on this street at this hour of the night. As short a time ago as only last month, Ollie would have found all these flashing legs and winking nipples and glossy wet lips . . . well . . . arousing. Even now, he felt a faint stirring in his groin, but he suspected that was a conditioned response and not anything generated by true desire. Or maybe it was because one of the girls had just grabbed his genitals and asked, "What you got here, Big Boy?"

"Nothing for you, honey," he said.

"Sure about that? I'm a virgin from Venezuela."

"And I'm a bullfighter from Peru," he said.

"Less see what you got there, *torero.*"

"Unzip him, Nina."

"Want me to suck your *espada?*"

"Come on, *torero,* less see that *acero* you got there."

"Or maybe juss a *puntilla,* eh?"

"Feels like a nice big package here, Anita."

"Wha' you say, *matador?*"

"We have our'sess a real *fiesta brava,* eh?"

"Some other time, girls," he said, and walked away.

"You'll beeee *sorrr*-eeeee!" they chanted in unison behind him.

Ollie wondered if he might be coming down with something.

For the past half-hour, he'd been looking for a girl named Wanda Lipinsky. From all accounts, Wanda was not Jewish. She had chosen the surname only because of its echoing proximity to the name Lewinsky, which slant rhyme seemed to promise all sorts of oral delights. Toward that end (and no pun intended) Wanda could be recognized, he'd been informed, by the thong panties she affected in imitation — if ever anyone got past her mouth to explore the hidden treasures under her skirt. But these were not the good old days, and these promised delectations, ah yes, were not what interested Ollie about Ms. Lipinsky, whose real name, he was further told, was Margaret O'Neill.

Little Margie, it seemed, was a freelance like the Carmela Sammarone who had possibly aced the pimp who'd given her up to the Boys of Grover Park. Little Margie, it further seemed, had gone on the town with Little Mela this past Wednesday night, cruising the hotels midtown, where Mela had scored, but not, alas, the thong-wearing Lewinsky sound-alike. Or so the grapevine maintained, and Ollie had no reason to doubt a story now corroborated by three skimpily dressed hookers freezing their asses off in what had turned into a somewhat chilling rain.

In the old days, there might have been something exciting about these girls — white, black, Latina, Asian, there was pure democracy in Ho Alley — shivering in their underwear and openly peddling their wares. But now, on this early morning in early June . . .

Surely he was coming down with something.

. . . they seemed only poor damn creatures who needed to be helped and comforted. Or perhaps even pitied.

Frowning, puzzled, he hunched his

shoulders and moved on through the falling drizzle.

He did not find Wanda Lipinsky until two that morning. She was backing her way out of a blue Chevy Impala where she'd undoubtedly just blown the little spic behind the wheel, her skirt halfway up her ass, exposing her buttocks and the red silk ribbon of a pair of thong panties buried in her crack.

He waited till she was clear of the car, waited until she turned, tugging at the short skirt, and began walking off.

"Wanda?" he asked.

She stopped dead on the sidewalk.

Turned toward him with a hooker's welcoming smile on her face. She was not an unattractive girl — woman, he guessed — in her mid- or late twenties, with long brownish hair and what he perceived in the near-dark to be blue eyes. Short tight skirt, the line of the thong panties clearly visible. Low-cut, swoop-necked blouse, uplift bra thrusting her breasts in his face. Eyebrows raising slightly. Do I know you?

"Police," he said, and showed the tin. "Few questions I'd like to ask you."

"Sure," she said wearily.

Another night in the cooler, she was thinking.

He wanted to know about last Wednesday night.

"Were you with Carmela Sammarone last Wednesday night?" he asked.

"Carmela . . . ?"

"Sammarone. You know who she is, Wanda. Were you with her?"

They were sitting in an all-night joint on Carson and McIntyre. Wanda was nursing a beer; she still had a long night ahead of her. She hoped. Ollie was sipping a club soda with a slice of lime in it; he was officially off duty, but he wanted to keep his wits about him. He had a feeling that Little Margie O'Neill here could turn out to be a slippery little customer.

"Carmela Sammarone," he said again.

Wanda said nothing.

"You *do* know her, don't you?"

"Never heard of her."

"Were you with her last Wednesday night?"

"Wednesday night, Wednesday night," Wanda said, rolling her eyes, thinking.

"Yes or no, Wanda?"

"I don't recall."

"Wanda," he said, "don't fuck with me."

"Language," she scolded.

"I need to find her. I understand you went downtown cruising . . ."

"I told you I don't remember."

"Think. The hotels downtown. Think, Wanda."

"Oh. You mean . . . ?"

"Yes? What do I mean?"

"Melissa? You talking about Melissa?"

"Is that what she calls herself? Melissa?"

"Melissa Summers, yes."

"Do you know where she is?"

"No, I don't. I'm not her fucking mother."

"Language," Ollie scolded.

"What'd she do?"

"That's what I'd like to ask her."

"I don't rat out friends."

"Then you *do* know where she is."

"I told you I don't."

"Where'd the two of you go last Wednesday night?"

"Who said we went anywhere?"

"Three girls so far. You want their names?"

"What'd Lissie do?"

"Tell me where she scored last Wednesday."

"Why? She rip off the guy, or something?"

"There *was* a guy, right?"

"You got me," she said, shrugging. "Was there?"

"How'd you like getting mugged and printed again tonight?"

Wanda said nothing.

"Wanna spend the night in a holding cell, Margie?"

Still nothing.

"You want some dyke forcing you to lick her pussy?"

"Been there, done that," she said.

"Okay then, we're through talking," he said, and stood up. "Let's go."

"Go where? Nobody solicited you."

"Gee, didn't somebody? I could swear you said you'd blow me for a C-note."

She looked up at him.

"Sit down," she said.

He kept standing.

"Sit down," she said again.

The bartender at the Olympia Hotel was washing glasses when Ollie got there at a little before three that morning.

"Sorry, sir," he said. "Last call was half an hour ago."

"How come?" Ollie asked.

He was surprised. In this city you could legally serve alcoholic beverages till four in the morning.

"We discovered traffic slows down after two, is all," the bartender said. "Sorry."

Ollie flashed the tin.

"Few questions," he said.

"Can't this wait?" the bartender asked.

"Afraid it can't," Ollie said, and pulled out one of the bar stools, and sat.

The bartender sighed, dried his hands on a dish towel.

"Wednesday night last week," Ollie said. "Were you working?"

"I was."

"Two hookers," Ollie said. "One blond . . ."

"We don't allow hookers here at the Olympia," the bartender said.

"Yes, I'm sure you don't. But you probably didn't recognize them as hookers. One was blond, short hair, what they call a feather cut, brown eyes. The other one had hair down to her shoulders, brown, with blue eyes. Good-looking girls, both of them. Probably well-dressed."

"We get lots of women in here could answer that description," the bartender said.

"This particular woman, the one with the brown hair, told me her and her friend were in here about ten o'clock last Wednesday night and that her friend, the blonde with the short hair, picked up some guy here and left the bar with him around eleven. Would you happen to remember that occurrence?"

"No, I don't."

"Big handsome guy, blond like the girl. Hearing aid in his right ear, would you recall now?"

"We get lots of . . ."

"Yes, I'm sure you get ten thousand blond guys wearing hearing aids every night of the week," Ollie said. "But on this *specific* night last Wednesday, this *particular* blond guy with the hearing aid paid for the bar tab with a credit card. According to my source, anyway, who I feel is a reliable one."

"What do you want to know?"

"His name."

"All that stuff went to the cashier that same night."

"All what stuff?"

"The credit card slips."

"Do you remember the man I'm talking about?"

"I seem to recall someone with a hearing aid, yes."

"Tall blond guy?"

"Yes."

"Do you remember the hookers, too?"

"I didn't know they were hookers."

"Of course not. Did you look at his credit card?"

"I must've checked the signature on the back, yes. When he signed for the tab."

"Would you recall the name on that card?"

"Come on, willya? How do you expect me to remember . . . ?"

"Or what kind of card it was?"

"We honor all the major credit cards here. How do you expect me to . . . ?"

"Is the cashier's office open now?" Ollie asked.

"The credit card slips from last Wednesday are long gone, if that's what you're think . . ."

"Gone *where?*" Ollie asked.

That Nazi bastard Deaf Man had kept him awake most of the night, so Meyer had come to work early this morning, arriving at the tail end of the Graveyard Shift, with only Fujiwara and O'Brien here in the squadroom, the rest of the 8-7's courageous team out preventing crime in these mean streets.

Now, in the comparative 6:30 a.m. stillness, no phones ringing, no keyboards clattering and clacking, he tried to make some sense of what they'd got so far. Copies of all the delivered notes were spread across his desktop. A copy of the list of plays plundered by Mr. Adam Fen was close at hand. All he had to do was piece it all together, ha!

Compared to all this Shakespearean lore, the earlier anagrams seemed elementary. Well, perhaps not. On their simplest level, the quotes were telling them:

1) This is going to be Shakespeare 101, kiddies.
2) I am going to dribble out the information bit by bit, piece by piece.
3) I am going to use darts as my weapon.

Perfectly clear.

But on the Deaf Man's turf, nothing was ever what it seemed. All was illusion and deception, a showoff smirking at them, telling them how goddamn smart he was while they were so goddamn stupid.

So what *else* was he trying to tell them?

Was there something here other than the obvious "Shakespeare, boys! Patience, girls! Darts, anyone?"

He set aside the anagrams, looked at the Shakespearean quotes again. Arranged them in order on his desktop. Okay. If the Deaf

Man had chosen to start with *shakes* and then *spear,* he was without question telling them "Shakespeare." Step to the head of the class. Shakespeare. We're finished with all the anagrammatic fun and games, kiddies, and now we're moving on to more scholarly matters. Graduate school, kiddies.

Okay.

So what next?

More *spear* quotes.

Spear-grass, boar-spear, and **venom'd spear.**

All right, separate the non-spear words, maybe there's something there.

Grass, boar, venom'd.

Anything?

Not that he could see.

Well, grass was pot, and a boar was a pig, and venom was poison.

Pot, pig, poison.

Still nothing.

He looked more closely at the *arrows* notes.

Broke his arrows.

Slings and arrows.

Narrow lanes.

The *arrow* buried in the *narrow* of the last note.

The unrelated words were *broke, slings,* and *lanes.*

Nothing there, either.

How about the darts?

Thither he darts it.

Darts envenomed.

Advanced and darts.

Thither, envenomed, and advanced.

Mean anything to you, Meyer, old boy?

No? Then how about the three kings he'd chosen?

Beats three jacks any day of the week.

Raise you a dollar.

Henry the Fourth, Richard the Third, Richard the Second.

Fourth, third, second.

Four, three, two.

Hold it . . .

The numbers were getting smaller.

Four, three, two.

Well, maybe that was an accident.

No, with the Deaf Man, nothing was accidental.

He was giving them information in *reverse* order!

Four, three, two. Spears, arrows, darts.

Moving from larger to smaller, in effect heading *backwards.* Zeroing in on the weapon he would use.

Their reasoning yesterday had been right on the mark.

The Deaf Man's weapon would be darts.

269

No question about it.
They had broken the code.

In America, it is not a crime to be a drug addict.

This means that you can walk into any police station and announce, "I am a drug addict," and they will tell you to run along, sonny. Unless you're in possession of drugs. That's another matter.

In this city, the subsections of Article 220 of the Penal Law define the various degrees of criminal offense for possessing any of the so-called controlled substances listed in Section 3306. There are a lot of them. More than a hundred and thirty of them. Some of them you never heard of. Unless you're addicted to them. Like, for example, Furethidine. Or Alfentanil.

In the eyes of the law, you can be a drug addict, but you cannot possess any of the narcotics that make you an addict. If this sounds somewhat bass-ackwards, consider the law that makes it a crime to solicit a prostitute. The pertinent section of the Penal Law's "solicitation" articles reads:

"A person is guilty of patronizing a prostitute when he patronizes a prostitute."

Swear to God.

This means you cannot go into a police

station to confess that you're either a prostitute or have just patronized a prostitute because then you're guilty of two separate crimes, whereas if you say you're a drug addict you're not guilty of anything but being a damn fool.

That's why the girl who delivered the first note that morning at 8:30 a.m. freely admitted that she was a drug addict who'd been approached in Harrison Park in Riverhead by a girl with long black hair who'd paid her a hundred and fifty dollars to deliver this here letter here, but she did not mention that she was also a prostitute who'd been working the park all night long the night before.

This was her prerogative here in the land of the free.

"Ah-ha!" Meyer said. "This time we're ahead of you, wise guy!"

The first note that Tuesday morning read:

"Yea," quoth he, "dost thou fall upon thy face?
Thou wilt fall backward when thou hast more wit"

"*Romeo and Juliet*," Willis said from the

computer. "Act One, Scene Three."

"Didn't he use that play before?" Parker asked. " 'To be or not to be?' Didn't he?"

"He's simply telling us he's doing it backwards. But we already *know* that, big shot!" Meyer said, and jabbed his extended forefinger at the air like a pistol.

"Now he's saying *hast,* the friggin faggot," Parker said, modifying his language in deference to the presence of a lady.

"He's telling us we're witless," Eileen said.

"Telling us when we smarten up, we'll fall over backwards."

"Is he gonna blow some poisoned darts at somebody's back?" Genero asked.

Luigi Fontero had boarded Alitalia's flight 0413 at Milan's Linate airport at 4:05 p.m. yesterday. He'd spent two hours and fifteen minutes on the ground in Frankfurt and was scheduled to arrive here at 9:00 a.m. It was now twenty minutes to ten, and he still wasn't here. Carella, waiting in the area just outside Customs with his mother and what appeared to be ten thousand other people, was beginning to get itchy. He'd told the lieutenant he'd be in by eleven o'clock latest. Now he was beginning to wonder.

"Do you think we should ask again?" his mother said.

"Mom, they said a half-hour late."

"That was forty minutes ago."

"He'll be here, don't worry."

For the occasion, his mother was wearing a simple pale blue suit and French-heeled shoes. She would not have her hair done until the day before the wedding; she was wearing it now in a youngish bob under a cloche hat Carella's grandmother had probably worn as a Twenties flapper, blue velvet with blue satin trim. Her brown eyes sparkled. She kept looking at the clock across the hall.

"You don't think anything's . . . ?"

"No, Mom, they'd've told us."

"Sometimes they don't," she said.

"Everything's fine."

"These days," she said, and let the sentence trail.

It had occurred to him, too.

He, too, looked at the clock.

Honey Blair had not told Hawes about the shooter's note, and she felt absolutely rotten about keeping such vital — well, probably not — information from him. But she justified this by telling herself the Note

273

wouldn't be of much value, anyway, fingerprint-wise, since it had been passed from hand to hand at yesterday afternoon's meeting. Besides, the overnights had shown that during her second defiant challenge to the shooter at a quarter past six yesterday, ratings had soared.

So, naturally, whereas she wanted Cotton to catch the guy who was trying to kill him, at the same time she hoped he wouldn't catch him too soon, not while she was enjoying the kind of celebrity she'd only dreamed about before now. It was one thing to have some guy ask you to sign his program at a concert; it was quite another to be stopped on the street, six seven times in a single morning, people telling her "Go get him, Honey!" or "We're with you, Honey!"

Celebrity was a funny thing.

People could turn on you in a minute — witness the whole Michael Jackson circus — or they could suddenly make you their darling. She enjoyed being their darling. But of course she didn't want anyone hurting her own precious darling, who at that very moment was on his way to the orthopedist's office building downtown, not because his foot was hurting him but because Jefferson Avenue wasn't the Eight-

Seven where nobody never saw nothing nohow.

Actually, Honey wished him luck.

Luigi Fontero came striding out of Customs wearing a brown silk suit with a matching brown-and-yellow striped tie over a beige shirt, a brown homburg tilted rakishly over one eye. He looked like Rossano Brazzi about to seduce Katherine Hepburn, all grins, hopeful expectation in his eyes.

When he spotted Carella's mother, he rushed to her at once. They fell into each other's arms like young lovers who'd been parted by war or famine. Luigi kissed her. Kissed Carella's mother. Not on the cheek, or even both cheeks the way Europeans did, but full on the lips, Carella's mother, a real smackeroo, right there in front of her own son.

"You are so beautiful," Luigi told her.

Carella wanted to retch.

"How are you, Steve," Luigi said at last, and offered his hand.

Carella accompanied them to the baggage claim area, listening invisibly to his mother's questions about the flight and the food on the flight, and the weather when Luigi left Milan, and when his relatives and friends would be arriving, listened to Luigi's answers, hearing him call Carella's mother "Luisa," his eyes never leaving her face, calling her *"cara mia"* and *"tesora bella,"* kissing her again and again, not on the lips, on the nose instead and the forehead and the chin, not offering to help when Carella yanked first one heavy suitcase, and then another, off the carousel, Luigi's arm around Carella's mother's waist, Luisa's waist, *cara mia*'s waist, *tesora bella*'s waist, her head on his shoulder, the big furniture-maker from Milan, Luigi Fontero.

Carella wheeled their luggage cart out to the curb for them, and hailed a taxi for them. He watched as the taxi pulled away. They both waved back at him through the rear window, beaming. It occurred to him that his mother really could have come out here by herself.

Alone, he walked back to the parking lot where he'd left the car.

574 Jefferson Avenue was a monolithic polished black granite structure flanked by a fur emporium on one side and a huge bookstore on the other.

When Hawes came walking up from the subway kiosk four blocks away, a full-scale demonstration was going on outside the fur place. The manager of the bookstore was out on the sidewalk, telling a police sergeant that these fur freaks were keeping customers away from his store. The sergeant was telling him this was a free country.

"Then you should be free to wear *furs* if you like," the manager said. He himself owned a raccoon hat that had cost him a hundred and eighty dollars, though not in the fur emporium next door.

Hawes walked through the line of chanting pickets and into the fur shop. A smartly dressed saleswoman in her fifties, he guessed, came over to him, the smile on her face belying the obvious concern in her eyes. Neatly coiffed hair. Blue eyes in a porcelain face. Eyes darting toward the plate glass windows fronting the store, afraid a brick would come crashing through at any moment. Store dummies wearing mink, sable, red fox, silver fox, raccoon, muskrat, coyote, and a veritable zoo of other animal furs stared eyeless at the protesters outside.

"Yes, sir, may I help you?" the woman asked.

Faint accent there? Nordic? He wondered if they protested the wearing of furs in Sweden or Denmark. He showed her his shield.

"Detective Hawes," he said. "I'm investigating the shooting outside last Friday."

"Why don't you do something about the *shouting* outside right this minute?" the woman said.

"Sorry, ma'am," he said, "but I'm not here about that. May I speak to the manager, please?"

"I *am* the manager," she said.

"I'd like to talk to whoever may have been working here last Friday morning at eleven o'clock," he said. "Whoever may have seen or heard anything at all."

"Do you realize what's happening here?" the woman said.

"Yes, ma'am, I have some idea. But someone tried to kill two people last Friday . . ."

"Someone's trying to kill *us* right now!"

"I'm sure the sergeant outside will keep it under control."

"I'm not talking about physical violence. They're too smart for that. I'm talking about ruining our pre-season *business*."

"Yes, ma'am," Hawes said.

It occurred to him that not too many good citizens were eager to help a cop investigating a crime, whether it was uptown in the asshole of creation or here in a fancy fur palace on the city's luxury shopping avenue. He was thinking he should have become a dentist, as his mother had suggested.

"Could I talk to your people, please?" he said softly.

She stared at him a moment longer, incredulously, and then said, "I'll see who was here," and walked off toward the back of the store.

Hawes stood there among all the dead animals, waiting.

The second note arrived at twenty minutes to one.

Hawes was just telling them he'd struck out at the fur salon, where everyone had either been deaf or blind last Friday, where nobody working in the place had heard any shots or seen anyone pumping a dozen or so slugs into the limo. The manager of the bookstore was so incensed about the marchers next door that he could hardly concentrate on anything Hawes was asking. In any case, there were thirty-eight employees in the shop and they serviced thousands of customers every day, so how did he expect them to have heard or seen a mere murder attempt right outside? Why don't you go get those freakin fur freaks off the sidewalk? he'd wanted to know.

Which was when a uniform brought in an envelope that had been delivered downstairs not five minutes ago, interrupting Hawes' doctoral dissertation on the indifference of the citizenry. At that very moment, Murchison was questioning the indisputable hophead who'd delivered it. The addict interrogations had moved from Captain to mere Sergeant in the space of a mere three days. *Sic transit gloria mundi*, even though it was Tuesday.

The note read:

**Why, you speak truth. I never yet saw
   man,
How wise, how noble, young, how
   rarely featured,
But she would spell him backward**

"There's *backward* again," Meyer said.

"Is he referring to Carmela Sammarone?"

"The *she*, you mean?"

"First time he's used the word *she*."

"His little hooker emissary."

"And all the 'wise, noble, young, rarely featured' goddamn junkies she's sending up here," Parker said.

"He may also be commenting on his

own bad spelling," Genero said. "All his 'haths,' you know."

Nobody thought the Deaf Man was commenting on his own bad spelling. Or Shakespeare's, for that matter.

In fact, Willis was of the opinion that the word *spell* as used herein referred to the woman in question placing a *spell* on someone, a hex, that is, causing him to fall backwards, as it were, as though in a charmed faint.

"Referring to the 'fall backward,' " Willis said. "In his first note today."

"In any case, the key word is *backward*," Meyer insisted. "Four, three, two. Spears to arrows to darts. In fact, he's telling us we've already cracked the code. 'Why, you speak *truth*,' he says. The truth is he's going to tell it to us backwards."

"Tell us *what* backwards?"

"Whatever he's going to do with these darts of his."

Sitting at the computer, Carella was already shaking his head.

So was Genero.

Two wops in concert, Parker thought.

"Can you imagine him throwing *darts?*" Carella said.

"Or blowing them from some kind of *pipe?*" Genero said.

"I can imagine that," Meyer said.

"When did you ever see that?" Hawes asked.

"I'm sure I've seen that," Meyer said. "This city?"

"In which case, who's the friggin *victim?*" Parker asked. "Who's he gonna blow these darts *at?*"

"Whom," Willis corrected.

"Thank you, Professor," Parker said.

"Well, he's right," Eileen said protectively.

Kling wondered what the hell was going on between these two all of a sudden.

"It's from *Much Ado About Nothing*," Carella said. "Act Three, Scene One."

"Which is exactly what this is," Parker said. "Much ado about nothing. A whole bunch of bullshit. He's not gonna kill anybody, he's not gonna rob a bank or blow up a building, he's just breaking our balls."

"Not mine," Eileen said.

Willis laughed.

Kling was sure now that something was going on here.

"Wanna get some lunch?" Hawes asked him.

The two men chose a diner a few blocks away from the stationhouse. Hawes ordered a grilled cheese sandwich, a coffee,

282

and a side of fries. Kling ordered the bean soup, a chicken salad, and an iced tea.

"Maybe the crime *already* took place," he was saying.

"Maybe so," Hawes said.

"Maybe he's just leading us back to Gloria Stanford. Go *back,* he's telling us. Rubbing our noses in it, you know? Nyaa nyaa, I killed her, and there's nothing you can do about it."

"That's possible, I guess."

Both men seemed preoccupied.

Even though they were discussing the Backward-Forward-*Whatever* machinations of the Deaf Man, Kling kept looking up at the clock behind the counter and Hawes kept using his fork to move French fries around in the ketchup on his plate.

"You gonna eat those or just play with them?" Kling asked.

"You want them?"

"No, I'm okay."

Hawes kept playing with the fries. At last, he looked up and said, "Bert . . . there's something I want to ask you."

Ah, Kling thought. *This* is why he wanted to have lunch. Never mind Mr. Adam Fen.

"It's about Augusta."

"Uh-huh."

"Will it bother you to talk about her?"

"No. All water under the bridge."

"You sure?"

"Positive."

"Actually, in fact, it's about Augusta as she *relates* to Honey."

"Uh-huh. Their names, do you mean?"

"No. Their names? What about their names?"

"Augusta Blair, Honey Blair. I was wondering if you . . ."

"No, that isn't . . ."

". . . thought maybe they were related or something."

"Never crossed my mind."

"Because Blair is a common name, you know," Kling said.

"Sure. Hey, *Tony* Blair, right?"

"Exactly. Anyway, Blair isn't Gussie's real name."

"What do you mean?"

"Blair isn't the name on her birth certificate."

"Then what is it?"

"Bludge."

"What?"

"Augusta Bludge."

"You're kidding me."

"No. She changed it when she went into modeling."

"Why does that always fascinate people?" Hawes asked. "Who cares *what* name is on a person's birth certificate? Nobody is *born* with a name, you know, there isn't a *name* stamped on anyone's forehead. A person is given a name by his or her parents. A person inherits a surname, like it or not, and then he's given a first name. That's why it's called a 'given' name. Because it's *given* to him. So if a guy wants to *give* himself a new name, that's entirely *his* business, isn't it? You think I like the name 'Cotton'?" he asked, gathering steam. "How would you like to go through life with the name 'Cotton'? Or 'Hawes,' for that matter. You know how many times I was called 'Horse' when I was a kid? You know how many times I've been tempted to change it? Cotton Hawes? So who cares *what* Augusta's real name was? Anyway, you don't mean her *real* name, do you? Because the minute she changed it, her *real* name became Blair, didn't it? You mean her *birth* name, don't you? Isn't that what you mean?"

"I guess so," Kling said, sorry he'd brought up the entire matter.

"Because Augusta Blair is her *real* name now," Hawes insisted. "What*ever* it used to be. Bludge, Shmudge, who cares?"

"I guess so," Kling agreed. "She even kept Blair when we got married."

"Bludge, who'da thought? What is that, German? She looks so Irish. I mean that red hair . . ."

"Auburn, actually."

"Who'da thought?" Hawes said, and moved some more fries around on his plate.

"Anyway, I don't think they're related," Kling said. "Her and Honey. If that's what you wanted to ask."

"Unless Honey's *real* name," Hawes said, landing hard on the *real* to make his point yet another time, "was Henrietta Bludge or something."

"Yes, in which case, they might be sisters," Kling said.

"Or cousins," Hawes said.

"Small world, sure," Kling said.

Both men fell silent.

"But what I wanted to know," Hawes said, and moved another fry, "is what it was like being married to a celebrity."

"Well, we're divorced now," Kling said. "I guess that tells you what it was like."

"I meant, the celebrity part. Cause Honey's something of a celebrity herself, you know. Not like Augusta, I mean she's on the cover of every fashion magazine you pick up. But lots of people watch Honey on the news . . ."

"Oh, sure."

"So I was wondering . . . I mean, I'm just a cop, we're both just cops . . ."

"I know what you mean, yes."

". . . and these two women make a lot more money than we do . . ."

"Yes."

". . . and are a hell of a lot better-looking than we are . . ."

"That's for sure."

"So I wonder . . . I can't help wondering . . . I mean . . . is it going to *work?* I know it didn't work for you, Bert . . ."

"No, it didn't," Kling said.

Neither of the men mentioned what was common knowledge in the squadroom: Kling had caught his wife in bed with another man.

"What I want to know . . . should I talk it over with Honey? The possible . . . you know . . . problems that may come up?"

"It's always best to talk it over," Kling said.

Same advice Carella had given him a long time ago, when Kling first began to realize there might be trouble in Paradise.

But, of course, talking it over hadn't helped a damn bit.

That hot summer.

The *heat* that summer.

"Let her know how you feel," Kling said, and looked up at the clock again.

"You got a taxi waiting?" Hawes asked.

"No, it's just I have to talk to this guy whose pawn shop was held up."

Hawes looked at his own watch.

"Tell her it bothers me, huh?" he asked. "Her being a celebrity?"

"Sure. If it really bothers you, sure. Talk it over."

"Well, actually that's not what's *really* bothering me, exactly."

"Then what is?"

"I just get the feeling . . . ah, forget it. I'm being a cop, that's all."

"What is it, Cotton?"

"I get the feeling she's not being completely honest with me."

"Uh-huh."

"Holding something back, you know?"

Join the club, Kling thought.

"So discuss it with her," he said.

"You think so, huh?"

"I think so," Kling said, and looked up at the clock again. "We'd better get a check, I don't want to be late. I told the guy two-thirty."

Hawes signaled to the waitress.

"Where you headed, anyway?" he asked.
"1214 Haskell," Kling said.
But he wasn't.

Sharyn was waiting outside her office building in Diamondback.

The address was 3415 Ainsley Avenue, and she wasn't waiting for Kling.

He had checked her appointment calendar last night.

For today, June the eighth, she had written in **Jamie**.

And below that: **My office. 2:30 p.m.**

He had supposed, or hoped, that the two of them would be meeting for some sort of medical consultation, in her actual office upstairs, her space. But it was now two thirty-five, and here was Sharyn standing outside her building, and up the street came Dr. James Melvin Hudson, wearing a neatly tailored gray suit this time, white shirt, dark tie. Nodding in greeting, he leaned down to kiss her on the cheek, as was apparently the custom between medical folk these days. Sublimely unaware of Kling's presence, they went ambling up the street together.

He followed behind at a discreet distance, the police term for keeping tabs on your girlfriend.

Or your significant other.

Or your lover.

Or whatever.

What goes around comes around, he thought.

They were going around the corner, he quickened his step, didn't want to lose them. Rounded the corner after them, almost bumped right into them, turned quickly away to avoid discovery. They were some ten feet ahead, checking out the lettering on a plate glass window.

Ye Olde Tea Room.

Ye *what?* Kling thought.

He didn't know they even *had* tea rooms in America, old or otherwise. In the heart of Diamondback, no less. Would wonders never? He hung back while they entered the place, two innocent colleagues out for their early afternoon tea, pip pip and all that. As soon as they were clear, he approached the plate glass window, put his face to it, hands cupped on either side of his head, alongside his eyes, and peered inside.

They were approaching a table on the right, a small table against the wall, under a sconce that cast scant light onto the woman already sitting there.

A white woman.

The moment they sat, one on either side of her, the woman reached for their hands. Sharyn's right hand, Dr. James Melvin Hudson's left. A hand in each of her own. She gripped their hands tightly, and then burst into tears.

Kling wondered what the hell he had stumbled into here.

It bothered Ollie that none of the credit card companies could help him on this thing. All he wanted was a damn name and address for the guy who'd picked up Melissa Summers — or vice versa — in the Olympia Hotel bar last Wednesday night, the second day of June. Now was that a big deal to ask?

Well, yes, they explained, it was a *very* big deal to ask. Because lacking the name of the card holder, it would be impossible to scan the thousands of purchases . . .

"This wasn't a *purchase*," Ollie told each and every one of them, American Express, Visa, MasterCard, even Discover. "This was a guy paying for drinks in a bar . . ."

Yes, well, whatever it was . . .

"A *particular* bar," he explained to one and all, "at a *specific* time. All you got to do is kick in your computer and zero in on the

Olympia Hotel bar at eleven o'clock last Wednesday night, and bingo, we've got our customer, ah yes."

But, ah *no*, they explained, that isn't the way it works, our computers aren't programmed that way. If you had the card holder's *name* . . .

"The card holder's name is what I'm *looking* for!"

And round and round the mulberry bush, but no cigar.

Ollie figured he'd have to hit the whores again.

The third note that day arrived a little early.

A quarter past two instead of the usual three-thirty or so.

And it wasn't addressed to Carella.

Instead, it was addressed to Detective / Third Grade Richard Genero.

Parker himself carried it into the squadroom.

"Desk sergeant gave me this," he said, handing the envelope to Genero. "Says a junkie dropped it off."

"Naturally," Meyer said. "Same m.o."

"Little early, though," Willis said, looking at his watch.

"And now he's picking on you, Richie."

"Richard," Genero corrected.

He was staring at the envelope as if it contained some malevolent evil chemical worse than anthrax, whatever that was, some kind of hoof and mouth disease?

"Well, ain't you gonna open it?" Parker asked.

"Here," Genero said, and handed the envelope to Carella. "You open it."

Carella was starting to pull on a pair of gloves when Parker said, "Murchison already dusted it."

Carella looked surprised. He put on the gloves, anyway, picked up a letter opener, slit open the envelope, pulled out the single sheet of white paper inside, and unfolded it. The note read:

37OHSSV 0773H

"What's that?" Parker asked. "Your license plate number?"

"Why's he sending us *numbers* all of a sudden?" Genero asked.

"Letters, too," Meyer said, leaning in for a closer look. "HSSV. Mean anything to any of you?"

"There's the *H* again," Eileen said. "At the end of the sentence."

"H for horseshit," Parker said.

"How about the 'oh seven seven'?" Hawes asked.

"That's James *Bond's* number!" Genero said.

"No, that's Double-Oh Seven."

They all kept staring at the message.

37OHSSV 0773H

"Well, it's addressed to you," Parker said. "So maybe he's trying to tell you something personal."

"I doubt that very much," Genero said, sounding somehow offended.

"Why don't you turn it upside down, Richard?" Parker suggested.

"What do you mean?"

"See if it makes any sense that way. Go ahead. Turn it."

Genero turned the letter upside down.

"Very funny," he said.

The Deaf Man's letter arrived some forty minutes later. Another junkie delivered it. It was carried up to the squadroom by a patrolman wearing latex gloves. They knew they'd find no fingerprints on either the envelope or the message inside it, but one couldn't be too careful these days. The envelope was addressed to Carella again,

294

the same personal challenge, one on one. The note inside read:

**And here have I the daintiness of ear
To check time broke in a disorder'd
string**

"Whyn't you turn it upside down again, Richard?" Parker suggested.

"Whyn't you go fuck yourself?" Genero said. "Excuse me, Eileen."

"Whyn't you guys stop tiptoeing around me?" Eileen said. "I'm a big girl now."

"I'll say," Parker said, and shot a glance at her chest.

Willis shot him a warning look.

Kling caught this.

He was positive now.

But why should he care?

Like a professor prodding a particularly dull class, Meyer asked, "So what's he telling us this time?"

Like an ass-kissing A-student (or so Kling thought) Willis said, "Well, time would seem to be the central theme, wouldn't you say?"

"*Broken* time," Meyer agreed.

At the computer, Carella said, "*Richard II* again, Act Five, Scene Five."

"Starting to repeat himself."

295

"He's jerking us off again," Parker said.

"No, he's going to tell us *when*," Hawes said.

"I'll bet," Eileen said.

"The exact *time*."

"But backwards."

"Time in a disorder'd string."

"And signs himself," Parker said.

"Huh?" Genero said.

"Daintiness of *ear*, Richard."

"Where were you, Melissa?" he asked.

It was only five o'clock, she didn't know why he sounded so pissed.

"The cops are looking for me," she said.

That got to him, all right. Eyebrows going up, eyes opening wide.

"How do you know that?"

"Friend of mine told me. Remember the girl I was with the night you picked me up . . ."

"Or vice versa," he said.

"Whatever," she said. "Do you re-member Wanda?"

"I remember her. She of the thong panties."

"How do you know that?"

"She showed me. When you went to the ladies room."

"So why'd you pick me instead?"

"Ah, but *you* picked *me*, little Lissie. You've got it backwards. The punto reverso!"

"The *what?*"

"Exact quote! Perfect, Benvolio!"

"I don't know what you're talking about."

"*Romeo and Juliet*, Act Two, Scene Four. The brittle exchange between Benvolio and Mercutio. 'The *what?*' says Benvolio. 'The pox of such antic, lisping, affecting fantasticoes,' replies Mercutio. 'These new tuners of accents!' "

"That explains it, all right," Melissa said.

"What'd she say? This Wanda person?"

"A fat cop was around asking about me. She had to tell him about Wednesday night."

"*Had* to tell him? Nobody *has* to do anything, Lissie."

"He was about to bust her!"

"So she told him *what*, exactly?"

"That the three of us were at the Olympia last Wednesday night, and I went home with you."

"Is that all?"

"She described you."

"Did she tell him my name?"

"She didn't know your name. Neither

did I, at the time." She hesitated, and then said, "I still don't know it."

"Adam Fen," he said.

"Sure."

"And this cop? Does he have a name?"

"Ollie Weeks. He's a detective up the Eight-Eight. They call him *Fat* Ollie Weeks, most people."

"Is he going to cause us trouble?"

"He's looking for me," Melissa said. "I suppose that could be trouble. If he finds me."

"If he finds you, he finds me," the Deaf Man said.

"Is what I meant."

"So make sure he doesn't find you."

"I got no desire to meet him, believe me."

"You still haven't told me where you were."

"Uptown. Lining up tomorrow's Junkie Parade. Talking to Wanda."

"I was worried you might have run out on me."

"And miss the big payoff?" she said. "*Whenever* that may be."

"Soon," he said.

"*Whatever* it may be," she said.

"You'll find out."

"Promises, promises."

"Meanwhile, there's something else I'd like you to do for me. Tonight."

"My place or yours?" she said, and tried a smile.

"There's a man I want you to meet," he said.

So what else is new? she thought.

10

The way Melissa understood this, there was this Greek violinist named Konstantinos Sallas, who was staying here at the Intercontinental Hotel with his wife, his violin, and his bodyguard. It was the bodyguard who interested Adam, the bodyguard who had information Adam needed, the bodyguard Adam wanted her to sleep with, if she had to, in order to gather this information.

Melissa had never slept with a bodyguard before.

Neither had she ever clasped *anyone* to her bosom, so to speak, with the express purpose of getting information from him. She felt a little bit like Mata Hari, especially wearing the black shoulder-length wig. Adding to this *femme fatale* image was a strappy little slinky little black silk shift Adam had bought for her that afternoon, on the assumption that she'd be coming back to the apartment, which of course she had.

It was now three minutes past midnight

on the ninth day of June.

According to Adam, it was the body-guard's habit to stop into the hotel bar for a glass or two of ouzo after he'd tucked in the violinist each night. Adam did not know the bodyguard's name — he had only observed him from a distance, here at the hotel and on his accompanying walks to the concert hall. But he gave Melissa a fairly good description of him, and she knew to expect a burly, bearded man some six feet four inches tall, barrel-chested and dressed entirely in black, including the black shirts and ties he wore with his black silk suits. He sounded less like a Greek bodyguard than one of the Hollywood agents she'd known on the Coast before she got busted that one time when she was but a mere slip of a girl just learning the trade, before Ambrose Carter taught her what it was really all about, girlfriend. She did not particularly enjoy sex with big hirsute men. But in anticipation of her share of the seven-figure payday, *whenever* that might come, *if* it ever came, she would have gone to bed with a gorilla.

So where the hell was he?

Ollie's reasoning was that if he couldn't find the john she'd picked up last

Wednesday night, then he just had to find Melissa Summers herself. No shortcuts this time, he guessed. Just the tireless legwork of the truly dedicated public servant.

It wasn't that he gave a damn about one dead Negro pimp more or less, which word he enjoyed using to describe so-called persons of color because he knew it pissed them off — not pimp, but Negro. Which words were eponymous, anyway. Or synonymous. Or whatever. Negro and pimp. In his experience, all the good criminal endeavors that used to be operated by decent white crooks were now the sole province of evil, grasping, upward-striving Negroes. He sometimes wished for a return to slavery. Wish in one hand, he thought, and shit in the other. See which you get first. One of his mother's favorite expressions, though not within earshot of his darling sister Isabel, who was probably still a virgin.

What primarily disturbed Ollie was that some little tart thought she could come into *his* neighborhood, *his* precinct, in the dead of night, and pump two nine-millimeter slugs into somebody, into some person's *back* and *head*, no less, white or black, *anybody*, it didn't matter to Ollie. What mattered was the violation of his *turf!*

So watch out, Melissa, he thought. Beware!

The Large Man is on the prowl, and he's gonna find you, you better believe it, ah yes, m'little chickadee.

In his mind, he sounded like W. C. Fields.

He wondered if Melissa Summers even knew who W. C. Fields was — what was she, twenty years old, something like that, in her twenties somewhere?

A prostitute.

In her twenties, and a prostitute.

No, a murderer.

Murderess.

Whatever.

And he was gonna get her.

He looked like that guy in the Harry Potter movies, whatever his name was, ask any ten-year-old. The big bearded guy with the pot belly and the gruff voice. Except that he was wearing a black suit, and a black shirt and tie, black socks, and highly polished black shoes. The Harry Potter guy dressed up like a gangsta, gee! Or a bodyguard, she guessed, if this was her man, which she had no doubt he was.

She was sitting at the bar when he came in. Big ox of a man barging into the hotel lounge like he owned it. Steely blue eyes flicking this way and that like a cop expecting street trouble. Satisfied that no one was about to jump him, he sat some two stools down from hers, giving her a quick once-over before he ordered a double ouzo. Just a sideward flick of those ice-blue eyes, but Melissa didn't miss such things, Melissa was a pro.

She was expecting some sort of Greek accent — wasn't he supposed to be Greek? The ouzo and all? — but no, he sounded as American as she did. Ordered the double ouzo, checked out the bar mirror as if he was scanning the room, but she caught that sideward glance at her again, he was aware of her.

"I never tasted ouzo," she said, bold as brass, turning toward him. "What's it like?"

"Do you like licorice?" he asked.

Turning to face her. Smiling encouragement. Nice smile. Blue eyes becoming warm and friendly . . . well, why shouldn't they? Good-looking girl sitting alone at the bar strikes up a conversation? Hey, what am I, a fool?

"Oh, it's like some kind of liqueur, is that it?" she said.

"Yes, that's exactly what it is," he said.

"Thank you," he said to the bartender, who had just put his drink down. "Would you care to taste it?"

"Not if it's sweet, no," she said.

"Depends on what you think is sweet," he said.

Little bit of come on there?

She smiled.

"Cheers," he said, and lifted his glass and sipped at it. "Actually," he said, "it's made from . . . may I?" he asked, and without waiting for permission, moved over a stool so that he was sitting right alongside her now, big shoulders crowding her. "Jeremy," he said, and extended one enormous paw.

"Melissa," she said, and took his hand.

"Nice to meet you. Sure you don't want a little taste?"

"Maybe later," she said, and smiled.

"I was saying," he said, picking up his glass again, holding it up to the light, "ouzo's a combination of pressed grapes, herbs, and berries. It's the star anise that gives it the licorice taste."

"That's what I don't think I'd like. The licorice taste. Candy's candy, booze is booze," she said, and smiled.

"Oh, this is *booze*, all right, believe me. Eighty proof."

"That strong, huh?"

Intending a little innuendo there, which he seemed to miss.

"Some ouzos are even stronger," he said. "Your Barbayannis is ninety-two proof. That's forty-six percent alcohol."

"That's strong, all right," she said, trying again.

"It's not produced in any other part of the world but Greece, you know. In fact, it's the Greek national drink."

"You seem to know a lot about it."

"Well, I spend a lot of time in Greece."

"Doing what?" she asked.

"My job."

Avoiding the question. She tried again.

"Doing what?" she asked.

"I'm a personal bodyguard."

"No kidding?"

"Yes," he said.

"Gee. I don't think I've ever met a body-guard before."

"Well, that's what I am."

"Come to think of it, that's what you look like. Big and . . . well, strong."

Get it? she thought.

"Thanks," he said.

"Though I guess you don't have to be big or strong if you carry a gun, am I right?"

He said nothing.

"Are you carrying a gun?"

"Shh," he said, and winked.

"I'll bet you are."

"It's licensed, don't worry," he said.

"I guess you'd have to. Carry a gun, I mean. I mean, if you're a bodyguard."

"Well, you never know."

"What does he do, anyway, your boss? Is he a diamond merchant or something?"

"No, no, nothing like that," he said, and smiled.

"So why do you need a gun?"

"Well, I'm a bodyguard. Like you said."

"Why does he need a bodyguard?"

"You never know," he said, and smiled again.

"Is he a movie star or something?"

"Not quite."

"How can you be 'not quite' a movie star? Is he a rock star?"

"Close. He's a musician."

"Ah."

"A classical musician. A violinist."

"What's his name?"

"Konstantinos Sallas."

"Wow."

"A mouthful, I know."

"Is he Greek?"

"Yes."

"Which is why you drink ouzo."

"Which is where I *learned* to drink it, yes. But he performs all over the world."

"That famous, huh?"

"Yes."

"Which is why he needs a bodyguard, I guess."

"Well, not only that."

"You sure he's famous? Cause I have to tell you, I never heard of him."

"Take my word for it."

"So you just follow him around day and night, is that it?"

"Not night," he said.

"Uh-huh," she said, and lifted her glass, and sipped at her drink, and looked over the rim at him, eyes raised like an innocent virgin.

"Are you a working girl?" he asked.

Busted.

"Yep," she said.

"How much for the night?" he asked.

The street was full of working girls.

Good-looking, too, many of them. This always surprised him. You expected scaly-legged whores, you got these sleek race-horses instead, they looked like they could be actresses or models, but here they were on the stroll. Selling themselves on the street. He could never figure it out.

Well, most of them were bag brides. Sold themselves to feed their habits. Most of them, in fact, it was their pimps got them hooked. So they'd be like slaves to the nose candy or the chick or the bazooka, whatever shit they were on, and that was it. They didn't care what they had to do to get the money to pay for it, or in most instances the shit itself, supplied by Mr. Pimp, that's a good girl, here's your tecata, baby, go do yourself.

Still . . . how could these good-looking young girls, most of them — well, some of them — let this happen to themselves? Where along the line did they . . . you know . . . *fall* into this? How did it happen? Well, he wasn't a sociologist, he was a cop, and a cop had to ignore such poking and probing, appropriate terms when a person was considering the plight of the poor downtrodden streetwalker, but that's the way it was, Charlie, and who gave a shit? Not me, Ollie thought. But still, he wondered.

He got his first lead to Melissa Summers from a black hooker who told him she'd spotted her Monday in Poison Park up on the Stem . . .

"Berrigan Square," she said.

"What was she doing there?" Ollie asked.

"Chattin up the poison people, you know."

"What do you mean, chatting them up?"

"Axin 'em diss an dat."

"Like what?"

"Some a dem cotton shooters, they do anythin for bread, you know."

Like you, Ollie thought, but didn't say.

"What was she asking them to do?"

"None of mah business."

"What time was this?"

"Monday afternoon sometime."

"Thanks, honey."

"Doan 'honey' me, Big Man. Juss lay a nice slice on me, you know whut I'm sayin?"

Ollie slipped her a double-dime.

Carella never used to worry about money.

Now he worried about money all the time.

Three in the morning, he was awake worrying about money. There used to be a time when he thought his salary was enough to satisfy all their needs. Well, not the base salary. But overtime boosted the base by a tidy little sum each year. Bought them anything they needed, everything, clothes, food on the table, vacations down by the shore, whatever. They never wanted for anything.

Then . . .

He didn't know how or why it happened, but all at once money seemed to be in scarce supply, to put it mildly. Maybe it was the kids growing up all of a sudden. April suddenly becoming a young lady before his very eyes, Mark growing at least two inches overnight, needing cell phones and laptops and zip sneakers and makeup kits and whatever else all the other kids in their class had. Almost thirteen years old. Seemed like yesterday the twins were born. Almost thirteen already, he could just imagine what it would be like when they were sixteen or seventeen, no money put aside yet for college, how'd he ever manage to get himself into such a tight financial situation?

Well, the wedding.

The wedd-*ings*.

Two of them.

He couldn't imagine what had possessed him to offer paying for them. Well, you couldn't let your mother pay for her own wedding, could you? Your father dead? You couldn't say, Gee, Mom, sorry, this one's on you, could you? You made your bed, Mom, now lie in it. What kind of son would that be? And if you offered to pay for *hers,* then you had to offer to pay for your sister's as well, didn't you? I mean, they were getting married *together,* it was going to be a double ceremony, two brides, two grooms, I do, I do, I do, I do. So if you were going to be a good son and pay for *one* of the weddings, then you had to be a good brother, too, didn't you, and pay for the *other* one as well? Why, of course! So Mr. Magnanimous, Mr. Generosity, Mr. Deep Pockets offered to pay for both. Gee, thanks, son. Thanks, bro.

Meanwhile, bro is broke. Sonny Boy, too.

Because Big-Hearted Bro, Loving Son and Benefactor, turned down Mr. Luigi Fontero's *subsequent* offer to pay for at least part of the double-bash. Luigi Fontero, the Furniture Maker of Milan, Future Husband of the Widow Carella, I will vomit!

I will vomit because I *still* don't understand how my mother could be marrying this big . . . *wop,* yes, excuse me . . . or how my sister could be marrying this . . . *inept,* yes . . . prosecutor who allowed Pop's murderer to . . .

Don't get me started.

Please.

I am broke.

I am awake at three in the morning.

And the double wedding will take place this Saturday at noon.

Sweet dreams, Big Shot.

He was asleep beside her, snoring like a bull, and she still hadn't found out what Adam needed to know. Yes, Jeremy Higel was a bodyguard. Adam already knew that, though not his name. And yes, he was protecting a violinist whose name was Konstantinos Sallas. Adam already knew that, too, name and all.

But the devil was in the details.

And details were what she needed.

What she figured she'd do was wake him up by playing with his dick — a very small one for such a large, hairy man — and then Deep Throat him, which would be a piece of cake, so to speak, in his case. Then, when he was close to imminent ejaculation, you should pardon the expression, she would start asking him questions which, if he didn't answer them, she'd leave him hanging here till next month at this time.

How does that sound, Jere?

Sounds good to me, she thought, and finger-walked the forefinger and middle finger of her right hand down his hairy chest and across his hairy belly and down into the wild bushiness of his crotch to discover at last, hidden there in the weedy black forest of his pubic hair, a weapon of mass destruction so formidable that it would have shocked and awed Bush, Blair, Cheney, Rumsfeld, and indeed the entire civilized world — all two and a half inches of it.

Wake up, Woolly Bear, she thought.

We've got some serious pillow-talking to do.

The first note was delivered at eight-thirty that Wednesday morning.

Another junkie, ho-hum.

When they unfolded the single sheet of paper inside the envelope, the message fairly leaped off the page:

87

"Gee, looka that," Genero said.

"That's us," Parker deduced.

The second note came at 9:30 that morning.

They didn't realize it as yet, but there would be a veritable parade of junkies today, one every hour or so. They questioned each new shabby messenger, hoping to pick up a fresh trail for Carmela Sammarone, but she seemed to be recruiting her people from all over town, wherever addicts congregated, which was virtually everywhere.

The second note read:

78

"That's us backwards," Parker calculated.

He felt he was getting good at this.

"Backwards again," Meyer said.

Carella searched for yesterday's notes, the ones that told them everything was going to be backwards from now on. He hadn't slept much the night before, and he had trouble finding them. In fact, he almost knocked over his second cup of coffee.

"Here we go," he said at last, and displayed the two notes.

The first one read:

"Yea," quoth he, "dost thou fall upon
thy face?
Thou wilt fall backward when thou
hast more wit"

The second one read:

Why, you speak truth. I never yet saw
man,
How wise, how noble, young, how
rarely featured,
But she would spell him backward

"You know," Willis said, "there are many
different meanings to the word *backward*. It
doesn't necessarily have to mean 'in reverse.'"

"It specifically says 'spell him *backward*,'" Brown said.

"Yes, but that could mean *cast* a spell on
him that would make him bashful or hesitant or shy. That's another meaning of
backward."

"*He's* certainly not bashful or hesitant,"
Hawes said.

"Or shy, either," Genero agreed.

"You think he might get her to hypnotize
someone?" Brown asked.

"Who?"

"The Sammarone woman. Carmela. Get her to cast a spell, you know?"

"Is she a hypnotist? Do we know that?"

"It's just, Hal said it could mean casting a spell."

"It *also* means 'late in developing,' " Willis said. "Backward. You say someone's backward, you mean he's retarded."

"Retarded ain't politically correct no more," Parker said.

"*Slow* then," Willis said. "Backward."

"Maybe he's telling us *we're* slow," Meyer suggested.

"Maybe we *are* slow," Carella said, and looked at the most recent note again.

Now they had **78**.

First **87** and now **78**.

Which was indeed **87** spelled backwards, or even *backward*, as the "she" in yesterday's second note would have it.

"Do *backward* and *backwards* mean the same thing?" Genero asked. "Cause I always said *backwards*. Is that wrong?"

"*Backwards* is the *plural* of *backward*," Parker explained.

"Is something going to happen in the Seven-Eight?" Eileen asked.

"Where *is* the Seven-Eight, anyway?" Hawes asked.

Meyer was already looking through his list of the city's precincts. It seemed there was a Seventy-eighth Precinct across the river, in Calm's Point.

" 'Him' spelled backwards is 'mih,' " Genero observed. " 'She would spell *him* backward.' "

"In Vietnamese, 'mih' means 'son of the crouching tiger,' " Parker said.

They all looked at him.

"Just kidding," he said.

But nobody was laughing.

You see a girl walking up the avenue at ten o'clock in the morning, wearing a slinky black silk dress and high-heeled black sandals with rhinestone clips, you know she's either an heiress or a hooker. And unless you're from Elk Horn, North Dakota, you know she didn't spend the night sleeping.

The Deaf Man was still asleep when Melissa let herself into the apartment. She went into the kitchen, poured herself some juice from the fridge, got a pot of coffee going, and then slipped out of her shoes and sat there at the kitchen table, waiting for the coffee to perk, looking out at the skyline, elbow on the table, chin resting on the heel of her right hand.

The aroma of the brewing coffee brought back memories of a childhood she'd almost forgotten. How'd I get here all these years later? she wondered. Whatever happened to little Carmela Sammarone? Where'd you go, Mela? she wondered. Mel? Where are you now, honey? Only place the name exists is on my passport, that one time Grandpa took me to Italy with him, to his hometown there, a walled city, she couldn't even remember the name of it anymore. Sort of sighing, she got up to pour herself the coffee.

"How'd it go?" he asked.

Startled, she turned from the stove.

He was wearing the black cashmere robe she'd bought him that made his eyes look very blue. Broad shoulders, narrow waist, belt around it. Blond hair tousled, made him look somewhat boyish.

"Good," she said. "Want some coffee?"

"Yes, please," he said. "Learn anything?"

"Oh, oodles," she said, and poured him a cup, carried it to the table, went to the fridge for milk, the cabinet for sugar. Sitting there at the table, in the sunlight streaming through the window, they could have been a cozy married couple having breakfast. She wondered what it was like to be a married couple.

"So tell me," he said.

"His name is Jeremy Higel, he's not Greek."

"He looked Greek. The beard, maybe. Or the association with Sallas."

"Are Greeks supposed to have beards?"

"Anyway . . ." he prompted.

"Anyway, he's not Greek. But he *is* Sallas' bodyguard."

"*That* I know."

"Who *is* a violin player."

"Correct."

"And the concert *will* take place at three o'clock this Saturday, you were right about that, too."

"So far, so good," he said.

"Oh, it gets much better."

"Tell me," he said, and smiled.

"They'll be picked up at the hotel at two o'clock. Sallas and his bodyguard."

"Why so early? The concert doesn't start till three."

"In case there's traffic. They're supposed to be at Clarendon by two-thirty."

"Who's picking them up?"

"A limo."

"Which company?"

"Regal."

"Good. You got that, huh?"

"Regal Limousine, yes. The car will be a

320

luxury sedan, is what they call it."

"That's very good, Melissa."

"I think so."

"Is he armed . . . Jeremy, is it?"

"Jeremy, yes. Jeremy Higel."

"Is he armed?"

"Yes."

"What kind of weapon?"

"A Smith & Wesson 1911."

"I didn't know you were that familiar with guns."

"I'm not. He gave me a guided tour. It's a forty-five caliber automatic, five-inch barrel length. Magazine holds eight rounds, plus one in the firing chamber. Satin stainless finish with a Hogue rubber grip. Very proud of that gun, he is. Nice-looking weapon, in fact. *Big* weapon, too. Which is more than I can say for the one in his pants."

"Did he give you a guided tour of that one as well?"

"A walking tour, let us say. Nothing to brag about, believe me."

"Par for the course, from what I gather."

"Meaning?"

"According to the e-mails I receive in the hundreds of thousands every day of the week, every man in America is deficient in that department and in serious need of enlargement."

"Present company excluded," Melissa said, and glanced shyly at where his legs were crossed in the black cashmere robe.

"Bust enhancement, too," he said. "According to my e-mails, every woman in the world needs her bust enhanced."

"Not me," she said.

"I noticed."

"Cause I already *had* them done."

"Oh?"

"Right after I started calling myself Melissa."

"Oh?"

"I thought I might become an actress, you see."

"I didn't know that," he said.

"Yeah," she said, and looked out at the magnificent skyline again. "Girlish dreams, right?"

87+78=165

"Well, now *there's* news," Parker said.

"But is it *correct?*" Genero asked, and began adding 78 to 87 on his calculator. Much to his surprise, eighty-seven plus seventy-eight did indeed add up to a hundred and sixty-five, more or less.

"What's he trying to *tell* us?" Carella asked.

"Why's he adding those two numbers?"

"Is there a One-Six-Five Precinct?" Eileen asked.

Meyer checked his list again.

"No," he said. "Highest is the Hun' Twenty-Third."

"*We're* slow, and *he's* getting faster," Parker said. "The notes are coming in faster and faster."

They all looked up at the wall clock.

It was now ten minutes to eleven.

The next note came at 11:47 a.m. It read:

$$165+561=726$$

Genero looked up from his calculator. "Right on the button!" he said triumphantly. "The arithmetic is absolutely *correct!*"

"The sums are getting bigger and bigger, too, did you notice that?" Hawes asked.

"Meaning?" Parker asked.

"Just commenting."

"Also," Brown said, "the *size* of the numbers is getting smaller and smaller."

"No, *bigger*," Hawes insisted.

"I don't mean the *numerical* value,"

Brown said, sounding like a mathematics professor all at once. "I mean the size of the *type*. Go ahead. Compare them."

$$\mathbf{87}$$

$$\mathbf{78}$$

$$\mathbf{87+78=165}$$

$$\mathbf{165+561=726}$$

"The Incredible Shrinking Deaf Man," Willis said, and Eileen laughed.

The door to Lieutenant Byrnes' office opened.

Scowling, he said, "Doesn't anyone have anything to *do* around here?"

They had plenty to do.

This was the 87th Precinct, and this was the Big Bad City.

So while in his apartment crosstown and further downtown the Deaf Man was calling Regal Limousine to arrange for a car and driver to pick him up at one-thirty this afternoon for what he'd described to

Melissa as a "trial run . . ."

. . . and while further uptown, Melissa herself was once again seeking out those poor deprived and demented individuals who were addicted to controlled substances of every stripe and persuasion to do her bidding for negotiable fees, the smaller the better . . .

. . . and while yet further uptown, in Berrigan Square, Detective Oliver Wendell Weeks was himself sitting on a bench in the midst of similarly depraved dope fiends, seeking information leading to the whereabouts of one Melissa Summers, presumed Slayer of Ambrose Carter, Infamous Procurer of Female Flesh . . .

While all these sundry people scurried about their busy little businesses, the men and women of the Eight-Seven scattered far and wide in pursuit of what was their usual daily routine when someone not quite as glamorous as the Deaf Man wasn't on the scene.

Angela was the only person here who knew sign language. But, of course, she was the bride-to-be, and there were thirty some-odd (some of them mighty odd, yuk yuk) women fluttering about her. And although she came over to Teddy every so often to exchange sister-in-lawly chitchat with her hesitant but well-meaning hands, she had to move on because there were other guests to welcome, other air-kisses to exchange, other . . . well, Teddy knew she was very busy. This was her shower, after all.

Sitting with the other women, Teddy could not hear their laughter or their speech, and she could not talk to them because her only language was in her hands. Whenever she used her hands, she mouthed the words as well, her lips matching her flying fingers. But without the signing, her mouthing came over as exaggerated grimacing, and people unaccustomed to reading lips merely frowned or smiled patiently in response. By reading lips herself, Teddy could catch words, or phrases, or sometimes even complete sentences, but at a gathering as large as this one, with so many people talking at once, it was impossible to keep track of any single conversation. So she sat essentially alone and apart in the midst of the chattering women, a fixed smile on her face, her dark brown eyes scanning the room, and the faces of the other women, and their lips, trying to read those lips, a silent spectator in a world she had never heard.

She had never heard her children's laughter.

She had never heard her husband's voice.

She imagined his voice to be soft and kind, the way his hands were soft and kind.

Smiling, she sat alone and apart.

Alone in the squadroom, Carella was manning the phones and the fax machines when the fifth note that day arrived. He pulled on the gloves, and opened the envelope:

$$726+627=1353$$

No surprises there. The Deaf Man was merely reversing the number each time out, and then adding it to the existing number. But why? And why was the font size getting smaller and smaller, while the numbers themselves got larger and larger? For comparison, he placed the numbers one under the other yet another time:

87
78
87+78=165
165+561=726
726+627=1353

Did this reversal and addition have something to do with the clues they'd already received from him? *If* you could even *call* them clues, the son of a bitch. Or were the numerals merely a preamble to what was coming? In much the same way the Deaf Man had prepared them for his Shakespearean quotes by sending them first a fistful of anagrams that culminated in **I'M A FATHEAD, MEN!**, the anagram for **I AM THE DEAF MAN!**

So put that in your pipe and smoke it, as Carella's mother used to tell him when he was a kid and she was exercising maternal authority, put *that* in your pipe and smoke it, Sonny Boy! His mother who was going to marry Mr. Luigi Fontero from Milano,

Italy, on Saturday, the twelfth day of June, *this* Saturday, his mother *Luisa*, mind you, not to mention his sister Angela, God bless us one and all!

Carella looked at the new note again:

726+627=1353

What the hell is he trying to tell us? he wondered.

Your average, run-of-the-mill, everyday office romance flourished around the water cooler or in the supply closet, secret glances, surreptitious touches, furtive kisses hastily exchanged. Rarely during the daily routine did lovers who worked in the same office find themselves alone in an automobile — unless they were detectives.

The burglary to which they'd responded was in a fish store off Seventh Street. The theft had probably taken place the night before but it hadn't been detected until late this morning, when one of the employees went into the freezer and discovered that thirty pounds of shrimp was missing.

"What kind of a world is this?" the owner of the store wished to know. "A person steals *shrimp?* Thirty pounds of *shrimp?* What's he going to do with thirty pounds of *shrimp?* He's got nothing better to steal? He has to steal thirty pounds of *shrimp?*"

"Well, these guys aren't rocket scientists, you know," Willis said.

"But thirty pounds of *shrimp?*"

"Anyone but you have a key to the place?" Eileen asked.

In the car later, Eileen driving, Willis riding shotgun, he said, "I can understand his point. Why would anyone bother? I mean, thirty pounds of *shrimp?* The guy's risking jail for thirty pounds of *shrimp?*"

"You and the owner ought to start a rock group," Eileen said.

"How so?"

"You've already got a name for it. Thirty Pounds of Shrimp. I hear that one more time, I'll scream."

Willis slipped his hand under her skirt.

"Hey!" she said. "I'm driving."

"So pull over."

"Why?"

"So I can kiss you."

"I'm a police officer, I want you to know."

"So am I."

"Stop that."

"Not until you pull over."

She checked the rear-view mirror, signaled, pulled the car over to the curb. He took her in his arms at once, kissed her fiercely. She yanked her mouth away, looked into his face, her own face flushed, fair complexion, the curse of the Irish. This time she kissed him, even more fiercely, pulled her mouth away again, checked the rear-view mirror, the side mirror, kissed him again, pulled back again, breathless.

"We'll get arrested," she said.

"Who cares?" he said, and pulled her to him again.

I AM THE DEAF MAN!

And accompanying the announcement that he had returned to plague them once again, he had included the first of his Shakespearean quotes:

We wondred that thou went'st so soon
From the world's stage, to the grave's
      tiring room.
We thought thee dead, but this thy
      printed worth,
Tells thy spectators that thou went'st
      but forth
To enter with applause.

331

An Actor's Art,
Can die, and live, to act a second part.

Though damned if Carella could find it anywhere on the web. Here in the office, and again at home on his son's computer (which had cost him $999, even discounted) he had gone to the RhymeZone Shakespeare Search again and again and again. He had typed in each and every key word or words he could think of, **went'st so soon**, and **world's stage**, and **grave's tiring room**, and **thought thee dead**, and on and on and on, ad infinitum, straight through to **Actor's Art**, and **act a second part**, with no hits at all. Zero. Shakespeare's Greatest Hits. None at all.

It suddenly occurred to him . . .

Christopher Marlowe.

One of the writers suspected of being the *real* author of Shakespeare's plays. Or his sonnets. Or whatever.

He went to the computer again, and Googled to the name.

The owner of the liquor store was certain that the man who'd come in wearing a ski mask and gloves was black.

"Big black man wearing a ski mask and gloves," he said. "In June. Didn't he know that'd look suspicious? A *ski* mask? And *gloves?* In *June?* How could anyone be so stupid?"

"How'd you know he was black?" Brown asked.

Being black himself — or rather, being more like the color of his name — he was naturally curious. Kling was curious, too, even though he was white and blond. They had responded to the call not ten minutes ago. The robber had cleaned out the cash register and taken a bottle of Johnny Walker Black from the shelf before he'd departed. Maybe that was why the owner thought he was black. The Johnny Black and all. Black by association, so to speak.

"You can tell," the owner said.

"You call tell a man wearing a ski mask and gloves is *black?*" Brown said.

"The voice," the owner said. "No offense meant."

"None taken," Brown said. "He *sounded* black, is that what you're saying?"

"Is *exactly* what I'm saying," the owner said. "No offense."

Kling tended to agree that black people sounded different from white people. Brown was inclined to agree as well. Both men could instantly identify a black person on the phone, even if he wasn't wearing gloves and a ski mask. So why were they both offended now — and they both were — by this scrawny little white man wearing a shabby maroon sweater and smoking a cigarette, telling them that he could tell the man who'd come in and stuck a gun in his face in broad daylight was black because he *sounded* black?

Was it because his identification was premised less on the robber's voice than on the fact that he was wearing a ski mask and gloves on the ninth day of June? Was the liquor store owner saying, in effect, "Only a black man would be stupid enough to wear a ski mask and gloves on a holdup in June?"

Neither Kling nor Brown knew exactly why they were offended, but they were. They went about their business, nonetheless, saying nothing about the possibly racist ID, taking down all the details of the robbery, and then telling the owner, who was already on his fourth cigarette in the past twenty minutes, that they'd get back to him if they got anything, to which he replied simply, "Sure."

Neither did they discuss the ID when they were alone in the car together, heading back to the stationhouse.

Kling wondered about this.

So did Brown.

★ ★ ★

Among the many quotes attributed to Marlowe were:

Comparisons are odious and **Who ever loved that loved not at first sight?** and **Come live with me, and be my love** and **Love me little, love me long** (which was an Elvis Presley song, wasn't it?) and **Was this the face that launch'd a thousand ships?**

But when Carella typed in the keywords in that first little poem they'd received, he got nothing again. So Marlowe hadn't written it, either. In which case, who *was* the culprit? Was it Sir Francis Bacon, another candidate for Shakespearean authorship, if Carella remembered correctly; college was a long time ago. Was it Edward de Vere, the Seventeenth Earl of Oxford, or the Tenth Earl of Warwick, or whoever he might have been?

He Googled over to Bacon, typed in the keywords, and got nothing. He typed in de Vere, went through the exercise yet another time. Nothing again. No hits, all misses. Something like a Broadway season in New York. So who had written those lines?

Or was the Deaf Man himself the author?

★ ★ ★

The family dispute had turned violent. That's why Genero and Parker were here. The woman, who'd had about enough of being slapped around by a husband half her size, grabbed a cast-iron skillet from the stove and swung it at her husband's head, splashing fried peppers and eggs all over his face together with the blood that gushed from the big gash the skillet had opened.

The uniforms who'd responded earlier were still at the scene. An ambulance had carted Agustin Mendez to the hospital, but his wife, Milagros, was still here in the apartment, her arms folded across ample breasts. The detectives had to watch where they were stepping because peppers and eggs were still all over the kitchen floor.

"He slipped and fell in the oil on the floor," Milagros said.

Perfect English, faintest trace of an accent. Damned if she was going to get sent up for finally striking back at her son of a bitch husband. Parker couldn't blame her. Neither could Genero.

"How'd the oil get on the floor, ma'am?" he asked.

"Agustin spilled it."

"Spilled the oil and then slipped in it, right?" Parker said.

"That's how it happened, yes," she said, and nodded defiantly.

In the street outside, walking back to the car, Parker said, "She's lying, you know."

"Oh, sure."

"They lie, these spics."

"Sure."

"Ollie's dating one, you know," Parker said.

"I didn't know."

"A mistake," Parker said, and shook his head gravely.

Carella looked at the note again.

726+627=1353

If the Deaf Man was reversing the number and then adding it to itself, then why not . . .

Well, let's try it, he thought.

He picked up a pen, pulled a pad in front of him, and wrote **1353** on it. He reversed the number . . . **3531** . . . and then added them together:

$$\begin{array}{r} 1353 \\ +3531 \\ \hline 4884 \end{array}$$

I'll be damned, he thought.

Unless he was mistaken, 4884 was the nonexistent postal box number the Deaf Man had used on his early messenger-service deliveries.

He was leading them back to the very beginning again.

He was telling them to go back.

Backward, men! Backward, you backward men!

And then something sprang off the pad, almost hitting Carella in the left eye.

4884

The number read the same forwards and backwards!

11

The driver from Regal Limousine was waiting outside 328 River Place South when his customer — a Mr. Adam Fen — came out of the luxury apartment building at precisely one-thirty that Wednesday afternoon. He tipped his peaked hat and immediately went to the curbside rear door, snapping it open, holding it open as his customer stepped in, and then closing the door behind him. Coming around to the driver's side of the car, he climbed in behind the wheel, and said, "I'm David, Mr. Fen."

"How do you do, David?"

"Nice day, i'n it, sir?"

Slight Cockney accent, the Deaf Man noticed. Or Australian, perhaps? Sometimes, they sounded alike. David was a man in his late forties, the Deaf Man guessed, some five-feet eight-inches tall, quite thin, a slight man by anyone's reckoning. He was wearing black trousers and a matching jacket, black shoes and socks, little black cap with a shiny black peak, white shirt, and black tie.

"And where shall it be this afternoon, Mr. Fen?"

"Clarendon Hall, please."

"Clarendon it is, sir."

The Deaf Man had ordered what Regal called its "luxury sedan" because this was the type of limo Konstantinos Sallas and his bodyguard would be riding to Clarendon this Saturday afternoon. He was not at all interested in the backseat reading lamps or vanity mirrors or any of the other amenities, preferring instead to concentrate on how much room there was in the front seat, where David sat behind the wheel with a blank smile on his face.

The weapon the Deaf Man had chosen was an Uzi submachine gun. Manufactured in Israel, the Oo-zee, as it was pronounced, was a boxy, lightweight weapon measuring only some 470 millimeters, and weighing but 3.5 kilograms. When converted to inches and pounds, this came to a sweet little firearm that was a bit more than eighteen inches long, and weighed a bit less than eight pounds. Certainly small enough to fit in a sports bag on the front seat alongside the driver. Glancing there now, he saw that David had placed on that front seat a folded black raincoat.

"I like the way Regal outfits its drivers," he said.

"Do you now, sir?"

"Indeed. Do they pay for the uniforms? Or do you . . . ?"

"Sir?"

"I asked whether *they* pay for the uniforms, or do you supply them yourselves?"

"They gives us an allowance, sir. We can go to any outfitter we choose, so long as the uniform meets Regal specifications, yes, sir."

"And where did you get your uniform?"

"There's a uniform supply house downtown on Baxter Street, yes, sir. That's where I was outfitted."

"The raincoat, too?"

"Yes, sir, the raincoat. They know Regal's specifications, they're most accommodating."

"What's it called?"

"Sir?"

"The supply house."

"Yes, sir. I'm sorry, I'm a bit hard of hearing."

"So am I," the Deaf Man said.

"Then you know what it's like."

More or less, the Deaf Man thought.

"It's Conan Uniforms, sir, the second floor at 312 Baxter. They have a full line of chauffeur, butler, maid, doorman, janitorial, security, and medical uniforms. Was Regal recommended them, in fact. They have all Regal's specifications. Nice people to deal with, too. Are you thinking of becoming a chauffeur, sir?" he asked, smiling at the absurdity of such a notion even as the words left his lips.

"Not just yet, no," the Deaf Man said, smiling with him, the oaf. "Are you from London, David?"

"Yes, sir. The part what's called Cheapside, do you know it, sir?"

"I do indeed."

"Yes, sir," David said. "Sir, we're about there now, would you care for the main entrance or the stage door?"

"The main entrance, please."

"Yes, sir."

David made his turn at the corner, and pulled up in front of the concert hall.

"I shouldn't be long," the Deaf Man said.

"I may have to move, sir, if the police come by. But I'll just circle the block till I see you."

"Fine, David, thank you," he said, and stepped out of the car.

In the glass-covered display frame to the right of the main entrance doors, there was a poster for this weekend's "Three at Three" series. It showed a black and white photograph of Konstantinos Sallas holding his violin by the neck, and grinning at the camera. Pasted across the lower half of the photo was a narrow banner that read SAT 6/12 AND SUN 6/13.

The Deaf Man nodded and walked into the lobby.

Berrigan Square was near the western-most end of the Stem, where a largely Jewish citizenry merged seamlessly with an increasingly Hispanic population that changed in a flash to what the real estate agents referred to in code as "a colorful neighborhood." Poison Park, as it was familiarly known to police and drug abusers alike, was a triangular-shaped patch of scrawny grass surrounding a bronze statue of Maxwell Wilkerson, Civil War general and later biographer of Abraham Lincoln.

Wilkerson was a witty man with a cheery smile (even in uniform) and graying hair (even in bronze) whose bravery and scholarship had enlightened an entire age. Standing at the apex of the triangle, surrounded by benches peeling dark green paint, sword upraised to the pigeons that soared overhead intent on defecation, and the traffic that zoomed on each of his flanks, east and west, he boldly dominated the small park and indeed the large thoroughfare itself. The shabby assortment of drug addicts and dealers assembled in the park didn't give a shit who Maxwell Wilkerson was or had been. Intent on scoring, each in his own way, they milled about the small triangle in the middle of the avenue, transparently exchanging folded bills for packets of white powder.

The cops in this city — and in most American cities — had long ago decided that the prisons were too full of petty drug abusers and had given up on making small busts. Being an addict was not a crime, but having in one's possession certain circumscribed amounts of controlled substances was. Even so, the law enforcement agencies concentrated instead on destroying the crops in South America and arresting the upper-level chieftains of the posses engaged in the traffic. They probably figured they were doing as good a job in the War on Drugs as the government was doing in its War on Terror even though they didn't have eighty-seven billion dollars at their disposal.

Fat Ollie Weeks figured it all had to do with money.

Not too long ago, he had busted a vast conspiracy linking counterfeit money to illegal drugs to terrorism. So you didn't have to tell him, thanks, that what was going on in Poison Park, or on the desert sands of Iraq, was all about money. Didn't have to tell that to his good buddy Steve Carella, either, who — Ollie had to admit — had helped a little in busting the big "Money, Money, Money Case," as he still fondly thought of it.

With the possible exception of Carella — and, well, Patricia Gomez now, he supposed — Ollie didn't like many people, and he didn't trust anybody at all.

He knew that any of the junkies here in Poison Park would sell his mother to an Arabian rug merchant if he thought the transaction would pay for his next fix. He knew that any of the dealers passing out drugs here would happily kill any of his competitors or indeed Ollie himself if he felt his lucrative livelihood was being threatened. None of these people cared about bringing democracy to Iraq because they knew that nobody gave a damn about sharing the pie with them right here in America.

None of these people had benefited from a tax cut because none of them paid taxes.

The junkies didn't vote because they didn't give a shit about anything but heroin or cocaine or meth or you name it. The dealers didn't vote because either they weren't citizens or they felt that whoever was President or Vice President didn't affect their lives in the slightest; in fact, if you asked them, they probably couldn't tell you who was now holding those elected positions.

Right here in America, the people here in Poison Park were as much slaves to using narcotics or selling narcotics as the black man had been a slave to King Cotton.

Right here in America.

So who cared what happened in Iraq?

Not Ollie, that was for sure.

Sitting on one of the benches as General Wilkerson's shadow slowly encroached on the tips of his brown shoes, Ollie merely hoped he was passing as either a junkie or a dealer because he had no intention of getting shot on this fine June afternoon.

True enough, he had never met a junkie of his size in his life. But he was dressed as seedily as every other addict in the park (the dealers fancied expensive leather, of course) and he had not shaved or bathed in preparation for the stakeout, and he tried to appear needy if not desperate. The addicts figured him for a new kid on the block; here in Dopeland, there was always a new kid on the block. The dealers approached him more warily; sometimes the new kid was carrying tin.

Ollie couldn't tell whether the man who sat down next to him on the bench was (a) an addict (b) a dealer or (c) an undercover like himself. This was the One-Oh-One Precinct; he knew some of the cops up here, but not all of them. In character (he felt) he scoped the man suspiciously. Neither said anything for several moments. Traffic whizzed by on either side of them, east and west. Another sort of traffic moved briskly in the park everywhere around them. Business as usual on this sunny June day.

At last, the man sitting beside him said, "You a cop?"

"Sure," Ollie said. "Ain't we all?"

The man laughed.

Five of him would have made one Ollie, he was that thin. Wearing jeans that hadn't been washed in months, it looked like, and a thin cotton sweater, its sleeves pulled down to the wrists to hide his track marks, Ollie guessed. Must've been twenty-five, thirty, hard to tell with some of these needle freaks. Hollow cheeks, darting blue eyes. The needy look Ollie was trying to emulate. Trying so hard he almost forgot he was here looking for a murderess. Murderer. *Whatever,* these days.

"You selling?" the man asked.

"No," Ollie said.

"So what're you looking to buy?"

Was he a dealer? He sure as hell didn't look like one.

"Actually, I'm a little short of bread just now," Ollie said.

"Ain't we all," the man said, and laughed again. "How about if you *wasn't* short?"

"I do a little Harry, is all. I just dip and dab."

"Don't we all," the man said again, but this time he didn't laugh. "I'm Jonesy," he said, but did not extend his hand.

"Andy," Ollie said.

A name he had used many times before. Andy. Sounded like a large man's name. Andy Fulton was the whole handle he often used on undercover. Big large name. "Reason I'm here . . ."

"Yeah, Andy?"

". . . is I heard some chick was handing out hundred-dollar bills . . ."

"Wish I knew a chick like that."

". . . for delivering letters, was what I heard."

"Right," Jonesy said.

Ollie didn't know whether the man thought he was shitting him or whether he knew something about Melissa Summers buying messengers. He waited. Nothing seemed to be forthcoming.

"Figured I might pick me up some change," Ollie offered.

"Right," Jonesy said again.

Ollie waited.

Traffic zipped by, horns honking, this city.

"You know who might know about that?" Jonesy said.

"Who?" Ollie asked.

Jonesy stood up abruptly. He swung one arm over his head, waved to a bench on the other side of the statue, and yelled out, "Emma? C'mere a sec, okay?"

Which is how Ollie came face to face with the man who'd stolen his priceless manuscript.

"Do I really have to read all this stuff?" Melissa asked.

He hated questions that did not require answers. Would he have gone to all the trouble of picking up a program and all these reviews if he *hadn't* wanted her to read them?

"It will familiarize you with what's about to come down," he said, falling into the vernacular, but perhaps that was all she understood.

Melissa pulled a face.

She looked at her watch.

In twenty minutes, she would have to leave here for Grover Park, where she would watch the stationhouse from across the street, to make sure the last letter of the day was delivered by the Chosen Junkie of the Hour. Meanwhile . . .

The title page of the program read:

Three at Three

"An inadvertent palindrome," the Deaf Man said.

"What's that?"

"A palindrome?"

"*All* of it."

"*Inadvertent* means accidental. A *palindrome* is something that reads the same forwards or backwards. I doubt very much that the people who designed that program realized that 'Three at Three' is a palindrome."

"Oh. Yeah," she said, her eyes widening.

"Three at Three! It *is* the same forwards or backwards."

"Actually, a palindrome should read forwards or backwards *letter* by *letter*. 'Three at Three' only partially qualifies. Then again, I'm sure its use was accidental."

"So what's 'Three at Three'?"

"Three concerts at three o'clock."

"Oh. Is this our Saturday concert?"

"The very one," he said.

"Well, well," she said, and opened the program.

There was a performance schedule and program for the first of the "Three at Three" concerts, which had taken place last Saturday and Sunday. She turned several pages and found the schedule for this weekend's performances. First, there was a full-page picture of Konstantinos Sallas, the guest soloist. He appeared to be a man in his late thirties, clean-shaven, very solemn-looking as he peered at the camera past the curved neck of the violin he was holding in his left hand.

The following page offered a biography of the man. Melissa skimmed it. Born in 1969 — she'd guessed his age about right — began studying violin when he was six, continued his studies at the Greek Conservatory, and then Juilliard in New York, won

351

an Onassis Foundation scholarship, made his concert debut in Athens when he was sixteen years old, won the International Sibelius Competition in Helsinki when he was seventeen, and won both the Paganini International and the Munich International while he was still in his teens. Before his concert debut with the London Symphony, he had also taken top prizes in the Hannover, Kreisler, and Sarasate violin competitions.

On the next page, there was a program of what would be performed at this weekend's "Three at Three" concerts. The first half of the bill would be Beethoven's Violin Concerto in D Major, opus 61 . . .

"That's the one Sallas will be playing," the Deaf Man explained.

The second half would be Brahms' Symphony No 4 in E Minor . . .

"Is he playing this one, too?" Melissa asked.

"No. Poor man would need a rest after the D Major."

"So he's just playing that one thing, is that it?"

"That's it. A lovely piece. Starts with four timpani beats . . ."

"What's a timpani?"

"A kettle drum."

"Oh."

"Four soft timpani beats," he said. "Read the man's reviews, he's truly phenomenal."

Melissa picked up the glossy sheet he'd handed her along with the program. She looked at her watch again. Sighing, she began reading.

"This wizard of the strings played Stravinsky's Violin Concerto and Ravel's Tzigane. His interpretations were humorous, fiery, and breathtaking . . ."

"Every sound that the extraordinary Sallas produced on his Stradivarius was like a shimmering crystal, which, against the heavy brass lines . . ."

"Konstantinos Sallas plays with consistent commitment, exquisite clarity and a thrilling . . ."

"It takes rare charm and brilliant execution for a solo violinist to hold the entranced attention of an entire . . ."

"Konstantinos Sallas brought singularly lustrous tonal effects and colors to the Sibelius . . ."

"I get the picture," Melissa said, and handed the program and the publicity sheet back to him.

"Anything else you get?" he asked.

"What?" she said.

"Look again," he said, waving the program back at her.

She turned to the schedule for this Saturday and Sunday.

Konstantinos Sallas, solo violinist with the . . .

"Oh," she said.

"Yes?"

"His name."

. . . Sallas, solo violinist . . .

"Yes?"

"It's what you said before. A whatchamacallit."

"Yes?"

"The letters," she said. "They spell the same thing forwards or backwards."

. . . Sallas . . .

"Sallas," she said. "His name."

"Good girl," he said, and wondered how many other people were beginning to catch on along about now.

"Don't you see?" Carella said. "It reads the same forwards or backwards."

They were all clustered around his desk now, studying the Deaf Man's final note of the day.

1353+3531=4884

"That number looks familiar," Willis said.

"It's the . . ."

"Right. The box number I tried to track down."

"Doesn't exist," Meyer said.

"But why's he taking us back there?" Eileen asked.

"Because he's leading us back to the beginning again," Hawes said.

"Also, the *size* of the numbers is very definitely getting smaller," Carella said. "Here, take another look."

They took another look:

$$87$$

$$78$$

$$87+78=165$$

$$165+561=726$$

$$726+627=1353$$

$$1353+3531=4884$$

"Backwards, and smaller and smaller," Carella said.

"So what the hell does that mean?" Parker asked, and looked at the clock, trying to figure how much longer this goddamn June the ninth was going to last.

For a man, Emilio Herrera was a damn good-looking woman.

In fact, the detectives up at the Eight-Eight whistled when Ollie marched him into the squadroom.

"Sit down, Emilio," he said, and indicated the chair alongside his desk.

"It's Emma," Emilio said, and sat, crossing his long splendid legs. Five feet seven inches tall in his high heels, weighing a hundred and ten in his padded bra, fingernails painted a glittery gold to match his frizzed blond wig, he tugged at his short blue skirt and then pouted a moist red look at Ollie, who indifferently pulled a pad toward him, and began writing.

Emilio watched.

If he wasn't higher than a hot-air balloon, he'd have at least recognized Ollie's name. But he happened to be floating on some very good Red Chicken and so he didn't know this phat phuck from any other detective up here.

"My book," Ollie said.

"Pretty," Emilio said, thinking he was referring to the pad he'd been writing in, which he now saw carried his hand-lettered name across the top of one page.

"The book you *stole*," Ollie said.

Emilio looked at him blankly.

"*Report to the Commissioner*," Ollie said. "Which I myself wrote."

"You did *not!*" Emilio said indignantly.

Ollie looked at him blankly.

"Olivia *Watts* wrote that report," Emilio said.

"I *am* . . ."

"Olivia *Wesley* Watts!" Emilio shouted.

"I am she," Ollie said. Or even her, he thought. "Where's my fucking *book?*"

"It is *not* your book! It is *Livvie's* book!"

"I *am* Livvie!" Ollie shouted.

"Sure! Same as I'm Emma!"

"Look, you little prick . . ."

"Oh, darling," Emilio said.

"If you don't tell me what you did with that book . . ."

"I got nothing to say to you about Livvie's book."

"There *is* no Livvie!"

"Ho ho."

"I made her up. Livvie is me, I'm Livvie,

357

but she doesn't exist! Olivia Watts is a synonym I . . ."

"Olivia *Wesley* Watts. And it's *pseudo*nym, not . . ."

"Don't get smart with me, you little . . ."

"And anyway, it *isn't*. A pseudonym. Because I saw her after the drug bust, and I told her . . ."

"You saw *who* after *what* drug bust?"

"Livvie. Detective Watts. The drug bust in the basement at 3211 Culver Ave, whenever it was. I saw her outside the building. I told her I'd burned the report so . . ."

"It wasn't a *report*, it was a *novel!*"

"It said *Report to* . . ."

"You *what?*"

"What?"

"You burned it? You telling me you *burned* it? You burned my *novel?*"

"To protect Livvie . . ."

"I'll give you protect Livvie."

"So the bad guys wouldn't get it."

"I'll kill you. I swear to God, I'll *kill* you!"

Ollie was out of his chair now, coming around his desk, his hands actually reaching for Emilio's throat.

"Do you know how long it took me to *write* that book? Do you *realize* . . . ?"

"Relax," Emilio said, "I memorized it."

Ollie looked at him.

"Was it really all fake?" Emilio asked.

"You *memorized* it?"

"Word for word," Emilio said. "Gee, it seemed so real. You're a very good writer, did anyone ever tell you that?"

"You think so?" Ollie said.

"You captured the thoughts and emotions of a woman magnificently."

Ollie almost asked, "How would you know?" But he recognized unadulterated praise when he heard it.

"Did the female viewpoint seem convincing?" he asked.

"Oh, man, *did* it!" Emilio said, and rolled his eyes and began quoting. " '*I am locked in a basement with $2,700,000 in so-called conflict diamonds and I just got a run in my pantyhose.*' "

"What comes next?" Ollie asked.

" '*I am writing this in the hope that it will somehow reach you before they kill me. You will recall . . .*' "

"Emilio," Ollie said, grinning, "I think this is the beginning of a beautiful friendship."

Standing across the street from Sharyn's apartment building, Kling saw the taxi when it pulled up, and recognized the girl the moment she stepped out of it. Same white girl Sharyn and Hudson had met with yesterday. Early thirties, he guessed. Black hair and brown eyes. Slim and svelte, five feet six or seven inches tall. She looked up and down the street before she went into the building, as if she suspected someone was following her . . . well, she was half-right on that score.

Sharyn had told him she couldn't see him until later tonight because she had a meeting at the hospital. He'd known even on the phone that she was lying. Didn't have to look into her eyes to detect the lie. So he'd followed her from her office, and sure as he was white and Sharyn was black, she didn't go to any damn hospital, she went straight home to her apartment here in Calm's Point.

He'd half expected Dr. James Melvin Hudson to pull up ten minutes later, but instead it was the dark-haired, dark-eyed beauty they'd had coffee with yesterday. He watched as she went into the outer lobby, studied the bell panel, found what she was looking for — Sharyn's apartment, he guessed, bright detective — pressed a button, and waited for the answering buzz. When it came, he could hear it faintly from across the street. The girl let herself in, and walked toward the elevator bank.

He looked at his watch.

It was almost five-thirty.

Ollie's manuscript was only thirty-six pages long, which he didn't realize was perhaps the length of a mere chapter in most mystery writers' novels, although there were some bestselling practitioners of the craft who seemed to prefer much shorter chapters, like say a page and a half long. In any event, reciting even a thirty-six-page book from memory was not an easy task, especially if you were a drug addict beginning to come down from a truly splendid high.

Almost unable to believe his good fortune, Ollie provided sweets and coffee for his thieving storyteller, and then set a tape recorder going. This was not unlike the good old days when wooly mammoths roamed the earth, and wise old men sat outside caves reciting tales of hunting valor and skill. The other detectives of the Eight-Eight pulled up chairs around Ollie's desk, not so much because they were dying to hear Emilio's story, but more because they wished to sneak a peek or two up Emma's skirt. But as the tale unfolded, they began to get more and more interested in the intricate plot development and intriguing characterization.

It took Emilio precisely an hour and forty-three minutes to recite Ollie's book word for word. By that time, the assembled detectives were all agog.

"Did you really write that?" one of them asked Ollie.

"Ah yes," he said.

"That is terrific stuff," one of the other detectives said, shaking his head in wonder and awe. "Absolutely terrific."

"You got a sure bestseller there."

"Make a great movie."

"And, little lady, you did a great job reading it."

Were it not for the presence of these other detectives, Ollie might have let Emilio go at that point, so grateful was he for the recitation, and the response to it. On the other hand, Emilio was just a no-good little cross-dressing whore who was a disgrace to his fine Puerto Rican heritage, and who, besides, had been pointed out as someone having knowledge pertaining to the hundred-dollar bills Melissa Summers was handing out in the drug community hither and yon, ah yes.

So Ollie picked up a throwdown dime bag of shit which he just happened to find under Emilio's chair, and he said, "Well, well, well, now where do you suppose *this* came from, Emilio?"

Which is how Emilio gave up Aine Duggan.

Waiting for the girl to come downstairs again, Kling visualized all sorts of things, none of them very pleasant.

First there was Sharyn and Hudson.

Sharyn in bed with a man blacker than she herself was.

Pornographic images of them doing all the things Kling felt only he himself did with Sharyn.

A black man fucking Sharyn.

(Was this a racist thought?)

A black man going down on her.

Sharyn slobbering the black man's Johnson.

An expression she had taught him.

A black expression.

(Was this damn thing, whatever it was, turning him racist?)

Well, *whatever* it was . . .

And at first it had appeared to be merely (merely!) Sharyn and Hudson alone, just the two of them, a sweet little love affair between a pair of colleagues, what the Italians called *una storia,* he would have to ask

Carella's intended stepfather if that was correct, *una storia,* some "story" here between these two black medical practitioners, some little goddamn fucking *story!*

But then it had turned into what appeared to be a genuine three-way, Sharyn, Hudson, and the so-far anonymous white woman, Hudson at the center of an Oreo, the cream on the outside this time around, black Sharyn on his right, the white woman on his left, or vice versa, who gave a damn, it was still lucky Pierre, always in the middle! Would the picture in his mind be less detestable if the man in the middle was white? And if Sharyn had longed for a three-way, why the hell hadn't she invited Kling himself?

And now —

Now this white woman rendezvousing with Sharyn on her own, the three-way turning into a possible lesbian relationship, the movie in his mind suddenly becoming black and white, the women hugging, the women kissing, the women fondling, the women muff-diving, Hudson excluded, Kling excluded, just the two women, black and white, locked in secret, steamy embrace.

The deception.

The deceit.

He snapped off the projector in his mind.

The screen went blank.

He looked at his watch.

Seven twenty-three.

It was starting to rain.

Aine Duggan was curled up in a fetal ball when Ollie found her in an alley off Thompson and shook her awake. It had begun to rain lightly. She blinked up at him.

He could barely recognize this woman with long stringy bleached blond hair and a few missing teeth, wearing blue jeans and a soiled gray sweatshirt, loafers without socks, scabs all over her ankles. The hooker he'd briefly questioned about Emilio Herrera shortly after his book was stolen had been wearing a cute short black skirt and a neat pink halter top and her hair was Irish-red and cut short and she looked like a teenager even though she was twenty-five at the time, which had not been all that long ago. She now looked thirty-five.

"Whussup?" she asked.

"I want to become a mailman," he said.

"Yeah?"

"I hear there's money in it."

"Who told you that?"

"Little birdie."

"I don't know whut the fuck you're talking about."

"A woman paying you to deliver a letter."

"Yeah?"

"To the Eight-Seven."

"Yeah?"

"Where'd you meet her, Aine?"

"How do you know my name?"

"Little birdie," he said again.

It was dark in the alley, but if she wasn't so down and out this very minute, she might have recognized Ollie, anyway, from their last encounter in a galaxy far far away. But the black tar had worn off, and she was no longer high, and she knew she didn't have any money and would probably have to jones her next fix, so who was this fat asshole kneeling beside her, with her face getting all wet from the rain? Was he maybe a prospective john?

"You wanna see my pussy?" she asked.

"I wanna see Melissa Summers."

"Yeah?"

"Where'd you meet her, Aine? Where can I find her?"

"Do I know you?" she asked, and peered at his face through the falling rain.

"Detective Oliver Wendell Weeks," he said. "You know me."

"Am I busted?"

"For what, Aine?"

"I don't know. I'm not a bad person, Detective."

"I know that."

"I'm just a person needs to be comforted and helped . . ."

"Sure," Ollie said.

". . . a person to be pitied."

"Sure, Aine."

"I'm just a sorry fucked-up piece of shit."

"I can help you, Aine."

"I need to make up. I need a fix real bad."

"I can see that."

"I need to find the candy man."

"I can help you do that."

She blinked at him in the falling rain.

"Tell me where you met Melissa Summers. Tell me where it was."

"Who?"

"Melissa Summers. Either a redhead or a girl with long black hair."

"I'm a natural redhead," Aine said. "Wanna see my pussy?"

"Focus, Aine. Melissa Summers."

"Black hair. Bangs."

"Yes."

"Slipped me a deuce to deliver a letter."

"That's her."

"Yeah," Aine said, and nodded in the falling rain.

"Where?" Ollie said.

"How much?" Aine asked.

"So how'd the meeting go?" Kling asked.

It was ten minutes past eleven. They were in his small studio apartment in the shadow of the Calm's Point Bridge. She'd been here waiting for him when he got home. Here in *bed* waiting for him, in fact. Wearing a white baby-doll nightgown.

"Boring stuff," she said.

"Like what?"

He was in the bathroom, brushing his teeth. In the bedroom, propped against the white pillows behind her, Sharyn was watching the Eleven O'Clock News on Channel Four.

"The new Medicare stuff," she said. "How we'll be handling prescriptions, who becomes eligible, da-da, da-da, da-da," she said, twirling her fingers in the air.

Lying.

She hadn't been at any hospital meeting. She'd been in her own apartment with a woman whose name was either C. Lawson, L. Matthews, or J. Curtis.

"What time did it end?" he asked.

"Around eight-thirty," she said.

Which was the exact time she and either Lawson, Matthews, or Curtis had come down from her apartment, walking together arm in arm to the bus stop on the corner, where Lawson, Matthews, or Curtis had hailed a taxi, and Sharyn . . .

"Come straight home?" he asked.

"Caught a bus," she said.

True enough. But not from any damn hospital.

In a second taxi, Kling had followed the white woman, no clue to her name as yet, just a tall, slender woman with dark hair and dark eyes, apparently comfortable enough to afford taxis all over the city, something Kling himself wasn't too cozy with. "Follow that taxi," he'd told his driver, and flashed the tin like a cop in a movie. Joined at the hip, they came over the bridge, yellow cab glued to yellow cab.

Like a cop in a movie, he'd followed Sharyn's three-way lesbian lover to her building after the taxis let them each off, waited till she entered the elevator, and then watched while the indicator showed her getting off on the fourth floor. He checked the lobby mailboxes, no doorman here, no need to conceal or reveal, all the time in the world to check the mailboxes at his leisure.

There were six apartments on the fourth floor. Three of the mailboxes carried men's names: George Santachiaro, James McReady, and Martin Weinstein. The other three carried androgynous, but most likely female, names: C. Lawson, L. Matthews, and J. Curtis. Kling didn't know why the women in this city thought an initial in front of their surnames would fool anyone into thinking a man lived here. Usually, that single letter was a good invitation to a would-be rapist. He jotted the three names into his notebook, and took the subway uptown. The time was nine-twenty.

He stopped in a Mickey D's for a hamburger and some fries.

Walked around in the rain a little, thinking, wondering what to do.

The city seemed glittery and bleak, bright white lights reflecting on black shiny roadways.

Black, he thought.

White, he thought.

Now, at fifteen minutes past eleven, Sharyn called, "Come look, it's Honey Blair."

Black skin against white nightgown

370

against white pillows. He climbed into bed beside her.

Honey Blair, blond and white, wearing a sexy little black mini and standing in her trademark legs-slightly-apart pose, was thanking all of the good citizens out there . . .

". . . for phoning or e-mailing tips on the man or woman who tried to kill me, I can't thank you enough. And mister, sister, who*ever* you may be . . ."

"Is that racist?" Sharyn asked.

". . . we're gonna *get* you!" Honey said, pointing her forefinger directly at the camera.

"I mean the *sister* part," Sharyn said.

"You'd better believe it," Honey said, and turned to the anchor. "Avery?" she said.

"Now why do I think that girl's lying?" Sharyn asked.

You should know, Kling thought.

12

He had been standing outside her building since eight this morning, but no sign of Miss (or possibly Mrs.) Lawson, Matthews, or Curtis. If she had a nine-to-five job, which was possible even though she'd met with Sharyn and her doctor boyfriend at a little before three on Tuesday, she'd be leaving for work sometime between eight and nine, was what he figured. But no sign of her yet.

A white girl, not her, came out of the building at eight-twenty, began walking off into what was shaping up as a sunny day, all that rain last night. Another white girl, again not the one he was looking for, came out at eight-thirty, and then a flurry of them a few minutes later, but still not his target. Was it possible she'd slept with the busy Dr. Hudson at his place last night? Nine o'clock, then nine-fifteen, and nine-thirty, no Lawson, Matthews, or Curtis. Maybe she'd overslept. The mailman arrived at a quarter to ten. Kling followed him into the building.

"Detective Kling," he said, and flashed the buzzer. "Eighty-seventh Squad."

The mailman looked surprised.

"Social Security checks?" he asked.

"Something like that. Do you know any of these women by sight?" he said, and showed the three names.

"Lawson's not a woman," he said. "Man name of Charles. Charles Lawson."

"How about these other two? L. Matthews? J. Curtis?"

"Lorraine Matthews is a blonde. Around five-six, sort of stout . . ."

"And Curtis?"

"Julie, yeah. Julia Curtis. Around thirty, thirty-five, long black hair, brown eyes. Five-seven, five-eight. That the one you're looking for?"

"No," Kling said.

But that was the one.

"What'd she do?"

"Wrong party," Kling said. "Sorry to've bothered you."

The first note was delivered at twenty to eleven that Thursday morning, the tenth day of June.

A rod not a bar, a baton, Dora.

This time they were ahead of him.

"It's a palindrome again," Willis said.

"What's that?" Genero asked. "A palindrome?"

"Something that reads the same forwards or backwards."

"Same as the 4884s he sent us yesterday," Carella said.

They felt they'd been ahead of him yesterday, too, but this time there was no doubt. The sentence read exactly the same, letter for letter, forwards or backwards.

"That's very interesting, the way that works," Genero said, clearly fascinated. "Look at that, Eileen. It's the very same thing, forwards or backwards."

"Oho!" she said, but nobody got it.

"*Dumb* Dora, he means," Lieutenant Byrnes said.

"Who's that?" Genero asked.

"It's an expression," Byrnes said. "Dumb Dora. He's telling us we're dumb."

"I never heard that, Dumb Dora."

"You're too young," Byrnes said. "It was a cartoon back in the Forties. Advertising Ralston."

"What's Ralston?" Genero asked.

"It used to be a breakfast cereal. I used to eat it."

"How old are you, *anyway*, Loot?" Parker asked.

"Old enough."

"Another palindrome, no question," Willis said, reading the note again, front to back and back again.

"Did I miss something?" Kling asked.

He was back in the squadroom now. About time, Byrnes thought. The clock on the wall read 10:48.

"He's sending palindromes now," Carella explained.

"Which are?"

"They read the same forwards and backwards."

Kling looked at the note.

A rod not a bar, a baton, Dora.

"Why?" he asked.

"That's what we're trying to figure out."

"Join the party," Brown said.

"A rod is a gun," Genero said. "Isn't it?"

"Used to be called that, anyway," Byrnes said, almost on a sigh. "Or even a gat."

"Has he given up on darts?"

"A gun *would* be a more practical weapon, you have to admit," Hawes said.

"Then why all that earlier fuss about

darts?" Carella asked.

"Slings to arrows to darts, right," Meyer said, nodding.

"What does he mean by 'not a bar'?"

"Nothing," Parker said. "He's full of shit. As usual."

" 'Not a bar,' " Eileen repeated.

"He's going to use a gun, not some kind of blunt instrument," Brown said.

They all looked at him.

"Well, *some* perps use crowbars," he explained.

They were still looking at him.

"As their weapon of choice," he said, and shrugged.

"You think he means a *police* baton?"

"What we used to call a nightstick," Byrnes said, again wistfully.

"Or does he mean a *conductor's* baton?" Willis said.

"Oh, Jesus, not another concert!" Parker said.

"Is it the Cow Pasture again?" Hawes asked.

"That was one of his very first references, remember?" Eileen said, nodding.

They scanned the scattered notes:

A WET CORPUS?
CORN, ETC?

"Remember what that became?"

COW PASTURE?
CONCERT?

"Is there a concert scheduled in the Cow Pasture?"

They scanned the city's three daily newspapers for possible events that might require the use of a baton, and came up with only five that possibly qualified. One was a performance by the Cleveland Symphony at eight o'clock tonight, at Palmer Center. Another was a performance by the city's own Philharmonic, again at eight, this one at Clarendon Hall. There were two jazz concerts in clubs downtown, and a student recital at the Kleber School of Performing Arts.

"So what do we do?" Kling asked. "Cover them all?"

"Well, if he's *really* gonna use a gun at one of these events . . ."

"None of them's in the Eight-Seven, did you notice?" Parker said.

"He's got a point," Genero agreed.

"So let's just alert these other precincts," Parker said, and shrugged.

Anyone but us, he was thinking.

★ ★ ★

Ollie was thinking like a novelist instead of a cop, but sometimes the two overlapped, ah yes. In crime fiction, there was an old adage that maintained "The Criminal Always Returns to the Scene of the Crime," or words to that effect, probably first uttered by Sherlock Holmes himself, a fictitional character created by Charles Dickens. In real life, however, as Ollie well knew, a criminal rarely if ever returned to the scene of the crime. What the criminal usually did was run for the hills, which was what Melissa Summers should have been doing instead of hiring assorted junkies to deliver the Deaf Man's messages, whoever he might be.

But he had been told by a truly sad specimen named Aine Duggan (who pronounced her name Anya Doogan, go figure) that a woman who answered the description he'd given of Melissa had approached her last Tuesday afternoon in Cathleen Gleason Park, a lovely patch of green close to the River Harb and the apartment buildings lining River Place South, where Aine had gone to sit and look out over the river and also to wait for her dealer. So this is where Ollie was on this sunny (thank God) Thursday at a little before noon, waiting for Miss Summers to put in a return engagement, either in her short red wig or her long black wig.

He doubted if she'd come back, but hope springs eternal, ah yes, and hope is also the thing with feathers. So he sat overlapping a park bench in the sunshine, watching the little birdies flutter and twitter, watching too the young mothers with their snot-nosed little toddlers scampering and scurrying, thanking the good lord that he was still a free and single individual, and then — suddenly and quite unexpectedly — wondering where Patricia Gomez was and what she was doing at this very moment.

"What I don't understand," Hawes said, "is how the shooter knew where I'd be."

Honey merely nodded.

He had gone to meet her outside Channel Four's offices on Moody Street, and they were now having lunch in a little Mexican joint two blocks away. Honey loved to eat. She was now eating *camarones cocoloco*, quite enjoying herself and not particularly eager to talk about whoever had tried to kill her. Despite the evidence of the Note, she had convinced herself by now that the shooter was after no one but herself. This notion was fortified by the thousands of letters, phone calls, and e-mails Channel Four had received, encouraging her to continue her crusade against the would-be assassin.

"Because first he had to know I spent the night in your apartment . . ."

"Well, that wouldn't take a rocket scientist," Honey said.

"I know. But it *would* take someone following us. And watching the building, waiting for me to come out."

"He probably thought we'd be coming out together."

"No, I came out alone. He could see you weren't with me. He started shooting the moment I stepped foot . . ."

"Well," Honey said, dismissing the notion and biting into another butterfly shrimp coated with coconut flakes.

"And next, he knew I'd be going to Jeff Ave. How'd he know that? How'd he know a limo would be dropping me off at Five-Seven-Four Jeff?"

"You're forgetting that *I* was in that limo, aren't you?"

"No, I'm not forgetting that at all. How could I? You broadcast it every night."

Honey wondered if she was only imagining his sharp tone. She looked up from her plate.

"Who ordered that limo?" he asked.

"I did."

"Personally?"

"No, my intern did. I asked her . . ."

"What intern?"

"A girl from Ramsey U. She's been working with me since the semester began."

"What's her name?"

"Polly Vandermeer."

"I'd like to talk to her," Hawes said.

"Fine, Sherlock," she said.

Hawes wondered if he was only imagining her sharp tone.

Look, sire, paper is kool!

"Another palindrome," Carella said.

"And it's Shakespeare again," Parker said.

Maybe he was right; the word *sire* certainly did sound like another sly reference to Shakespeare.

"At least he spelled *kool* right," Genero said.

"Reads the same backwards and forwards," Willis said.

"I love the way that works," Eileen said.

"But why?" Meyer asked. "Is he directing us backwards?"

"To *where?*" Brown asked.

He was scowling. He always looked as if he might be scowling, but this time he really was scowling. He remembered the last time the Deaf Man had graced them with his presence, causing a race riot in Grover Park. Brown did not like race riots, and he did not like the Deaf Man. However much these little messages seemed to promise fun and games, Brown was fearful the games would turn sour soon enough.

"To the early messages, that's where," Kling said. "The ones he used that box number on. 4884. The same backwards and forwards. He's saying go *back*."

"To the anagrams."

"To Gloria Stanford's murder."

"And the first of the Shakespeare poems."

"I can't find that damn poem anywhere," Carella said. "I've Googled everywhere, I just can't find it."

"Maybe he made it up, sire," Genero suggested.

"It's too good for him to have made up," Eileen said.

"Let's have another look at it," Willis said.

We wondred that thou went'st so soon
From the world's stage, to the grave's
    tiring room.
We thought thee dead, but this thy
    printed worth,
Tells thy spectators that thou went'st
    but forth
To enter with applause.

An Actor's Art,
Can die, and live, to act a second part.

"Sure as hell *looks* like Shakespeare," Parker insisted.

"But why's he taking us back to 4884?" Carella said.

"Could it be a street address?" Eileen said.

"Must be thousands of 4884's in this city."

"Let me see that new one again," Willis said.

They all looked at it:

Look, sire, paper is kool!

"Well, this is off the wall, I know . . ."

"Let's hear it," Hawes said.

"In this first quote. The third line . . ."

We thought thee dead,
but this thy printed worth

"The last three words . . ."

thy printed worth

"What I'm thinking," Willis said, "is . . . well . . . I know this is far out . . . but if you *print* something, you've got to have . . ."

"Paper!" Eileen said, and felt like kissing him, he was so smart.

Look, sire, paper is kool!

"Hey, kool!" Genero said. "He's telling us to look at the newspapers, see what's playing around town."

"Find the concert."

"If it's a concert."

"We've already done that," Parker said sourly.

Polly Vandermeer was a cute little twenty-two-year-old blonde wearing a pleated plaid skirt and a white long-sleeved blouse with a tie that matched the skirt. Looking more like a preppie freshman than a senior in Communications at Ramsey University, she greeted Hawes with a wide smile and a warm handshake. Miss Blair, as she called her, had already told her that a detective investigating the shooting wanted to talk to her. She did not seem at all intimidated; she'd already spoken to two detectives from the Eight-Six Squad.

"It seems incredibly awesome," she said, "that anyone would want to kill Miss Blair. I mean, she's like so *nice*."

"She is indeed," Hawes said.

They were in a small room that served as a coffee-break area for members of the Channel Four staff. A coffee machine, a refrigerator, a four-burner stove top with a tea kettle on it, a soft-drinks machine. One other woman was in the room when they sat down, drinking coffee, absorbed in the morning paper. A white-faced clock on the wall, black hands, gave the time as 11:10.

"Miss Vandermeer," he said, "I wonder . . ."

"Oh, please, *Polly*," she said.

"Polly, do you remember Miss Blair asking you to order a car for her last Friday morning?"

"Yes, sir, I do," Polly said, blue eyes wide now, face all serious and attentive.

"Do you remember the exact request?"

"Yes, sir, she asked for a pickup at her

apartment and a drop-off here at the studio."

Hawes looked at her.

"No interim stops?" he asked.

"No, sir."

"A stop at the 87th Precinct, for example? 711 Grover Avenue? And another one on Jefferson Avenue?"

"No, sir, this was the same as every morning."

"When did she make this request?"

"When she left for home Thursday evening."

"For the next morning, correct?"

"Yes, sir. For Friday morning, the fourth of June."

"Didn't mention my name, huh?"

"*Your* name, sir?"

"Cotton Hawes, yes. Did she say she'd be picking up and dropping off Detective Cotton Hawes? On her way to the studio?"

"No, sir, she certainly did not," Polly said, sounding suddenly disapproving.

"So when Miss Blair gave you this request, what did you do with it?"

"Phoned it down to Transportation."

"On Thursday evening."

"Yes, for the next morning."

"Who took your call there?"

"Rudy Mancuso."

"Is Transportation in this building?"

"Yes, sir."

"Where, Polly?"

BORROW OR ROB?

"Clearly, it's another palindrome," Willis said.

"Front to back or vice versa," Brown said.

"Well, he's certainly not about to *borrow* anything," Meyer said.

"Then why does he say so?" Genero asked.

"He doesn't say for sure," Carella said. "He asks us to guess. Is he going to borrow or is he going to rob?"

"Right," Kling said. "He's asking us to guess which."

"Teasing us again," Meyer said.

"But why a palindrome?" Willis asked.

"Are we forgetting his first note today?" Eileen said.

A rod not a bar, a baton, Dora.

"Right," Parker said. "A baton. He's going to stick a baton up somebody's ass."

"No, he's going to rob the box office at a *concert* someplace."

"That's *rob*," Parker said. "You stick somebody up, you ain't *borrowing*, you're *robbing*."

"The only concerts are the ones we found in the paper," Carella said. "And we've already alerted the local precincts."

"Good," Parker said. "So let's forget it."

"Remember when there used to be those big rock concerts at the Hippodrome?" Genero said, misting over.

"Circus just left there," Kling said.

"I love circuses," Eileen said, and glanced at Willis as if she expected him to buy her a balloon.

"Anyway, a palindrome isn't a hippodrome," Kling said.

"They used to have hippos in them big arenas, you know, back in Roman times," Parker said. "That's how they got the name hippodrome."

No one challenged him.

Rudy Mancuso was a squat burly man, dark-haired and dark-eyed, who sat in shirtsleeves behind a cluttered desk in an office where two other men sat at equally cluttered desks across the room. He was entirely sympathetic to Hawes' quest for the shooter, but he seemed totally unaware that Hawes himself had been the target in the first rifle assault. In fact, he didn't even know there'd *been* a previous shooting. He kept clucking his tongue over "poor Miss Blair," becoming all business — "Transportation, Mancuso" — each time the ringing phone interrupted Hawes' questioning. In a comparatively peaceful ten minutes, Hawes managed to get some answers.

Mancuso corroborated essentially what Polly had already told him. The telephone request last Thursday evening was for a Friday morning pickup at ten, at Honey's building, and a drop-off here at Channel Four. No interim stops. Same as every morning.

"If there *were* interim stops . . ."

"None were ordered, Detective."

"But *if* there were . . ."

"Okay?"

"Who would have known about them?"

"You mean like if Miss Blair, after she'd been picked up, told the driver to stop someplace on the way here?"

"Yes."

"Well, the *driver* would have known . . ."

"Who else?"

"He might've called in to say he was stopping at such and such a place before . . ."

389

"Who would've taken that call?"

"Either Eddie or Frankie. Right there across the room."

You'd have thought Eddie and Frankie were a ventriloquist and his dummy. Everything Eddie said, Frankie repeated. Eddie's full name was Edward Cudahy. He watched while Hawes wrote it down in his little notebook. Frankie's full name was Franklin Hopper. He watched, too. Eddie told Hawes he didn't remember any driver calling in to say he'd be making any interim stops on Honey Blair's way to the studio last Friday morning. Frankie said the same thing. Eddie said he didn't remember which drivers were on call last Friday morning. Frankie said the same thing. Hawes thanked them both for their time. Both men said, "You're welcome," almost simultaneously.

Hawes went back to Rudy Mancuso's desk, and asked for the name of the driver who'd picked up Honey Blair last Friday morning, the fourth of June.

Mancuso told him the driver was off today.

"Then give me his home address," Hawes said.

"I don't know if I should do that."

"Would a court order change your mind?" Hawes asked.

The last note of the day arrived at a quarter to four. It was another palindrome. It read:

MUST SELL AT TALLEST SUM

"Now just what the hell is that supposed to mean?" Parker asked.

No one knew what the hell that was supposed to mean.

Besides, the night shift was just coming on, so they all went home.

When you're in love, the whole world's Italian.

Or so it seemed to Carella.

Here they all were, ta-ra!, the prospective brides and grooms and their whole *mishpocheh* or *meshpocheh* or however "family" was spelled in Italy, all gathered in a restaurant called Horatio's, in the city's midtown area, not too distant from where Luigi Fontero had put up all his relatives. Carella wondered who had paid all those air fares to the U.S. and whether or not the visiting Italians all had to be fingerprinted before gaining entrance to these fiercely protected shores — thank you, Bulldog Tom Ridge, and the ever-alert Homeland Security team.

Representing the Fontero family was a small army of relatives from Milan, Naples, Genoa, and/or Rome, kinfolk near, far, or even remote, but certainly numerous and clamorous. Representing the Carellas were Steve and Teddy (minus the children, or "*i creatori*," as he and his sister used to be called when they themselves were small, ah so long ago); and Uncle Freddie who was a casino dealer in Vegas and who had flown east especially for the wedding this Saturday; and Carella's Aunt Josie and his Uncle Mike, who'd come all the way up from Orlando, Florida, hadn't seen them in years, but hey, this was a big double wedding! Aunt Josie loved to play poker. Uncle Mike used to call Angela "The Homework Kid" when she was small because she always had her nose buried in a book, but now — hey, looka here! — all grown up and about to be married for the second time.

Aunt Dorothy was here, too, summoned from wherever she was living in California with the third of her husbands, Carella's beloved Uncle Salvie having died of cancer shortly after Carella joined the force. He missed Uncle Salvie, a cab driver who'd known the city better than any cop, used to tell stories abut the hundreds of passengers he carried to every remote neighborhood. Carella's grandmother always kept telling him he should have become a writer. Carella guessed he'd've made a good one, too, some of the phony novelists around these days.

Aunt Dorothy was the one who'd first tipped to the fact that young Carella was enjoying what to him at the time was a wildly erotic relationship with Margie Gannon, a little Irish girl who lived across the street from the Carella family in Riverhead. This steamy adolescent byplay amounted to nothing more than copping a feel every now and then, or sliding his hand under Margie's skirt and onto her silken sexy panties, but oh, such ecstasy! Aunt Dorothy teased him relentlessly about her, referring to her as Sweet Rosie O'Grady, Carella never could figure why.

Aunt Dorothy was telling a dirty joke now. She loved dirty jokes. Carella suspected the joke fell upon deaf ears as regarded most of the Fontero tribe. For that matter, Henry Lowell's stiff Wasp relatives didn't seem to be enjoying his aunt's ribald sense of humor, either. His sister's in-

tended sat holding her hand and smiling
tolerantly as the joke unfolded endlessly,
something about the Pope, sure to be a
winner among the Fonteros, the Pope
being stopped by a prostitute outside the
Vatican (Careful, Aunt Dotty!) and then
running back inside to ask the Mother Superior "What's a blowjob?" (Watch it!)
and the Mother Superior telling him . . .

Carella suddenly wondered if his mother
and Luigi . . .

No, he didn't want to go there.

All at once, everyone was laughing.

Even the Fonteros, who, Carella now realized, understood more English than he'd
earlier supposed.

The laughter swelled everywhere around
him.

He wondered why he couldn't find it in
himself to share it.

13

The eleventh day of June dawned all too soon.

At six-thirty a.m. on what looked like the start of a sunny Friday morning, Melissa and the Deaf Man were sitting in the breakfast nook of his seventeenth-floor apartment, overlooking River Place South, Gleason Park, and the River Harb beyond.

"Your job tomorrow," he was telling her, "will be a very simple one."

She was thinking that her job *today* wouldn't be a simple one at all. If she didn't get out of here soon to start lining up her junkies . . .

"The luxury sedan from Regal will be arriving here at half past noon tomorrow," he said. "All you have to do is deliver the driver to the Knowlton."

So what else is new? she thought.

"And what will *you* be doing?" she asked.

Far as she could see, all he'd done so far was sit on his brilliant ass while she ran all over the city doing his errands. And he still hadn't told her what her cut of the big seven-figure payoff would be, if there ever *was* a big payoff, which she was honestly beginning to doubt, now that he was into palindromes and all. If he was so intent on screwing up the 87th Precinct, why was he bothering with word games? Why didn't he just lob a hand grenade through the front door? Good question, eh, Adam? What *is* this thing you have with them, anyway?

"What is this thing you have with them, anyway?" she asked, venturing the question out loud, what the hell.

"By this *thing* . . . ?"

"This messing around with their heads."

"Let's just say our ongoing relationship has been a frustrating one," he said.

"Okay, but why . . . ?"

"I wouldn't trouble my pretty little head over it," he said, a line she had heard in many a bad movie, a line she had in fact heard from the late unlamented Ambrose Carter while he was still training her, so to speak, his exact words being, "I wouldn't trouble my pretty little head over it, swee'heart, just suck the man's cock."

"Yes, but I *do* trouble my pretty little head over it," she said now, somewhat defiantly. "Because it seems to me you're

396

spending a lot of time and money telling these jerks exactly what you're about to do . . ."

"Exactly what I'm *not* about to do is more like it," he said.

"Whatever," she said. "Why are you *bothering*, that's the question? Why not just do the gig and get out of town?"

"That's precisely what I plan to do. Tortola, remember?"

"Who's Detective Stephen Louis Carella?" she asked, straight out.

"A dumb flatfoot."

"Then why are you addressing these letters to him? If he's so dumb . . ."

"It's personal. I shot him once."

"Why?"

"He was getting on my nerves."

"Did he send you away, is that it?"

"I've never done time in my life."

"Did he bust you? Did you beat the rap?"

"Never. Neither Carella nor the Eight-Seven has ever laid a hand on me."

"Then . . . I don't get it. Why *bother* with them?"

"Diversion, my dear, it's all diversion."

"I don't know what that means, diversion."

"It means smoke and mirr . . ."

"I *know* what it *means,* I just don't see how it applies here."

"Try to look at it this way, my dear," he said patiently. She did not like it when he got so tip-toey patient with her. It was more like condescension when he got so patient. "In these perilous times of High Alert, with a terrorist lurking under every bush — please pardon the pun — one can't be too careful, can one? So, even *with* the assistance of policemen from other precincts, they'll *still* be too late."

"Who'll be too late?"

"The stalwarts of the Eight-Seven."

"Too late for *what?*"

"The foul deed that smells above the earth — to paraphrase Mr. Shakespeare in his brilliant *Julius Caesar* — shall already have been done. Too late, my love. Altogether too late."

"I still don't get it," she said.

"Well," he said, and sighed heavily, "I wouldn't trouble my pretty little head over it."

Which pissed her off all over again.

The driver who'd been behind the wheel of the limo last Friday was named Kevin Connelly, and he did not appreciate being awakened at seven in the morning. Associating Hawes at once with the bullets that had come crashing into the car last week, he immediately looked into the hallway past him, as if expecting another fusillade. Satisfied that Hawes was alone, he stepped aside and let him into the apartment.

He was still in his pajamas. He threw on a robe, led Hawes into the kitchen, and immediately set a pot of coffee to brew on the stove. Like two old buddies about to embark on a hunting trip, they sat drinking coffee at a small table adjacent to a small window.

"I want to know about the Honey Blair call last Friday," Hawes said. "What'd the dispatcher give you?"

"Pickup and delivery for Miss Blair," Connelly said. "Same as always."

"So how come you picked me up on the way?"

"Miss Blair told me to stop by for you."

"Gave you 711 Grover?"

"No, she didn't know the address of the precinct. I had to look it up in my book. This little book I have."

"How about 574 Jefferson? Did she tell you we'd be dropping me off there?"

"Yes."

"How long did you figure it'd take from her building to the precinct?"

"About ten minutes."

"And from there to Jeff Av?"

"Another twenty."

"Plenty of time for someone to get there ahead of us."

"Well, sure. As it turned out."

"But you and Miss Blair were the only ones who knew where we were going."

"Until I called it in to Base."

"Base?"

"The Transportation office. At Channel Four. I called in to give them the new itin."

"Who'd you speak to there?"

"One of the guys."

"Which one?" Hawes asked.

And after me, I know, the rout is
    coming.
Such a mad marriage never was be-
    fore:
Hark, hark! I hear the minstrels play.

"God, does he know about the *wedding*?" Carella asked out loud.

"How could he?" Meyer asked.

"He could," Genero said knowingly. "He's evil."

Carella was thinking, It *is* a mad marriage. *Two* mad marriages! Like never was or were before. He was already at the computer, searching for the source of the quote. It was eight-thirty in the morning. The other detectives all clustered around the first note that day as if it were a ticking time bomb. Which perhaps it was.

"There's *hark,*" Willis said. "I *told* you it meant listen, didn't I?"

" 'Hark, hark!' " Kling quoted. "He's harking us to death."

"*Hokking* our *chainiks,*" Meyer said.

"Which means?" Parker demanded, sounding insulted.

"Which means 'breaking our balls,' excuse me, Eileen."

"It's from *The Taming of the Shrew,*" Carella said. "Act Three, Scene Two."

"Think the Minstrels might be a rock group?" Brown asked.

"Here, check it out," Willis said.

The June 11–18 issue of *Here & Now* magazine had appeared on the newsstands early this morning. Published every Friday, it covered the city's cultural scene for the following week, alerting its readers to what was happening all around town. Handily divided into sections titled Art, Books, Clubs, Comedy, Dance, Film, Gay & Lesbian, Kids, Music, Sports, and Theater, the magazine offered a neat little guide to all that was going on that week.

The Music section this week . . .

The Deaf Man's note this morning seemed to confirm that his target was a concert someplace . . .

. . . was divided into subsections titled "Rock, Pop & Soul," "Reggae, World & Latin," "Jazz & Experimental," "Blues, Folk & Country," and "Cabaret." A separate section listed "Classical & Opera" events. The variety of offerings was overwhelming. For this weekend alone, there were 112 listings in the "Rock, Pop & Soul" section; this was not Painted Shrubs, Arizona, kiddies.

The magazine's **DON'T MISS!** column highlighted the "dashing singer-guitarist" **John Pizzarelli** and his trio, appearing nightly at 8:30 p.m. in the Skyline Room of the Hanover Hotel; "soul legend" **Isaac Hayes,** performing at 8:00 and 10:30 this Friday and Saturday nights at Lou's Place downtown; **Kathleen Landis,** "lovely pianist and song stylist," nightly at 9:00 p.m. in the lounge of the Piccadilly; **Konstantinos Sallas,** "renowned violin virtuoso, guest-starring with the Philharmonic" at Clarendon Hall this Saturday and Sunday at 3:00 p.m.; and **William Christie** leading the Paris National Opera and his "stellar early-music ensemble" in *Les*

Boréades at the Calm's Point Academy of Music, this Friday at 7:15 p.m. and this Sunday at 2:00 p.m.

There were groups named the Hangdogs, and Cigar Store Indians, and the Abyssinians, and Earth Wind & Fire, and the White Stripes, and Drive-By Truckers, but nobody named the Minstrels was performing anywhere in the city anytime during the coming week.

"Think there's a group called 'A Mad Marriage'?" Kling asked.

"I wouldn't be surprised," Meyer said.

"Here, you check it out," Brown said, and tossed him the magazine. "There's only ten thousand of them listed."

"How about 'Never Was Before'?"

"Or 'A Rout Is Coming'?"

"Good start," Willis said. "Know any lead guitarists?"

"Anybody got a garage?" Eileen said.

"What's a rout?" Genero asked.

"A disorderly retreat," Kling said.

"I thought it was some kind of rodent."

"He's telling us he's got us on the run," Parker said.

"Maybe he has," Carella said.

It bothered him that somehow, in some damn mysterious way, the Deaf Man may

403

have learned about tomorrow's impending wedding, *weddings,* and was planning some mischief for them. Carella hated mysteries. In police work, there were no mysteries. There were only crimes and the people who committed them. But the Deaf Man insisted on creating his own little mysteries, taunting them with clues, making a humorous guessing game of crime.

On Carella's block, there was nothing humorous about crime. Crime was serious business, and the people who committed crimes were nothing but criminals, period. He didn't care if they came from broken homes, he didn't care if they'd been abused as children, he didn't care if they had what they believed were very good reasons for beating the system. The way Carella looked at it, there *were* no very good reasons for beating the system. Maybe President Clinton should have kept his zipper zipped, but he was right when he suggested that everyone should work hard and play by the rules.

Carella worked hard and played by the rules.

The Deaf Man didn't.

That was the difference between them.

Well, maybe the Deaf Man *was* working hard at concocting these riddles of his, but he sure as hell wasn't playing by the rules.

Carella had to admit that there was nothing he'd have liked better than for someone — *anyone* — to pop out of his seat and raise his hand when the priest asked the gathered witnesses to speak now or forever hold their peace. But he did not want that someone to be the Deaf Man. He did not want any surprises at tomorrow's ceremony, *ceremonies*.

He wanted all of this over and done with.

The weddings and whatever the Deaf Man was planning.

All of it.

Toward that end, the Deaf Man's next note was no help at all.

So glad of this as they I cannot be,
Who are surprised withal; but my
  rejoicing
At nothing can be more. I'll to my
  book,
For yet ere supper-time must I perform
Much business appertaining.

"No, wait," Willis said. "I think he's trying to tell us something, after all."

"Yeah, what? There's nothing at all about a concert this time," Parker said.

"But he's back to something *printed* again. 'Thy printed worth,' remember? Now he's specifically mentioning a book. 'I'll to my *book*.' There it is, right there, in black and white. A *book*."

"I looked at all Shakespeare's plays in the library the other night," Genero said.

"Good, Richard, you get a gold star."

"Well, maybe he's telling us to go to the library. To find that missing quote, or whatever."

"Of course he is," Parker said, encouraging him. "Maybe in the very same book you looked at the other night."

"Maybe so."

"Maybe you can even borrow the book, Richard. Ponder it at your leisure."

"Well, wait a minute," Eileen said. "He *did* say 'borrow or rob,' didn't he? In one of his notes? And that's where you borrow a book, isn't it? A library?"

"First book I ever owned," Parker said, "I *stole* from the lib'ery."

"Where's that *Here & Now*?" Eileen asked. "Is there anything about a library in it?"

In a section of the magazine titled . . .

AROUND TOWN

406

. . . they found a subsection titled:

LAST CHANCE DEPARTMENT.

Headlined there was an article titled . . .

Bye Bye, Bard

It read:

To mark the departure of the 6.2-million-dollar First Folio edition of Shakespeare's plays, on loan from the Folger Collection in Washington, D.C., Patrick Stewart — renowned Shakespearean actor and subsequent captain of the starship *Enterprise* — will read from selected plays in a farewell tribute. Saturday, June 12, at 3:00 p.m. The Molson Auditorium at Langdon Library.

This time, they Googled directly to *First Folio*. And this time, they found the source of what until now they'd believed was a Shakespearean quote:

**We wondred that thou went'st so soon
From the world's stage, to the grave's
tiring room.**

We thought thee dead, but this thy
  printed worth,
Tells thy spectators that thou went'st
  but forth
To enter with applause.

An Actor's Art,
Can die, and live, to act a second part.

The lines of verse had been written "To the memory of Master William Shakespeare" by a contemporary poet and translator named James Mabbe. It appeared in the 1623 First Folio of plays as one of several introductory dedications.

"Never heard of him," Parker said.

But it now seemed possible that the Deaf Man was directing them to the valuable book that would be leaving the Langdon Library this Saturday. And it seemed further possible that he planned to steal it.

"And hold it for ransom," Eileen suggested. " 'Must sell at tallest sum.' "

"He's gonna kidnap a *book?*" Genero said.

"*Whatever* he's gonna do, he's doing it before suppertime," Kling said.

"Sure, look."

For yet ere supper-time must I perform

Much business appertaining.

"Three o'clock would seem to qualify," Brown said.

"Where's the Langdon Library?"

"Midtown South Precinct, isn't it?"

"We'd better alert them."

"You think they don't already know they've got a six-million-dollar book on their hands?"

"Six million *two*."

"Security there must be thicker than bear shit."

"But that's it," Willis said. "We doped it out, right?"

"Thank you, Mr. Deaf Man," Genero said, and bowed from the waist.

You are welcome, gentlemen! come, musicians, play.
A hall, a hall! give room! and foot it, girls.

"Friggin guy's a mind reader," Parker said.

"What's he mean *'girls'*?"

"I'm a girl," Eileen said, and beamed a Shirley Temple smile.

"He's back to music again."

" 'Musicians.' "

" 'A hall, a hall!' "

"A *concert* hall!"

"Where's that magazine?"

"Wasn't there something about . . . ?"

"Here."

Under **DON'T MISS!**, they once again found:

Konstantinos Sallas, "renowned violin virtuoso, guest-starring with the Philharmonic" at Clarendon Hall this Saturday and Sunday at 3:00 p.m.

"Three o'clock again," Eileen said. "That's still 'ere suppertime.' "

"What does he mean by *air?*" Genero asked.

"Before."

For yet ere supper-time must I perform

"That would seem to indicate a concert, don't you think?" Carella said. "The word *perform?*"

"No, he's saying he *himself* has to perform," Meyer said. "He has 'much business appertaining.' "

"But it doesn't sound like a book anymore, does it?"

"The son of a bitch is asking us to *choose!*" Parker said.

"Which? The Sallas concert or the

Folger First Folio?"

"The concert," Eileen said.

"The book," Genero said.

"Both," Kling said.

It was Brown who tipped.

"A palindrome!" he said. *"Sallas!"*

And now they all jumped in like a Greek chorus.

"Sallas!"

"Sallas!"

"He's going after the violinist!"

"He's going to kidnap the friggin *violinist!"*

"And hold him for the tallest *sum!"*

"Or maybe the book," Genero insisted, raining on their parade.

"Which?" Carella asked.

The next barrage of notes — seven of them in all — arrived in the same envelope at two that afternoon. They were all Shakespearean quotes, which in itself seemed to indicate the Deaf Man's target was not some palindromic Greek fiddler, but the pricey book containing thirty-six of the bard's plays. Contrariwise, as was the Deaf Man's wont, the content of the notes seemed to be challenging the detectives to choose. Either or, lads. You pays yer money, and you takes yer choice.

411

It is "music with her silver sound,"
because musicians have no gold for
    sounding:

But on the other hand:

Was ever book containing such vile
    matter
So fairly bound? O that deceit should
    dwell
In such a gorgeous palace!

Then again:

And those musicians that shall play to
    you
Hang in the air a thousand leagues
    from hence,
And straight they shall be here: sit, and
    attend.

Unless:

A book? O rare one!

However:

If music be the food of love, play on

But perhaps:

Devise, wit; write, pen;
for I am for whole volumes in folio.

Thanks for nothing, they were thinking.

You are very welcome, sir,
Take you the lute, and you the set of
    books

And now there seemed to be an urgency
to the Deaf Man's notes. A sense of impending accomplishment. A certainty that
time was running out, the deed would
soon be done, and if they didn't catch on
soon, it would be too damned late.

The previous envelope had contained
seven notes.

This one arrived a half-hour later, and
there was just a single note in it:

And she goes down at twelve.

"Party's getting rough again," Parker
said, and winked at Eileen.

The thing was, Ollie was looking for either a redhead with short hair, or a bru-
nette with long hair. He wasn't looking for
the feather-cut, elegantly dressed blonde
who came into the park at three that after-

413

noon and took a bench facing the river. He had no idea that this was Melissa Summers.

Nor did Melissa have any idea that the fat guy sitting on a bench near the playground equipment here in Cathleen Gleason Park was a detective. Most detectives she'd known worked out in the gym and had muscles on their muscles. This guy looked more like a pedophile, but she didn't have any kids here in the park, so let their mothers worry. Besides, after chasing junkies all day long, all she wanted to do was sit here peacefully and listen to the sound of the distant river.

In any case, neither of the two paid the slightest bit of attention to the other.

At three-fifteen, Melissa got up, heaved a gentle sigh, left the park, and started back for the apartment on River Place South. She was thinking that on Sunday at this time, she'd be basking on a beach in Tortola.

Some five minutes later, Ollie got off his bench, farted, and headed back for the Eight-Eight. It never once occurred to him that he should give the Eight-Seven a little buzz, mention that Carmela Sammarone was going by the name Melissa Summers these days. Neither did he realize how close he'd come to nailing her, whoever she might be, or even whomever.

Tomorrow's another day, he thought, and nothing's over till it's over.

The next envelope arrived at the end of the day.

It, too, contained just a single note:

Come on; there is sixpence for you: let's have a song.

"A song," Carella said. "The violinist again. Sallas."

"The ransom's gonna be *sixpence!*" Genero said.

"Brilliant, Richard. You know what sixpence is?"

"Of course I know what it is! What is it?"

"Six *pennies*, Richard."

"Then why didn't he say so?"

"But you notice he's gone from twelve to six?" Willis said.

"That's right," Meyer said. "It was twelve in the last note."

"Now it's six."

"He's going *backwards* again," Kling said.

"Six-twelve," Meyer said.

" 'And she goes down at twelve,' " Eileen quoted.

"Yes, *ma'am!*" Parker said, and waggled his eyebrows at her.

"Get your mind out of the gutter, Andy. Maybe he's using a *different* kind of slang."

"Who, Shakespeare?" Genero asked.

"No, the Deaf Man. Maybe he's telling us when the *crime* will go down."

"Twelve noon, you mean?"

"No. Six-twelve."

"Huh?"

"Maybe that's what all the backwards bullshit was about. Maybe he's saying June twelfth. Maybe he's saying *tomorrow.*"

"*When* tomorrow?" Parker asked.

"Sometime before supper?" Willis said.

"How about three o'clock?"

"That's both the library reading *and* the concert."

"So let's dog *both* events," Carella said.

The lieutenant in command of Midtown South totally dismissed the idea of anyone trying to breach the security at the library's Folger Exhibit. *Primo,* there were armed guards all over the room that housed the alarmed case in which the book was exhibited. *Secondo,* there was state-of-the-art technology in the alarm system itself. If

416

anyone so much as *breathed* on that case, alarms would sound all over the museum, *and* at the offices of Security Plus, who would call Mid South at once. There was no way anyone could even *approach* that book, no less get it out of that room.

"How about at the reading tomorrow?" Carella asked.

"What reading?" the lieutenant asked. His name was Brian O'Ryan. Carella figured he'd had a father as comical as Meyer Meyer's.

"The reading Patrick Stewart will be doing," he said.

"I don't know anything about any reading."

"Three o'clock tomorrow," Carella said.

"I'll check it out," O'Ryan said. "If I feel it calls for a police presence, I'll supply it. Provided the Captain will authorize overtime pay."

"I'll let you know if we get anything further from the possible perp," Carella said.

"The possible perp, uh-huh," the lieutenant said.

The Chief of Security at the library said much the same thing. The case containing the book was alarmed and there were armed guards in the Elizabethan Room . . .

"Is that where the reading tomorrow will

417

take place?" Carella asked.

"No, no. Do you mean Captain Picard's reading? No, that'll be in the Molson Auditorium."

"And where will the book be at that time?"

"Right where it is now."

"The Elizabethan Room."

"Yes. Under armed guard. In an alarmed case. Moreover, the case is on steel ball bearings. After the reading — which should end around four o'clock, he's only scheduled to read for an hour or so — the Head of Special Collections will accompany the guards when they wheel it out of the Elizabethan Room and into a steel vault, where it will remain locked up and secure until the Folger people came to recover it on Sunday."

"In other words . . ."

"In other words, the book will not be taken from the case until armed guards remove it and carry it to an armored car that will transport it back to Washington."

"I see," Carella said.

"However — since you seem so *terribly* concerned, Detective Coppola — we'll make sure our security staff is watching for any suspicious-looking characters lurking about the library at three o'clock tomorrow afternoon."

Carella didn't much appreciate the sarcasm, but he thanked the man, and then called Clarendon Hall.

The Director of Events there was entirely more understanding, perhaps because not too long ago there'd been a terrorist attack at the hall itself. He told Carella that ever since that devastating assault, security had been on red alert at all times. Certainly, no one intent on mischief could conceivably get past the armed guards and metal detectors at the main entrance. And if any attempt was made to do harm to the performing musicians, he would first have to get past an armed guard outside the stage door entrance, and then a battery of guards posted on either side of the stage itself.

However . . .

The director would personally phone the Eight-Four Precinct, to alert them to possible danger at tomorrow's three o'clock concert, and to ask for bulkier police protection. "Bulkier" was the exact word he'd used. Carella told him he planned to do that himself, but it never hurt to get a request straight from the horse's mouth.

So now there was nothing else the Eight-Seven could do. It was no longer their baby; they could even throw away the bath water. If the Deaf Man was after the Folger First Folio, Mid South would be there at the library to stop him. If he was after the Greek violinist, the Eight-Four would nab him at the concert hall.

Either way, the end of a brilliant career.

Confident that he'd done all he could do for now, Carella left the squadroom at six that Friday night.

As Fat Ollie himself might have said, tomorrow was indeed another day.

Ah yes.

14

Predicting a busy night tonight — because in this city Saturday night was when all the loonies came out to howl — Byrnes assigned only a skeleton crew to the day shift. Arriving at 7:45 a.m. to start their eight-hour stint were Detectives Meyer, Parker, and Genero. Meyer might have wished for slicker partners, but Carella had a wedding to attend, and Hawes was off chasing whoever had tried to kill him twice, and Kling had called in sick, so he was stuck with these two.

The first message came fifteen minutes after they'd signed in. It was delivered by a Caucasian drug addict, aged eighteen, nineteen, in there. The sealed envelope was addressed to Carella.

"I thought we were through with this guy," Parker said.

"Apparently not," Meyer said, and called Carella at home. Carella was already up and having breakfast. The wedding was scheduled for noon.

"Want me to open it?" Meyer asked.

"Be my guest," Carella said.

There was a single note in the envelope. It read:

GO TO A PRECINT'S SHIT!

"He spelled *precinct* wrong," Genero said. "Didn't he?"

Meyer read the note to Carella, misspelling and all.

"He doesn't make spelling mistakes," Carella said.

"Unless he's quoting Shakespeare."

"This isn't Shakespeare."

"What do you think?"

"An anagram," Carella said. "He's starting all over again."

"Or is he just telling us it's going to happen right here," Meyer said. "In the Eight-Seven Precinct."

"Maybe that, too. Let me talk to my son."

"Huh?" Meyer said.

The name in the mailbox was Edward Cudahy.

Hawes had not got the address until eight this morning when finally he'd reached Rudy Mancuso, who'd told him Saturday was Eddie's day off, and wanted to know why Hawes wanted to talk to him again. Hawes told him he needed to confirm some information he'd got from Cudahy's partner, Franklin Hopper. A total fabrication, but Mancuso gave him the address.

The apartment number was 3B.

There was no lock on the glass-paneled inner lobby door. Hawes opened it and found himself facing a steep flight of stairs. A narrow corridor to the right of the steps led to an apartment at the end of the ground-floor level. He began climbing. It was now eight-thirty in the morning, and the building was heavy with sleep. On the third floor, he took his gun from its shoulder holster.

There was no sound from behind the door to apartment 3B. He listened a moment longer, and then tapped at the door. Waited. A voice called, "Yes?"

"Federal Express," he said.

"Fed . . . ?"

A puzzled silence.

He waited.

The door came open some four inches, held by a night chain. Eddie Cudahy's face appeared in the narrow opening. His eyes widened the moment he recognized Hawes. The door was already starting to close again. In that single instant, Hawes had to decide whether or not to kick it in. He was not armed with a No-Knock warrant, but the guy in there might have fired a rifle at him on two separate occasions. Possibly blow the later court case, or lose the perp now? Which? Choose!

His flat-footed kick snapped the chain and sent the door flying inward. He followed it into the room, saw Cudahy running for the window and the fire escape beyond, saw too in those next immediate sudden seconds that the walls of the single room were covered with photographs of Honey Blair.

"Stop or I'll shoot!" he shouted, and was grateful when Cudahy stopped and put his hands up over his head.

It's easy to find things when you're a kid.

It's even easy to find 1,253 anagrams for the words **GO TO A PRECINT'S SHIT!** because that's exactly how many there were on the internet site Young Sherlock Holmes called up for his big detective father. Scattered among those that made no sense at all were some actual phrases or sentences that seemed to mean something:

GO STOP A CRETIN!

"He's calling himself a cretin," Mark said.

"That, he ain't," Carella said.

A NICE GROT STOP!

"What's a grot?" Carella asked.

"British slang," Mark said. "Brit kid in my class says that all the time. 'I feel a bit grot today.'"

"So what's a 'grot stop'?"

"A break when you're not feeling too good?"

"I'm not feeling too good right this minute," Carella said, and rolled his eyes.

GRITS TO A PONCE!

"What's grits?" Mark asked.

"Some kind of Southern dish," Carella said. "Made out of corn, I think. What's a ponce?"

"That's British, too," Mark said. "It's somebody who's gay." He turned from the computer. "Is this guy gay? The one who's sending you these notes?"

"I don't think so."

A NEGRO COP TITS!

"Well, hello," Mark said, and grinned.

But the anagram the Deaf Man seemed to be indicating, the words that seemed best to fit **GO TO A PRECINT'S SHIT!,** was all the way down near the end of the list:

PROGNOSTICATE THIS!

He was asking them to predict.

He was asking them to forecast exactly *what* precinct shit would go down in *which* precinct on the twelfth day of June.

Today.

And she goes down at twelve.
GO TO A PRECINT'S SHIT!
PROGNOSTICATE THIS!

But *when* on the twelfth?

And *where*?

If not the library or the concert hall, then *where* in their very own precinct?

Hawes marched his prisoner into the stationhouse moments after the second note that day was delivered. The clock over the muster desk read 9:10 a.m.

"You want to take this upstairs?" Murchison asked him, and handed the envelope across the desk. He was not wearing gloves. They had given up wearing gloves when handling these envelopes because they knew there'd be no prints on them except those left by the delivering junkies.

On the second floor, Hawes dropped the envelope on Meyer's desk, and then said, "This way, Eddie."

"Who's that?" Meyer asked.

"Guy tried to kill me," Hawes said.

"He's dreaming," Cudahy told Meyer, but he accompanied Hawes down the hall toward the Interrogation Room.

Meyer shrugged and opened the envelope.

One, two, three: time, time!

"What's that supposed to mean?" Parker asked.

"It means three o'clock," Meyer said, "what do you think it means? One, two, three, bingo! He's giving us the exact time, the *time!* It's either the folio or the violinist."

"Or something else at one, is a possibility," Parker said. "Or even something at two."

"I thought it was supposed to be precinct shit now," Genero said.

He had gone outside to look at the word lettered across the top of the entrance doors, and sure enough the Deaf Man had spelled it wrong.

"Maybe it *is* something in the precinct," Parker said. "At one or two o'clock."

Actually, he didn't care where it was or when it was. All he knew was that at four o'clock he'd go home.

Meyer was already on the phone with Carella, reading him the note.

"What happened to the anagrams?" Carella asked.

"This is what we got," Meyer said.

"Call me if anything else comes in," Carella told him. "I'll be here till eleven."

"I saw you the first time you came up to the station," Cudahy told Hawes. He had decided that maybe it was best to cooperate here. Maybe if he explained his side of it, Hawes would understand. On television, there were sympathetic cops who understood a person's side of it.

"This was after she taped the Valparaiso kidnapping last month," Cudahy said. "I spotted you going into the screening room together to watch the tape. The screening room is right down the hall from Transportation. I saw you when you went in, and

I saw you when you came out together. I knew something was going on right then. Knew it right off. Figured I had to stop it."

"Why?" Hawes asked.

"Why? Because I have an investment in her."

"Oh, you do, huh? What kind of investment, if you don't mind?"

"An *emotional* investment. I watched her from the very beginning, from when she first came to the station from Iowa, when they had her doing these remotes from godforsaken places all over the city, in weather you could freeze yourself, those little skirts she wears, in rainstorms, snowstorms, even places that were dangerous, drug dealers, hookers, they sent her everywhere! And I was watching her. So I wasn't about to let somebody step in and take my place, not after all those years of her paying her dues."

"Take your place, huh?"

"Yes! My rightful place!"

"Did she even know you *existed?* Does she know you exist *now?*"

Hawes was trying to keep this from getting too personal here. But this little son of a bitch had tried to kill him, *twice*, no less.

"Oh, she knows I exist, all right. You think she doesn't stop in Transportation every now and then, thank us for the good service we provide, the cars we send her? You think she doesn't know I'm taking good care of her? She gave me a signed picture last Christmas. Autographed personally to me. 'To Eddie, With Warmest Wishes, Honey.' Warmest wishes. You think that means nothing, warmest wishes?"

"So you decided to kill me."

"Only when you started sleeping over. Until then . . . listen, she's entitled to friends, that's okay with me. I didn't mind you taking her to restaurants, to movies, that was okay. But . . ."

"What'd you do, follow us?"

"Just to make sure you didn't harm her."

"Followed us all over the city, is that it?"

"To *protect* her! But when you started staying at her place nights . . . no. That wasn't right. It just wasn't right. No."

He was shaking his head now, convincing himself that this wasn't right, trying to convince Hawes as well that this simply wasn't right.

"Did you know I was a cop?"

"Not at first."

"How about later?"

"Yes."

"But you didn't think I could protect

her, huh? A police officer? Couldn't protect her, huh?"

"*You're* the one I was trying to protect her *from!*"

"So you tried to kill me."

"Tried to keep you away from her."

"And almost killed her in the bargain!"

"I didn't know she was in the car. I thought the driver had dropped her off at Four, and then gone to pick you up. I was waiting for you on Jefferson Avenue, but I didn't know she was with you."

"Waiting to *kill* me," Hawes said.

"To *warn* you."

"But *killing* me would've been all right, too, huh?"

"You should have kept away from her. It was your fault I almost hurt her. I apologized for that."

"Oh, you did, huh?"

"In the note I wrote."

"What note?"

"I sent her an apology. Told her I was sorry, I didn't know she was in the limo."

"When was this?"

"Right after what happened on Jefferson Avenue. The incident there."

"*Incident!* Attempted *murder,* you mean!"

And then, suddenly, what Cudahy had just said sunk in. If he'd really written

431

Honey a note of apology, then she'd known all along that she hadn't been his intended victim. All that stuff on television . . .

"Go ask her, you don't believe me," Cudahy said.

Hawes guessed he'd have to.

Meyer and his two brilliant sleuths were still pondering the first two notes when the third one arrived at twelve minutes to ten. It read:

Why, sir, is this such a piece of study? Now here is three studied, ere ye'll thrice wink:

Meyer called Carella at once.

"He's zeroing in on three," he told him.

"Going backwards, too," Carella said. "Halving the numbers each time. First twelve, then six, now three."

"Backwards and *smaller.*"

"Right. Spears, arrows, darts, remember?"

"If he's saying three o'clock," Meyer said, "then it's still either Clarendon Hall or the library."

"Neither of which is in our precinct."

"So what was all that about 'a precinct's shit'?"

"Might've had nothing to do with anything. Just an anagram for 'prognosticate this.' Just him telling us to predict."

"*Or* . . ." Meyer said.

"Yeah?"

"Did you notice he said '*a* precinct's shit'? Not '*the* precinct's shit.' What he said was 'Go to *a* precinct's shit.' "

"So?"

"So . . . if it's three o'clock, then it's Clarendon Hall or the library. It's either the Eight-Four's shit, or Mid South's. Not ours."

"Yeah, I get what you're saying."

"Although . . ."

"Yeah?"

"He says, '*Go* to a precinct's shit.' *Go* to it. Maybe he's telling us to send some of our own people to both venues."

"Yeah, maybe."

"It's a thought, isn't it?" Meyer said.

Carella could almost see him smiling.

"It's a good thought," he said. "Let's see what he sends next."

"You put on your tuxedo yet?"

"Just about to."

The next note came at 10:27 a.m.

My lord, I was born about three

"Three o'clock for sure," Meyer told Carella on the phone. "That still makes it either Sallas and the Eight-Four, or the folio and Mid South."

"We're covered either way," Carella said.

"Right."

Both men fell silent.

"The thing is . . ."

"I know."

"If it's either Mid South or the Eight-Four, why's he breaking *our* balls?"

"Maybe we're reading this all wrong," Meyer said.

"You think?"

"No, I think we've got it right."

"But, you know . . ."

"Yeah."

"All that tight security."

"Right."

"He can't *really* be telling us it's three o'clock, can he?"

Both men were silent again.

"So how do you want to work this?"

"I've got a wedding to go to."

"You know what I think?"

"Say."

"We have nothing to worry about. The

434

Eight-Four is sending its people over, and so is Mid South."

"Right. So we're okay."

"I think so."

"Me, too."

"Don't you think?"

"I guess."

"What?"

"I don't know. It's just . . . with this guy . . ."

"I know."

"He may be planning to blow up the Calm's Point Bridge, who the hell knows? All the rest of it may be bullshit, just like Parker says."

"Yeah, well, Parker," Meyer said, lowering his voice.

Carella looked at the clock again.

"I gotta get out of here," he said.

"Good luck," Meyer said.

NOSTRADAMUS!

It was writ large. And the slanted exclamation point lent urgency to the word, demanding attention.

"Another anagram, right?" Genero said.

"Wrong," Parker said. "Nostra Damus is a college in the Midwest."

Meyer was thinking about the anagram

they'd received first thing this morning:

GO TO A PRECINT'S SHIT!

Which they'd rearranged as:

PROGNOSTICATE THIS!

He'd been taught by his grandfather that Nostradamus was a sixteenth-century French physician who'd become famous during his lifetime and afterward because of his talent for prophesying the future. Prophecies. Prognostications. Prognosticate *this*, amigo! And now Nostradamus, who had fascinated Meyer's grandfather only because he'd been born of Jewish parents.

"Nostradamus was . . ." Meyer started to explain, but Genero said, "There's 'SUM' again."

"Where?" Parker asked.

"Backwards," Genero said. "Don't you remember?"

"Remember *what?*" Parker asked impatiently.

"All those notes we got. Where are those copies, Meyer?"

Meyer found the copied notes, spread them on his desktop.

"Here you go," Genero said. "Here's the one I mean."

But she would spell him backward

"So?" Parker said.
"And this one," Genero said.

MUST SELL AT TALLEST SUM

"*So?*" Parker insisted.
"So here's 'SUM' *again*," he said. "*Backwards*," he said, and tapped the most recent note:

NOSTRADAMUS!

"Start at the end of the word," he said.
"It's not a word, it's a *name*," Meyer said. "Nostradamus. He was . . ."
"Whatever," Genero said. "M-U-S is S-U-M backwards. The last four letters of the word . . ."
"The *name*."
". . . are an anagram for 'A SUM.' "
Parker was nodding. He had to admit the little jackass was right. "A sum," he said. "The ransom he'll be asking."
"In fact," Genero said, if you *keep* going backwards . . . look at this, willya? . . . you

get 'DARTS.' Isn't that what he was telling us a long time ago. Arrows to slings to darts? Here . . . where is it?" he said, and began rummaging through the notes on Meyer's desk. "Here. Here you go."

Filling the air with swords advanced and darts,
We prove this very hour.

"Three o'clock is the hour he gave us," Meyer said, and looked up at the clock; this very hour was now a quarter to twelve.
"The point is," Genero said, beginning to enjoy his role as visiting lecturer, "we've got anagrams for both 'A SUM' and 'DARTS' . . . so what *else* might there be in this single word?"
"It's a name," Meyer told him again.
"The name of a college," Parker agreed.
They all looked at the note again:

NOSTRADAMUS*!*

"As a matter of fact," Parker said, "it's '*NO* DARTS.' "
"We're back to him using a gun again," Meyer said.
"A rod, right."
"At a concert."

438

"Maybe."

"Let's see what that looks like," Parker said, beginning to have a little fun here himself. " 'NO DARTS' and 'A SUM,' " he said, and lettered the words on a sheet of blank paper:

NO DARTS A SUM!

"Try it backwards," Meyer said. "He keeps telling us to go backwards."

A SUM NO DARTS!

"Add a comma to it," Meyer suggested.
"Where?"
"After 'SUM.' "
Parker pencilled it in:

A SUM, NO DARTS!

"Pay a *sum*," Genero said, "a *ransom*, and I won't shoot you with poisoned *darts*."
"That's ridiculous," Parker said.
"He says so right in this other note here," Genero said, and found it, and, using his forefinger, tapped it with great certainty:

**For piercing steel and darts
    envenomed**

Shall be as welcome to the ears

"Poisoned *darts*," he said, nodding in agreement with his own deduction. "If you don't pay the ransom, I'll shoot you in your *ears* with poisoned *darts!*"

"No, he's talking *music* there," Meyer said.

"Where?" Parker asked.

"Here."

Shall be as welcome to the ears

"He's referring to music. 'Welcome to the ears.' The violinist again."

"Sallas."

"Clarendon Hall."

"Three o'clock," Meyer said, and again looked up at the clock.

The time was now 11:56 a.m.

Here come the brides, Carella thought, all dressed in white, one on each arm, mother and daughter looking somewhat alike in their nuptial threads and short coiffed hairdos, neither wearing a veil, each radiant in anticipation.

And there at the altar, looking up the center aisle of the church as Carella approached with their imminent wives . . .

440

There at the altar were the two grooms, Luigi Fontero and Henry Lowell, each looking serious albeit nervous, the priest standing behind them and between them and looking happier than either of them.

The organ music stopped.

They were at the altar now.

Carella handed off his mother to Luigi on his left, and his sister to Lowell on his right . . .

So long, Mom, he thought. So long, Slip.

. . . and went to sit beside Teddy in the first row of pews. Teddy took his hand and squeezed it. He nodded.

He listened dry-eyed as the priest first told the gathered assemblage that they were here today to join in holy wedlock not just Louise Carella and Luigi Fontero, but *also* Angela Carella and Henry Lowell . . .

Someone in the pews behind Carella tittered at the novelty of it all; some novelty, he thought.

. . . and listened dry-eyed as the priest first recited the words for his mother and Luigi to repeat . . .

. . . and watched dry-eyed as Luigi slipped the wedding band onto his mother's hand and kissed his bride, Carella's mother . . .

. . . and listened again dry-eyed as his

sister and Henry Lowell repeated the same words . . .

. . . and watched dry-eyed as the man who'd allowed his father's killer to walk sealed their marriage with a golden circlet and a chaste kiss . . .

Till death us do part, Carella thought.

Teddy squeezed his hand again.

Again, he nodded.

He felt no joy.

15

It was almost twelve-thirty when Sharyn got back to the apartment. Kling was waiting for her, waiting to confront her. He'd known she was lying the moment she told him she was going to her office this morning. He knew the office in Rankin Plaza was closed on Saturdays, and he knew her private office on Ainsley Avenue was similarly closed. So while she was in the shower, he yelled to her that he was heading out, and then he went downstairs and waited for her to come out of the building. He then followed her not to Rankin and not to Ainsley but to a coffee shop on Belvedere and Ninth where who should be waiting for her but Dr. James Melvin Hudson himself in person.

Kling had watched them through the plate glass windows fronting the street.

Hudson leaning over the table.

Sharyn's head close to his.

Talking earnestly, seriously.

Taking her hands at one point.

Crying?

Was he *crying?*

Now, at three minutes to one, he waited for her in his own apartment, waited for the sound of her key in the latch, the key he had given her, waited to confront her.

He was sitting on the couch facing the entrance door. On one end of the couch was the small pillow she'd had needle-pointed with the words:

Share
Help
Love
Encourage
Protect

. . . the first letters of which spelled out the word SHLEP, a Yiddish word that translated literally as "to drag, or pull, or lag behind," but which in this city's common usage had come to mean "a long haul," a "drag" indeed, as in "a shlep and a half."

The words on Kling's pillow were needlepointed in white on black. Those on the identical pillow in Sharyn's apartment were black on white. They were in this to-gether, for the long haul. Or so he'd thought. They knew it would be a shlep and a half, a white man and a black woman. But they knew they could get through it if they merely respected those five simple rules: **S**hare, **H**elp, **L**ove, **E**ncourage, **P**rotect. Or so he'd believed until now.

He heard the key turning in the lock.

The door opened.

When the doorman called upstairs to tell her the driver from Regal was here, Melissa said, "Ask him to wait, please. I'll be right down."

She checked herself in the hall mirror . . .

Sweater tight enough to warrant admiration, skirt short enough to inspire whistles, strappy high-heeled sandals, altogether the image of either a top fashion model or a high-priced call girl, often indistinguishable one from the other these days. Satisfied, she picked up her purse, and went downstairs to meet whatever destiny awaited her on this bright Saturday afternoon.

Luigi's brother was talking to Carella. Or rather, the brother — who possessed another fine old ginzo name, Mario — was talking *at* him, regaling him in broken English with stories about Luigi when he was young.

Mario Fontero was telling him they'd been born into a poor family in Milan. Luigi and Mario, the Nintendo brothers. Mario was telling him that even when he was a boy, Luigi had been a hard worker. Mario was telling him that Luigi had gone to university and graduated with honors. Mario was telling him that Luigi had started his own furniture business.

On the dance floor, Luigi was holding Carella's mother close.

His wife now.

Luigi Fontero's wife.

Sharyn closed the door behind her.

Locked it.

"How'd it go at the office?" Kling asked.

"I didn't go to the office," she said.

He looked at her.

"Why'd you follow Julie?" she asked.

"What?"

"Julia Curtis. Why'd you go to her building and ask her letter carrier . . . ?"

"Why'd *you* go meet Jamie Hudson this morn . . . ?"

"What the hell is going on, Bert!"

"You tell me!"

The room went silent.

"Have you been following me?" she asked.

"Yes," he said. "Have you . . ."

"Why?"

". . . been *lying* to me?"

"Yes."

"Why?"

"Because . . ."

She cut herself short.

"Yes, tell me. Why'd you lie to me?"

"To protect Julie."

"Who the hell *is* she, Sharyn? Have you and Hudson been . . . ?"

"She's a very troubled girl . . ."

"Oh, please, spare me the . . ."

". . . who has to make the most difficult decision in her life. And if she decides the wrong way . . ."

"Is she in trouble with the law?"

"Of *course* not!"

"Then why do you have to protect her from me?"

"Because you wouldn't understand the situation."

"What situation? You and your *colleague* Dr. Hudson meeting her on the . . ."

"What's wrong with you? You surely don't think . . ."

". . . sly? You mean you and your little *Jamie* boy . . ."

"Is *that* what you th . . . ?"

"What am I *supposed* to think? You go

447

sneaking around . . ."

"Julie has a serious problem!"

"Oh? Does her Mama disapprove of a three-way with two black . . . ?"

Sharyn slapped him.

"I'm sorry," she said at once.

The room went utterly still.

"It's not what you think," she said.

"Then tell me what it is," he said.

The driver's name was Jack.

"Is it still Burtonwood's, ma'am?" he asked.

Burtonwood's was a department store downtown on Jefferson. Adam had given this as the destination when he'd called Regal.

"Yes, but I have to make a stop first," she said.

"Yes, ma'am," he said.

"I have to pick up a lamp," she said. "To return to the store."

"Very well, ma'am," he said.

She was sitting on the backseat, positioned so that he could see her in the rearview mirror. She wasn't wearing panties, and her skirt was high enough on her thighs for Jack here to see China 'crost the bay.

"Will it fit in the trunk, ma'am?" he

asked. "The lamp?"

"Oh yes," she said, and gave him the address of the Knowlton Hotel on Ludlow Street.

The game was afoot.

NOSTRADAMUS!

"Here's *another* one spelled backwards," Genero said.

"Where?" Meyer asked.

"Right here," Genero said, pointing. " 'MAD ARTS.' That's 'STRADAM' spelled backwards."

Indeed it was:

STRADAM
MAD ARTS

" 'STRADAM' ain't even a word," Parker said.

"Who said it was?"

"Just what *are* you saying, Richard?"

"I'm saying 'MAD ARTS' is a word. *Two* words, in fact."

"And just what is 'MAD ARTS' supposed to mean?"

"A crazy modern painting."

"Right," Parker said. "He's gonna kidnap the Mona Lisa."

449

"Or some *other* crazy modern painting," Genero said.

Meyer looked again at the anagram in Parker's handwriting:

A SUM, NO DARTS!

He still didn't get it.

"Knowlton Hotel, ma'am," Jack said. "Shall I just wait here?"

"Can you help me carry it down?" she asked. "The lamp?"

He looked as if he didn't fully understand, but his role in all this would be over in the next ten minutes or thereabouts, so it didn't matter whether he quite got it or not.

"It's sort of heavy," she said, and uncrossed her legs to afford him a better view of the dawn coming up like thunder.

"Of course, ma'am," he said, thinking he was beginning to get the drift. "I'll be happy to."

He followed her into the elevator and up to the sixth floor. He followed her down the hall to room 642. He waited behind her while she inserted a key into the lock. She felt certain he was checking out her splendid ass in its short tight skirt.

"Come in, please, Jack," she said, and smiled over her shoulder in blatant invitation.

He stepped into the room, thinking there wasn't a lamp at all, and grinning in sly anticipation, when all at once all the lamps in the world went out because that was when the Deaf Man hit him on the head with a somewhat blunt instrument.

At two o'clock sharp, a uniformed driver from Regal Limousine pulled up to the parking area in front of the Intercontinental Hotel, stepped out of the luxury sedan, and told the doorman he was here for Mr. Konstantinos Sallas.

The doorman went inside, buzzed the suite upstairs, and told Mr. Sallas that his car was here. Sallas, in turn, rang his bodyguard's room, told him the car was here, told his wife he'd see her backstage after the concert, kissed her goodbye, and picked up his violin case. He met Jeremy Higel at the elevators, and together they went down to the lobby and out into the street, where the uniformed driver was standing outside the black car, waiting for them.

"Mr. Sallas?" he asked.

"Yes?"

"Nice to meet you, sir," the driver said, and rushed to open the rear door for them. When they were comfortably seated, he climbed in behind the wheel, turned to them, and asked, "Would you be more comfortable with the violin up front, sir?"

"Thank you, no, I'll keep it here," Sallas said, and gave the case a little proprietary pat.

"Clarendon Hall then," the driver said, and started the car.

Neither of them noticed that there was a hearing aid in his right ear.

Luigi Fontero's sister was telling Carella all about the gardens of Rome, where she lived. He gathered this was what she was talking about since he heard the word *Roma* and also the word *giardini*. Otherwise, he caught little else of what she was saying because she was speaking in rapid-fire Italian.

"Uh-huh," he said.

"*A Roma,*" she said and rolled her eyes, "bella *Roma, ci sono molti giardini . . .*"

"Uh-huh," he said.

"*Per esempio,*" she said, "*ci sono i giardini della Villa Aldobrandini a Frascati, ed anche i giardini . . .*"

"Uh-huh," he said.

". . . *della Vila d'Este a Tivoli. Ma, se-cundo me . . .*"

"Excuse me," Carella said.

"*. . . i piu belli giardini . . .*"

"*Scusi,*" he said, "excuse me," and got up and moved through the dancers on the crowded floor — his sister dancing with Uncle Mike now, all suntanned and bald from Florida, his mother dancing with her new son-in-law, the assistant district attorney Henry Lowell — and worked his way to the men's room. On his way back to the table, where he now saw Alberta Fontero was bending somebody else's ear about the fabulous gardens of Rome, he stopped in the banquet hall's office, and asked a twenty-year-old kid behind the desk there if he could use the phone.

"There's a pay phone in the men's room," the kid said.

"This is police business," Carella said, and showed his shield. The kid looked at it as if he thought it might be fake, but he indicated the phone, shrugged, and walked out.

Carella began dialing the squadroom.

"Eighty-seventh Squad, Meyer."

"It's me," Carella said.

"Is that music I hear?"

"Yeah, let me close this door."

He got up, came around the desk, closed the door on the Sonny Sabatino Orchestra, and came back to the phone again.

"I'm glad you called," Meyer said. "Have you got a pencil?"

Carella took a pencil from a cup on the desk. He found a crumpled sheet of paper in the wastebasket, pulled it out, smoothed it, and said, "What've you got?"

"Nostradamus," Meyer said. "That's N-O-S . . ."

"T-R-A . . ." Carella said, nodding.

"You know it?"

"Nostradamus, sure. The Greek prophet."

"French," Meyer said.

"Whatever."

"Write it down."

Carella wrote it down:

NOSTRADAMUS

"Okay, got it," he said.

In the movies, this was that stretch of turf alongside the river, under the bridge, where the nasty bad guys pulled up in their big black cars for a face-off about dope or prostitution.

In real life, this was that very same spot.

454

And Konstantinos Sallas knew this was not Clarendon Hall.

"Driver?" he said, and tapped on the glass partition separating them from the front seat. The glass slid open. "Where are we?" he asked. "Is something . . . ?"

And realized he was looking into the barrel of an automatic weapon.

Jeremy Higel, the Greek's bodyguard, was already reaching under his jacket.

"No, don't," the Deaf Man said.

The hand stopped.

The Deaf Man gestured with the Uzi.

"Get out," he said. "Both of you."

"Wh . . . ?"

"Get out of the fucking *car!*"

Sallas reached for his violin case.

"Leave it," the Deaf Man said.

NOSTRADAMUS

"That's the latest from our friend," Meyer said. "Nostradamus."

"Just the name?" Carella asked.

"That's all. We've been juggling it around up here. So far, we've got 'A SUM' backwards . . ."

"Uh-huh, 'A SUM,' I see it . . .' "

A MUS

455

"Backwards, right?"

"Right. Backwards."

A SUM

"And 'DARTS' is buried in there, too. You see it there? 'DARTS'?"

"Right," Carella said, "I've got it."

DARTS

"The way *arrows* was buried in *sparr* —" Meyer started, and then interrupted himself. "Help you?" he asked. Carella heard a muffled voice on the other end, away from the phone. "Thanks," he heard Meyer say.

"What've you got?" he asked.

"Another one."

"Another what?"

"A letter. A note. Addressed to you again."

There was a crackling silence on the line.

"Well, *open* it!" Carella said.

Outside the closed door to the office, he could hear the Sonny Sabatino Orchestra playing *Mezzo Luna, Mezzo Mare* . . .

Heard wedding guests joining in with the lyrics . . .

Heard Meyer ripping open the envelope . . .

"Meyer?"

"Yeah."
"What does it say?"

To-day, to-day, unhappy day, too late

"Meyer?"
Meyer read it to him.
"What's he mean?" Carella asked.
"Mama mi, me maritari . . . ."
"I don't know," Meyer said.
"Figghia mi, a cu . . . ."
Carella glanced at the note on his desk:

NOSTRADAMUS

"Damn it, what's he . . . ?"
"Mama mi, pensaci . . . ."

A SUM

"Si ci dugnu . . . ."

DARTS

"Oh, Jesus, it's DARTS *backwards!*"
Carella said.

STRAD

"It's the violin!"

★ ★ ★

The violin in the case now tucked under the Deaf Man's right arm was one of a precious few created by Antonio Stradivari, the master violin-maker, in the early 1700's — the so-called Golden Period during which he made only twenty-four violins. Sallas's violin was one of them, a year older than the so-called "Kreutzer" Stradivarius that had recently sold at auction for $1,560,000. The "Taft," another Stradivarius violin made in that same period, sold at Christie's for a million-three. The "Mendelssohn" Strad had sold for a million-six. The "Milanollo" of 1728, conserved rather than played over the centuries, was largely considered to be worth at least that much. By a conservative estimate, the Deaf Man calculated that Sallas's precious little fiddle here was worth something between a million-two and a million-seven — not bad apples for a few weeks' work, eh, Gertie?

He had driven back to the Knowlton Hotel to make certain that Jack the driver was still securely bound and gagged, had patted him on the head, smiled, and gone to change out of the chauffeur's uniform he'd purchased last week at Conan Uniforms on Baxter Street. Driving the Regal

458

luxury sedan to a side street some ten blocks from his apartment, he'd bid the car a fond farewell, and left it there locked. The last words he'd heard on the car radio were, "Jack? Are you there, Jack? Have you got your passenger? What the hell is going *on*, man?"

Now, at twenty minutes to three — wearing a blue suit with the faintest gray shadow stripe, wearing as well a gray shirt that picked up the stripe, and a blue tie that echoed the suit, black shoes, blue socks, the black violin case tucked under his arm — the Deaf Man whistled a merry tune as he strolled jauntily back to the apartment on River Place South — where Melissa Summers was busy cracking his computer.

On the phone to Midtown South, Carella told the lieutenant there what he thought was about to happen; the Deaf Man was planning to steal Konstantinos Sallas's priceless Stradivarius violin. The lieutenant promised to send a contingent of his detectives over to Clarendon at once. He called back five minutes later to say the boys were on the way. But he'd also called Clarendon and the director there was concerned because Sallas hadn't shown up yet, and it was already twenty minutes to three.

"Where was he coming from?" Carella asked.

"The Intercontinental," the lieutenant told him.

"Right here in the Eight-Seven," Carella said, and remembered the Deaf Man's first note that Saturday morning:

GO TO A PRECINT'S SHIT!

"How was he getting there?"

"Car and driver."

And Carella remembered another note from what now seemed a long time ago:

**Even such, they say, as stand in narrow lanes
And beat our watch, and rob our passengers.**

"Carella? You still there?"

"I'm still here," he said.

Outside, he could hear the Sonny Sabatino Orchestra starting another set, saxophones soaring. The words of the Deaf Man's final note echoed in his mind:

To-day, to-day, unhappy day, too late

. . . and he realized all at once that the violin had *already* been stolen, yes, right here in the old Eight-Seven.

Outside, the orchestra was playing a sad sweet song.

For no good reason he could discern, Carella put his head on his folded arms and began sobbing.

The thing about a computer was that it not only told you where to find things, it also told you where you'd *gone* to find those things. So right here in Adam's little office at the rear of the apartment, there was a pretty good record of all the sites he'd visited in the past few weeks, especially those he'd marked as favorites. Which showed he trusted her. She guessed. Leaving them there for her to see. Or maybe he wasn't as smart as she thought he was.

All this stuff about violins made by this guy Stradivari. Oh my! So *that's* what Adam was after, the Greek's fiddle. My, my, my. Page after page of computer information about Stradivari and Amati and Guarneri and the 18th century, and the prices all these various violins had fetched at various auctions, and who owned which violin when, or even now, and even what kind of varnish was used on them, my, my, my, Melissa thought.

So that's what he'd meant about a seven-figure payday. My, my. A violin. Who'd've imagined it? A mere violin. And, oh my, lookee here. All the sites he'd visited while composing the little notes she'd delivered for him, and folders he'd made to store files from those sites, folders with titles like **SPEARS**, and **ARROWS**, and **DARTS**, and more folders titled **ANAGRAMS**, and **PALINDROMES**, and yet more folders titled **NUMBERS**, and **TIMES**, and on and on, oh my oh my.

There was also a folder titled **SKED**, and when she opened that she found a file titled **CALENDAR**. She thought at first that this might tell her something about their trip to Tortola, but no, it was just a sort of coded timetable for the past week:

MON 6/7   **DARTS**
TUE 6/8   **BACK TO THE FUTURE**
WED 6/9   **NUMBERS**
THU 6/10 **PALS**
FRI 6/11 **WHEN?**
SAT 6/12 **NOW!**

But he'd been serious about taking her to Tortola once this was all over, because sure enough here was a folder titled **TRAVEL**, and inside that was a file called **AIR**. And there before Melissa's very eyes, right there on the computer screen, was a flight itinerary:

Date:	13JUNE–SUNDAY
Flight:	AMERICAN AIRLINES 1635
Departure:	SPNDRFT INTL 9:30 AM
Arrival:	SAN JUAN PR 2:11 PM

. . . .

Date:	13JUNE–SUNDAY
Flight:	AMERICAN AIRLINES 5374
Departure:	SAN JUAN PR 3:00 PM
Arrival:	TORTOLA BEEF IS 3:39 PM

Which made her wonder if he'd already booked the flights.
So she kept surfing.

Carella was sitting there at the desk with his head on his folded arms, wondering why this wedding today had been so joyless for him, wondering why he hadn't danced with either his mother or his sister today, wondering why both the champagne and the music had seemed so flat today. And he thought, My father should be here today. He thought, My father should still be alive. But of course, his father was dead.

Luigi Fontero stopped in the doorway to the banquet hall's small office, looked in, puzzled, and then went to the desk, and came around it, and put his hand on Carella's shoulder.

"Steve?" he said. "*Ma che cosa?* What's the matter?"

Carella looked up into his face.

"*Figlio mio,*" Luigi said. "My son. *Dica mi.* Tell me."

And Carella said, "I miss him so much," and threw himself into Luigi's arms, and began sobbing again.

She was waiting for him when he got back to the apartment with the violin. He set it down on the hall table, next to the phone there, as casually as if the Strad were worth a nickel instead of more than a million. He put the blue sports bag containing the Uzi on the floor then, just under the table. Turning to her, he said, "I see you got back all right."

"Oh, yes," she said. "Took a taxi over from the Knowlton. Hardly any traffic at all." She nodded at the violin case. "I see you got back all right, too," she said.

"Indeed." He came across the room to her, arms outstretched. "What've you been doing?" he asked.

"Surfing your computer," she said.

"Oh?"

"Yes."

He looked at her. Arms still stretched to embrace her, but not so sure now. She couldn't tell whether the look on his face was quizzical or amused or just what. She didn't much care what it was; she knew what she knew.

"Now why'd you do that?" he asked.

Quizzical, she guessed. The look. Or amused. Not at all menacing. Not yet, anyway.

"Oh, just keeping myself busy," she said. "A girl can learn lots of things from a computer."

"And did you learn lots of things?"

"I learned how much the fiddle there is worth."

"I told you how much it's worth."

"Seven figures, you said. Isn't that right?"

"Yep."

"That's what the computer said, too."

"Why'd you have to go to the computer to learn what I'd already . . . ?"

"You didn't tell me you were stealing a

precious violin, Adam."

"There was no need for you to know that."

"No, there was only a need for me to socialize with junkies . . ."

"You were free to choose your own messeng . . ."

". . . and fuck a bodyguard, and let a chauffeur think I was *about* to fuck him."

"Is something wrong, Lissie?" he asked, trying to look concerned and pleasant and caring.

"Oh yes, something is wrong," she said, and reached into her handbag, and pulled out an American Airlines ticket folder and flapped it on the air. "*This* is wrong," she said.

"Where'd you get that, Liss?"

"Top drawer of your office desk. Right under the computer."

"You *have* been busy."

"It's a one-way ticket to Tortola," she said. "Made out to Adam Fen."

"There's another ticket in that drawer, Liss."

"No, there isn't. I turned it upside down and inside out, I looked through that whole damn desk, *and* your dresser, too, *and* all the pockets in all the suits and jackets in your closet, and there is no other ticket. There is just this one ticket, Adam. *Your* ticket. You never planned to take me with you at all, did you?"

"Where'd you get such an idea, Liss? Of *course* you're coming with me. Let me find the other ticket. Let me show you . . ."

"There is no other ticket, Adam."

"Liss."

"There *is* none!" she said, and shook the folder on the air again. "You never planned to give me any part of that million-whatever, did you? You just used me, the same way Ame Carter used me. I was just a handy little whore to you, wasn't I?"

"Well," he said, and smiled, and spread his hands reasonably, "that's what you are, isn't it, Liss."

Which was perhaps a mistake.

He realized this when he saw her dip into her bag again and come up with not another airline ticket, but with what looked instead like a small nine-millimeter pistol.

"Careful," he said.

"Oh yes, careful," she said, and waved the gun recklessly in the air. "Know what else I found on your computer, Adam? I found . . ."

"I can assure you, Lissie, there *is* another ticket in my desk. Let's go look for it, shall . . . ?"

"No, I don't think so."

"We'll look for it togeth . . ."

"No, we *won't* look for it together because it doesn't *exist.* Would you like to know what else I found?"

He said nothing.

He was wondering how he could get to that blue sports bag under the hall table, wondering how he could get his hands on the Uzi in that bag before she did something foolish here. He was not eager to get shot again. It had taken too long for Dr. Rickett to fix him up after the last time a woman shot him. He did not think she was going to shoot him, but he did not like the way she kept tossing that gun around so negligently.

"I found a file titled 'PROSPECTS,' " she said, "and another one titled 'BUYERS,' which had some of the same names and addresses in them, little bit of duplication there, Adam? Little redundancy?"

He said nothing.

He was wondering how he could back slowly away from her, toward the sports bag, without tipping his hand. He certainly did not want to get shot here. Not again.

"I'm figuring these are the names of people who might care to *own* that little

Stradivarius across the room, Adam, am I right?"

He still said nothing.

"Names and addresses of all those prospects and buyers, I don't think they'd give a rat's ass *who* they bought that fiddle from, you or me, so long as they get their hands on it, am I right?"

"Backups, Liss. Merely backups. In case the fiddler refuses to pay the piper."

"Meaning?"

"We'll offer the Strad to Sallas first. If he pays what we want for it . . ."

"We?"

"Of course, Liss. You and I. We. Us. If he gives us what the fiddle's worth, it's his again. If not, as you surmised, there are all those redundant prospects and buyers out there. Can you imagine such people in this world, Liss? People who don't know how to play the violin, who don't care at all about music, people who just want to own something beautiful and precious."

"I can imagine them, yes."

"Like you," he said, and tried a smile. "Beautiful and . . ."

"*Bull*shit!" she said, and waved the gun again.

"Careful with that thing," he said, and spread the fingers of his right hand on the air, sort of patting the air with them, urging caution.

"What I'm going to do right now," she said, "is buy myself a ticket to Paris or London or Rome or Berlin or Buenos Aires or Mexico City or Riyadh, where all these backups seem to live, and see which one of them might care to take this fiddle off my hands. I feel sure . . ."

"Why don't we just do that together?" he suggested.

"No, why don't we just *not* do that together!" she said, and rattled the gun on the air again. "I want to be on that plane alone. Without you, Mr. Fen. Just me and the Strad, Mr. Fen. And then I'll see about all these violin-lovers all over the world. Maybe they'll be willing to pay a handy little whore even *more* than . . ."

"I never called you a . . ."

"Oh, didn't you?" she said, and waved the gun at the floor. "Lie down, Adam. Face down. Hands behind your head. Do it!"

"Liss . . ."

"*Do* it! Now!"

"You're making a big mis . . ."

"I said *now!*"

He turned swiftly and moved closer to the hall table, and then got down on his knees, and then lowered himself flat on the floor, positioning himself so that his head and his hands were close to the hall table. He could feel her presence behind him, the gun level in her hand. If he did not make his move now . . .

In that next crackling instant, she realized he was reaching into the blue sports bag on the floor under the table, and she saw what was in that bag, saw his hand closing around the handle of the automatic weapon there. And in that same crackling instant, he saw from the corner of his eye the little gun leveling in her hand, steady now, no longer uncertain, and he tried desperately to shake the Uzi loose of the bag before . . .

Almost simultaneously, they thought exactly the same thing: *No, not again!*

She meant getting fucked by yet another pimp.

He meant getting shot by yet another woman.

Actually, she did manage to say just that single word aloud, *"No!"*, before she shot him in the back the same way she'd shot that other pimp, Ambrose Carter.

Twice.

The same way.

16

In this city, there are beginnings, and there are sometimes endings. And sometimes those endings aren't quite the ones imagined when you and I were young, Maggie, but who says they have to be? Where is it written that anyone ever promised you a rose garden? Where is it written?

"I understand someone sent you a note," Hawes said.

"I get notes all the time," Honey said.

"This note was an important one," he said.

They were in her apartment. The apartment on the seventeenth floor of the building where Eddie Cudahy had taken a potshot at him on Wednesday morning, the second day of June. *Several* potshots, in fact.

It was now three o'clock on the afternoon of the twelfth, ten days and some eight hours later, but who was counting? Hawes had already arrested, questioned, and booked Eddie Cudahy, but Honey

Blair was still in her nightgown and peignoir, trying to look innocent when she knew exactly which note Hawes was talking about. He was talking about *the* Note.

DEAR HONEY:
PLEASE FORGIVE ME AS I DID NOT KNOW YOU WERE IN THAT AUTOMOBILE.

"According to a man named Eddie Cudahy," he said, "who works for Chann . . ."

"Yes, I know," she said.

"You know *him* . . . ?"

"Vaguely."

". . . or you know the *note* I'm talking about?"

"Both."

"Why didn't you tell me about it?"

"Because Danny decided not to broadcast it."

"Who's Danny?"

"Di Lorenzo. Our Program Director."

"That was withholding evidence," Hawes said.

"Well, it certainly wasn't truth in broadcasting," she said, and smiled.

"This isn't funny," he said. "The man

473

was trying to kill me."

"Yes, well, me too, you know."

"No, *not* you too."

"Well."

"He specifically wrote . . ."

"I know."

". . . that he didn't know you were in that limo. He was after *me*, Honey. Me and me alone."

"Well, probably. Yes."

"So why'd you suppress that note?"

"I didn't. Danny suppressed it."

"But you went along with it. You went on the air every night . . ."

"Well, yes."

"Why, Honey?"

"Be good for my career," she said, and shrugged.

"But bad for my health," he said.

"Well, that too."

"Uh-huh," he said.

They looked at each other.

"This note," he said. "Was it hand-written?"

"Yes."

"Where is it now?"

"I have no idea."

"I'll need it."

"Why?"

"For evidence. We've charged Cudahy

with attempted murder."

"That's a shame. He seemed nice."

"Murder would've been a bigger shame," Hawes said.

They kept looking at each other.

"Why don't we go back to bed?" she asked.

"No, I don't think so," he said.

"Cotton . . ."

"See you," he said, and walked out.

They were on the thin edge of ending it here, and they both knew it. Sharyn had lied to him, and Kling had followed her like the detective he was, and both transgressions were grounds for packing toothbrushes. So they sat together in his apartment, silent now, Sharyn having explained (sort of) and Kling having defended (sort of), each waiting for more because each still felt betrayed.

Someone had to break the silence here.

If this thing was going to work here.

They both knew they *had* to make this thing work, because if it couldn't work right here, between this white man named Bertram Alexander Kling and this black woman named Sharyn Everard Cooke, then maybe it would never work anywhere in America between any two people of different colors. It had got down to that between them; thinking of each other as two people of different colors. But someone had to break the silence here, someone had to reach across this widening chasm.

So, reluctantly, but like the good detective he was, he weighed in his mind which had been the heavier offense, lying or following someone you were supposed to love, and he guessed his breach had been the greater one. So he cleared his throat and looked across the room to where she sat turned away from him in stony silence, arms folded across her chest, and he said, "Shar?"

She did not answer.

"Shar," he said, "I'm sorry, but I still don't quite understand."

"What is it you don't *quite* understand, *Bert?*" she said.

"If Jamie Hudson *really* wants to marry this Julie person . . ."

"She's not this Julie *person*. She's a woman named Julia *Curtis*, who happens to be a physician, just like Jamie and . . ."

"Oh, forgive me, a *physician*, please, do I need an appointment here?"

"Go to hell, Bert."

"How was I supposed to know she's a doctor? I see the three of you running around like spies in . . ."

"Yes, go to hell."

"If he wants to marry *her*, why's he meeting *you*?"

"He asked me to talk to her."

"Why?"

"Damn it, she's not *sure!*"

"Not sure of *what*, damn it!"

"That she *wants* to marry a black man!"

"So what are you, a marriage broker all of a sudden?"

"No, I'm Jamie's friend. The girl has serious doubts. She loves him, but her entire life . . ."

"Oh, I get it. You're the shining example, right? You and me. Black woman, white man, you're supposed to show her it can work, is that it?"

"You still don't get it, do you?"

"No, I'm sorry, I don't. Are you sure that's the *only* reason she won't marry him? Because he's black and she's white? Or is there . . . ?"

"She's black, too," Sharyn said.

"What?"

"I said she's black. We're all three of us black. Jamie, Julie, and me. We're all black. Get it now?"

He let this sink in. She watched him letting it sink in.

"She looks as white as . . ."

"Yes, Bert?"

"She looks white," he said.

"White enough to pass ever since she turned sixteen. She left home, left the south, went to Yale Med. She's afraid if she marries Jamie, she'll lose her white practice, lose everything she's worked so hard for all these years."

The room went silent again.

"You should have told me," he said.

"I'd have broken her trust."

"How about *my* trust?"

"How about mine, Bert?"

She said his name softly this time.

"You shouldn't have followed me," she said.

"You shouldn't have lied to me."

"Here we go again," she said.

There was another silence.

He wondered if they could ever again breach the silence.

"Whatever happened to **SHLEP?**" he asked, and picked up the needlepointed pillow, and held it against his chest so she could read it:

**Share
Help
Love
Encourage
Protect**

"I should've had them put a *T* on the end," she said. "For Trust."

"Sharyn . . ."

"You don't trust me, Bert. Maybe it's because you don't love me . . ."

"I love you with all my . . ."

". . . or maybe it's because I'm black . . ."

"Sharyn, Sharyn . . ."

"But whatever it is, the *T*'s missing, Bert. It should've been **SHLEPT.** Maybe that's what it should be now," she said, and took the pillow from his hands. "**SHLEPT.** Past tense."

He looked at her.

"Should it?" he said.

"I don't know," she said. "Should it?"

For Eileen and Willis, this was still the beginning, and this was still Saturday, the start of a weekend off for both of them, and so they were still in bed together.

"What do you think?" he asked.

"About?"

"Us?"

"Oh."

"You. Me."

"Uh-huh."

"Does that mean 'Uh-huh, I think this will last forever, we'll get married one day, and have kids, and . . .' "

"Uh-huh."

"Or does it mean 'Uh-huh, I understand your question, and I'm thinking about it'?"

"It means 'We'll see,' " she said. "But meanwhile," she said, and rolled over into his arms, and kissed him on the mouth.

Under her lips, Willis grinned.

Ollie saw her coming up the street in her tailored blues, the nine on her right hip, the weight of it giving her a sort of lop-sided gait, long black hair tucked up under her cap, silver shield pinned just above her left breast, eyes casually checking out the perimeter as she came sailing toward the diner, good cop, he thought, beautiful girl, he thought, woman. Her name tag, white letters on black plastic, read: P. GOMEZ. Who'd have thunk it? he thought. Gomez.

Her eyes lit up when she saw him, who'd have thunk *that*, either? The sun was shining, her eyes sparkled in the sunlight. Beautiful brown eyes. Patricia Gomez. He almost shook his head in wonder.

"*Hey,* Oll!" she said. "What're *you* doing here?"

Oll, he thought. Only person in the universe who calls me Oll. Not even my sister calls me Oll. Not even my *mother* called me Oll, may she rest in peace. Oll.

"Thought we could have a late afternoon snack together, ah yes," he said.

"Hey, that's terrific!" she said.

He knew she'd just been relieved on post. Knew that before she headed back in to change out of uniform, she usually stopped for a cup of coffee either here or in the coffee shop up the street. He knew all this. He prided himself on being a good cop.

She opened the door to the diner, holding it open for him to follow her inside. The proprietor knew her, of course, made a big fuss out of showing *Officer* Gomez to a fine booth in the corner. She took off her cap, hung it on one of the racks flanking the booth. Her hair was all pinned up, like.

"Well, this is a nice surprise," she said.

"I was hoping you'd be here," he said. "I'm glad I caught you."

"Me, too."

"How's it going today?"

481

"Quiet. How about you?"

"I'm off today. Put in a long week, though."

"You working something big?"

"Yeah, some pimp got aced."

"Lucky you," she said.

"Yeah. All day yesterday, I was sitting in that pocket park off River Place, you know the one?"

"Sure. Gleason Park."

"Waiting for this girl to show up, but she never did. This woman."

"That's too bad, Oll."

"Yeah."

"Kinda sad, these girls," he said.

She looked at him.

"Which girls is that, Oll?"

"These hookers, you know. I spent a lot of time in Ho Alley, too. These hookers. Standing out there, you know. Half naked."

She kept looking at him.

"Raining, too," he said.

She put down the menu.

"You okay, Oll?" she asked. "You seem kind of . . ."

"Yeah, I'm fine," he said.

"Oll?"

He nodded. Waited a long time. Then he said, "Patricia, I have to ask you something, and I want you to tell me the God's honest truth."

"You're scaring me, Oll."

"No, no. I . . ."

"Oll?"

"Patricia . . . am I a person to be comforted and helped?"

"You need a little comfort and help, Oll?" she asked, and smiled faintly. "Is that it, honey?"

"Am I a person to be . . . pitied?" he asked.

"Pitied?" she said. "No. What are you *talking* about, Oll? *Pitied?*" She almost reached across the table to grab both his hands, but then she remembered she was in uniform, and reached across with her eyes, instead, her eyes fastening to his. "What is it, Oll?" she asked. "For God's sake, what *is* it?"

He shook his head.

"Oll, Ollie, *please,*" she said.

"Am I a sorry fucked-up piece of shit?" he asked.

"Ollie, Jesus, don't say such . . ."

"Am I a fat person?" he asked.

She reached across the table, anyway, the hell with the uniform. Took both his hands in her own. Held them tight.

"Tell me the truth," he said.

She almost said, No, you're not fat, who's been telling you that, Oll? She almost said, You're a good dancer, Oll, very light on your feet.

"Yes," she said. "You're fat."

He nodded.

"But that's just eating," she said.

He nodded again.

"Cut back a little," she said, and tried a smile. "Don't order four burgers for an afternoon snack."

"How many are *you* going to have?" he asked.

"You folks decided yet?" a waitress asked.

"Just a glass of skim milk," Patricia said.

Ollie hadn't even looked at the menu yet.

"I'll have what the lady's having," he said.

"Thank you, folks," the waitress said, and swiveled off in her pink uniform.

"Remember that movie?" Patricia asked. "Where Meg Ryan fakes the orgasm? And the woman across the room says, 'I'll have whatever . . .'?"

"Yeah, that was funny," Ollie said. He was silently thoughtful for a moment. Then he said, "I never tasted skim milk in my life."

"You'll like it," Patricia said.

"I doubt it," he said glumly.

"But you know, Oll," she said, "fat, thin, who cares? I don't mind, really."

"You like going out with a fat person, huh?"

"I like going out with *you*," she said.

"Wanna go out tonight?" he asked.

"Yep."

"Why?"

"Because I *like* you," she said. "I find you creative, and . . ."

"Creative? No, Patri . . ."

"*Yes*, Oll! You wrote a *book!*"

"Well . . ."

"How many people can write a book? *I* can't write a book!"

"Well . . ."

He almost said, "I caught the faggot spic hump who stole it," but he didn't say that out loud because Patricia probably'd had lots of people calling her a spic in her lifetime, and he didn't think she'd appreciate the word coming from his mouth, although it probably was short for Hispanic, what writers called an elision, he supposed.

"I caught the guy who stole it," he said.

"Get out!"

"I did. He recited the whole thing for me. I taped it. I can start all over again, Patricia.

I can listen to it, and find out what's good or bad, and make it really work this time."

"You see what I mean? That's *so* creative, Oll, and inquisitive, and . . ."

"Come on, you'll make me blush."

"So blush," she said. "I'll bet blushing burns calories. And lively and . . . and . . . yes, you *are* a good dancer!"

"Who said I wasn't?"

"Well . . . nobody."

"So are you, Patricia."

"Thank you, Oll. I really do like the way we dance together, don't you?"

"Yes, I do."

"Maybe we can go dancing again tonight. Burn some more calories."

"Better than exercise, that's for sure," he said.

"But it *is* exercise. Dancing. You know what else you should do, Oll?"

"No what?"

"You should think about going down the police gym, run the track, lift some weights. Be good for you."

"I'd have a heart attack."

"Nah, come on, a *heart* attack! What's the matter with you? A little *exercise?* Come on!"

"Exercise is boring."

"Sure. So?"

Ollie shrugged.

"By the way," she said, "tonight's my treat. I owe you one."

"Okay, I accept," he said.

"Be a cheap date," she said, and winked. "Now that you're on a diet, right?"

He hadn't realized he was on a diet.

"And, by the way, when are you gonna learn 'Spanish Eyes' for me?" she asked.

"I almost have it down pat."

"The Al Martino version, right?"

"Right."

"*Not* the Backstreet Boys."

"Right. My piano teacher says I'm almost there."

"I want you to play it for my mother."

"Maybe I should lose a few pounds first."

"Nah, *she's* fat, too," Patricia said, and burst out laughing.

Ollie found himself laughing, too.

"Two skim milks," the waitress said, and set them down. "Anything else?" she asked, and looked at Ollie expectantly.

"Thank you, no," he said.

"You know," Patricia said, "fifty percent of all Americans want to lose twenty pounds, did you know that?"

"Yeah, well not me," he said.

"I want to lose weight, too," she said.

"You do?"

"Sure. Ten pounds or so. I would love to lose ten pounds or so."

"You think I should lose ten pounds or so?"

"Well . . . to start."

"Then what? *Twenty* pounds? Like fifty percent of Americans want to lose?"

"No, *fifty* pounds. Like *twenty* percent of Americans want to lose."

Ollie looked at her.

She grinned, shrugged.

"I made up that last statistic," she said.

"Good thing. Cause I don't plan to lose no fifty damn pounds."

"Okay, start with ten."

"Ten, I could maybe manage."

"Good, we'll both lose ten pounds."

"Both of us, huh?"

"Sure. We'll lose ten together."

"Together," he repeated.

Somehow, together sounded good.

This was all very strange.

"Patricia?" he said.

"Yes, Oll?"

"If *Report to the Commissioner* is ever published . . ."

"Yes?"

"I'm gonna dedicate it to you."

Her eyes went suddenly moist.

She squeezed his hands across the table.

This was all so very strange.

He sipped a little of the skim milk.

It tasted like goat piss.

Meyer was just about to sign out when the phone call came. He looked up at the wall clock. 3:43 p.m.

"Eighty-seventh Squad," he said. "Detective Meyer."

"May I speak to Detective Carella, please?"

"Not in today. May I take a message?"

"Yes. Will you tell him Adam Fen called . . . ?"

Meyer immediately looked at the caller ID number flashing on his screen. A 377 prefix. Right here in the precinct. He signaled to Parker across the room, waved him over to the desk. On a sheet of paper, he scribbled the single word:

ADDRESS!

Parker nodded, wrote down the caller ID number, and went back to his own desk.

"Are you still there?" the Deaf Man asked.

"Still here," Meyer said.

"I hope you're not doing what I think

you're doing. I'll be gone long before you get here."

"What is it you think I'm doing?"

"Please, dummy," the Deaf Man said, "you're way out of your league. Give this message to Carella. Have you got a pencil?"

"Ready," Meyer said.

"Tell him a woman named Melissa Summers may try to leave the country in the next few days. Tell him . . ."

At his own desk, Parker was talking to a phone company supervisor, trying to get an address for the 377 number. With his free hand, Meyer gestured *Hurry up!*

". . . to watch the airports. She's in possession of . . ."

"How do you spell that name, please?"

"*Summer* with an *s* on the end!" the Deaf Man shouted. "Melissa *Summers*. Stop . . . stop trying to keep me on this line!"

He seemed to be suddenly struggling for breath.

"Are you okay?" Meyer asked.

"No, as a matter of fact, I've been shot. But don't . . ." He struggled for breath again. "Don't bother putting out . . . a med alert, I've got my own doctor, thanks."

"Why don't you let us come help you?" Meyer suggested. We'll get you to a hos . . ."

"Please don't be ridiculous," the Deaf Man said, and caught his breath again.

Across the room, Parker was just getting off the phone.

"Tell Carella she has the Strad."

"The what?"

"Tell him I hope he gets her."

There was a click on the line.

"It's 328 River Place South," Parker said.

Genero kicked in the door to apartment 17D at four-fifteen that Saturday afternoon. It was the first time in his life he'd ever kicked in a door. It made him feel like a television cop. He was not alone — in storming the apartment, that is. Parker and Meyer had both done this sort of thing before, and they did not feel like television cops at all. In fact, they felt more like firemen, breaking down the door this way.

Whoever had lived here —

According to the super, the man renting the apartment was named Adam Fen, though recently a good-looking blonde had begun living with him. They figured this had to be the Melissa Summers the Deaf Man had mentioned, but the super didn't know her name.

Whoever had lived here had left in a very big hurry.

There were blood stains in the entry hall, on the carpet near the hall table. Heavy stains. They figured this was where he'd got shot and where he'd done most of his bleeding. There was also a trail of blood leading first to the bathroom, where a roll of cotton gauze on the sink seemed to indicate he'd tried to stanch the blood and bind the wound, and next to a small office at the rear of the apartment, where blood smears on the computer keyboard seemed to indicate he'd been typing something before he left.

When they booted up the machine, they discovered that all the files had been deleted. The only thing that popped up on the screen was a yellow Stickie note that read:

I'LL BE SEEING YOU, BOYS!

"Guy's bleeding all over the floor, he stops to write us a note," Genero said.

"That's his style, all right," Meyer agreed.

"I'll be seeing you, huh?" Carella said into the phone.

"Is what the Stickie said."

"And you think he's wounded, is that it?"

"No question. He told me he'd been shot, and there's blood all over the place here."

"Better put out a Med alert."

"He said not to bother. He's got his own doctor."

"So you think he's gone again?"

"With the wind."

"How about the girl? Summers, is it?"

"Melissa Summers. He says she's heading out of the country."

"Where?"

"Didn't say."

"With the Strad?"

"That's what he told me."

"Has anyone heard from the Greek yet?"

"Not us. Maybe he called Mid South."

"Be nice to know what happened."

"Oh yes."

"Better contact Homeland, Meyer."

"I already did. *And* all the airlines. They'll be watching for her and the fiddle."

"*If* that's the name on her passport."

"If she even *has* a passport."

There was a long pause on the line.

"So what do we do about him?" Meyer asked.

"Wait, I guess. If we get the girl . . ."

"*If.*"

"She may be able to tell us something about him. If not, we grab him when he pops up again."

"*If* he pops up again."

"He always does, Meyer."

"Death and taxes."

"Same thing," Carella said.

There was another pause.

"Well . . . I've got work to do here," Meyer said.

"Go easy."

"See you Monday."

"See you," Carella said, and hung up.

He stood by the phone with his hand on the receiver for a moment, looking down at the phone, wondering when next they'd see the Deaf Man, thinking never was soon enough. He almost sighed.

Teddy was waiting for him in the bedroom.

He undressed silently, went into the bathroom to brush his teeth and floss, and then went to the bed, and climbed in beside her.

Her hands moved in the air.

It was a lovely wedding, she signed.

He read her hands, nodded.

Didn't you think so? she signed.

He nodded again.

Steve?

He looked into her eyes.

Are you ever *going to get over this, or what?*

"Get over what?" he asked mischievously, signing the words at the same time, grinning. Then he took her in his arms, still grinning, and kissed her, and held her close, and she remembered a beginning, long long ago, when a detective named Steve Carella stood hatless and gloveless in the falling snow and offered a girl named Theodora Franklin a single red rose on St. Valentine's Day — and filled her life with roses forever.

She turned off the bedside lamp, and snuggled close to him again.

At 3:00 p.m. the next day, a young blond woman checked in at Spindledrift International Airport for Air France's 5:10 p.m. flight to Paris. Passport Control had been alerted to stop and detain a woman named Melissa Summers. The name in the blonde's passport was Carmela Sammarone. The inspector merely glanced at her photo, stamped the passport, and said, "Have a nice flight, Miss Sammarone."

Melissa smiled demurely, and walked towards the security gate, where she placed the violin case she was carrying on the scanning machine.

Yesterday, a Homeland Security officer had listened to Meyer on the telephone, had written down the pertinent information about some valuable violin, asked if this constituted a bomb threat, and when told that it did not, shrugged and thanked Meyer for the "heads-up," were the exact words he'd used.

The airport security people who opened and examined Carmela Sammarone's violin case were similarly looking for bombs or guns or knives or tweezers, and in any event would not have known a Stradivarius from a Budweiser. All they did was pat down the case and shake the violin to see if anything suspicious rattled around inside there.

One of the guards remarked, "My uncle used to play the fiddle."

"That's nice," Melissa said, and watched while they closed the lid on the case, and snapped the clips shut.

"Have a nice flight," the other guard said.

Waiting for takeoff in the first-class section of the plane, Melissa sipped at a glass of ouzo and leafed through the June issue of *Vogue*.

"First time to Paris?" the flight attendant asked.

"Yes," Melissa said, smiling.

It was a beginning.

Acknowledgments

Ever since 1982, a man named Daniel Starer has been doing my research for me. Whether I was writing about life in a convent, or the vicissitudes of the music business, or what it's like to be eaten alive in a lion's cage, he has always been there when I needed him. My research requests for *Hark!* were particularly demanding, but — as always — he came through with patience, good humor, boundless energy, and limitless creativity. I cannot begin to thank him enough. He can be found at http://www.researchforwriters. com.

About the Author

In 1998, Ed McBain was the first American to receive the Diamond Dagger, the British Crime Writers Association's highest award. He also holds the Mystery Writers of America's prestigious Grand Master Award. His most recent 87th Precinct novel was *The Frumious Bandersnatch*. Under his own name — Evan Hunter — he has enjoyed a writing career that has spanned five decades, from his first novel, *The Blackboard Jungle*, in 1954, to the screenplay for Alfred Hitchcock's *The Birds*, to *Candyland*, written in tandem with his alter ego, Ed McBain, to *The Moment She Was Gone*, published in 2002.